· BEFORE THE BATTLE

Perry shook the woman's arm quite violently, but still she didn't stir.

The manager appeared, a small balding man with a bristling mustache. "Anything wrong here?"

"This woman," said Perry. "I can't wake her up."

The manager tried shaking her arm, too. "Ma'am? Can you hear me, ma'am? This is the manager!"

When she didn't respond, he carefully took hold of her head and turned it sideways so that they could see her face. Her eyes were wide open, but the pupils were dilated, and she was plainly dead. She must have been quite pretty once, years and years ago.

Springer laid a hand on her forehead. "She's cold," she said. "Feel how *cold* she is."

"That's okay," said Perry. "I'll take your word for it." He had never seen a dead body before, not even his mother.

Springer came back to their table. "No question about it," she said.

"The Winterwent?"

She nodded. "He must be aware that we're preparing ourselves to fight him. I think he's going to give us a whole lot of trouble."

One by one, the lights blinked back on. Sasha said, "My God, I'm frightened. Why can't I wake up?"

John laid a plump, reassuring hand on her shoulder. "You *are* awake, honeycakes. It's when you fall asleep that you have to start worrying."

NIGHT WARS

GRAHAM MASTERTON

LEISURE BOOKS NEW YORK CITY

A LEISURE BOOK®

September 2006

Published by

Dorchester Publishing Co., Inc.
200 Madison Avenue
New York, NY 10016

ISBN 0-8439-5427-2

The name "Leisure Books" and the stylized "L" with design are
trademarks of Dorchester Publishing Co., Inc.

Printed in the United States of America.

Visit us on the web at www.dorchesterpub.com.

NIGHT WARS

CHAPTER ONE

Sasha was woken up at three o'clock in the afternoon by an earsplitting thunderstorm. It sounded as if the city were being bombarded from the other side of the Ohio River by heavy artillery. She could hear rain cascading from the broken gutter above her bedroom window and clattering into her window box. Fortunately, she had long ago given up trying to grow geraniums in it. Like everything else in her life, she had never remembered to take care of them.

She buried her head under the pillows, but she knew that it was no use. She turned over and lay on her side for a while, watching the rain trickling down behind the blinds, but then she said, "Shit," under her breath and sat up.

She had promised herself that she would sleep all day. But the thunder was too calamitous and she simply wasn't tired anymore. Apart from that, she didn't like the dreams that she had been having. She had dreamed that a woman in a white coat had crept into her bedroom with a sackful of albino squirrels and let them all loose.

She went to the window and let up the blind. The surface of Third Street was dancing with rain, and people were hurrying across the intersection with umbrellas and newspapers held over their heads. Huge brown clouds were moving slowly across the city from the southwest, and it was so gloomy that cars were driving around with their headlights on.

She pressed her forehead against the glass. She wished that this were yesterday, and that she hadn't left for work yet. She wished that this were the day before yesterday—before she had filed that story about the ninety-one-year-old woman in St. James Court who had been so neglected by her children that she had survived only by frying and eating her nine pet cats. The old woman had even devised recipes to make her kitties more palatable, and Sasha had quoted the recipes in detail.

It was a terrific story, and it would have been even more terrific if it had been true, and if Sasha hadn't inadvertently used the same apartment number as the mayor's mother.

Regrettably, it wasn't the first time that the accuracy of one of her scoops had been challenged. There was the story last June about the Butchertown man who had concealed himself and his surfboard inside a large cardboard box and tried to FedEx himself to Oahu because he thought he deserved a vacation. Then there was the story about the fifteen-strong girls' choir who were so depressed about their failure to win a bluegrass contest that they had decided to join hands and throw themselves off the George Rogers Clark Memorial Bridge, only to be saved by a passing entrepreneur who offered them a $50,000 recording contract.

Yesterday, less than an hour after the *Courier-Journal* had hit the streets, and less than ten minutes after a phone call to her editor Jimmy Berrance from the mayor's office, Jimmy had ordered her to clear her desk.

"What does it matter if it's true or not?" she had protested. "It *could* have happened, couldn't it?"

"It could, sure," Jimmy had agreed. "But the problem is, it didn't."

Lightning flickered over the shiny wet rooftops, followed

by another barrage of improbably loud thunder. Sasha went across to the small divided-off kitchenette in the corner of her room and opened up her refrigerator. Two bottles of white wine, a wrinkly apple, three slices of pepperoni pizza, and a can of tuna. At this rate, she was going to end up like her fictitious old lady, eating Cat Creole.

She closed the refrigerator. On the door was Scotch-taped a poster that the *Courier-Journal* had brought out when she first joined them, two-and-a-half years ago. It showed a pretty, smiling girl of twenty-four in a cream designer jacket. She had a beautifully cut blonde pageboy, and wide-apart blue eyes that just sparkled sincerity. Sasha Smith, the Tender Heart of Kentucky.

She didn't look like that now. Her hair was cut short and messy, her eye makeup was smudged, and she was wearing nothing but a grubby T-shirt with a picture of Alfred E. Neuman on the front and a scarlet lace thong.

Her room was at the very top of the house, so that it had steeply sloping ceilings, and it was a catastrophe. The bedsheets looked as if they had been knotted together, ready for a prison break. The couch was heaped with cushions and discarded sweaters and bottles of nail polish remover and cotton wipes and candy wrappers. The polished wood floor was strewn with shoes and bras and shopping bags and worn-out jeans and CDs all out of their cases. On the walls she had stuck posters of her heroes and heroines: Bob Woodward, James Thurber, Erica Jong, Hunter S. Thompson and Paris Hilton. Well, Paris Hilton wasn't exactly a heroine, but Sasha considered that a total lack of self-awareness was an achievement worthy of respect.

She decided to take a shower and wash her hair and dress up in the new honey-colored Max Mara sweater that she had bought at the Fourth Street Live! Mall, if she could find it. Then she would meet her friend Laurel and go to Freddie's Bar, where the *Courier-Journal* staff usually hung out after work. Screw them, she thought. I'll show them what they're missing.

She had just stepped into the small triangular bathroom when she heard her cell phone playing "Wake Up, Little Susie," somewhere on the couch. No, ignore it. It wasn't going to be Jimmy Berrance, apologizing for firing her, and it wasn't going to be WHAS, offering her a job as a roving TV reporter. It wasn't going to be her father, either, that was for sure. But it kept on playing and playing, and after the tenth play she hesitated in the middle of the bathroom with her arms crossed and her T-shirt half-lifted over her head. Maybe it was Joe Henry, her kind-of-boyfriend, back from Seattle two days early.

She went back into the living room and rummaged through the magazines and sweaters on the couch. She found her cell phone studded with caramel popcorn.

"Hello? Joe Henry?"

"Is that Sasha? I tried to call you at the office, but they told me you didn't work there any longer." It wasn't Joe Henry. It was a woman's voice, and she sounded as if she were panicking.

"No, that's true, I don't work there any longer. Who is this?"

"Jenny Ferraby. Do you remember me? You wrote an article about me last year."

"Jenny Ferraby? Oh, sure, yes." It would have been difficult to forget Jenny Ferraby. She had fought the State of Kentucky for the right to use her late husband's sperm to conceive a child, even though he had been executed three years before for a triple homicide. It had become known in the media as the "Demon Seed" case.

"You must be due pretty soon, huh?" said Sasha. "I have a note somewhere to call you about that."

"The baby was born two days ago, three weeks premature. He's a little boy."

"Congratulations. Is he okay?"

"That's why I'm calling you. There's something wrong with him. He won't stop screaming and he won't sleep. He hasn't slept for even a second since he was born."

"You're kidding me. All babies sleep. I mean, that's what they do, isn't it? Cry, crap, eat and sleep."

"Not this one. He opened his eyes as soon as he was born and he hasn't closed them since."

Sasha cleared herself a space on the edge of the couch and sat down. "So what do the doctors say?"

"They don't understand it any more than me. At first I thought—well, you can imagine what I thought. Maybe it was a punishment from God, for going against nature."

"Oh, come on."

"I know. It wasn't very rational, but then I wasn't feeling very rational. It was only when another baby was born, about seven hours later, and *she* wouldn't stop crying, either—and then another, and another."

"What do you mean?"

"I mean that every baby born here in the past forty-eight hours is exactly the same. Seven babies so far. They won't stop screaming and they won't sleep. They're having to feed all of them on a drip."

"Well, I have to admit, that is very strange indeed. Listen—if I remember, you were going to have your baby where? At the Ormsby Clinic, wasn't it?"

"That's right. That's where I am now."

"And the doctors can't work out what's wrong?"

"They're going frantic. Everybody here is going frantic."

"Who else knows about this?"

"Nobody. They asked us not to tell the media, in case the whole thing turns into a circus. But it's obvious that they don't have the first idea what to do, and I thought that if you published a story about it ... well, some specialist might read it. Somebody who has experience with cases like these."

"Ms Ferraby—Jenny—I don't work for the *Courier-Journal* anymore. They fired me. Why don't you call the editor, Jimmy Berrance? He should be able to help you."

"But surely you can still write a story about it? When I wanted to have George's baby, you were the only one who understood. You were the only one who didn't treat me as if I was some kind of ghoul."

"I'm sorry. I'm finished with the *Courier-Journal*. I'm looking for a career change. Maybe TV, or movies. Maybe I'll join a rock band."

"Sasha, I'm desperate. I wouldn't have called you if I wasn't desperate."

"I'm sorry, Jenny. What can I say?"

"Wait up," said Jenny Ferraby. Sasha could hear voices, and a door opening and closing and a phone ringing. Then another door opened and she heard babies crying.

"Just listen," said Jenny Ferraby. "Listen to them, and my boy is one of them. Listen, and tell me that you're not going to help me."

Sasha listened, and the sound she heard made her feel as if the skin around her scalp were shrinking. An appalling chorus of naked, helpless fear. Seven babies, every one of them way beyond hysteria, screaming and screaming as if something so terrible was about to happen to them that they would never be able to catch their breath.

The thunder had cleared away toward St. Matthews by the time she reached the Ormsby Clinic, and the red asphalt driveway was wreathed in steam. As she climbed out of her ten-year-old sky-blue Mustang, Jenny Ferraby came down the front steps of the clinic and hurried toward her. She was a thin, fretful-looking woman of thirty-five with wild gingery hair, wearing a pale green summer dress and Birkenstock sandals.

"Thank you so much for coming. You have no idea how worried I am. If Kieran doesn't stop crying ... I'm sure he's going to die of exhaustion."

"You didn't tell the doctors I'm a reporter? Well ... *was* a reporter?"

Jenny Ferraby took hold of her arm and clung to it tightly. "I said that you were a very close friend of mine, that's all."

"What about the other parents?"

"They've all agreed to keep this out of the media. None of them really wants the publicity. It's distressing enough as it is."

They went through the revolving door into the clinic's reception area, which was chilly and modern, with cream marble floors and bay trees in woven straw containers. The words ORMSBY OBSTETRIC CLINIC were written in shiny stainless steel letters on the wall, and in the center of the reception area stood a bronze sculpture of a faceless mother and a faceless child.

The receptionist glanced across at them, and Jenny Ferraby pointed at Sasha and said, unnecessarily, "My friend. She's come to see my baby."

She led the way along the corridor to the maternity wing. Sasha could hear the babies crying as soon as they walked through the swing doors. A harassed-looking nurse hurried past them and gave Jenny Ferraby a sympathetic grimace.

Outside the intensive care ward, nine weary mothers and fathers were sitting, drinking coffee or trying to read magazines or simply sitting with their heads in their hands. One or two of the mothers looked around as Sasha and Jenny Ferraby came past, and tried to smile, but the rest of the parents ignored her. They were too worried and too tired.

Through the large glass window, Sasha could see the babies lying in their transparent plastic cribs, all of them crimson-faced and all of them crying. A drip had been attached to each of the babies to keep them hydrated and fed, and each of them was wired-up to an LCD screen to monitor their vital signs. Two doctors and four nurses were gathered around one of the screens, talking and shaking their heads.

"That's my Kieran," said Jenny Ferraby, pointing to the third baby along the row. "Look at him, the poor little darling."

"Haven't they tried *sedating* them?" asked Sasha. "I

mean, I know they're very little, but they can't let them go on crying like this."

"They've tried everything. They've tried music, they've tried dolphin noises, they've tried flashing lights and they've tried keeping them in total darkness. They gave them as much antihistamine as they dared, but it didn't have any effect at all."

"So what do they plan to do next?"

"I'm not sure. They've told us that they're going to try hypnosis, but I don't see how you can hypnotize a premature baby."

"Can I talk to one of the doctors?"

"Sure, I don't see why not. So long as you don't tell them what you're really doing here."

Sasha approached the window and looked into the IC unit at all the wriggling, screaming babies. They were so dehydrated by their crying that they no longer had any tears.

Jenny came and stood beside her and said, "I feel so helpless. Kieran is depending on me to protect him and take care of him, and I can't."

She waved to one of the doctors, a short African-American woman with glasses and hair cropped like a blacksmith's anvil. The doctor waved back, and after a moment she came out through the double doors.

"Hello, Jenny. How are you holding up?"

"Dr. Absalom, this is my friend, Sasha. I brought her along for some moral support."

"Right now, I think we could *all* use some moral support," said Dr. Absalom.

"This is so strange, isn't it?" said Sasha. "All of these babies crying like this and not sleeping."

"Well, we're working on a couple of possible treatments," said Dr. Absalom. "One theory is that they've somehow been traumatized while they were still in the womb, but why this condition should only have affected babies born here at Ormsby, we simply have no idea."

Sasha watched one of the nurses taking a blood sample

from the baby next to Kieran. "Were the mothers given any kind of prescription medication prior to their giving birth?"

"Nothing stronger than vitamin supplements."

"Were they following any specific diet?"

Dr. Absalom raised one eyebrow. Sasha realized that her question might have sounded too professional, so she shrugged quickly and said, "I'm just wondering, that's all. Like, I heard that unborn babies can even get a taste for garlic, if their mothers eat a whole lot of it."

Dr. Absalom nodded. "We've been recommending the same diet plan to thousands of mothers for more than sixteen years. It's not mandatory, though, and so the mothers have all been following different regimes. Three Hot Browns a day, in one case."

"Hey—that's what I *call* a diet."

Jenny Ferraby said, "Do you think I could take Sasha in to see Kieran?"

"Provided you both wear caps and masks, and you don't touch him, sure."

Dr. Absalom called for one of the nurses to bring them surgical masks and caps to cover their hair. "When you go in there—well, the noise is very upsetting. But please understand that we're doing everything we possibly can to relieve these babies' distress."

"I understand that you're not telling the press about it, though," said Sasha, through her blue mask.

"That's because we don't want the parents to suffer any more than they are already."

"And you wouldn't want the Ormsby Clinic to be associated with inexplicable infant insomnia, would you?"

Dr. Absalom said, sharply, "Our priority, Ms.—"

"Edison."

"Our priority, Ms. Edison, is the welfare of these children. Nothing else."

"I see," said Sasha. "I'm sorry." She didn't want to annoy Dr. Absalom before she had the chance to go in and see baby Kieran, and take his picture, too. This story might even get her job back for her.

"Okay?" said Dr. Absalom, and opened the outer door. Sasha and Jenny Ferraby followed her.

Even before she opened the inner door, Sasha found the screaming was almost unbearable—the terrible, quivering anguish, and the knowledge that she couldn't do anything to stop it.

"You'll have to be brave, I'm afraid," said Dr. Absalom.

Jenny Ferraby walked through the inner door, and then Sasha. Every one of the seven babies were crying and gasping and frantically waving their arms. Every one of them had its eyes open, with its pupils darting from side to side, as if it were desperately frightened, but powerless to escape.

"Oh God," said Sasha. "If you're a baby, this is what hell must be like."

That evening, Sasha sat on the couch with an open can of cold spaghetti bolognese and her laptop on her knees and started to type up her story. Humidity was over ninety-one percent, and even though she had opened her window wide, the grubby pink calico drapes hung motionless. It was raining again, softly but very steadily, and car tires sizzled on the wet street outside. In another apartment, somebody was practicing the cello, starting and stopping and then starting again.

By midnight, most of her story was done, but tomorrow she would have to call the Ormsby Clinic and give them the opportunity to make a comment. Using her cell phone, she had managed to take three reasonable photos of the screaming children. In one of them, Jenny Ferraby was leaning over Kieran's crib with tears in her eyes—tears for the tears that little Kieran himself could no longer cry.

She looked through the photos two or three times, and she was just about to put down her phone when she hesitated. She knew there was no point in calling her father's number. He had never picked up before and there was no reason for her to think that he would pick up now. He had walked out on her mother thirteen months ago and vanished altogether three-and-a-half months prior. No phone calls, no letters, no e-mails. Eventually, Sasha had used her contacts at the *Courier-Journal* to trace him to an engineering company in Manitoba. She must have called him a hundred times since then, and left dozens of messages, but he had never answered. *Dad. This is Sash. Just call me and tell me you're happy.*

She pressed his number, but after it had rung twice she disconnected. Even if he did answer, she didn't really know what she wanted to say to him, not after all this time.

When she had finished rewriting her story, she got up, dropped the half-empty spaghetti can into the trash, tossed the fork into the sink, and then fell onto her bed, too tired even to brush her teeth. It was nearly two in the morning, and even though she had slept for most of yesterday, she felt emotionally exhausted. She wound one of the sheets around herself, punched the pillow into shape and closed her eyes.

She couldn't wait to finish off her story in the morning. And she was dying to show it to Jimmy Berrance. "Not only is this the greatest human-interest story in the history of Louisville, it actually happens to be true. So, nyardy, nyardy, nyah."

He would have to give her job back. He might even give her a raise. He might even promote her to chief features editor.

She dreamed that she was standing by the cast-iron fountain in Central Park. Although the path was sunlit, the sky was low and very dark, and when she looked up she saw that it was filled with thousands and thousands of ravens, all flying northeast. Their wings made a horrible rustling noise, and Sasha was sure that she could *smell* them, dry and fetid, like the desiccated corpses they picked on.

As she was standing there, a small boy came pedaling toward her on a tricycle. Although he was pedaling very hard, it seemed to take him forever to reach her. She had time to look around: at the diagonal pathways, along which people in white topcoats were walking at a measured pace, some of them ostentatiously smoking; and at the trees, which were thickly laden with purple blossom; and at the water in the fountain, which glittered in the sunlight like a golden horse's tail.

At last the boy arrived. He was naked except for red and white Keds. He looked up at her and she recognized him almost at once as Kieran, Jenny Ferraby's son. But how had he grown up so quickly, and why wasn't he crying any more?

"Kieran?" she asked him. For some reason she found it necessary to talk into a crumpled brown paper bag. It was something to do with hyperventilating, which was always a risk in dreams.

"They took the insides out of our heads," said Kieran, although he was speaking sideways language, and Sasha found it very difficult to translate. Sideways language was extremely oblique, made up of hints and suggestions and implications, rather than straightforward words. She knew that it was usually spoken in places where space was at a premium, like coal mines.

"I think you'll have to explain that more clearly," she said. "I don't want to let you down by misinterpreting you."

"They took the animals and the balls and the dancing," Kieran told her. "They took the morning and the moon and all of the answers."

"Who did?"

"They did. The cold people."

"And is that why you cry all the time, and why you can't sleep?"

Kieran nodded. "Find the insides of our heads, and then we can sleep."

He climbed back onto his tricycle and sped away so fast

along the diagonal path that she was sure that he had gone to Warp 9. She felt the fountain spray softly against her cheek. She pressed her hand over mouth, not sure what she was supposed to do next. But she knew that she was supposed to do *something*.

She turned around and she was back in bed. An urgent voice whispered, *"Sasha?"* She opened her eyes. It was still dark, but she could see that there was somebody standing in her room.

CHAPTER TWO

With exaggerated Oliver Hardy–style finger flourishes, so that he racked up his anticipation layer by layer, John unwrapped the warm greaseproof paper around his roast beef triple-cheese melt. He had already opened his mouth to take his first bite when the intercom blurted, "John? Pickup at SDF. Dr. Charlie Mazurin, coming in from Atlanta on Delta 5145, touching down at thirteen-fifteen."

"Leland, I'm on my lunch break, for chrissakes. Somebody else will have to take it."

"John, there is nobody else. And you don't have lunch breaks."

"What do you mean I don't have lunch breaks? That must be illegal."

"You work a six-hour shift nine through three, which doesn't include lunch breaks. Besides that, lunch is about the last thing you need. Not to mention breakfast and dinner."

"Leland, my devotion to the joys of Kentucky's cuisine is my business. You don't expect this vehicle to drive around

Louisville all day without fuel, and you shouldn't expect the same of me."

"What's your location, John?"

"East Louisville Park, parked."

"In that case, you'd better move your sizeable butt. You have sixteen minutes to make it to the airport and the traffic on I-65 is backing up as far as Liberty."

John closed his eyes and took five deep breaths. "Om," he intoned. "Ommmmmm." He was sorely tempted to tell Leland to stick his taxi-driving job in the night garage, but he knew in his heart that this wasn't the time. His salivary glands told him that he badly needed this roast beef triple-cheese melt, but his frontal lobes had to accept that he needed the money more.

"Ten-four," he said. He carefully rewrapped his sandwich and pushed it into the storage box underneath the armrest. Then he started up the engine of the bright yellow seven-seater Voyager and pulled away from the curb without making a signal, so that a KFC truck almost collided with him. The KFC truck driver blasted his klaxon and yelled something politically incorrect about John's mother and his physical size, but John did nothing except dismissively flap his arm. As far as he was concerned, traffic was like the weather. There was nothing you could do about it, so you might as well ignore it.

He turned right on South Clay and right again on East Muhammad Ali, accompanied by a barrage of protesting horns. He couldn't stop thinking about the sandwich in his armrest and whether he should take a bite to keep him going.

"Absolutely not," he argued, looking at his own eyes in the rearview mirror. "That would be treating the sandwich with no respect."

"What are you talking about, respect?" he retorted. "It's only a sandwich, for chrissakes. Six seventy-nine from Dooley's."

"It doesn't matter. Eating is spiritual. Eating demands one hundred percent concentration. You wouldn't clean your bicycle during Mass."

"No, *you* sure wouldn't. You don't own a bicycle and you never go to Mass."

"Well, maybe it's time you started."

"Which?"

"How should I know? Either. Both. A little pedaling, a little prayer. You might lose fifty pounds and get to meet God."

"If I lost fifty pounds, God wouldn't recognize me."

He was probably wrong. He had a gelled-up pompadour with a distinctive white streak in it, and he was wearing a peacock-blue shirt with pink flamingos all over it, as well as flappy brown safari shorts and bright yellow desert boots.

He whistled tunelessly between his teeth as he steered one-handed down South Preston Street. It was starting to rain again, just a few warm freckles on the windshield. He had calculated that he needed to work for Louisville Sunshine Cabs for nineteen weeks and three days to make enough money to continue his journey home to Baton Rouge. The engine had dropped out of his beloved Mercury Marquis three weeks ago while he was crossing the John F. Kennedy Bridge, and it was still in the shop at Blue Grass Lincoln-Mercury, waiting for a new transmission. Well, it had probably been fitted with its new transmission by now, but he hadn't been to the shop to find out. That would mean having to pay for it, $875 and change.

Traffic on South Preston was stopping and starting, so without making a signal, John turned sharply right on East Jacob Street and headed for the interstate. As he drove up the ramp, tailgating an elderly couple in an old blue Honda, he flicked his intercom switch.

"Leland? What's the name of that pickup? Dr. Marzipan?"

"Mazurin. The flight's early so put your foot down."

*   *   *

He waited in solid traffic on the Henry Watterson Express-
way at the intersection known to local radio reporters as
"the horse barns," with the rain drumming on the roof of
his taxi. He no longer wondered how his life had come to
this, but now and then he wished that things had turned out
different. His weakness had always been food. Not just
food, but the kind of food that went straight to the waistline.
He had joined the U.S. Quartermaster Corps in 1974, at
the age of nineteen, and served for seventeen years as an
army cook, during which he had won the Fort Lee Prize for
Culinary Excellence three times in succession. But he had
never been able to resist Southern fried chicken with
crunchy bits and mustard-barbecued pork chops with spicy
crackling and rolled oysters, and in 1986 he had virtually
been invalided out of the service on account of weighing
377 pounds and not being able to find a uniform to fit him.

After his discharge, he had been deeply depressed, but he
had managed to get his weight down to 273 pounds, mainly
by eating nothing with the letter "c" in it for six months,
such as chicken, catfish, soft-shelled crabs, corn bread,
cookies and ice cream. Eventually, his Uncle Desmond had
bought him a powder-blue double-breasted suit with dark
blue piping and wangled him a position with the Louisiana
Restaurant Association. He had been happily underworked
and pretty much his own boss, driving from town to
town and making cursory checks on restaurant hygiene—
ensuring, for example, that if steaks were dropped on the
kitchen floor they were always swished under the faucet
before they were returned to the customers' plates. But
there had been political jiggery-pokery in the Louisiana
Restaurant Association, and after three-and-a-half years
Uncle Desmond had been obliged to resign and John had
been replaced overnight by the sallow, drawling son of the
association's secretary, even though the boy didn't know a
muffulata from a muffler.

Last month, on a kind of pilgrimage, John had driven all the way from Baton Rouge to Presque Isle, Maine, a distance of 2,307 miles, to attend the funeral of his old army buddy, Dean Brunswick III. On the way back, his car had broken down once in Calais, Maine, and now here, in Louisville, with 886 miles still left to go. He wondered if the Lord were trying to explain something to him.

The rain began to clear, and John was suddenly dazzled with silvery sunshine. Almost at once, the traffic started to move.

He was standing by the arrivals gate holding up a hastily-written sign saying MAZURIN when somebody tapped him on the shoulder. He turned around and found himself confronted by a tall African-American woman. She was wearing a loosely woven white silk dress with very long sleeves, and her hair was braided with scores of tiny white beads. She had high cheekbones and slanting eyes, like a Masai, and the look was enhanced by her silver and copper bracelets, and the complicated copper collar that she wore around her neck.

"Sunshine Taxis?" said the woman, with a smile.

"That's correct, ma'am. But I'm already booked." John squinted around the terminal, but there was still no sign of anybody who looked remotely like a doctor. "If you need a ride into the city, though, you're welcome to join us, just as soon as my fare gets his sorry ass together and makes an appearance."

"This is who you're waiting for?" she said, pointing to his placard.

"Dr. Charlie Mazurin, that's the man."

"Dr. Charlie Mazurin, that's me."

"*You're* Dr. Charlie Mazurin? Oh, it's Charlie like in Charlotte, right? Jesus, I'm sorry, it's my boss. He never thinks it's worth telling me small details like what gender my fare is."

Dr. Mazurin had only one piece of luggage, a large shapeless carpetbag in dark brown and black, with brown beads hanging from the handle. John picked it up for her and it clanked as if it were filled with scrap metal. "What do you have in here?" he asked her. "Auto parts?"

She smiled, but she didn't answer him. "The cab's right out here," he told her. "There—the yellow Voyager. Hey, look, the sun's shining just for you. We've had some weird weather these past few days. Thunder, lightning, hailstones, you name it. The only thing we haven't had is snow."

He helped her into the front passenger seat. As he climbed in beside her, she sniffed and wrinkled up her nose.

"Oh," he said. "Sorry. That's my lunch. Listen, I'll get rid of it."

"No, no. You don't have to do that."

"No, listen. It's gone cold now anyhow." He tugged the greaseproof packet out of the storage box, walked across the curb and tossed the sandwich into the nearest trash can.

"There," he said. "That's settled it."

"That's settled what?"

"I've been arguing with myself if I should eat it." He pulled out in front of a black stretch Lincoln limousine, and the driver blasted his horn at him. "These people, no insight. They never anticipate what you're going to do. I'm driving a taxi, he thinks I'm going to stay here all night and never move?"

"Do you argue with yourself very often?" asked Dr. Mazurin, fastening her seatbelt and stretching out her very long legs.

"Not always. Sometimes I *agree* with myself. But mostly I argue. Especially when it comes to food. 'I think I'll stop for a double-cheese cheeseburger.' 'What? A double-cheese cheeseburger? How fattening is that?' 'Well, not exactly slimming, I agree, but I'm two-ninety already, so who's going to notice if I put on a couple of extra pounds?' 'But that's sheer greed. You're not even hungry.' 'Hunger doesn't come into it. I've been driving this taxi all day and I *deserve* it. Besides, the cheeseburger was invented in Louisville, and all I'm doing is honoring a great civic tradition.' "

Dr. Mazurin shook her head so that her long copper earrings swung. "And this is how you talk to yourself all the time?"

"I don't have anyone else to talk to, that's the problem."

"You don't have a partner?"

"I don't currently have a woman in my life, if that's what you mean."

"You say that as if you think you don't deserve to."

"Look at me."

"Well, I'm looking at you. You're a good-looking man."

"How do you know? I'm fat. All fat people look the same. If fat people could run fast, they'd all be bank robbers, because nobody can tell them apart."

"I think you're being unfair to yourself. You know who you remind me of? Brad Pitt."

"I remind you of Brad Pitt? Ha! Are you sure you don't mean Marlon Brando?" John had rejoined I-65 and was heading back north toward the city. The slate-gray rain clouds had almost disappeared now, off to the east, and the sky was a deep renaissance blue. Ahead of them the tall office buildings along the Ohio River waterfront were glittering like castles.

"It's your eye movements," said Dr. Mazurin. "It's the way you keep glancing upward, and sideways. That's the sure sign of somebody who thinks that their inner personality is quite different from the way they appear to the outside world."

"I see. Inside, I'm anorexic? Well, you know what they say. Inside every fat man there's about twenty-three skinny guys desperate to get out. You haven't told me where you want to go."

"The Ormsby Clinic. You know where that is?"

"Sure."

Dr. Mazurin was quiet for a moment. Then she said, "I'm sorry. I hope I didn't upset you."

John wobbled his jowls. "No. The only person who ever upsets me is me. How could I throw away that roast beef triple-cheese melt? I mean actually *throw it away*, without even taking a single bite? 'I don't know, John, how could you do that? Maybe you didn't want the taxi to smell like an orangutan's outhouse. Maybe you were thinking of your figure at last.' Ha! That'll be the day!"

"You'd make a good ventriloquist act," said Dr. Mazurin.

"Not a hope. I'd always have my mouth full of fried shrimp."

Dr. Mazurin opened her purse and took out a card.

"What's this?" John asked her.

"My cell number. I was wondering if you wanted to talk, later."

"Talk about what?"

"About you. About the you who wants to eat and the other you—the you who doesn't want to eat."

"You think there's only two of me? There's another me who wants to be a world-class gymnast."

"I'm serious."

John frowned at her. "What are you, some kind of shrink?"

"I'm a hypnotherapist."

"You mean you can put me to sleep and when I wake up I won't ever feel like another oyster po' boy again?"

"Maybe."

John turned off the interstate and headed east on Oak Street. He turned into the Ormsby Clinic and switched off the Voyager's engine.

"Well?" said Dr. Mazurin.

"I don't know. I think I'm frightened of trying to improve myself."

"Why's that?"

"I might succeed, and then what?"

Dr. Mazurin touched his arm. "Listen, I have quite a lot of work to do here, from what they've told me, but why don't you call me this evening, around eight? You could take me someplace good to eat, and we could talk."

"I, uh—I'm kind of embarrassed for funds right now, I'm afraid. About the most I could afford is the Hill Street Fish Fry, and that's mostly takeout."

"Don't worry, it'll be my treat."

John hefted Dr. Mazurin's carpetbag into the reception area. Two worried-looking doctors and a nurse were waiting for her already, and they ushered her away before John had a chance to say anything more to her.

"That's eight seventy-five," said John to the now-deserted corridor. "Gratuity is at your own discretion."

He turned to the receptionist with her upswept spectacles and the receptionist stared back at him unblinking, like a chameleon. Well, he could always collect his fare later. And if Dr. Mazurin was going to take him out for dinner, it didn't seem very gentlemanly to ask for a fare at all. He walked back out of the reception area with his desert boots squelching on the marble tiles.

It was a busy afternoon. He had to ferry five cackling seniors out to the Beargrass Golf & Country Club, and then he had to go back to SDF to pick up a couple who quarreled all the way to their hotel about something the husband had allegedly promised the wife but had now decided was much too expensive. Even after twenty minutes, John still couldn't work out if it was an electrically adjustable bed or a boob enlargement.

He did a school run to St. Polycarp Elementary at 3:15 and then drove back to the Sunshine Taxi garage on East Jefferson Street. After he had parked, he looked under the seats, as he always did, to make sure that nobody had left anything behind, like money. It was then that he saw something gleaming in the black shag carpet. He picked it up and saw that it was one of the silver-and-copper bracelets that Dr. Mazurin had been wearing. Its catch must have snagged on her purse when she gave him her card

He jiggled it thoughtfully in the palm of his hand and then dropped it into his shirt pocket.

"You got something on your mind, John?" Leland asked him as he handed over his keys.

"What makes you say that, Leland?"

Leland was skinny and white, with one eye permanently closed against the Kent Light that dangled between his lips. Whatever family he had come from, he looked as if he had been the runt of it. His white short-sleeved shirts always had a faintly pink hue, as if he had accidentally washed them with his red socks.

"As a general rule, John, you're always laughing."

"I'm sorry, Leland. I forgot that fat guys have to be jovial by law."

"You got something on your mind, John, I can tell."

"I'm hungry, Leland, that's all. I was just about to do justice to a roast beef triple-cheese melt when you gave me that Dr. Mazurin job and I haven't stopped since."

"Nah, John, it's not that." He coughed. "I'd say you got woman trouble."

"Me, Leland? Woman trouble?" But John suddenly realized that he had glanced sideways and up, like Brad Pitt.

On his way home, he called in at Dizzy Whizz on West Catherine Street and bought himself the twelve-inch Sub-Whizz Melt with turkey, ham, extra bacon and cheese, hot peppers and honey mustard, an order of four Inferno Wings and a Southern Cream Pie. It was a long time until 8:00 P.M., and in any case he didn't seriously believe that

Dr. Mazurin would remember her offer to take him out for dinner.

"You on a diet, John?" asked Mary, his server, with twinkly green eyes and a freckly smile. "No onion rings today?"

"Thinking about my breath, Mary," John told her.

"Don't tell me ... you got a date!"

John took out his brown plastic wallet and shrugged. "Maybe. Maybe not. You never know your luck."

He took the bus back to his apartment building on Riverside. It was a yellow-painted concrete block that had been put up in 1947 and was long overdue for demolition. At one time the upper rooms must have had views all the way across Sand Island to the Indiana shore, but whenever he drew back the grimy net curtains, all that John could see out of his bedroom window were the black-streaked concrete piers of Route 150.

His room was completely square, and there was just enough room for a double bed, a red Formica-topped kitchen table with a small refrigerator hidden underneath it, and an old brown armchair with fraying fringes. In one corner, three-quarters of the way up the wall, a Zenith television set was fixed on a bent metal arm, so that John always had to watch TV with his head tilted to the right, which gave him a crick in his neck. In the opposite corner there was a dark damp patch in the shape of a winged creature. John had decided that it was the Angel of Mute Desperation.

He unwrapped his Sub-Whizz Melt and took a large bite. For some reason he wasn't as hungry as he had imagined. He stood in the center of the room chewing, and he had to chew for a long time before he could swallow. He crouched down on the floor so that he could reach the refrigerator, and he wrestled out a half-frozen can of Coors. He popped the top and took a swallow. The beer was so cold that it made his eyes water, as if he were crying.

*   *   *

He dressed himself for dinner well before 8:00 P.M. He took a shower in the bathroom across the hall and sprayed himself with a free sample of Davidoff aftershave that he had been given at the airport while he was waiting for the quarreling couple. He chose his cherry-red shirt and his red and green plaid golfing pants. He thought about wearing his white double-breasted coat but the cuffs were grubby and there was a button missing and both lapels were decorated with loops of dried gravy.

"All right, God," he said, looking up at the ceiling. "I've had enough of this fucking destitution. Can I go back to an ordinary life now?"

"You really think that God's going to listen to you? You with your foot-long submarine sandwich with extra bacon? God's too busy taking care of the starving millions in Africa."

"I'm only asking for a new sport coat, for chrissakes. What use is a new sport coat to the starving millions in Africa? 'Look at me, bwana, you can see my ribs but how natty am I?' "

As soon as his bedside clock said 8:00 he punched out Dr. Mazurin's cell phone number. *The person you are calling is currently unavailable.* Goddamit, he thought. She must still be busy at the Ormsby Clinic.

He sat in his brown fringed armchair for another five minutes, drumming his fingers. Then he tried Dr. Mazurin a second time. Nothing. Still switched off. Even though the air-conditioning worked reasonably well, he was beginning to perspire. He always perspired when he was anxious, or guilty.

He tried again at 8:11, 8:16, 8:23 and 8:35. Still switched off.

"She's a doctor. Something must have come up. I should have given her my number, too."

"You're deluding yourself, John."

"Oh, you think so? You heard what she said about people's appearance. She could see me. She could see what I really look like."

"What you really look like, John, is a big sweaty lard-ass with a stupid pompadour."

He called the Sunshine Cab company and Nico came to pick him up.

"I never saw you dressed up like this before, man," said Nico, his eyes glittering under his black leather cap. "You got a date or something?"

"More like 'or something.' "

"You angry or something, man?"

"No, I'm insouciant."

"Insooshant? What's that, like, drunk or something?"

Nico drove him to the Ormsby Clinic and John asked him to wait. Inside, there was a different receptionist, a blonde girl with her brown roots showing and elaborate braces on her front teeth.

"Is Dr. Mazurin still here? Dr. Charlie Mazurin?"

"Yes, sir, but I'm afraid she's tied up right now. Can I help you at all?"

"I, uh, I have something of hers. She accidentally left it in my car. Something of value, I believe."

"If you want to leave it with me, sir, I'll make sure that she gets it."

"I'd rather give it to her personally, if you don't mind."

Before the receptionist could reply, though, Dr. Mazurin came along the corridor, walking very quickly. She came up to the reception desk and said, "I need my bag."

"Dr. Mazurin?" said John.

She stared at him as if she had never seen him before. Her eyes were wide and glassy and she looked to John as if she were in shock.

"Dr. Mazurin, I just came to say that it doesn't matter about dinner. But I brought your bracelet back. It must have dropped off in my cab."

John held it up. Dr. Mazurin came slowly across the reception area and stared at it.

"I'm sorry," she said. "I've been trying to carry out some hypnosis ... It always makes me distracted."

"That's all right, Dr. Mazurin. As it happens I made alternative dining arrangements."

She didn't seem to understand what he was talking about. She turned back to the receptionist and said, "My bag?"

The receptionist dragged the carpetbag out from behind her counter. Dr. Mazurin took hold of the handle, but John took hold of it, too, and said, "Here. Let me. You don't want to be carrying that."

"All right, thanks. Can you bring it along to the IC unit for me?"

"Sure. Sure thing."

John followed her along the corridor with the bag clanking and banging against his knees.

"I was just glad that I found your bracelet," he said. "Like, anybody could have picked it up, you know, and you never would have seen it again. Whatever happened to honesty?"

Don't mention a five-dollar "thank-you," of course, or the $8.75 fare you owe me, plus fifteen percent tip.

Dr. Mazurin turned and gave him a ghostly little smile, but that was all.

When she pushed open the swing doors to let him through, he heard the babies crying for the first time. "Jesus. Sounds like somebody's hungry."

"No. Not exactly. Can you·bring the bag through here, please?"

She led the way past the waiting area, where six or seven parents were still haggardly hunched in their chairs or stretched out on the couches, trying to sleep. John gave one or two of them an awkward smile, but none of them smiled in return. He followed Dr. Mazurin farther along the corridor, past a large inspection window, and it was then that he saw the babies for the first time. Five of them were still crying loudly and jerking their arms and legs, but two of them were lying very quiet, except for an occasional shudder.

"What's wrong with these little guys?"

Dr. Mazurin didn't answer him, but walked ahead of him through another pair of swing doors to a quiet, turquoise-carpeted area marked RESIDENTIAL SUITES: PRIVATE. She opened one of the side doors, where there was a bedroom, with a desk and a couch and a flat-screen TV, and a bathroom off to one side. John dropped the bag down onto the floor with a complicated clank and said, "So ... you're what? A part-time plumber or something?"

Dr. Mazurin shook her head. "The equipment in this bag—well, I hope you never have to find out what I designed it for."

"You and me both. I hate hospitals, and surgery, and all that kind of stuff. I can't even watch *ER*."

Dr. Mazurin said, "You know where this equipment is, though, if you should ever need it."

John didn't have the faintest idea what she was talking about. Why should *he* ever need it, whatever it was? "Sure," he told her, and turned to go.

"Listen," said Dr. Mazurin. "I'm so sorry about dinner. I do remember asking you, it's just that—well, I'll try to make it up to you."

"*Fah,* you don't have to do that. It's obvious you got your hands full." He hesitated by the door and then he said, "Those babies ... is that who you've been trying to hypnotize?"

"It's a very unusual problem. I'm sorry, I shouldn't have said anything, really. Ormsby is trying to keep this crisis as

low-key as possible. You know—for the sake of the parents.
You saw for yourself how worried they are."

"Sure. But how do you hypnotize babies?"

"So far, I haven't been able to, I'm afraid."

"Oh. But, like, why *would* you?"

"Because they were all born with a life-threatening condition and the doctors here have tried everything else that they can think of."

"Oh, I see. I didn't mean to talk out of turn. Do you mind if I ask what's wrong with them?"

"So long as you can keep it to yourself."

"Sure, I'll tell all my hundreds of numerous friends that I don't have."

Dr. Mazurin hesitated for a moment, and then she said, "The simple fact is, none of these babies can dream."

On the way back to Riverside, John sat frowning out of the taxi window like a man searching for a lost child. Nico kept glancing over at him and saying, "You okay, man? Something happen in that clinic or something? Somebody die?"

"No, nobody died. Not yet, anyways. But there was something going on there. I don't know why it should bother me so much, but it really bothers me."

"What's that, man?"

John shook his head. "I'm not really supposed to tell anyone."

"Hey, man. A problem halved is a problem cut in two, right? Something like that."

"Yeah."

Nico pulled up to the curb and John gave him a crumpled twenty. "Keep the change, okay?"

"Thanks. The change is minus three dollars and twenty-five cents."

"That much? Don't spend it on anything frivolous."

For the first time for as long as he could remember, John went to bed that night without eating anything. He couldn't stop thinking about those screaming babies, although he couldn't understand why they had upset him so much. For some inexplicable reason he felt responsible for them.

It was ridiculous. He didn't even *like* babies. Yet their helpless distress had disturbed him more than anything had ever disturbed him before. He felt like Holden Caulfield in *The Catcher in the Rye,* which was the only book he had ever read that wasn't a restaurant guide or a cookbook.

I keep picturing all these little kids playing some game in this big field of rye and all ... I mean they're running and they don't look where they're going and I have to come out from somewhere and catch them.

He undressed and hung up his shirt and pants on the clattering wire hangers in his closet. After he had pulled on his old gray T-shirt, he looked for a long time at the Sub-Whizz Melt congealing on the table. He couldn't persuade himself to take even a single bite.

"I've lost my appetite, that's all. It's not a federal statute that I have to have an appetite."

"Excuse me? What does having an appetite have to do with it?"

"Having an appetite has everything to do with it. And just look at it. That cheese has turned into candle wax."

"Is this the same man who ate two portions of Dutch Potato Scramble, two days old, with a serving spoon?"

"It's too big. It's bigger than my head. And you should never eat anything bigger than your head."

"In that case, cut it in half."

John took out his one-and-only kitchen knife, a foot-long serrated carver that he had liberated from the Ramada Inn in Natchitoches, Louisiana, and cut the sandwich in half, and then into quarters. It was no good. He still couldn't eat it.

"All right. You're temporarily relieved of ingestion duty.

Save it for later." He wrapped up the sandwich in crinkly aluminum foil and wedged it into the refrigerator. Then he brushed his teeth and gargled with turquoise mouthwash and rolled into bed.

He watched TV for a while—a strange black and white movie about people walking through a formal park, in 1910 or thereabouts. It was French, with subtitles, and it was so slow-moving that he found himself staring at it with his mouth open, mesmerized.

"*Mon chien à besoin d'un oculiste.*" My dog is short-sighted.

"*Une caniche avec des lunettes? Vous êtes fou!*"

Shortly after midnight, he suddenly blinked himself back into focus. He had been dribbling onto his T-shirt, and he wiped his mouth with the back of his hand. He switched off the television, but he lay awake for almost an hour, listening to the sounds of the city and the distant rumbling of thunder. He was sure that he could hear babies crying, but when he lifted his head from the pillow and strained his ears, it faded and mingled with the sound of the traffic.

"You're losing your marbles, my friend."

"I'm suffering from extreme malnourishment, is all."

"Okay, tomorrow you get up early and go to Lynn's Paradise Café for breakfast. Hot buttermilk biscuits with sausage gravy, country ham eggstravaganaza and sweet potato fries with cinnamon spice, the whole works."

"John, my friend, you got yourself a deal."

He slept for a while. He dreamed that he was walking through the formal park with the French people. A woman in a white bonnet nodded to him as he passed, and said, "*Bonjour, Monsieur Dauphin, comment allez-vous?*" He smiled back, although he wasn't at all sure that he ought to, especially since one of the men was staring at him with undisguised venom. The pathway was lined every few yards with decorative stone urns, and every urn was filled to the brim with silvery herring.

He turned over, and as he turned over he opened his eyes and squinted toward the window. The drapes didn't quite meet in the middle of the window, and he could see that somebody was standing right in front of them. Somebody tall, and silent, and very dark.

CHAPTER THREE

"Perry!"

"Just a minute, Dad!"

"Perry, you get your rear end down here right now!"

"Okay, Dad! Wait up just a minute, okay?"

"Not 'just a minute'! *Now!*"

"Okay, Dad! Wait up just a minute, okay?"

On his computer screen, Perry was filling in a deep purple shadow between Steel Sister's enormous breasts. Steel Sister was the heroine of the animated adventure that he was creating on his computer, *Trash Planet*. She was an android, with arms and legs constructed out of scrap metal and old auto parts, but a torso that had once belonged to America's second most famous porn star (after Jenna Jameson). Perry called her "part woman, part junkyard."

He pressed Save, and switched off his computer. Steel Sister vanished from the screen just as his bedroom door opened. His father came in, hot and sweaty and red-faced, his denim overalls covered with brick dust.

"What the heck have you been *doing,* boy? I've been calling your cell phone for over an hour!"

33

"Sorry, Dad, it's switched off. Saving the battery."

"I called the house number, too!"

"Sorry, didn't hear it."

"So, what have you been doing? Gawking at that computer screen, I'll bet you."

"I was looking up stuff for my science project, that's all. Lava flow, out of Mount Hualalai."

Perry's father glowered at the computer and then wiped his nose with the back of his hand. "When I was your age, it was down to the library if I wanted to look anything up."

"That was then, Dad. This is now. These days, books are like, irrelevant."

"Well, there's one book that isn't, and that's the book that says 'If any would not work, neither shall he eat.' Dunc has been helping me for hours."

"Okay, Dad. I'm coming, okay?"

"You got two minutes. And when you come home tonight, you tidy up this room, you hear? Looks like the seventy-four tornado in here."

"Yes, Dad."

When his father had left the room, Perry found his Levis tangled up in his bedclothes and pulled them on, hopping on one leg. Then he put on his favorite T-shirt, which was black with a large X on the front of it made up of white skulls. He looked at himself in the mirror over his dresser and scruffed up his hair with his fingers. His chin was sprouting but he couldn't be bothered to shave, and besides, he had used his last disposable razor to scrape paint from a plastic model of the Millenium Falcon. He squeezed a large dollop of mint toothpaste onto his tongue, squirted himself with D&G aftershave, and then hurtled down the stairs five at a time.

His father was waiting for him in the hallway, with the sun shining through his thinning fair hair. "Do you have to come swinging down the stairs like a baboon?"

"Sorry, Dad. Must be genetic."

His father didn't rise to that, although Perry could tell that he wasn't at all amused. George Beame was a staunch Creationist, and he believed that God had made man in his own image, just like it said in the Bible. He didn't hold with any of that man-is-descended-from-the-apes blasphemy.

But all he said was, "Glad to see you dressed to impress."

"X-Skulls, Dad. Coolest band since Alice in Chains."

"Never heard of them."

"They're cool. You'd like them. Well, you never know."

They left the house and walked down the neat brick path together to his father's old blue Chevy truck. The thunderstorm had just passed over and the streets were dazzling. A stranger wouldn't have immediately recognized them as father and son. George Beame was short and thickset, with a face like a pugnacious baby, while Perry was tall and skinny, with long, El Greco features—a bony, complicated nose and dark eyelashes that any girl would have died for.

Perry looked exactly like his older sister Janie, and both of them looked exactly like their mother. But their mother had died of ovarian cancer on Christmas Eve seven-and-a-half years ago, and Janie had left home seventeen months ago after a summer of screaming matches with her father. Perry was now the only reminder that George Beame had of the woman he had loved so devotedly, and for so long. Although he would never have admitted it, that was why he was so possessive about Perry, and wanted him to stay at home, even though he was a leading candidate for the world's most annoying seventeen-year-old. Even now, Perry often caught his father staring at him across the room with an expression of such sadness that he always felt the urge to say something stupid, or laugh like a jackass at the television, just to remind his father that he wasn't his mother, reincarnated, and that he wasn't Janie, either, returned to the fold.

They climbed into the truck and George Beame drove them the seven blocks to the store. "Frank Reddy's lending me his concrete-mixer Monday. We should have all the flooring finished by the end of the week."

"Cool."

"There's a church barbecue Sunday. Nancy Bedford said that Trisha's going to be there."

"Oh, really?"

"Trisha's a really nice girl."

"You think so?"

"She's always polite. That's a real rarity these days, polite."

"I agree with you, Dad. She's polite. She is also totally flat-chested and her favorite band is the Country String Pickers."

"Have some respect, will you?"

"I'm respectful, Dad. It's just that I'm not blind or deaf."

Beame's Provisions stood on the corner of Ray Avenue and Grinstead, in the Highland District. It was an old-fashioned store with a nineteenth-century frontage and brass lamps all along the fascia. George Beame had kept up his profits by providing traditional-style groceries that few of the supermarkets stocked, as well as a deli counter that offered some of the best braunschweiger sandwiches in Jefferson County.

Six months ago, George had bought the store next door, Smells Better, a failing aromatherapy business. Now he was busy knocking out the interior so that he could enlarge his kitchen and provide his customers with tables and chairs. He always said that "The Lord didn't give us hands so that we could sit on them."

He parked the truck outside and Perry climbed down. Inside the half-demolished shell of the aromatherapy store, his older brother Dunc was happily tearing up floorboards with a crowbar. Dunc was just twenty-three, and looked much more like his father, except that he was even shorter and squatter, and his fair hair stuck up like a scrubbing brush. You could tell at once by the enthusiastic smile on his face and his wide-open pale blue eyes that something was wrong with Dunc. After he was born, the doctor had said,

"Think of Dunc's mind as a jigsaw, with several pieces of sky missing."

"Hi, Perry!" he enthused. "Boy, you should have been here about ten minutes ago."

"Oh, yeah? Why's that, Dunc?"

"Sue Marshall came in and she was wearing the shortest little red skirt "

"Dunc," George Beame snapped at him. "Perry's view of girls is disrespectful enough without you encouraging him."

"She's got the greatest bongaroobies, don't she?" said Dunc, shaking his head in wonder. "She sits down and five minutes later they're still bouncing."

"Dunc!" snapped his father. "I won't have any of that locker room talk here. Get on and finish that floor before I make you wash your mouth out with carbolic. Perry—you can mind the store while Dora has her lunch break."

Perry stepped over the joists and slapped his brother on the shoulder. "You take it easy, Dunc. No harm in looking."

"Hmh," said Dunc, wriggling his fingers like incey-wincey spiders. "Be nice to *touch,* though, once in a while."

"Yeah, well, maybe one day."

Perry climbed the makeshift steps that led through to the main store and pushed his way through a heavy curtain of plastic sheeting. Inside the store, two red marble counters ran the length of the store from the front to the back. The right-hand counter was taken up with glass-fronted cases containing Kentucky hams and Italian salamis and pickles, as well as baskets filled with fresh, fragrant, salt-topped bread. It was here that Morris and May worked, making the sandwiches. Morris was a bony sixty-five-year-old with cropped gray hair and a bulbous nose. He was a notorious sourpuss, although the left corner of his mouth had been known to twitch up a little when a discerning customer asked for his braunschweiger on rye bread with mayo and raw onions. May was twenty-one: tall and black and skinny with a green and white spotted scarf on her head and huge hoop earrings, and she was always bopping as she spread the sandwiches.

Behind the left-hand counter, where Dora worked, the shelves were stacked to the ceiling with every kind of exotic grocery you could think of, from cans of pâté de foie gras to bottles of sour cherry syrup. There were over thirty-two different varieties of tea, from Ahmad's to orange pekoe, and more than a hundred brands of cookies and crackers, from Willingham Manor peach pecan cookies to Duchy Original oatcakes, from the Prince of Wales's own factory in England.

The smell in the store was extraordinary—woody and aromatic, with a deep underlying note of very ripe cheese.

Perry went up to Dora and said, "Hi, Dora. Dad says you can take your break now."

Dora was a tiny, birdlike woman who had worked for Perry's dad since a week after Beame's had first opened. She was probably the only person who knew where everything in the store was kept. She took off her rimless spectacles and polished them on her apron. "About time, Perry. My son and my daughter-in-law brought my new granddaughter home this morning and I can't wait to go over to see her."

"Hey, congratulations. Look—I'm sorry I'm late. I kind of lost track of the time. Stay away as long as you want, I'll cover for you."

"That's very sweet of you, Perry. You always were an understanding boy."

George Beame battled his way through the plastic sheeting from the store next door. "Perry, I need to go out again. I have to pick up some plaster moldings from Alcott and Bentley. Keep your eye on things, will you … especially Dunc."

"Yes, sir. No problem."

"Off to see the new addition?" George asked Dora.

"I can't wait. Even if it does mean that I've become a grandma."

*   *   *

George Beame drove off, leaving Dunc happily banging and hammering and wrenching up floorboards. Dora took off her apron and brushed her hair.

"Later," said Perry as she left the store. He watched her cross the street to her green Honda Civic and climb in, but while he was doing so the phone rang. He tossed the receiver up in the air like a cocktail waiter, caught it, and announced, "Beame's Neighborhood Stores, and if we ain't got it, believe me, you seriously don't want it."

An anxious voice said, "Is Dora there? Dora Crawford?"

"I'm sorry, she just left. Take a message for you?"

"This is her son, David. I'm down at the Kosair Children's Hospital. Her new granddaughter's very sick and I need her to get here right away."

"Listen—wait—she's still here, right across the street. I'll see if I can catch her."

"Please. The doctors don't think that our little girl has very long to live."

Perry dropped the phone. He ran out of the store and into the street, shouting "Dora! Dora! Dora, wait up!" He was almost hit by a bright red Corvette, and he slammed his hand on its hood and shouted, "Out of my way, asshole!"

The driver peeled off his designer sunglasses and retorted, "Who are you calling *asshole*, asshole?"

But Perry ignored him and dodged across to Dora's Honda. She had started up the engine and she was pulling away from the curb when he banged on the roof.

"Dora!"

She wound down the window. "Perry—what's wrong?"

"Your son was on the phone. He said you should go down to the children's hospital, fast as you can. Your new granddaughter's sick. He says she might not make it."

"Oh, my God." Dora covered her mouth with her hand. Then she looked up at Perry; he had never seen anybody look so distraught. "Oh, my God, that's awful."

"Listen," said Perry, "I'll drive you. Let me just go back and tell Dunc what's happening."

He ran back across the street. The Corvette driver had pulled into the side of the road and was leaning over sideways, examining his hood for dents. "Hey! Asshole! Don't you think for one moment you're going to get away with this!"

Perry burst back into the store. "Dunc!" he shouted, wrestling his way back through the plastic sheeting. "Dunc ... I have to go out! I won't be long, but I need you to take care of the store, okay? Can you do that? Can you go out front and take care of the customers for me?"

Dunc frowned at him, and then carefully laid his crowbar down on the floor, as if it were made of porcelain. "Sure, Perry. I can do that."

"You're sure? Morris and May will help you."

"You want me to take care of the customers?"

"That's right. The customers are going to come into the store and tell you what they want, and all you have to do is give it to them."

"That's all I have to do?"

"That's right, Dunc. That's all you have to do. They say, 'Give me some of that Gethsemani cheese,' and what you do is, you give them some of that Gethsemani cheese. How hard is that?"

"That's not hard."

"Good. Now, I won't be too long, okay?"

"Okay."

"And wash your hands first, okay?"

"Okay."

On his way out, Perry went up to Morris and said, "I'm leaving Dunc in charge until I get back, okay?"

Morris was spreading Benedictine on a kaiser roll. "What you mean is, you're leaving *me* in charge, in the middle of the lunchtime rush."

"Don't worry, I'll watch out for Dunc," said May. "So long as he keeps his hands to himself."

"He'll be okay, I promise. He can manage pretty good, just so long as he doesn't get flustered. Now I really have to go. Dora's new granddaughter is in the hospital and they think she might die."

"Oh, Jesus. In that case, you go."

Perry drove down to East Chestnut Street as if he were Steve McQueen in *Bullitt,* running red lights and slewing the car around corners. Dora gripped the door handle so tight that there were white spots on her knuckles, but she didn't complain.

"Don't you worry," said Perry. "These days, what these doctors can do, it's amazing."

Dora was too upset to answer, but she nodded.

At last, Perry swerved the Honda up to the steps of Kosair Children's Hospital. A hospital attendant came up to them and said, "Sorry, folks. You can't park here. The garage is around the back, on Flexner."

Perry shouted, "This is an emergency, okay? This is Mrs. Crawford, okay? Her baby granddaughter's real sick. The doctors told her to hurry."

"Okay, sir. No need to panic. I'll take her up to neonatal while you park your vehicle."

Perry retorted, "This lady's baby granddaughter is dying, and all you care about is your goddamned parking regulations?"

"I'm sorry, sir, but you cannot leave your vehicle unattended directly in front of the hospital entrance."

"Did you take lessons to be a pompous pontificating asshole or were you just born that way?"

"Sir, I have to warn you, if you're going to be abusive—"

Dora laid a hand on Perry's arm. "It's all right, Perry. You go find a place to park and I'll see you in the clinic." She climbed out of the car, but before she went up the steps into the hospital entrance she said, "*Calm,* Perry. You understand me? Nobody never got noplace by waxing angry."

Perry drove around to the parking garage, still fuming. Screw all rules and regulations and whoever enforces them. This was supposed to be a free country, right? Instead, what? You can't park here and you can't skate-board there and you can't even scratch your balls without somebody making a song-and-dance about it.

He had to drive around and around to the fifth level be-fore he could find a place to park, the Honda's tires scream-ing in a cats' chorus, and by the time he found his way to the elevators he was arguing out loud. He stabbed the button for neonatal care. If Dora's granddaughter had breathed her last gasp while that pompous pontificating asshole was pontificating, and Dora had been too late to see her alive, Perry was going to make sure that he paid the price for it.

When he stepped out on the fourth floor, however, the atmosphere was so calm and the air-conditioning was so cool that his adrenaline began to subside.

"Pompous pontificating asshole," he repeated, but a passing nurse gave him such a beatific smile that he felt em-barrassed, and said, "Hi," and smiled back.

Kosair was a specialist children's hospital, with some of the most advanced neonatal care in the country. The floors were white and shiny and there were splashy abstract prints on the walls and everything smelled new. Every now and then, a soft chime sounded, and a warm, seductive voice called for a doctor. "Dr. Kasabian, please come to pul-monology for a blow-job." That's what Perry thought it sounded like, anyhow.

There were fifteen or so people in the waiting area out-side of the neonatal unit, men and women, most of them in their late twenties or early thirties. As he approached, Perry couldn't help noticing how haggard they looked, and that the women's eyes were red from crying. Nobody was drink-ing coffee or reading a magazine, and none of them were talking. Perry felt as if he had walked into an airport lounge after a plane crash.

The swing doors opened and a nurse came out, looking grim-faced. For a brief second, Perry caught the sound of babies crying. Not just crying, but screaming hysterically. The nurse came hurrying down the corridor toward him, and as she came closer he could see that she was red-eyed, too.

"Nurse? I'm trying to find Mrs. Dora Crawford."

The nurse stared at him, totally distracted.

"Mrs. Dora Crawford? Her daughter-in-law's in here, having a baby. Her son called her up and said it was sick."

"They're all sick," said the nurse.

"What?"

"They're *all* sick. I'm sorry—I have to make a very urgent phone call."

"But Mrs. Crawford—?"

"I'm sorry. You'll have to wait like everybody else."

Perry walked slowly up to the waiting area. One or two of the men glanced at him sympathetically, but still nobody spoke. He mooched around for a while, wondering if it was worth him hanging around. If Dora's granddaughter were suffering from some life-threatening illness, or already dead, then she would probably stay here for hours. He sat down in front of the aquarium and watched some stupid angelfish circling around for a while, and then he decided that he would write Dora a note and leave it at the nurses' station, telling her where her car was parked, and apologizing because he hadn't been able to stay. It was twenty-five minutes to three now, and he had left Dunc in charge of the store. The same Dunc who believed that spaghetti grew on bushes (well, only because Perry had told him it did).

He went to the nurses' station to borrow a pen and a piece of paper. He had just written, "Dear Dora, sorry to be a pain and everything," when the door from the intensive care unit opened and Dora appeared with her son, David. She had both hands raised to her cheeks, as if she had just witnessed something horrific. David wasn't much taller than she was, with black slicked-back hair and a dark blue chin. His face was yellow and he looked as if he hadn't slept for days.

Dora came up to Perry and said, "She died, Perry. They did everything they could, but she died."

"I'm sorry," said Perry. He looked at David and said, "I'm real sorry, sir."

"The poor little scrap," said Dora. She was so tearful that she had to take her glasses off. "She was so tiny. But she was screaming and screaming and she couldn't seem to stop. And all the other babies are the same."

"Do the doctors know what's wrong with them?" asked Perry.

David shrugged, his mouth puckered with grief.

"It's something to do with their brains," said Dora. "One of the doctors said that they couldn't dream properly."

"Do what?" asked Perry.

"We don't really know," said David, putting his arm around Dora's shoulders. "They said it was some kind of syndrome, I didn't really catch the name of it. But if you can't dream properly, you panic. And that's what our baby died from, and all the rest of these babies are going to die from. Panic."

Perry drove Dora's car back to the store. He drove slower and slower until the cars behind him started to blast their horns. He drew over to the right and let them pass, and didn't even turn to look at them when they gave him the finger and shouted, "Ya moron! What do you think this is, a funeral?"

He parked opposite the store, but he didn't get out of the car right away. He sat frowning at the steering wheel, wondering why he felt so shaken. He didn't know Dora's family, and he hadn't seen their baby, either alive or dead, so why did he feel that he was somehow involved?

He could almost believe that he had been fated to go down to the Kosair Hospital today, as if time and destiny had secretly arranged for him to be there, and to witness Dora's grief.

After a while he climbed out of the car and crossed the road to the store. Morris and May were still making sandwiches for five or six late-lunchers, while Dunc was talking about cookies to a fat woman in a poppy-print dress. "We got chocolate chip, nutty chocolate chip, oatmeal raisin, peanut butter, white chocolate, pumpkin chocolate chip, gingersnap, pumpkin raisin and Lucky-in-Kentucky pecan chocolate chip."

Perry had to hand it to Dunc: some of his wiring might have been faulty, but he could remember anything and everything. He could tell you the telephone number of the Animal Rescue Center or the number of graves in the Evergreen Cemetery or every single winner of the Kentucky Derby since it began in 1875, *and* their odds.

The fat woman said, "Okay, son. Give me some of those oatmeal raisin, and maybe some of those gingersnaps, too. No, forget the gingersnaps. Got to keep down to my fighting weight."

Dunc handed them over and winked at her, and said, "You have a good day now, and come back! You'll always find a beam at Beame's!"

Perry watched her leave the store, and then he turned to Dunc and said, very slowly, "You didn't ask her for any money."

Dunc smiled at him, and nodded.

"Dunc—you didn't ask her for any money!"

"Of course not. I was doing like you said. You said, 'The customers are going to come into the store and tell you what they want and all you have to do is give it to them.' "

"Jesus, Dunc, not without *paying* for it!"

But Dunc was adamant. "I did exactly what you asked me to do, Perry. If they want Gethsemani cheese, give them Gethsemani cheese."

"But not *free,* Dunc! Dad's going to kill us. Well, he's going to kill *me!*"

"Got a problem?" asked Morris, looking up from his Benedictine-spreading.

"No," said Perry. "Nothing that a little ritual suicide couldn't sort out."

*   *   *

That night, while Perry was washing the supper plates, his father came into the kitchen. He stood directly under the overhead light, which made him look even more haggard than he really was.

"I don't blame you for what happened," he said. "But you could have thought to call me."

"I guess so. I'm sorry. I got kind of carried away."

George picked up a towel and started to dry the saucepan lids. "You took quite an emotional knock there, didn't you?"

Perry looked at him and said, "I don't know why. She wasn't *my* baby, was she? But it wasn't just her—it was *all* of those babies. I could hear them all crying and ..." He lifted his hands out of the dishwashing water, wearing two foam gloves.

"You wished there was something you could do to help them, but you couldn't."

"I don't know, Dad. I can't explain it."

His father laid a hand on his shoulder. "It's called Christian spirit, son. We all have a duty to look out for others, but these days, most of us choose to look away. What you felt today—well, that shows me what kind of a person you really are, and I hope it shows you, too."

"Dad—I don't want you to read too much into this, you know?"

"Oh, I know. You wouldn't want to ruin your credentials as a right royal pain in the rear end."

"It's not that, Dad. It's just that—I don't know—I feel like I'm *responsible,* you know?"

His father cleared his throat, and then said, "It's time I told you something about your mother. I guess I should have told you years ago, but I never did. I guess I wasn't confident that I could say it without breaking down."

"Dad?"

His father tried to smile again, but it was the same puckered smile of grief that David Crawford had given him at the hospital.

"Linda—your mother—when she died, she was going to have a baby."

Perry stared at his father, but he didn't say anything. The foam in the sink softly crackled, and upstairs he could hear Dunc playing one of his video games.

"She was three months gone when we found out that she had a malignant tumor on her ovary. The doctors gave her a choice. If she underwent a course of intensive radiotherapy, it would give her a fifty-fifty chance of beating the cancer, but the baby wouldn't survive. If she *didn't* have the radiotherapy, the baby would have a better chance, but she would die. Simple as that.

"She didn't hesitate. She said that God had created life within her, and it wasn't her place to take it away. If this was to be a test of her faith, then so be it."

George Beame's eyes were brimming with tears. Perry tore off a sheet of paper towel and gave it to him. "What happened to the baby?" he asked.

His father wiped his eyes and blew his nose. "Baby died, too. Wouldn't take nourishment after he was born. Wouldn't sleep, wouldn't stop crying. Doctors could never find out what was wrong with him. He died in his mother's arms, and twenty-four hours later she died, too."

"What was his name?"

"You want to know his name?"

"Sure. He was my brother, after all."

"Joe. That was what we christened him. Joe."

Perry stayed up late that night, long after Dunc and his father had gone to bed. He was creating a scene in *Trash Planet* in which Steel Sister prowls through a scrapyard, hunting for her archenemy, Acid Boy. But as she searches through the heaps of crushed cars, she is being followed by more and more fragments of scrap metal, tumbling along the ground behind her, like rats following the Pied Piper.

The fragments of metal gradually collect themselves together into a giant child, five times as big as Steel Sister, but with the mental simplicity of a three-year-old. This was

Junk Toddler, who would follow Steel Sister everywhere she went. Sometimes Junk Toddler would unintentionally save her from perilous situations, but more often than not he would be a liability, crawling into car-crushers or falling into blast-furnaces, just when Steel Sister was desperately needed elsewhere.

Perry was hunched over his computer screen, wearing one of the black Soundgarden T-shirts he always slept in, a droopy pair of red and white-striped boxer shorts and a huge pair of hairy Bigfoot slippers with plastic claws in the toes. He was having trouble with his Maya software. Every time he got the fragments of scrap metal to assemble themselves together into a human form, they fell apart.

"Come on, you son of a bitch," he swore, his fingers flying over his keyboard.

It was then that the screen abruptly went black.

"Shit," he said. "Please, God, don't tell me that I've lost all of this."

His computer was still running, and as far as he could make out the Maya program was still running. But the screen remained totally black. All he could see was his own pallid face with his hair sticking up.

"If this is God punishing me, then can I please ask You to think of some other punishment, because I have been working for months and months on this freaking animation and if I lose it then I will lose the will to live, I swear it, and You will have me on your conscience for all eternity. Amen."

Gradually, a dim oval light appeared on the screen. Perry leaned forward over his keyboard and frowned at it, as if the power of frowning could bring it into sharper focus.

The light became brighter, and little by little it seemed to form itself into a recognizable shape. After a few minutes, Perry found himself staring at a pale, ethereal-looking face, with bottomless shadows where his eyes should have been. Or *her* eyes; he couldn't decide if it was a man or a woman or an androgynous child.

The face didn't move, or blink, or speak. Perry punched

CTRL/ALT/DELETE, but the face stayed on the screen. He even switched off the power, but the face didn't even waver.

"Who are you?" he said. He was so scared that he thought he was going to wet his shorts. "Are you going to talk to me or what?"

He stood up, stumbling over his chair. The face continued to stare at him, placid and pale.

"Who are you?" he screamed at it. "What do you want? Say something, for Christ's sake!"

The face opened its mouth, as straight and tight as a mailbox. It spoke, but it didn't move its lips.

The face said, "Joe sent me."

CHAPTER FOUR

"Who's there?" said Sasha.

The figure moved sideways, to the left, but it *slid* rather than walked, as if it were on wheels.

Sasha sat up and scrabbled for her bedside light. She switched it on and was just about to shout, but found that she couldn't. The figure was her father. Her father, who had walked out on his family all those months ago and was now supposed to be working in Manitoba. But here he was, right in front of her, in her apartment.

"Dad?" she said hoarsely. "Dad, what are you doing here?"

Her father was standing only about three or four feet from the end of her bed. He looked older and grayer, and his face was almost silvery. He was wearing a loose-fitting gray suit and a gray T-shirt. He *flickered,* too, very subtly, as if it were a projected image rather than a real person. He reminded Sasha of the girl who had crawled out of the television screen in *The Ring.*

He had lost a lot of weight. His eyes were dark, more like

pools of oil than eyes, and his cheekbones were very finely carved. His expression was utterly remote.

Sasha was so frightened that she felt as if her skin were shrinking. Shivering, she shifted herself off the edge of the bed and stood up. She was wearing only her T-shirt, which made her feel even more vulnerable.

"Dad, is this really you?" she demanded. Her voice was high-pitched and ragged, and she didn't even sound like herself. "How did you get in here?"

"I thought you'd be pleased to see me," said her father. His voice was oddly hollow, like a draft blowing under a door. "It's been such a long time, hasn't it?"

"Dad, you're scaring me. You're you, but you don't look like you. There's something wrong, isn't there?"

"Well, you're right, sweetheart. I'm not exactly what I appear to be. I'm a *messenger*, in a way. I thought that if I looked like somebody you really wanted to see, it would make things easier for both of us."

"What are you talking about? What do you mean, 'messenger'? Are you my dad, or aren't you?"

"Yes, I am. And, no, I'm not."

Sasha picked up her cell phone. "I think you'd better leave. If you have anything to say to me, I think you'd better find some other way of doing it."

Her father lowered his eyes for a moment, and then looked up at her with a very serious expression. "I can't leave, Sasha, I'm sorry. I've come about the babies."

"The babies? What are you talking about?"

"You know what I mean about the babies. You saw them yourself, didn't you, crying their hearts out?"

"How do you know about that?"

Her father attempted a smile. "You don't have to be afraid of me, Sasha. You can call me Dad if you like, or you can call me Springer, which is what people usually call me. I've only come to talk to you about the babies, nothing else."

"I'm going crazy," said Sasha. "This isn't real, and you're not here, and if I close my eyes you're going to disappear."

"I'm sorry, Sasha. You have a duty, just like your father does, and just like I do."

Sasha squeezed her eyes shut, hoping that the figure would disappear, but then she suddenly got frightened that he might come up close to her when she wasn't looking, so she opened them again. He was still there, although he hadn't come any nearer.

"Tell me I'm dreaming."

Springer shook its head. "No, Sasha, you're not dreaming, although it wouldn't make any difference if you were."

"Please, go away," said Sasha. "Whatever your message is, I really don't want to hear it."

"I'm afraid that you don't have any choice."

Springer's dry, understated intonation was so much like her father's that Sasha could hear it in her memory as well as her ears. There was something infinitely regretful about it, something that reminded Sasha of early winter evenings, long ago, when she had walked by the river with her father, hand in hand, hardly ever speaking, but as close as a father and daughter could possibly be.

"All right," she said. "Tell me."

"As I said, Sasha, it's time for you to do your duty—the duty that you were born for. You saw those babies, how they cried. They cried because they can't sleep; and the reason why they can't sleep is because somebody took their dreams away."

"Oh, come on. This is insanity. This is total insanity."

"You don't believe that babies can have their dreams stolen?"

"Of course not. And who would want to do it, and how could they?"

Springer moved around to the end of the bed, much closer to her. "Sasha, do you believe in good and evil?"

"In what sense?"

"Do you believe that a constant battle is going on, between harm and salvation, between kindness and hatred, between love and hostility?"

"I don't understand the question."

"Yes, you do. You've seen what's happening in the waking world, how terrorists are trying to destroy our sense of security and tear apart everything that makes us feel comfortable and happy. The same thing has been going on for centuries in the world of dreams, but in the world of dreams the struggle has been much more devastating. Whole cultures have been destroyed. Why do you think Greek civilization collapsed? Why do you think Rome fell?"

Sasha said, "Who cares why Rome fell? It's the middle of the night and if you don't leave I'm going to call nine-one-one. I really don't want to listen to any more of this stuff."

"Wait, Sasha. Remember those babies today and hear me out."

"Listen—I feel sorry for those babies, okay? But there's nothing that I can do to help them, is there?"

"You don't think so?" Somehow, Springer had managed to come much closer, so that he was standing only two or three feet away. "Babies, when they're born, know *everything*. They know the secrets of true innocence, and the secrets of true evil. Babies know the whole meaning of human existence."

"What?"

But Springer pointed to his forehead and said, "In here, babies know exactly why they were born, and what their future is going to be. They have a complete grasp of time and space—the stars, the positions of the planets, everything. They know how matter was made out of nothing at all and how the universe was put together. When you think about it, it's completely logical that they know, because they were born in the image of the all-seeing, all-knowing force which created everything.

"What happens is—they dream about this universal knowledge in their very first dream, but as soon as they wake up, they forget it, almost all of it, except for the faintest resonance. Their minds are wiped clean, for their own protection. *Knowing* is one thing, but *understanding* is quite another. If babies knew how the universe worked without understanding *why* it worked, or what for, they would suffer from total overload. They would short out every synaptic circuit in their entire brain."

"I still don't see what this has got to do with me."

"It has everything to do with you, Sasha, because you are one of the few people in this world who can protect newborn babies from having their first dream taken away from them."

"*Me?*"

Springer reached his hand out as if he were going to stroke Sasha's hair, the way her father used to. He looked so much like her father that she almost let him, but then she jerked her head away. "*No*," she said. "I might be going mad, but I'm not stupid."

Springer shrugged, and said, "You could have gone through your whole life without ever knowing about this. But because of what's been happening, we need you, Sasha, and we need you urgently. You are directly descended from a long line of people who were trained to defend humanity's dreams against the incursion of evil. You have a dream name and a dream identity, just like your father does, and your father's mother and her mother before her."

Sasha shook her head in disbelief.

Springer was suddenly standing by the window with his back to her, although Sasha could have sworn that she hadn't seen him move. He looked back over his shoulder and said, "There is a dazzling force of purity in the universe, which some call God, and others call by many different names. In the world of dreams it is known as Ashapola, and it is Ashapola who sent me."

"So, what, you're like an angel, sent by God?"

Springer smiled. "If that makes it easier for you to understand what I am, then yes."

Sasha sat down on the bed. "So you're an angel. I'm

falling apart. God help me, I'm losing my mind. It's the stress, isn't it, of losing my job? Shit—why am I asking you? You're not even real." She gripped her cheeks with both hands and twisted them hard to wake herself up. But she didn't wake up. She couldn't, because she wasn't asleep.

Springer was silent for a moment, but then said, "Reality comes in many different guises, Sasha. You assume that your waking life is real. Your job, this apartment, your friends. But there is a far greater reality than the one with which you're familiar. When you come to understand who you actually are, *Sasha* will seem like nothing more than a character in a play, and this waking world will seem like a stage set."

"I'm perfectly happy as I am, thank you. I don't want to feel like a character in a play. Why don't you leave me alone?"

"I can't, Sasha. You're needed."

"To do what, exactly? How can I help those babies? I'm not a pediatrician."

"They don't need doctors, they need you. They can't sleep because they can't dream, and they can't dream because the forces of darkness have tried to rob them of their very first dream, and in doing so, they have irrevocably damaged their ability ever to dream again.

"This isn't fantasy, Sasha. This is science. People visit the dream world every night to make sense out of their waking lives, and if they can't do that, they become severely disturbed. They are unable to function as human beings, and in a very short space of time they die, like those babies are dying."

Sasha said, "Excuse me—*'forces of darkness'*?"

"I'm sorry. I didn't mean to sound like a politician. But ever since the earliest days of creation, there have always been negative forces in the universe. Good is unable to exist without evil—otherwise, it would have no meaning. The greater the good, the greater the evil, by definition."

"So what exactly are they—these 'forces of darkness'?"

"I suppose you would call them demons or devils or evil spirits. They are trying to destroy the universe that Ashapola has created. They are only interested in their own greed and their own lust for power. For centuries, they have believed that humanity is only good for serving them or for satisfying their perverted appetites. They have regarded humanity only as slaves, or as objects of torture or extreme sexual abuse, or as food.

"But this time, they are seeking much more than the subjugation of human beings. They have gradually come to understand that newborn babies possess the knowledge of the universe, and they want this knowledge for themselves. Don't you see? If they can learn how the universe was put together, they will be able to take it apart. We're not just talking about the end of the world, Sasha. We're talking about the stars falling and the sky disassembling and the entire material universe flying into atoms. Everything that exists now will exist no longer. People, planets, galaxies—everything. Gone. And nothing in its place but total chaos."

Sasha turned her head away. She really didn't want to hear any more of this. It was giving her a headache. But Springer persisted. "Ashapola has managed to hold back the forces of darkness for so many centuries because of people like you—people who can take up arms in the world of dreams and fight for purity and light and justice."

"And what if I say that I don't believe you?"

"It doesn't matter if you believe me or not, it's not going to change anything. The forces of darkness will still try to unravel everything that Ashapola has created. But the plain fact is that you *do* believe me, because I look exactly like your father. I *am* your father, in the physical sense, and you know that your father would never lie to you or mislead you or put you in any mortal danger, not without a just cause."

Sasha said nothing at first, but she knew that Springer was right. His appearance was so impossible that it had to be true. He waited patiently for her to reply, still smiling, and it was agonizingly hard to believe that he wasn't her father. She wanted so much to put her arms around him and hold him close.

"If I *do* agree to help you," she said, "what will I have to do?"

"Do you want to see?"

"I don't understand what you mean."

"Come here, stand in front of the mirror."

Sasha hesitated, but then she got up and walked over to the mirror that was screwed to the wall next to her closet. The surface of the mirror was dusty and covered in lipsticky fingerprints, and there were scores of Post-It notes clustered over the top of it with scribbled reminders of dental appointments and phone numbers. She could see herself clearly enough, but strangely she couldn't see Springer, even though he was standing right next to her. She looked around, but he was still there.

"In the dream world," said Springer, "your father is known as Zerak, the Illusion Engineer. To put it simply, he is capable of visually altering a landscape so that it looks as if a faraway range of hills is suddenly close, or a forest has vanished. He can make the most treacherous of swamps look like the driest of deserts. Very useful, that, for drowning an entire battalion of advancing barbarians. You have inherited many of his talents. You are a natural deceiver, although you usually mean well with your deceptions. You can alter facts to suit your own interpretation of the truth. You are Xanthys, the Time Curver."

"I'm *who?* The *what?*"

"You are Xanthys, spelled with an X, and you are a Time Curver. You have the ability to bend the time-stream, so that you can alter almost any sequence of events to suit your own purposes."

"And what does that mean?"

"It means that you can bring forward an event which has not yet happened so that it happens now, or bring back an event which happened some time ago so that it happens again. Believe me, it is a wonderful tactical gift. It allows you to use your enemy's own deviousness against him, or to manipulate ordinary events to influence any conflict. For instance, your enemy may be standing on an empty highway, but you can curve time so that an automobile which passed along that highway yesterday passes along it again and knocks him down."

"Xanthys?" said Sasha, peering into the mirror.

"Look more closely," Springer urged her.

Sasha stepped right up to the mirror. All she could see at first were two curved shadows under her eyes, but then she realized that they were not shadows at all, but a large pair of crystal-clear goggles, which gave her a grasshopper appearance. She had a pair of earphones, too, like seashells. Her hair was no longer tousled but clustered with hundreds of tiny silver beads.

She was wearing upcurved epaulets made of jointed metal and elaborate metal boots with V-shaped metal wings in front of her ankles. Around her waist hung a heavy metal belt from which dozens of complicated keys were dangling. Apart from that she was naked, although her skin was burnished all over with some kind of copper paint.

In spite of her doubts, Sasha began to feel a rising surge of recognition. It was like seeing herself for the first time as she really was. Her reflection didn't look strange or outrageous at all. Quite the opposite: it was like discovering that, ever since she was a child, she had always been dressed up in the wrong clothes. She reached out and touched the mirror, and the reflection in the mirror reached out to her, too—greeting her, saluting her.

Gradually, the image of Xanthys faded. Sasha turned back to Springer and said, "My God. That was me, wasn't it? I felt like that was really *me*."

"It *is* you. You have always been Xanthys, as well as Sasha."

"But how can I be two people at once?"

"You're not, really, any more than I am. You have a waking identity and a dream identity, that's all. Everybody does, except that not everybody is chosen to serve Ashapola, any more than everybody in the waking world is chosen to serve in the armed forces."

Sasha looked back at the mirror. "But how do I become Xanthys? I've never been Xanthys in any dream that I can remember."

"All you have to do is invoke the power of Ashapola before you fall asleep. Then, when you dream, you will become Xanthys. I will teach you the meditation that you will need to undertake and the incantation that you will need to recite. It was in Latin, originally, but it was translated into English when it was brought to the New World in the seventeenth century."

"But what do I do then? How do I fight these forces of darkness?"

"You will rise up from your sleeping body and go hunting for them in other people's dreams, which is where they will be hiding themselves."

"Other people's dreams," Sasha echoed him. "That sounds ridiculously easy—not."

"Don't worry," said Springer. "I will train you well before you first go out as Xanthys. And you will not be alone. There will be other Night Warriors with you, with different abilities and different weaponry."

"Is that what you call them? Night Warriors?"

Springer nodded. "The Night Warriors are a fierce and noble calling. They have never been recognized in the waking world, but they have kept humanity safe since time began. I will teach you their history, and their traditions, and their lore. I will tell you of their greatest victories and their most terrible defeats. By the time you have finished your training with me, you will feel that your real self is the self which exists in dreams. As a Night Warrior, you will begin to realize your true potential and your true power. No matter how meanly other people regard you, no matter how you have failed during the day, in your dreams you will be a heroine."

He looked around her apartment. "Here," he told her, "I can give you an example. What time is it?"

Sasha peered at the big brass alarm clock on her nightstand. "A quarter of three, just gone."

"Lift your arm and point at your clock. That's right. Now slowly circle your finger clockwise."

Hesitantly, Sasha did as she was told. "What's supposed to happen?" she asked, but Springer said, "*Concentrate*. And keep on rotating your finger."

She continued to circle her finger, and as she did so the clock hands gradually started to turn, too. Springer was right: it did take enormous concentration. It made the veins in her forehead throb and her shoulder muscles lock up, but she could do it. The clock hands moved on to twenty after three, then half-past, then ten after four, then a quarter of five.

Not only did the clock hands turn, but the sky outside her apartment window began to lighten, and suddenly she could hear traffic and birds singing. In the distance, she could hear an airplane thundering its way westward, but when she turned her finger faster, it was gone.

Springer said, "I think you can stop now. Try to turn it back."

"I can turn it *back*?"

"Why not? You turned it forward, didn't you?"

Sasha circled her finger counterclockwise. The clock hands began to rotate the other way, and as they did so, she heard the airplane thundering back again. The sky rapidly grew dark and the traffic noises died away. In less than a minute, they were back to 2:46.

Sasha stared at her fingertip in amazement. "That's just incredible. I never knew I could do that."

"Well … to be truthful, it wasn't a very subtle demonstration. If you turn your clock forward, the whole world has to turn with it. It's rather like unscrewing the wheel-nut on a car by keeping the wheel-nut still and rotating the whole car round and round. You also had more than a little help from Ashapola, through me. But it was *you* who directed it. And once you become Xanthys, you will be able to curve time entirely by yourself, and in far more sophisticated ways than that. You will be able to select specific incidents and move them backward or forward or sideways through time in almost any way you choose."

"And what if I select the moment that you first appeared in my apartment, and send that moment so far forward in time that it never gets to happen? Not in my lifetime, anyhow."

"Well, you *could*, but you won't."

"How do you know that?"

"Because you are Xanthys, the daughter of Zerak. You are a Night Warrior, and a Night Warrior's first concern is the safety of the universe, and all those who live in it."

The sky had grown naturally light before Springer left. Sasha went over to her kitchen counter to make them both a cup of coffee, but when she turned back he had simply vanished.

"Springer?" she said. "Springer, where are you?" She crossed her apartment and tried the front door but it was still locked from the inside. She checked her small triangular bathroom, but he wasn't there, either. All she could see was her own reflection in the medicine cabinet mirror, Sasha or Xanthys, or maybe both of them, looking pale.

She walked slowly back into her living room. She felt drained, both mentally and physically. Springer had talked to her for more than three hours about the Night Warriors, and how her training as Xanthys would change her life forever.

"Once you have realized how much power you possess in the world of dreams, you will be able to use much of that power during the day. Look at what you did with your alarm clock. Your life will change immeasurably, whether you want it to or not."

"Hey, maybe I'll find myself a great new job."

Springer had given her a sly, sideways smile, just like her father used to. "Yes, maybe you will. But all the same, you will find that whatever success you achieve during the day, it will count very little compared to the success you achieve during the night. The greatest of adventures is waiting for you, Sasha, as soon as the sun begins to set."

She stood in front of the window, slowly rotating her head to ease her neck muscles. Below her, the sunshine was gleaming on Third Street like warm, slowly poured syrup. It was the same intersection that she had looked over yesterday morning and every morning since she had moved here, but today the streets looked distinctly artificial, as if the Italianate houses of Old Louisville were only stage sets, and at any moment the trees could all be picked up and taken away by scene-shifters. Springer had been right: now she knew about the world of dreams, the real world didn't look so solid anymore. That old couple who were crossing the street, she could make them cross it again and again; or else she could make them return to their home, before they had even set out for their walk. Those birds that had just exploded out of that white oak tree, she could make them burst out of those branches over and over as many times as she wanted.

Even after all of Springer's explanations, Sasha still wasn't completely clear how her newfound talents as a Time Curver were going to work, but she was excited and eager to give them a try. For the first time in her life, she felt as if she were going to achieve something really significant, something dramatic, something that would change the lives of thousands of people. There was no longer any need for her to make up stories about bluegrass singers jumping off bridges or starving widows living on cat fricassee. Not when she was saving defenseless babies from the forces of darkness; and maybe the universe, too.

* * *

She went back to bed and slept until one o'clock in the afternoon. When she woke up, she felt drowsy and hungry and unaccountably depressed. Her mug of greasy-looking coffee was still sitting on the kitchen counter, and for some reason her room looked even untidier than ever, as if a gang of uncontrollable children had been romping around in it, throwing all her clothes everywhere.

She took a carton of orange juice out of the refrigerator and sniffed it suspiciously. It was only two days past its sell-by date, but it was thick and woolly and it smelled like carpet felt. She would have to go out for something to eat.

She showered, her eyes closed, leaning her shoulder against the tiles for support. Then she dried herself and dressed in a pale blue skinny-rib sweater that only had one orange smear of foundation on the sleeve and her short denim skirt. While she brushed her hair and put on her makeup, she listened to the news on Channel 3.

A bald, bespectacled doctor appeared on the screen, with sunburn freckles on his head. He was looking tired and grim, and his left eye kept twitching.

"… Here at the Norton Hospital, in the last twenty-four hours, three newborn infants have died and seven more are still in a highly critical condition."

A woman reporter held up her microphone to ask, "Do you have any idea what's wrong with them, doctor?"

"Our preliminary tests suggest that all of them are suffering from Charcot-Wilbrand Syndrome, or agnosia. In technical terms this means that for one reason or another, they are incapable of revisualizing images in their brains. In simpler language, they don't have the ability to dream.

"Charcot-Wilbrand Syndrome sometimes follows a stroke, although there is no indication that any of the infants in our care at Norton have suffered any such trauma. However, an inability to dream can cause great psychological distress, since dreaming is the way in which we all keep our thinking in order and prevent our minds from descending into total chaos."

The reporter asked, "If these babies didn't all suffer from strokes, doctor, do you have any theories at all about why they should have been born without the capacity to dream?"

"None whatsoever, I'm sorry to say. We're looking into every conceivable possibility. We're checking their mothers' diets, so far as we can. We're checking to see if they were exposed to radiation from cell phone towers. We're checking incidents of water pollution and air-quality advisories. We're checking mosquito activity in the past nine months, and the activity of several other parasites. We're even checking the local incidence of solar flares."

"What would you to say to any woman expecting the imminent birth of a baby in Louisville, doctor? What words of reassurance could you give her?"

"None at all, I'm afraid. I know that there are dedicated doctors and nurses in every hospital in Louisville who are working twenty-four/seven to give these babies a chance to survive. But my only advice is to leave Louisville, or Jefferson County, or even the state of Kentucky altogether, and arrange to give birth to your baby elsewhere."

"So this condition is specifically related to Louisville, and nowhere else?"

"So far, yes. But it's made an appearance now in five different postnatal units around the city, one after the other, and who's to say that it won't spread further afield?"

"That was Dr. Allan Kleinman," said the television reporter, turning toward the camera. "Dr. Kleinman and his team are doing everything they can to find out why the newborn babies of Louisville are unable to dream, so that they can prevent the joy of parenthood from turning into the most poignant human tragedy that this city has ever experienced.

"What does Dr Kleinman need? He needs all of the

medical expertise for which Louisville is nationally famous. Most of all, however, he needs a miracle."

Sasha turned around and peered at Dr. Kleinman on the TV screen. "A miracle?" she said, and she thought about her alarm clock, and the sky growing light in the middle of the night. "Dr. Kleinman—I think you're in luck."

CHAPTER FIVE

John said, "If you've come to rob me, help yourself. I have about eighty-seven dollars in small denomination bills in my wallet, if it's any good to you, and about thirty-two cents in change in my back pants pocket. And while you're at it, you can relieve me of my maxed-out Visa card—oh, and there's a Bacon's store card with about three dollars and seventy cents of credit left on it."

The figure came closer. "I haven't come for your money, John."

John heaved himself up onto one elbow. "Who is this? I know that voice."

"I should think you do, after all of these years."

John took three wheezy breaths. It couldn't be. But his room was so dark that all he could see was a dark, sloping-shouldered shape, and he hesitated to switch on his bedside lamp. I mean, if he switched it on, he was going to see for sure who it was, and if it was who it sounded like …

"You *sound* like him, I can't deny that. But you can't be. Not unless I'm having some kind of nightmare on account of ingesting insufficient nourishment before I turned in."

"Turn on the light, why don't you? Then you'll see."

John rolled over and reached for the dingly-dangly little cord that hung below his bedside light. "If this is some kind of a leg-pull—"

"No leg-pull, John, I promise you."

John switched on the light and blinked at the man who was standing in the middle of his room. The man was about five-feet-nine, heavily built, with tangled white curls and a face crimson with alcohol. He must have been quite handsome once, but his blue eyes were weeping and his skin was rough with eczema and he hadn't shaved for several days. He was wearing a sagging blue pullover with the elbows fraying, and camouflage pants, and worn-out canvas sneakers and no socks.

"I don't know what to say," said John. "Was that all some kind of a practical joke, then, that funeral?"

"No, John, nothing like that. It was a proper funeral, no trickery whatsoever."

"I drove two thousand, three hundred and seven miles to see you cremated," John protested. "If you weren't really dead, I warn you—I'll frigging *kill* you."

"No, no, John. Don't upset yourself. What you went to see, that was the genuine article, I promise. Real casket, real flames. Real body inside. It's just that I had to pay you a visit, you see, and I wanted to come in some kind of a guise that wouldn't alarm you. Dean Brunswick III was the only person I could find who really liked you."

John sat up. The night was intolerably hot, and even though the air conditioner was squeaking and whirring away like two hamsters in a treadmill, his T-shirt was soaked in sweat. "What are you trying to say to me, Deano? Are you dead, or aren't you?"

Dean nodded. "Dean Brunswick III is dead, John, yes. I look like him. I *am* him, in a way that I can't really explain to you. But I'm not actually *him*."

John sat on the edge of the bed, his chest rising and

falling like an asthmatic. "What did Deano do in Colonel Wrightman's cigar box?"

"What? I don't have any idea what Deano did in Colonel Wrightman's cigar box. I don't even know Colonel Wrightman."

"You really don't know? Then maybe you are who say you are and not who you look like."

"My name's Springer. I haven't come here to take your money or to harm you. I've only come here to ask for your help."

"How do you manage to look like Deano? How do you do that? What is it, plastic surgery? No—don't be stupid, nobody would undergo plastic surgery to look like Deano. The whole point of plastic surgery is to look as little like a penniless wino as possible, *n'est-ce pas?*"

"Are you asking me?" said Springer.

"I'm just discussing it. How about a beer? I know it's the middle of the night. What is it, two-thirty? Jesus. Are you *sure* you're not Deano? That wasn't just an empty coffin they were burning, was it, on account of you could get away from the people you owed money to, and your parole officer?"

"My name is Springer. I have this—*facility,* if you like. I can look like other people."

"That's some furshlugginer facility. How about a beer?"

"You already asked me that."

"No, I asked *me,* not you. Do you want one, too?"

"No, thanks."

"Okay. But you don't mind if I have one?"

"No, go ahead. You'll sweat it all out, anyhow." John knelt down under the table, wrenched open his diminutive refrigerator and took out a frosted can of beer. "You scared the living crap out of me, you know that?"

"I'm sorry."

"It's sufficiently unnerving to have a strange individual appearing in your bedroom unannounced in the small hours of the morning without that person having an identical similarity to somebody you've just driven all the way to Presque Isle, Maine, to see reduced to ashes. They don't have a way of reconstituting ashes, do they, to bring people back to life? Look at my goddamn hand. It's trembling."

"I'm sorry."

John popped the top of his beer and took an icy-cold swallow. He punched his stomach with his fist and burped, and then he said, "Springer? Is that what you told me your name was? What is it you want, Springer?"

Springer nodded. "You might say that I've come from the draft board."

"They want me back in the army? That's it—now I'm *convinced* that I'm dreaming."

"I'm not talking about the army that you remember, John. There's another army, and you've always been one of its reserves."

"Another army? What the hell are you talking about? It wasn't that time I drank those two bottles of tequila, was it, in Tijuana? Don't tell me I accidentally enlisted in the *caballeria*. There isn't a horse that could carry me, and I could never fit into a tank. Do they have tanks, the Mexican Army?"

"John," Springer interrupted him, "you remember those babies today, at the Ormsby Clinic?"

"Of course I do. It was terrible. Poor little guys were screaming their heads off."

"Those babies had all been attacked. Not physically, but mentally. A malevolent influence climbed inside their minds as soon as they were born and tried to ransack their dreams. So far, thank Ashapola, this malevolent influence has not been successful in extracting the knowledge that it has been searching for. But as a consequence of what it has done, those babies have lost the capacity to dream altogether, and because of that they will almost certainly die."

"Excuse me? Are you making any sense or should I go back to sleep and try waking up again?"

Springer smiled. "I'm afraid it's true, John." Choosing

his words carefully, he told John about Ashapola, and the world of dreams, and the endless war between good and evil. When he had finished, he said, "There are very few people who can help to combat the forces of darkness, and you happen to be one of them."

"So I didn't enlist?"

"No. You don't have to. You were born to be a Night Warrior. Your father wasn't one, but your grandmother was, and your great-grandmother, and her father before her."

John said, "Do I look like any kind of warrior to you—night, day, afternoon or anything?"

"Oh, you'd be surprised. Some of the most unexpected people make the very best Night Warriors. Some of them have been seriously disabled in waking life, but in their dreams there's no stopping them. Remember Christopher Reeve? By day, he could hardly move a muscle, but during the night he could run and swim and ride horses."

"So what you're saying is, when I'm asleep, I could run the four-minute mile and then make passionate love to Halle Berry all night without even breaking a sweat?"

"Technically, yes."

John sat on his bed for a long time without saying anything. A man who looked exactly like his dead friend Deano had appeared in his room in the middle of the night and told him that he had been selected to fight the forces of evil and save a whole clinic full of screaming babies. He had often suspected that it would come to this, but he hadn't thought that it would come so soon. He wondered what kind of food they served in the nuthouse.

But Springer said, "You haven't lost your mind, John. This is actually happening. The first time you enter the dream world as a Night Warrior, you won't believe how solid and real everything feels, and how insubstantial all of *this* will suddenly seem to you—this room, this city, this job that you do."

"How about the food that I eat? I'm finding it hard to imagine an insubstantial turkey and bacon sandwich."

"Well, you'll see for yourself."

"Okay ...," said John, suspiciously. "So how do I manage it, entering the world of dreams?"

Springer described the meditation and the incantation to Ashapola.

"I see. I ponder for a while, right? Then I say the magic words, right? Then I fall asleep and I'm some kind of a Jean-Claude Van Damme? Right?"

"Right, right, and wrong. You won't be Jean-Claude Van Damme, you'll be Dom Magator, the Armorer."

"Dom Magator? You're pulling my leg, right?"

"Not at all. Dom Magator is the greatest armorer in dream history. You'll be carrying a collection of weapons such as no waking soldier has ever dreamed of—not only for your own use, but for the use of your fellow Night Warriors. For instance, you will have more than two hundred different kinds of knives—from a Sonic Bowie, which can cut through flesh and bone by sound alone, to a Spatial Stiletto, which can actually cut a hole in one reality and allow you to escape into another.

"You will also have thirteen different guns, such as a Density Rifle, which compresses everything it hits into the greatest density possible, and a Successive Detonation Carbine, which knocks down your enemy target and at the same time charges up his body with a massive amount of latent energy. When his companions come to help him, the charge jumps to them, too, and after thirty seconds there is a chain of explosions which blows them all to shreds."

John said, "That's who I am, then? Dom Magator, the walking arsenal?"

"Do you want to see?"

"How do you mean?"

"Do you have a mirror in here?"

"Sure." John stood up and opened the rickety closet door. There was a cracked mirror screwed to the back of it, next to a pinup of a big-breasted brunette with her mouth stretched wide open, looking as if she were trying to fellate a huge crayfish po' boy.

"There you are," said Springer, laying a hand on his shoulder, although the odd thing was that John couldn't see Springer's hand reflected in the mirror. John peered at himself short-sightedly. He didn't look any different. A fat man with a wildly disarranged pompadour, wearing a sweaty T-shirt and droopy shorts.

"Terrific," he said. "One look at that and the forces of darkness are going to be heading for the hills, running all the way."

"Look closer," Springer encouraged him.

John leaned closer, and as he did so, he thought he could see a smudgy outline around his head. He wiped the mirror with his fist, but the outline stayed where it was. In fact, it began to grow clearer and sharper, and he realized when he leaned back again that he was wearing a helmet. It was heavy and black and cubelike, and studded all over with nuts and bolts and small metal attachments, like rings and switches and control knobs. The visor was little more than a slit covered with darkly tinted glass.

He turned around. "Can you see this thing on my head?" he asked Springer. "I look like somebody's old radio set."

"That's your protective helmet, full of communications gear. It also holds all of your target-imaging equipment. You can see your enemy through twenty feet of solid granite."

"Can it see through shower tiles? There's this nurse who lives across the hall, Nadine—"

"John, be serious. This is a serious business, believe me."

John turned back to the mirror, and as he did so he became aware that his shoulders were draped in a vast black-metallic cape, made of some very soft, heavy fabric, which reached almost down to his ankles. Underneath the cape he was wearing complicated armor, leathery and multijointed, like a black beetle. Around his waist hung a wide metal belt, from which six or seven of his guns were suspended—

revolvers with extravagantly sculptured handgrips and very long barrels, automatics with five different slides and triple sights, semiautomatics with foot-long magazines and twelve contra-rotating barrels.

On his back he wore a curved metal harness with row after row of black silver-topped knife handles sticking out of it, and a horizontal rack with five rifles in it, all of them looking as sinister and high-tech as the handguns that hung around his waist.

His outfit was finished off with knee-high boots, each one of them encircled with even more knife handles. There was hardly an inch on his body that didn't have a weapon attached to it.

"That's one hell of an outfit, isn't it?" said John, turning this way and that to admire himself. "If I saw me coming dressed like that, I think *I'd* run for it, too. And don't you think it makes me look thinner?"

Springer stepped back and looked him up and down. "I never thought the time would come when I would actually see Dom Magator, in person."

"Well, me neither," said John. But after he had finished inspecting himself and primping up his pompadour, he said, "No."

"What do you mean, 'no'?"

"This is all very impressive, Deano, or Springer, or whoever you are. It's great to see myself looking like somebody who might be able to make a contribution to the sum of human happiness. But the sad fact is that I don't have the first idea how to use any of this fancy cutlery. I'm extremely dexterous with a cake fork, and you should see my action with a lobster pick. But as for a space-age stiletto, and a—what was it?—successful detoxifying carbine? Sorry, *signor*. I wouldn't have the first idea."

Springer was unperturbed. "Don't worry, John. I will train you well. Apart from that, when you enter the world of dreams as Dom Magator, you will discover that you have inherited from your grandmother all of the skills and all of the technical expertise that you require to be an armorer. In your dreams you will be Dom Magator. He is your *alter ego,* your dream personality. Dom Magator is just as real as John Dauphin, if not more so."

John studied himself in the mirror. He glared at himself through his tinted visor, even though his tinted visor wasn't really there. But Springer was right. He *was* Dom Magator. At school, he had been mercilessly teased and bullied because he was so fat. In the Army they had flicked him with wet towels and called him lard-ass and Mount Buttmore. Even when he was working for the Louisiana Restaurant Association, people had said in stage whispers whenever he walked into the door, "Jesus H. Christ. The earth shook."

But all that time, without anybody knowing it, he had not only been fat and easygoing John Dauphin; he had been Dom Magator, too. Powerful, wise, one of the mainstays of the Night Warriors, with the most sophisticated armory of personal weapons ever devised by man, sleeping or waking. Seeing himself in this armor, his whole life suddenly made sense. His patience, his endurance, his self-protective jokes. He had been waiting for this moment, when he would realize at last how important he was and why he had been born the way he was.

Gradually, his illusory armor began to fade, and soon he was looking at the same fat greasy-haired man in the same sweaty T-shirt.

"So when do I go into action?" he asked Springer.

"After your training, and after you have met your fellow Night Warriors."

"And when will that be?"

"As soon as possible, Dom Magator, believe me. This is a race against time. The forces of darkness will need only to be successful in stealing the dream of one baby before they can take the universe to pieces."

John cleared his throat. "What will you do, call me? I can give you my cab company number."

John rummaged through his closet until he found his

plaid pants, which had dropped off their wire hanger onto the floor. He took two dog-eared business cards out of the back pocket and carefully straightened one of them out. "Here you go ... Sunshine Taxis. If I'm not in the office, ask for Leland. Leland will know where I am."

He held it out, but Springer had vanished.

John looked around the room, bewildered. "Hey, Deano! Deano? Where the hell did you go?" He swung back the closet door. Springer wasn't hiding behind it. He dragged the drapes aside, but Springer wasn't there, either, and when he tried the window, he found that it was locked. Grunting with effort, he bent down and peered under the bed. Hmm. A whole warren of dust-bunnies, a Mounds wrapper and one shriveled fawn sock, but no Springer.

He stood up again, blowing out his cheeks. "You're losing it, John. It's all that chloresterol, it's clogged up your brain. Two hundred-sixty cheeseburgers a year for twenty years, that's four thousand, seven hundred-twenty cheeseburgers and you think anybody could stay sane on a diet like that? Not to mention all that fried chicken and spicy chorizo and onion strings. It's a well-known medical fact that indigestion gives you nightmares, and that's what's happened to you. What a poor sad mook you are. Springer wasn't a messenger from Ashapola. Springer was a half-melted blob of mozzarella cheese."

He looked at himself in the mirror. "See? No helmet. No armor. No guns. Who the two-toned tonkert did you think you were kidding? Dom Magator, the Armorer. In your dreams."

Yet it had all seemed so real. And not only that, it had all seemed so *right*. For the first time ever, John had really believed that his life had some purpose and some meaning apart from finding fifty different ways to feel sorry for himself and stuffing his face with food by way of compensation. If he really *was* Dom Magator, the Armorer, what a blast that would be. If he really could go into battle in other people's dreams, with all of those weird and wonderful knives and all of those ritzy guns …

He lay back down on his sweaty, tangled sheets. It was no good. He must have been hallucinating or dreaming. Maybe he should see a doctor. That Charlie Mazurin, she was a shrink, wasn't she? Maybe *she* could help him.

He was about to switch off his bedside light when he noticed a large black spider walking across the ceiling, right above his head. He swallowed. He wasn't particularly afraid of spiders. After all, when it came to comparative size, there was no contest. But he had a justifiable phobia about them dropping into his mouth when he was asleep. It had happened to him once when he was ten years old and he only had to look at a spider and he could imagine it struggling down his throat.

He reached across and picked up his kitchen knife. Lying flat on his back again, he held the knife right in front of his eye, aiming it, and then he threw it up at the ceiling as hard as he could.

In the split-second that he did it, he knew that it was a damn fool thing to do. If the knife didn't stick in the ceiling, it would drop back and stick into *him*. He rolled over, lifting his left shoulder to protect his face. But there was a sharp *chukk!* and the knife stayed where it was, quivering. Not only that, it had struck the spider dead center, so that the creature's legs surrounded the knife blade like a hairy black star.

John stared at it in disbelief. He had never been any good at throwing knives before—not that he was aware of, anyhow. Yet he had nailed that creepy-crawly as accurate as a lizard spitting at a mayfly.

He stood up, balancing himself on the bed, and pulled the knife out of the ceiling. The spider came with it. John turned it this way and that and said, "Thought you'd tickle *my* tonsils, did you, you loser?"

On the opposite wall hung a calendar with a photograph of Louis the Ex-Vee-One on it, the French king after whom

Louisville was named. John lifted up his knife again, tilted it over his shoulder, and threw it. The point hit Louis right between the eyes, with the spider still attached to it.

John clambered down from the bed and went over to the calendar. He tugged out the knife, and then he walked back to the other side of the room and threw it again. It hit exactly the same spot.

"There, you see. I wasn't hallucinating, was I? Springer *was* here, and I *am* Dom Magator."

"Lucky shot, that's all."

"You think so? Watch this."

John took out the knife and threw it again, and again it hit King Louis between the eyes. Just to make absolutely sure, he did it a fourth time.

"Look at that. I can't miss. I'm a Night Warrior."

"All right. You've discovered a talent for knife-throwing that you never knew you had. Go join a circus. You're fat enough."

"I can't miss, goddammit! I'm Dom Magator! I'm a Night Warrior!

CHAPTER SIX

Perry said, "*Joe* sent you? You mean my baby brother Joe—the one my dad was telling me about? The one who died?"

The pale face on his computer screen slowly blinked its eyes. Its voice was slow and blurry, like a tape recording playing at half-speed. "You heard those babies at the Kosair Hospital, Perry. They've been hurt, and they're distressed, and they're never going to get well. Joe was killed by the very same thing."

"What are you talking about? I saw it on the TV news. Nobody has a clue what's killing them, not even the doctors."

"Nobody in the waking world, I agree. But they are not being killed by anything from the waking world. They are being attacked in the world of dreams."

"Say what?"

"The world of dreams, Perry. All of those places you visit when you sleep. In its own way, it's just as real as the waking world."

"What is this hooey? And who are you, anyhow? Hey—I'll bet you're some kind of a computer virus. I'm right, aren't I? You're not a person at all. You're nothing but a fancy new version of Netsky, or BackDoor, something like that."

The face gave another placid blink. "I suppose you could call me a virus. After all, what is any kind of virus but a messenger, carrying information? And that is what I am—a messenger."

"So if you're a messenger, what's the message?"

"The message is that you must try to help those babies. Not many people have the power to do so, but you are one of them."

"I'm sorry, bro. I don't have the first idea what you're babbling about."

"Of course you do. You've already had the feeling that you are somehow responsible for what happens to those babies, haven't you?"

Perry was just about to make a smart retort, but he opened and closed his mouth and no words came out. Like, wait up a minute, he thought. How does this face on my computer know about *that?* His feeling that he had some kind of duty to help those babies hadn't even been a fully formed thought, more like walking into a room and forgetting why you went in, although you're sure that you came in there for *something*. After all, what was Dora's granddaughter to him, really? What were any of those babies at the Kosair Hospital?

The face said, "Let me explain who I am. More important, let me explain who *you* are."

"Forget it," said Perry. "If you think that I'm going to sit here talking to my monitor, you're crazy. If I can't switch you off, I'm going to throw a blanket over you. You're welcome to babble to yourself all night if you want to, but don't think that I'm going to answer you, because I seriously don't appreciate people invading my hard drive, especially when I'm trying to work on something real important."

"Listen to me, Perry. In the whole of your life, nothing that you do will be as important as this. Ever."

"Oh, really? *Trash Planet* is going to make me rich and/or famous. What could be more important than that?"

"Unless you listen to me, you will never be either of those things. In fact you will never be anything. If the forces of darkness continue to attack these babies, and eventually find a way of stealing their dreams, then the entire universe will cease to exist, and you with it."

"I see. And which comic book did you swipe that particular evil scheme out of?"

The face abruptly vanished and the computer screen went black. Perry shook his head. Some goddamned virus. He had come across worms that infected his e-mail and viruses that had slowed his animation software to a crawl, but he had never come across a face that wouldn't allow him to switch his computer off, and insisted on talking to him, and even seemed to know what was happening inside of his head. It was totally nuts. He would have to e-mail his geek friend Hubert Bahr and find out what kind of a virus it was, and how to disinfect his hard drive.

But it was then that a girl's voice said, right behind him, *"The trouble is, Perry, it's all true."*

"Dah!" Perry jumped out of his chair, knocking it over. *"Jesus choking Christ!"* To his horror, his older sister Janie was standing beside his bed.

"Janie?" he said, and he could hardly breathe.

"Hi, Perry. Been a long time, hasn't it?"

"Janie—Jesus—what are *you* doing here? How the hell did you get into my room?"

Janie was tall and pretty in a pale, undernourished, pre-Raphaelite way, with very long black hair that flew around her face as if she were standing in the wind. She was wearing a short gray dress, and that was ruffled by the wind, too—even though there *was* no wind. Her eyes were closed, but she was smiling, as if she were very aware that he was standing in front of her.

"How long have you been here?" said Perry. "Have you been—*what?* Have you been hiding under my bed?"

"Of course not, Perry. I don't need to hide. You seemed to be having trouble in believing that I was real, so I thought that it would be easier for me to talk to you in some recognizable shape."

"So that was you on my monitor? It didn't look like you."

Janie swept back her hair, but still she didn't open her eyes. "I can be anyone, Perry. Two-dimensional, three-dimensional, man or woman. Anyone who makes you feel comfortable. Anyone you'll listen to and believe."

"So ... you're *not* Janie?"

"Not exactly, no. I thought that if I appeared on your screen, you would pay more attention to what I had to say to you and take it more seriously. But I forgot that you're something of an expert when it comes to computer generated images, and you know what visual trickery can be done. Plainly, I needed to look more convincing. So here I am."

With that, she opened her eyes. They were totally yellow, like a rattlesnake's eyes, and they had no pupils at all.

Perry opened his mouth, and then closed it again.

"Don't be frightened," said Janie. "I've only come here to ask for your help."

"Janie's okay, isn't she? You haven't hurt her?"

"Of course not. Janie's well. She may even be coming back to see you soon. Meanwhile, I'm afraid that you'll have to make do with me."

Perry paced around his room. Every now and then he stopped and looked at Janie and said, "I don't freaking believe this. I really don't. Tell me you're not here."

"I'm afraid I am, Perry. I'm as real as you are. In some ways, I'm even *more* real."

"So what's this all about? What's this message?"

"Well," said Janie, "it's more of a revelation than a message. My name is Springer, and I have been sent to you by Ashapola."

"Ashapola? Never heard of him."

"Well, listen, and you will."

Softly and simply, with her hands outlining patterns in the air, Springer told him about the creation of the universe and the never-ending battles in the world of dreams. Perry listened, but all the time he kept on shaking his head.

"And you think that by turning yourself into a hologram of my sister, I'm going to believe you?"

"I'm not a hologram, Perry. Here—feel how solid I am."

Perry jammed his hands under his armpits. "I'm not touching you, man. No way in the world, waking or dreaming. What if I catch something?"

"With any luck, you'll catch a large dose of reality. You're *needed*, Perry, urgently. Your skills and your abilities. This has now become a war to the very finish, with the whole of creation at stake, and we are having to call on everybody who can help us to win it. Which includes you."

"What skills? Oh, sure, I can skateboard. I can play the guitar. I can do animation on my computer. That's about all."

"You can *invent* people. People like Steel Sister and Acid Boy and Junk Toddler."

"Yeah right, sure, but they're only in stories."

"In the world of dreams, Perry, there is no difference between stories and reality."

"I'm not following you."

Springer came up close to him and touched his shoulder. "You can *invent* people, Perry. It's something that you've inherited. Your grandfather could invent people, too."

"I don't believe this. I really don't believe it. If this is true, why didn't my dad ever tell me about it?"

"Because he doesn't know. For a very complex genetic reason these abilities only appear in alternate generations, and only on the male side. Your grandfather had them, and your great-uncle also had some wonderful skills, but not your father."

"Only on the male side?"

"That's correct. For some reason, they don't translate to women."

"Wait up ... you're not talking about *all* the males?"

"That's right."

"So if *I* have this talent to invent people ... Dunc must have some kind of a talent, too."

"Dunc? Yes, your brother Duncan has a very special ability. Not the same ability as yours, but very impressive all the same."

"So how does this work?"

Springer said, "Go back to your computer and switch it on."

"Now what?" said Perry. "Another trick?" But he did as Springer asked him, and switched his computer back on. His screensaver appeared, dozens of purple mice running races from one side of the screen to the other.

Springer sat down on the desk beside him. "The men in your bloodline belong to a very select group of people— people who can enter the world of dreams and fight any enemy that they may find there."

"Oh, really?"

"Yes, really. They're called Night Warriors, although their original Sanskrit name meant 'Army of Dreams,' and the Romans called them 'The Legions of Sleep.' They have been guarding humanity from the forces of darkness ever since Ashapola created the very first human. It is written in the *Great Book of the Night* that the first human was a dreamer and the second human was a Night Warrior, to protect her."

"Her? The first human was a woman?"

"What good is a seed without a bed to plant it in?"

"Oh, yeah, right, got you. No good having the P without the U."

"Here," said Springer. She touched the screen of Perry's computer, and an image appeared almost instantaneously. It was a young man sitting on a rock in a grainy red desert. He was dressed in a skintight suit made of some shiny scarlet material, with a chrome breastplate covered in scrolls and oak leaves and a chrome codpiece fashioned in the shape of a lion's head. On his head he carried an extraordinary chrome helmet that made him look like a monstrous hammerhead shark, with dozens of colored lenses over his eyes—pink, yellow, purple, green and red. An elaborate system of brackets and hinges made the lenses interchangeable.

The young man was holding a long-barreled rifle with a Y-shaped stock that fitted around his upper arm, just above the elbow, and a series of slides and handles and switches.

"So, who's this character?" asked Perry. "He looks kind of minty to me."

"That's you," said Springer. "The Zaggaline, the Character Assassin."

"You're putting me on. I can go into the world of dreams, but I have to walk around looking like that?"

"You'll need that outfit, believe me, and all of that equipment. The helmet is fitted with all the visual and auditory equipment you require for creating any kind of character you want to. The suit will give you some measure of protection from your own characters, in case your enemies try to turn them against you."

"What about that rifle?" Perry peered at it closer. "That looks pretty neat."

"It's not actually a weapon in itself. It's a Lethal Energy Transmuter, or LET. Your invented characters will be carrying invented weapons, and the LET will load them or arm them or power them up, depending on what they are. You might have devised a crossbow, for instance, which shoots a thousand bolts at once in a thousand different directions; or a gun which turns daylight into instant night; or a grenade which can re-arrange your enemy's molecular structure and convert him instantly into atoms. The LET will give these weapons the power to work."

"Yeah, but what characters am I supposed to think up?"

"Any character you need. For example, suppose that your enemies try to deceive you by disguising themselves as children, or innocent bystanders, or even animals. You can invent a Sin Sensitive who can sniff out the faintest whiff of evil. Or suppose that you are trying to hunt down one of your enemies in a forest of razor-sharp swords. You can invent an Armadillo Man whose armored skin will protect him from being cut to pieces.

"You will be restricted only by the limits of your own ingenuity. All you have to-remember is that some of the characters you create may turn out to be just as dangerous to you and your fellow Night Warriors as they are to your enemies."

"My fellow Night Warriors? How many of us are there?"

"So far, no more than a handful, I regret. Dom Magator, the Armorer, who will be carrying all the weapons that you will need. Xanthys, the Time Curver, who can alter the sequence of any event. Yourself, The Zaggaline. Your brother. And one other."

Perry counted on his fingers. "That's only one-two-three-four-five of us, right? And the five of us, we're supposed to fight a full-scale war against the entire forces of darkness? Like, two words come to mind, man. One of them is 'hopelessly' and the other is 'outnumbered.' "

Springer said, "I can't lie to you and say that it won't be dangerous. There's always a risk that you could be killed inside somebody else's dream, in which case your waking body would appear to go into a coma, from which it would never wake up."

"Oh, terrific."

"Perry, nobody lives forever. And this is your chance to do something really significant. There may only be five of you so far, but I think you will find that your skills and tactical abilities will make you a very formidable task force."

"What about Dunc? I mean, Dunc has *real* skills and tactical abilities, doesn't he? I left him in charge of the store and he was giving cookies away for free."

"Do you want to see him, in *his* Night Warrior manifestation?"

"Okay, then. So long as he doesn't have a special gun for blowing his own feet off."

At that moment, Perry's bedroom door opened and Dunc appeared, blinking, even more tousle-headed than usual. He was wearing blue and white striped pajamas with the pants on backwards.

"Perry? What do you want?"

"I didn't call you, dude."

But Dunc said, "*Janie!* What are you doing here? We thought you were gone forever and ever!"

"This isn't Janie, dude."

Dunc shuffled across the room and gave Springer a hug. "Janie! It's so good to see you! Where have you *been?* Why didn't you write us and tell us where you were?"

"This isn't Janie, dude," Perry repeated.

Dunc frowned at him and scratched his head. "Of course it's Janie. You can't fool me! This is one of your practically jokes, isn't it?"

"I know she looks like Janie, but she isn't Janie. She's like—well, she's kind of like a ghost who's pretending to be Janie so that she doesn't scare us."

Dunc reached out and squeezed Springer's shoulder. "She's not a ghost. You can't feel ghosts. I saw it on TV. If you try to grab a ghost there's nothing there."

Springer said, "Perry's right, Duncan. I'm not really Janie. My name's Springer and I've come to ask you to help me."

"You're pulling my chain again, dude," Dunc insisted. "Of course it's Janie. I'm so pleased you came back, Janie. You're not going to go away again, are you? I know you had all those bad fights with Dad and all, but I know that he's going to be over the moon that you came back. I'll go wake him and tell him you're here."

He turned around and he was about to walk out of the door when Springer said, "Duncan, what is the chemical composition of breast implants?"

Dunc blinked again. "What?"

"I thought that would get your attention. You like big bouncing Pamela Anderson–type breasts, don't you? Well, can you tell me what's in them?"

"Well, sure," said Dunc, slowly. He closed his eyes and recited, "Methyl ethyl ketone, cycolhexanone—both of which are neurotoxins—isopropyl alcohol, ethanol, acetone, urethane, polyvinyl chloride, amine, toluene, dichloromethan—which is a carcinogen at any level of exposure—freon, silicone, sodium fluoride, solder, formaldehyde, talcum powder, trisodium phosphate, Eastman 910 Glue, ethylene oxide, carbon black, xylene, hexone, 2-hexanone, thixon-OSN-2, rubber antioxidant, stearic acid, zinc oxide, naptha, phenol—which is another neurotoxin—benzene—which is also a neurotoxin and a carcinogen—lacquer thinner, epoxy resin, expoxy hardener 10 and 11, printing ink, metal cleaning acid and color pigments as release agents."

Dunc opened his eyes again. All Perry could say was, *"Whoa."* Like, Dunc had always had a knack for memorizing lists, but how and when and why had he learned the thirty-seven ingredients of silicone gel, as well as their deleterious effects on the human body? Even Dunc himself was stupefied. He kept pulling at his lips, as if his mouth had taken on a life of its own and he was worried that it might suddenly start reciting something else that he didn't know.

He turned to Perry and said, "This is some kind of a joke, right?"

"Dude, you're the one who knows all that stuff, not me."

"But I *don't* know it."

"Obviously, you do. Otherwise, how would you know it?"

Springer said, "Duncan, you have a comprehensive knowledge of every branch of science, from anatomy to zoology. In the world of dreams, anyhow."

"What do you mean? I'm awake, right?"

"Of course," said Springer, "but I was just giving you an example of how much you know. You are Kalexikox, the Knowledge Gunner."

"What do you mean?"

Perry said, "You and me, dude, we can go into other people's dreams. It's something we got from grandpa. In real life, when we're awake, we're just two ordinary guys, okay? But at night, if we say the right words, we can put on this really cool armor and we get to carry guns and everything. We're like soldiers."

"We don't have to go to Iraq, do we?"

"No, no, nothing like that. Like I say, it's all going to happen in other people's dreams. We get to fight these bad guys who are trying to hurt all of these newborn babies."

"Why are they trying to do that?"

"Let me show you," said Springer. She touched the computer screen again and another image appeared. Dunc immediately said, "Lookit, that's me!" And it *was* him, standing on a balcony at night. Far below him—like the scattered embers of a windblown fire—Perry could dimly see the lights of a sprawling settlement.

Dunc was wearing a suit of armor of mind-boggling complexity. It was constructed entirely out of brass and stainless steel, and it was thickly covered all over with scientific instruments—slide-rules and compasses and protractors, as well as a forest of sextants and astrolabes and theodolites and other calibrated measuring devices. Perry couldn't even begin to guess what most of them were intended to calculate.

Dunc's helmet was a shining glass globe, inside which tiny sparks of dazzling light were constantly weaving patterns around his head, like fireflies. His only weapon appeared to be a heavy pistol hanging from his belt, with five or six shiny metal balls lined up along the top of the barrel, about the size of golf balls.

"There," said Springer. "Kalexikox the Knowledge Gunner."

"Don't you think I look cool?" said Dunc. "Lookit that suit, man, covered in all those knobbly bits. How cool is that?"

"That's seriously cool, dude," said Perry. But he looked at Springer and said, "So—he knows a whole lot. How is that going to help us fight these forces of darkness?"

"Knowledge is power, Perry. Even you know that."

"Sure. But I still don't see what this Kalexikox can do. You're not going to scare the forces of darkness just because you happen to know the ingredients of a boob job, are you?"

Springer smiled. "Of course not. But think about it. Every dream has a different logic and a different physical construction. Every dream has its own particular landscape, its own particular weather, its own particular flora and fauna. Kalexikox knows almost everything there is to know about the science of dreams, and what he doesn't know, he knows how to find out.

"In a dream, a craggy mountain may be nothing more than a craggy mountain, made out of real rock. But it might just as easily be a painful memory of a lost romance, or a hiccup in the dreamer's finances, or maybe a work colleague that the dreamer finds obstructive.

"In a dream, a pot of honey may be a pot of honey, but it could equally be a musical instrument, or a crystal ball that can tell you the future, or a specimen jar or a bomb. Kalexikox knows the scientific difference between one thing and another, and that could easily save your life."

"I would really know that?" Dunc asked her.

"Yes, Duncan. You would really know that. And you would really know that the boiling point of beryllium is two thousand, four hundred, seventy-one degrees Celsius; and that the witch crabs which live under the Arctic ice have such slow metabolisms that they outlive tropical crabs by more than double; and that the atmosphere of Jupiter is eighty-six percent hydrogen and fourteen percent helium."

"Hey," said Dunc, and punched Perry's shoulder. "So nobody can call me dumb anymore."

"You *were* never dumb," said Perry. "Your brain was wired up all the wrong way, that's all."

"Oh, yeah? I'll bet that *you* don't know the boiling point of billion."

"Dude—why don't you wait until we get into a dream before you start trying to show off, okay?"

Springer said, "I will continue to recruit more Night Warriors, as and when I can locate them. But for the moment, you five will need to go out tomorrow night on your first mission."

"As soon as that? I thought you said you were going to train us."

"I am. But the threat from the forces of darkness is too great for us to wait any longer. I will have to train you in the field. However, almost all of your skills are inherited, and mostly I will need to do nothing more than explain to you what you are capable of doing."

"One thing," said Perry. "What exactly are they, these 'forces of darkness'?"

"I will tell you everything tomorrow," said Springer. "Now I have to go. Both of you should try to get some sleep."

Dunc said, "You're really not Janie, are you?"

"No, Duncan," said Springer. "But one day, who knows?"

With that, she touched the computer screen again, and as she did so, she instantly vanished, as if she had switched herself off.

"That's amazing," said Dunc. He opened the door and looked out onto the landing, as if he expected to see Springer standing out there.

"That's *amazing*," he repeated.

Perry said, "Listen, Dunc, we don't have to do this Night Warrior stuff. All we have to do is say no. That Springer person, whoever she is, whatever she is, she can't force us, can she?"

"I *want* to do it," said Dunc. "I want to know all about honey, and craggy mountains and boob-jobs."

"Dunc—it could be really dangerous. Springer said that

we might go into somebody else's dream and get killed. If that happened, our bodies would still be lying in bed like we're sleeping, but we would never wake up."

"So? I never did anything dangerous in all of my life. You and dad and Janie, you never let me do anything dangerous. You never even let me ride a bike. Not without training wheels, anyhow."

"Riding a bike without training wheels isn't exactly as dangerous as fighting the forces of darkness."

"I still think we ought to do it."

"Well, let's go to bed and think about it, okay?"

"Okay."

Dunc left the room and Perry stood in front of his computer for a while, half-expecting Springer's face to reappear. But then the door opened again and it was Dunc.

"Perry?"

"What is it?"

"Which crabs live under the Arctic ice?" asked Dunc.

"Witch crabs," said Perry.

"I just asked *you* that."

CHAPTER SEVEN

Fat, warm droplets of rain were starting to speckle the sidewalk as Sasha walked along Fourth Street to the Starks Building on the corner of Muhammad Ali Avenue. Although it was only two in the afternoon, the sky was growing darker and darker, and fluorescent lights began to flicker in most of the downtown offices. She had to push her way through a small crowd of sheltering shoppers to get in through the revolving door, and as she did so there was a train crash of thunder overhead and the rain began to bucket down in earnest.

She crossed the echoing lobby and went down the stairs to the basement, to the Colonnade Cafeteria. The Colonnade was a wide, low, institutional-looking room with mirrors on every wall so that it appeared to be infinitely larger than it actually was. In between the huge square pillars that held up the fourteen-story building above, there were shoals of Formica-topped tables and red leatherette chairs. At lunchtime, the cafeteria would have been packed, but now there were fewer than a dozen other customers. One elderly lady in the corner was actually asleep, her head resting on her open book. There was a lingering smell of over-steamed cabbage and a faint whiff of disinfectant.

Sasha sat down at a table in the corner. A bus person came up to her, collecting dirty plates and wiping tables. "Was that *thunder* I heard?" the cleaner asked her.

"That's right." Sasha was rummaging in her woven bag, trying to find her purse.

The bus person stacked some more coffee cups. "I'll tell you something, Sasha, I've always been stone scared of thunder. Makes me think that the entire sky is going to fall down on top of me."

Sasha looked up. She wasn't especially surprised that the woman had used her name. After all, Sasha's picture had appeared twice weekly in the *Courier-Journal* and her face had frequently been featured on posters and in local TV commercials for the *Courier-Journal*.

The woman was black, about thirty years old, with one of those unusual faces with very widely spaced eyes that sometimes look beautiful and sometimes look almost alien. She was wearing a caramel-colored wig and a large gold crucifix around her neck.

"It's pouring," Sasha told her. "Maybe we ought to start building an ark."

"You think so? I don't think no outsized boat is going to save us."

"What do you mean?"

The cleaner gave her an extraordinary look, both knowing and challenging. "The end of the world is nigh, Sasha. The question is, what are we going to do about it?"

"So—what's good today?" Sasha asked her, trying to change the subject.

"Roast beef, corned beef, Mexican spaghetti and English meatloaf. The special is gringo-style burritos."

"And what do you recommend?"

"I'd go for the English meatloaf."

"Okay." Sasha got up and went across to the U-shaped counter where the lunch selections were laid out. She picked up a tray and chose tomato aspic—two wobbly round molds of jellied tomato juice served on a tired-looking lettuce leaf—and a portion of English meatloaf with green beans, carrots, fried okra and cornbread. Then she went to the self-service dispenser for a glass of iced tea. The cashier rang up a tab for $6.04.

When she returned to her table she found that a fat man was sitting in her place. He had a high cockatoo-style pompadour and was wearing a bright pink Hawaiian shirt with bright yellow flowers and bright green palm leaves on it. He was shouting at somebody on his cell phone.

"Leland, I had to stop for nourishment. You can't expect me to drive around for six whole hours without some kind of sustenance to keep body and soul together. Leland, I can't hear you very well, you sound like your head is buried in a box of Rice Krispies. I'm in a basement, Leland, the signal is bad. Yes. I'll call you later. But I have to eat first, got it?"

As Sasha approached, he snapped his cell phone shut and said, "Sheesh, I thought we abolished slavery in 1865."

"In Kentucky, as a matter of fact, the Thirteenth Amendment wasn't actually ratified until 1976."

"That figures. Even then, I think they omitted to tell my boss about it."

"You'll have to excuse me. You're sitting in my place."

The fat man looked around in mystification, as if he had heard disembodied voices coming out of thin air. "Pardon me? Did you say that I was sitting in your place?"

"Well, I know that there are quite a lot of empty seats here, but I was actually sitting right there. That's my shopping bag."

"Oh, I'm sorry. I didn't see it. It's almost the same indeterminate color as the carpet. I'm sorry. I'll move."

With that, the man heaved himself up and sat on the next chair.

"What's that you _have_ there?" he said, peering at Sasha's tray.

"English meatloaf." She sat down two chairs away and reached over for her shopping bag.

"I meant that red wobbly stuff like two bosoms, if you don't mind my saying so."

"Tomato aspic. It's kind of a Louisville specialty. It tastes like V-8 if V-8 was jelly."

The fat man wrinkled up his nose. "Really? And that's a specialty? You know, I've only been here three weeks now, but I've decided that you Looh-a-vullians don't actually have a cuisine. I mean not like New Orleans or Baton Rouge, which is where I come from. We have barbecued shrimp that people fly across the world for. And what do you have? Benedictine—cream cheese and cucumber sandwich spread? I wouldn't feed that stuff to my dog, even if I had one. And look at this venue! It looks like Hitler's Bunker. It even *smells* like Hitler's Bunker."

Sasha didn't much like the Colonnade, either, but like most of the people who ate there, she came because it was cheap and quick, and there were always plenty of choices. Not only that, she had been coming here for so long that it was almost like eating at home. Her mother used to bring her when she was little.

She started eating her tomato aspic. It didn't look very appetizing, but it had a distinctive taste of celery and a sharp, refreshing tang.

"I can't work out why I came in here," the fat man told her, still looking around.

"I thought you were hungry."

"Yes. But I felt like deep-fried scrod."

"So why did you come in here?"

"Because I couldn't find anyplace else to park, and it was raining, and for some reason I get the feeling that I'm *supposed* to be here."

Sasha put down her spoon. "That's really weird. I had that feeling, too. I haven't been here in at least two years, but I suddenly thought ..."

The fat man waited for Sasha to finish her sentence, but

she couldn't actually put her feeling into words. After a while, he said, "Well, I was never in here before, and by the look of that Tomato Wobble, I don't think I'm ever going to come in here again."

At that moment the bus person came over. "It's self-service. You have to take a tray and make your own selections."

"Give me a moment," the fat man told her. "I'm just girding my loins. That meatloaf, that doesn't look like something you could rush at headlong. You would have to catch it unawares, wouldn't you? Position yourself downwind of it and kind of creep up on it."

"That's all right, John. You take your time."

The cleaner walked away and disappeared from sight behind one of the pillars. The fat man frowned at Sasha and said, "Did I hear that right? Did she call me by my name?"

"If your name's John, then yes."

The fat man held out his hand. "John Dauphin, restaurant inspector and winner of many prestigious culinary awards, currently employed in the bespoke carriage business."

"Sasha Smith, newspaper columnist, currently freelance."

"Hey—yes. Sasha Smith! Didn't I read one of your pieces? Some old biddy who was cooking her cats to stay alive?"

"That's the one. My editor thought it was a little too colorful, and that's the reason I'm currently freelance."

"Too colorful? You mean you made the whole thing up? That's a pity. I was wondering if you had that recipe for Siamese Stir-Fry. No, I'm kidding you, really. It was such a great article, I don't think they should have given you the rush for that, whether you made it up or not. That deserved a Pulitzer."

"You're here for the same reason as me, aren't you?" said Sasha.

"I'm sorry?"

"Well, you said you had the feeling that you were supposed to be here. I had exactly the same feeling. And that

woman. She called me Sasha and she called you John. And
there's something about her, something about the way she
looked at me. It's there, in her eyes. She can change her appearance but she can't change that look."

John leaned back in his chair, so that it creaked under his
weight. "If I said the word 'Springer'—would that mean
anything to you?"

"Springer, yes. That's who she is, and that's what both of
us are doing here."

"Then it's true," said John, lowering his voice. "Or even
if it isn't true, then both of us have been duped in exactly the
same way."

At that moment, two young men in khaki raincoats came
walking across the room, both of them drenched. One of
them was tall and dark and very skinny, with a bony nose
and big, soulful eyes. The other was sandy and chunky, and
he was grinning and ducking his head and pretending to
shadow-box. Although so many tables were empty, they
came directly up to Sasha's table, pulled out two chairs and
sat down opposite.

John stared at them. "Hey, fellers," he said after a while.
"I don't like to be unfriendly or nothing, but there is such a
thing as personal space, and you just happen to have impinged on mine."

The sandy-haired young man turned to the dark young
man and said, "Perry? What's 'impinged'?"

The dark young man tugged a paper napkin out of its
holder and wiped rainwater from his face. "It comes from
the Latin 'impingo' meaning 'I'm a pinhead.'"

John shifted his chair back. "Listen, o hilarious juvenile,
take a hike."

"Why should I? This is a free country, isn't it? Where
does it say in the constitution that I'm not allowed to sit at
any cafeteria table that happens to have an available seat?
All right, I'm impinging on your personal space, I admit it.
But look at the goddamned size of you, man. Your personal
space reaches as far as Speed, Indiana."

"Okay, punk, that's it," said John, and stood up.

Neither of the two young men stood up, but the cleaner reappeared and came up to their table, and said, "Is there a problem here, people?"

John raised his hand. "Nothing that I can't personally take care of myself, thank you. Such as by forcibly propelling these two young smartass kids into the rain, out of which they shouldn't have bothered to come in from in the first place."

"But they didn't have a choice, John," countered the woman. "They both knew that they were supposed to be here. Just as you did."

John said nothing for a moment or two, although he was breathing like an asthmatic. Eventually, however, he said, "You *are* Springer, aren't you? And this whole preposterous cock and bullshit Night Warrior stuff, it's all *true,* isn't it? It's all going to happen, for real, and we're the Night Warriors. This young lady here, and these two smartass kids and me. 'It's freaking *insane,* man.' 'No, it's not.' 'You saw those screaming babies, didn't you? You saw yourself in the mirror, man, wearing all of that armor, and toting all of those guns and all of those knives.' But why us? I mean, for *chrissakes,* look at us. Fatty and Blondie and the Soaking-Wet Caped Crusaders."

Springer waited until he had finished arguing with himself. Then she said, "John—a Night Warrior's abilities are never compromised in any way by his or her deficiencies in the waking world. In fact, most of the time, somebody who is disadvantaged when they are awake will be much the greater in the world of dreams."

"Well, that's good to know," said John. "I'd hate to think I was going into battle with a comedy act."

"Who are you calling a comedy act, fatso?" Perry demanded. "Listen to you, talking to yourself! You're like the Three Stooges all rolled up into one enormous stooge."

"That's enough," said Springer, sharply. "Whatever you think of each other in the waking world, you will have to trust each other implicitly in the world of dreams. You will be in battle together, facing terrible dangers. You will often find yourselves making instantaneous decisions that could mean the difference between life or death or mutilation."

"Mutilation?" said John. "Hey, come on—you never said nothing about mutilation. I really, *really* dislike that word. I nearly dislike it as much as the word 'maim.'"

"Yeah, I was wondering about that, man," Perry put in. "Like, what happens if we get wounded in the world of dreams?"

"I won't lie to you," said Springer. "If you get injured in any way in the world of dreams, you will suffer some equal disadvantage in the waking world. For instance, if you were to lose your leg in a dream battle, you would discover when you woke that you still had your real leg, but couldn't feel it. It would remain numb and useless."

"Bummer," said Dunc. "What would happen if you lost your head?"

"Nothing that *you'd* ever notice," said John.

"Hey," said Perry. "My brother is mentally challenged, if you don't mind."

"I don't mind. I think we're *all* mentally challenged, coming to this cabbage-smelling cellar to talk about waging war on the forces of darkness."

Perry turned to Springer. "That's right ... you said you were going to tell us what these 'forces of darkness' actually are."

Sasha stood up. "This is a joke, right? In a minute you're going to show us where the cameras are hidden."

Springer pointed at her. "Didn't you single-handedly make the morning come early, Sasha? Or was that a joke? And how about you, John? Didn't you see yourself, wearing the armor of Dom Magator? And you, Perry. You saw yourself dressed up as The Zaggaline. And Duncan—what are the ingredients of hot dogs?"

"*What?*" said John. "Get real—nobody knows that."

But Dunc frowned and said, "Hot dogs are a semisolid.

Skeletal muscle meat, usually pork, is comminuted into a paste with thirty percent fat, ten percent water, dried milk, cereal or isolated soy protein, plus legally permitted colors, flavors and preservatives. Turkey or chicken frankfurters are allowed to contain skin and fat in natural proportions to that found on a turkey or chicken carcass, and may contain comminuted poultry feet."

"God," said John, pulling a face. "Don't take me out to the ball game ever again."

Springer said, "Meet Kalexikox, the Knowledge Gunner. Not so dumb as he appears to be, is he? Now, please sit down now, all of you. There is one more Night Warrior yet to arrive. Tonight you will be going out on your first training exercise, and this lady is somebody you will really need to take with you."

"Lady, hunh?" said John, tweaking up his pompadour.

Sasha said, "Listen—my boyfriend could be coming back from the West Coast tonight. I know you said that this Night Warriors thing is really important, but if he does … well, I don't think I'll be doing much sleeping, if you know what I mean, let alone dreaming."

"I'm sorry, Sasha. Tonight it will be essential for you to sleep alone."

"So what am I going to say to him? 'You can't stay over, Joe Henry, because I'm too busy fighting the forces of darkness'?"

"If you think that he will believe you—then, yes. Tell him exactly that."

Perry slapped the table and said, "Woo-hoo! That has to be the least believable excuse for not putting out that I ever heard!"

Dunc laughed, too, slapping his thigh, although he didn't really understand what he was supposed to be laughing at.

They were still laughing when a tall African-American woman came down the staircase and weaved elegantly and without hesitation between the empty tables toward them. She was wearing a loose white sweater with batwing sleeves, very tight jeans and pointy brown boots. Her hair was elaborately decorated with tiny white beads.

"Well, well, well," said John. "If it isn't Dr. Charlie."

"John Dauphin," said Dr. Mazurin, with a smile. "I never would have had *you* down as a Night Warrior."

"John is Dom Magator, the Armorer," said Springer. "I made sure that he took you to the clinic, so that he could see the babies for himself."

Perry looked at Dr. Mazurin, and then back at Springer. "So when I took Dora to the Kosair Hospital ...?"

"That's right," said Springer. "I'm afraid that I reorganized *your* life, too. I knew that you would be much more motivated if you could see for yourself the reason why I was asking you to fight."

"You can *do* that? You can change people's lives like that?"

Springer mimed a find-the-lady pattern with her hands. "Let's just say that I can shuffle them a little. For instance, why did you all come here? You were all hungry, weren't you, and you were all looking for someplace to eat. But I was the one who made you choose the Colonnade."

John said, "Okay, we get the picture. But next time you decide to meddle with my gastronomic destiny, can you make sure that we meet up at Stan's Fish Sandwich?"

Dr. Mazurin sat down next to Dunc. She said, quietly, "Springer called on me because I already have experience with attacks like these on newborn babies. It happened about seven years ago, in New York, but back then we were able to drive off the forces of darkness before any of the babies were killed or permanently disabled. This time, though ... this time the situation is much more serious."

"So ... you've been a Night Warrior before?" said Sasha.

Dr. Mazurin nodded. Her copper earrings swung as she held out her hand. "Amla Fabeya, the Ascender."

Springer said, "Amla Fabeya's specialty is climbing. Any imaginary obstacle that the forces of darkness can put up to isolate themselves—cliff, or castle, or wall, or drawbridge,

Amla can scale it. You will be surprised how often you need her."

"Not me," said John. "I get short of breath going up escalators."

Dr. Mazurin said, "What is happening today is critical because we are not just fighting against one of the forces of darkness, as we were in New York, but *two,* which is historically unheard of."

"That's right," explained Springer. "Two of the fiercest and most barbaric forces of darkness have decided to put aside their differences and become allies. Usually, they are deadly rivals, and their hatred of each other keeps them from forming any kind of coalition and becoming too strong.

"Obviously, though, the forces of darkness have been taking lessons from human warfare. Divided, they're always dangerous and destructive, but we can usually keep them under control. United, however, they can rip the universe apart.

"They are stealing the dreams of every newborn baby they can lay their hands on, in the hope that they can completely understand how Ashapola created the universe, and how they can disassemble it, atom by atom. Their intention is to make their own dark universe out of the matter that they destroy. To put it in terms that you can understand, they want to demolish heaven and rebuild it as hell. Nothing beautiful or gentle or inspirational will survive, and that includes humanity itself, except maybe as slaves or food.

"As I told you all last night, they haven't yet succeeded, but it is only a matter of *when,* rather than if."

Sasha said, "Is there any reason they chose to attack babies here in Louisville? I mean, it's not exactly the center of the known world, is it?"

Springer smiled. "In a way, it is. Why do you think that United Parcels use Louisville as their international hub? Louisville might seem as if it's nowhere, but it's the nearest place to anywhere else. Once the forces of darkness have acquired the knowledge of all creation, they will be able to spread their destructiveness all around the world within a matter of hours."

Perry said, "Don't you think it's time you told us what these 'forces of darkness' actually are? I mean, it's been difficult enough, getting our heads around the idea that we're some kind of dream warriors, but we don't even know what we're supposed to be warrioring against."

"That is why I gathered you here," Springer agreed. "Seven years ago, in New York, Amla Fabeya was fighting the Night Cobra."

"The Night Cobra?" said Perry. "Sounds like something which Sasha won't be getting tonight!"

John shook his head in despair. "Did some sadist once erroneously tell this kid that he was amusing?"

Springer said, "The Night Cobra was the original serpent, which was supposed to have tempted Eve in the Garden of Eden. The reason why so many people dismiss the serpent as nothing more than Biblical myth is because it appeared in the world of dreams, rather than the waking world. The Night Cobra was trying to penetrate Eve's consciousness because she was the first human that Ashapola created, and like newly born babies, she knew everything that Ashapola knew—until her very first dream, anyhow, when she forgot it all.

"The Biblical story of the serpent is correct in some ways, but fundamentally wrong in others. The Night Cobra wasn't *offering* knowledge, it was trying to *steal* it. But it didn't succeed. When the first woman slept for the very first time, Ashapola created the very first Night Warrior to protect her, and to protect the secret of creation. The Night Cobra was seriously wounded and learned nothing; and when the first woman woke up, all she knew was that she had forgotten something huge and extraordinary.

"That is why humans are forever seeking more and more knowledge. They are always aware that for one split-second, when they were born, they completely understood how the universe was made."

Dr. Mazurin said, "The Night Cobra tried to attack newborn babies in New York, but we had sixteen Night Warriors there, and eventually we destroyed it. We lost three Night Warriors and five were wounded, but considering what we were up against, those were quite acceptable casualties."

"Oh yeah?" said Perry. "Acceptable to who? I wouldn't find it acceptable if one of them was me."

"I wouldn't like it, either," said Dunc. "I'd be pretty damn mad about it."

John covered his face with his hands. "Ashapola, wherever you are, sir or madam, give me strength."

Springer said, "Now we have discovered that two forces of darkness have risen up and formed an alliance known in the world of dreams as the Ice Axis. The most terrible of the two forces is the Winterwent, who travels through dreams in a sledge drawn by a thousand frozen wolves with ice splinters instead of fur. He is capable of freezing any dream through which he passes, and that is why people sometimes find that they are dreaming of blizzards in the middle of summer, or why they wake up shaking with cold. If he encounters any opposition in the dream world, he freezes it solid, and he can actually lower the brain temperature of sleeping people so much that he kills them.

"In the dream world, the Winterwent can freeze you simply by touching you, and then he can shatter your frozen body with the Kattalak, which is his ice-ax, fashioned out of frozen mercury."

"Minus 38.844 degrees Celsius," said Dunc. Everybody stared at him, and he turned around himself, as if somebody standing behind him had said it. Then he turned back and explained, "That's—that's the freezing-point of mercury. Minus 38.844."

"So what does this Winterwent look like?" asked Sasha.

"Tall, skeletal, with a sharp elongated skull and a cloak

made of rags and crackling ice. Six arms, like a frozen spider, and claws. Think of what it feels like to be frozen to the bone, and that's what the Winterwent looks like."

"So who's his ally?"

"The High Horse. He rides three enormous horses, one on top of the other. He's a barbarian out of your very worst nightmares. He wears a helmet with three living stags heads on it, which are constantly screaming in pain, and his fur cloak is made of living animals like foxes and otters and raccoons, all fastened together with metal hooks so that they scream, too. You can always tell when the High Horse is coming, because you can hear such a cacophony of suffering.

"The High Horse is unconditionally brutal and relishes other people's despair. He takes pleasure out of twisting children's arms off and then throwing them down wells to see how they can swim, and out of cutting men open and nailing their intestines to trees, and then pushing flaming torches into their faces so that they have to back away and disembowel themselves rather than be burned. Most of what he does to women is too disgusting to tell you, but he likes to force live rats up inside them, five or six at a time with their tails tied together, and then set fire to their tails."

Now, for the first time, the small company of Night Warriors was silent and serious.

At last, John cleared his throat and said, "So, these are the guys we're up against? The Winterwent and the High Horse?"

"They don't sound real, do they?" said Springer. "And of course, in the waking world, they're not. But when you arrive in the world of dreams, they will both be as real as you are. I'm not going to lie to you, they are two of the most formidable opponents that any Night Warriors have ever had to face. The Winterwent is utterly coldhearted and ruthless. The High Horse is sadistic and mad. They have their differences, but they both want to destroy the real world and everything in it, so that they can have their own world of cold and pain and unrelenting cruelty."

"Well, if you want my opinion," said John, "we should all go to sleep tonight and get into those dreams, and then we should collectively whup their asses." He turned to Perry. "How about you, o hilarious kid?"

Just then, however, the cafeteria's lights flickered and dimmed until they could hardly see each other. Not only that, they felt a sudden chill, as if a huge cold storage unit had been opened.

"Brownout?" Sasha suggested.

But Springer was worriedly looking around the room. "There!" she said, after a moment. "That old woman— shake her awake!"

"What?" said Perry.

"That old woman, sleeping in the corner. Shake her awake!"

"Okay, but—"

"She's been dreaming, and the Winterwent has been listening to us in her dream!"

Perry went across to the woman's table. She was wearing a green blouse with tiny little flowers on it, and her shoulders were bony and hunched up. Her wavy white hair was pinned back with a green plastic barrette. Her face was pressed flat against the pages of her book, as if she had been trying to stare right through the printed words to the imaginary world beyond. Perry hesitated for a moment and then he shook her arm. "Ma'am? Pardon me, ma'am!"

Springer came over and joined him. "Shake her harder!"

Perry shook the woman's arm quite violently, but still she didn't stir.

The manager appeared, a small balding man with a bristling moustache. "Anything wrong here?"

"This woman," said Perry. "I can't wake her up."

The manager tried shaking her arm, too. "Ma'am? Can you hear me, ma'am? This is the manager."

When she didn't respond, he carefully took hold of her

head and turned it sideways, so that they could see her face. Her eyes were wide open, but the pupils were dilated and she was plainly dead. She must have been quite pretty once, years and years ago.

Springer laid a hand on her forehead. "She's cold," she said. "Feel how *cold* she is."

"That's okay," said Perry. "I'll take your word for it." He had never seen a dead body before, not even his mother. Dunc started to amble toward them, frowning with curiosity, but Perry intercepted him and led him gently away. "You don't want to see this, dude."

Springer came back to their table, too. "No question about it," she said.

"The Winterwent?"

She nodded. "He must be aware that we're preparing ourselves to fight him. I think he's going to give us a whole lot of trouble."

One by one, the lights blinked back on. Sasha said, "My God, I'm frightened. Why can't I wake up?"

John laid a plump, reassuring hand on her shoulder. "You *are* awake, honeycakes. It's when you fall asleep that you have to start worrying."

CHAPTER EIGHT

Perry put away the last dinner plate and hung up the dish towel.

"Well," he said with an exaggerated yawn. "I think I'll turn in."

His father said, "You're kidding me, aren't you? It's not even nine o'clock yet."

"Is that all? Oh. Guess I've had a hard day."

"Doing what, for instance? Dunc was down at the store at seven o'clock, tearing up floorboards and shoveling up rubble. You didn't even show up until halfway through the afternoon."

"It's been *intellectually* hard."

"Don't tell me. You read the funny papers."

"Dad, I really want to get good grades. I want you to be proud of me for a change."

George said, "Yes, well," as if he wasn't at all convinced, and switched off the kitchen light. In the living room, Dunc was lying on the brown velvet couch with his feet drawn up like a small child, his mouth sagging open, snoring. George stood over him for a while, watching him, and then he said,

"I wonder what he dreams about. I wonder if he's clever in his dreams."

"The way he's snoring, he probably thinks that he's sawing up floorboards."

The nine o'clock TV news had just started, and George turned up the sound and sat down in his armchair. A worried-looking woman reporter was standing outside the Kosair Children's Hospital with her hair blowing over her face, while flashing red ambulance lights were reflected on the wet streets behind her.

"Tonight the death toll among newly born infants at Kosair and other Louisville hospitals and clinics stands at twenty-seven, with a further thirty-four babies still in intensive care. Pediatric specialists have been flown in from nine other cities in a desperate attempt to save these children's lives."

"My God," said George. "This is like the Massacre of the Innocents."

Perry was tempted for a moment to tell his father what was really happening, and why all of these babies were dying, but he knew that he wouldn't believe him. He would probably say that he was being blasphemous, or tasteless, or both. And he couldn't really blame him. He was still finding it hard to believe it himself.

The reporter was saying, "Specialists have agreed that the babies appear to be suffering from a rare brain condition which leaves them incapable of dreaming. So far, however, none of the medical experts has been able to suggest how infants so young could have been stricken by this syndrome, which is usually only seen in adults, after a stroke.

"Various special interest groups are trying to lay blame on particular causes. Environmentalists are blaming water table pollution. Vegetarians are blaming chemical additives in processed meat. And alternative medicine enthusiasts are blaming the anti-depressant Diazepam, which many women continue to take during their pregnancies, in spite of their physicians' warnings.

"So far, however, no single cause has been scientifically identified, and meanwhile the babies continue to cry—and to die."

George shook his head. "The same thing happened to little Joe, but your mother never took any kind of medication. Maybe it's God's will and there's nothing that anybody can do about it."

"Dad—I don't think God wants a whole lot of babies to die before they even have the chance to live."

George turned his head and stared at Perry in surprise.

Perry said, "I don't know. Maybe God has some special plan. Maybe He wants more babies in heaven—you know, because it's mostly geriatrics up there, and He's sick of all of their moaning and groaning about their back pains and their arthritis. But I don't see it, myself. I don't think He would ever be that selfish."

George said, "Maybe you should turn in. Maybe you *have* been straining your brain."

Perry took a shower. He had just lathered his hair with shower gel when the water ran cold, and by the time he had rinsed himself his teeth were chattering. "Jesus," he said, dancing across the landing to his bedroom.

He tugged on one of his baggy T-shirts and a pair of plaid shorts while he was still only half-dry, so that they stuck to him. As he was scruffing up his hair in his mirror, he glanced across at his computer. He was tempted to spend some time on his *Trash Planet* animation to see if he could sort out the problems he had been having with Junk Toddler. Once he started, however, he knew that he would probably still be messing around with spinal structure and rendering when the sun came up, and by that time his first opportunity to be a Night Warrior would have passed him by.

Maybe, if he really told himself the truth, he *wanted* the opportunity to pass him by. Now that the time had arrived for him to enter the world of dreams and put on the protective armor of a Night Warrior, he was beginning to feel increasingly unsure about it. Suppose it was all for real? Suppose he got killed, or lost the use of his legs? For all of his bravado, he was only a seventeen-year-old kid. He hadn't even *lived* yet. The furthest he had traveled on his own was to Indianapolis, to an X-Skulls concert. And apart from that messing-about last Christmas holiday with Helen Emmerich, he was still technically a virgin. What if he got killed, and never even, you know, *did* it?

He sat on the end of the bed and unfolded the piece of paper that Springer had given him, bearing the invocation to Ashapola. It was written in faded black ink in a scrawly, forward-sloping script, as if a spider had scuttled across the paper. "You're nuts," he told himself. "You know what's going to happen. Precisely zip. You're going to go to sleep, wake up, and that'll be it. The Zaggaline, my ass."

He was feeling so undecided about this whole Night Warrior thing that he hadn't yet gone downstairs to shake Dunc awake. Dunc was asleep already, but of course he hadn't yet recited the invocation to Ashapola. Until he did, he couldn't change into Kalexikox, the Knowledge Gunner.

Maybe it would be better if he left Dunc out of this altogether. Dunc was so childlike, so defenseless, he would probably blunder into the first ambush that the Winterwent and the High Horse had set up for them.

"*The Winterwent,*" he repeated, under his breath. "*The High Horse.*" He knew that they were only imaginary, but they still made him feel chilly and frightened. In the far distance, he thought he could hear animals screaming.

He was still sitting on the end of his bed when his father knocked on his door.

"Just came to say good night," said George.

"Oh, sure. Good night, Dad."

His father stayed where he was for a few moments, still holding the doorhandle. "Just wanted to say ... well, you and me haven't always gotten on too good, have we? But I think that we can."

"Sure, Dad, whatever you say."

"I had a dream about your mother last night, and little Joe. I dreamed that I was walking down by the river, and there they were. She was throwing a bright blue ball and little Joe was catching it, and he was laughing."

Perry didn't know what to say. His father was clearly feeling emotional, because he had to stop and swallow hard before he said anything else.

"It wasn't like any dream I ever had before. I felt like I was really there, and *they* were there, too. When I woke up ... I couldn't believe for a long while that it hadn't actually happened."

Perry hesitated, and then he said, "Somebody told me that the dream world is the real world, and the waking world is only like a dream."

"Oh, yes? Who told you that?"

"Just some dude I was talking to."

"Well, maybe that dude was wiser than he even knew."

His father gave Perry an awkward salute and left the room, closing the door behind him with exaggerated care.

Perry climbed slowly into bed, pulled the sheets around him and stared unfocused at his purple pillowcase. He suddenly thought: *Shit, Perry, you're growing up.* It was an appalling sensation, really scary, as if he had discovered that his bed had floated out to sea and nobody was ever going to put a boat out to rescue him.

He looked at the piece of paper. He didn't *have* to read out the invocation. He didn't *have* to dream that he was The Zaggaline. But what was the alternative? A whole life of not knowing if he could have saved those babies or not. Or no life at all, if Springer had been telling the truth. Blackness, nothingness and pain. The whole world, ripped apart at the seams.

He was still trying to make up his mind what to do when his door opened again, and this time it was Dunc, yawning and stretching and scratching his behind.

"Sorry, dude," said Dunc. "I was watching *Stargate Atlantis* and I must of closed my eyes for a minute."

"Don't worry about it," Perry told him. "Why don't you go to bed and I'll see you in the morning?"

Dunc blinked at him. "What are you talking about, dude? We're supposed to be Night Warriors. We have to say the words and fall asleep and then we have to fight that cold person and that person on the horse."

"Dunc, you don't really want to do that, do you?"

"I'm Kalexikox, Perry. I know everything. I know what everything's made of. Boob jobs and hot dogs and craggy mountains."

"Sure, Dunc. But this is really going to be dangerous."

"We have to say the words, Perry. That's what the lady told us."

Perry sat up in bed. "Okay, then. But let me tell you, I don't think anything is going to happen."

"We still have to do it, dude. We promised."

Perry looked at the piece of paper. Then he said, "Okay … we'll do it. So long as you go to bed right afterward."

Dunc came over and sat down on the bed, bouncing up and down to make himself comfortable. "Are you excited? I'm excited."

"Sure, I'm excited."

"I'm scared, too," said Dunc. "But that's what makes it exciting, right? It's like when I was a kid and I climbed right up on top of the garage roof and I couldn't get down."

Perry held up the piece of paper. "Say this after me, okay? 'Now—' "

"*Now*," said Dunc, immediately.

"You don't have to repeat every single word as soon as I say it. Let's try to do it in phrases, okay? 'Now when the face of the world is hidden in darkness—' "

Dunc repeated it, and then waited. Perry thought, This is going to work. I have a really bad feeling that this is going to work.

"Go on," Dunc urged him.

"Okay, okay, don't rush me, all right? '—let us be conveyed to the place of our meeting, armed and armored; and let us be nourished by the power that is dedicated to the cleaving of darkness, the settling of all black matters, and the dissipation of all evil, so be it.' "

They repeated the invocation three times and Dunc didn't stumble once, not even over a word like "dissipation."

When they had finished their recitation, Dunc said brightly, "That's it?"

"That's it. All we have to do now is go to sleep."

Dunc stood up and briskly chafed his hands together. "Okay, then, that's it?"

"That's it."

Dunc looked around the room. "You know what the trouble is?"

"What's the trouble, Dunc?"

"I don't feel sleepy anymore."

"Well, go to bed anyhow, and think about Sue Marshall's bongaroobies. See if you can count how many times they bounce up and down before they finally come to a complete standstill."

"Okay, dude."

"Later, dude."

When Dunc had left the room, Perry lay back in bed and stared up at the ceiling. Quite unexpectedly, he wondered what his mother would have thought of him if she could have seen him now. For the first time in years and years, he felt the pain of missing her, and the sound of her voice, and his eyes filled up with tears.

John eased himself into bed a little after 10:30 P.M. He was suffering from serious heartburn. After they had found that gray-haired woman dead at the Colonnade, he hadn't had the appetite to eat anything there—especially not that English meatloaf—and because he was late back on duty, Leland had refused him even a five-minute cheeseburger break. When his shift was over he had went to Stevens & Stevens for one of their "Me Turkey, You Jane" turkey and bacon sandwiches, and he had wolfed it down without chewing it properly, with bits of lettuce dropping onto his T-shirt, and now his digestive system was paying the price.

Although he kept burping, he felt steady and determined and ready for action. He believed in Springer—or at least he *wanted* to believe in Springer, even though for most of his adult life, most of the things that he had ever wanted to believe in had turned out to be lies or scams or wishful thinking. Springer had shown him that he was so much more than an overweight, self-deprecating clown. He was Dom Magator, the Armorer, and he wasn't going to be late and let down his fellow Night Warriors. He was the kingpin, and they were going to be relying on him for all of the weapons. They were going into the dream world to kick some serious ass, and he was going to provide them all of the high-tech guns and all of the fancy knives they needed to do it.

The thunderstorms had rolled away now, off to eastern Indiana, but the rain had done nothing to clear the humidity. John was perspiring so much that he had to dab his face with a rancid brown towel, and press it underneath his armpits.

"Okay," he said, tossing the towel into the chair on the other side of the room, "you believe in this, right? You're going to say these sacred words and when you fall asleep you're going to be a Night Warrior."

"You genuinely believe this is genuinely going to happen?" he retorted.

"Yes, as a matter of fact I do. If I don't believe in this, feller, then what *do* I have to believe in?"

"Something tangible. Fried chicken, for instance, with a spicy crumb coating, served with hot biscuits and gravy."

"Get thee behind me, Satan."

He picked up the piece of paper that Springer had given him and tilted it toward his bedside lamp. He was sure that his eyesight was getting worse. Maybe he needed glasses.

Very slowly, he read out the words of the invocation. "Now when the face of the world is hidden in darkness, let us be conveyed to the place of our meeting, armed and armored; and let us be nourished by the power that is dedicated to the cleaving of darkness, the settling of all black matters, and the dispissation—I mean, the disposition—I mean, the dissipation of all evil, so be it. "

He paused for a moment, and then he added, "And may Deano be forgiven for all of his transgressions. Not just the cigar box but that other thing with the vacuum cleaner and the sausage links, Amen."

He repeated the invocation twice more, and then he switched off his bedside light and lay flat on his side. *Okay, now sleep. You never have trouble going to sleep.*

He lay there for twenty minutes, not moving, and not sleeping. His air conditioner rattled, his refrigerator whinnied, and the couple in the upstairs apartment had started one of their muffled, door-slamming arguments. Out on the river, the stern-wheel paddle-steamer *Belle of Louisville* sounded her calliope; and in the street below, six or seven cars blasted their horns at each other in an ever-increasing display of aggression. John had never realized how noisy the city could be until now. He could even hear *bicycles* going past, with a smug, self-satisfied *zizzing* noise.

He sat up and switched his bedside light back on. He hoped that Springer hadn't been making a fool of him, and that this Night Warriors business wasn't some kind of elaborate practical joke. He heaved himself out of bed, left his room, and went across the hall to the bathroom. He took a leak, one hand pressed up against the wall to support himself. When he had finished, he filled up his glass with tepid water from the bathroom faucet, so that he could dissolve two Alka-Seltzer and settle his stomach.

He had almost made it back to his room when the door opposite his apartment opened and the nurse who lived next door stepped out into the hall wearing a tight black sequined top and a very short black skirt. Her red hair was all swept up and she smelled strongly of J-Lo perfume.

"Oh, *hi*, John. How are things with you?"

"Getting by, Nadine. Getting by."

"You going off to dreamland already, John?"

He rubbed his stomach. "Truth is, Nadine, I don't feel so good."

"You should take more care of yourself, John. Take more exercise."

"You're right, Nadine. Matter of fact, I was thinking of taking up the trapeze."

"John, are you ever going to be serious?"

He went back to his room and closed the door behind him. He took a deep breath and then punched the wall with his fist. He felt so humiliated and belittled that he could have burst into tears. Of all the times that Nadine had to come out of her room it was then, when he was sweaty and smelly and his pompadour was tilting off to one side.

He sat on the edge of the bed and drank two Alka-Seltzers, which fizzed right up his nose and made him sneeze. If Springer had been lying to him and there was no such person as Dom Magator, and it turned out that the Night Warriors were some set-up by *Candid Camera*, or some reality TV show like that, he promised himself that he was going to find Springer and wring his neck like a chicken, even if Kentucky did have the death penalty.

Sasha took a long hot shower and then wrapped herself up in her biggest bath towel and blew her hair dry. She put on a stripy man-sized shirt and propped herself up in bed with a large glass of red wine and a copy of *The Secret South*, which she had been promising herself for months that she would read. The book was supposed to be an exposé of how the South was still in the hands of old money and old power, and was still secessionist in everything but name. It would make a great newspaper feature if she could find enough Old Southerners to admit that they still regarded themselves as Confederates, and that Lee's surrender at Appomattox had been nothing but a gentlemanly way of preventing any further loss of life.

If she couldn't find any real interviewees, of course, she could always invent them. She could see the headline now: SCARLETT O'HARA LIVES ON!

After a while, however, she put her book down. She was kidding herself. Whether she liked it or not, she had to accept that, from tonight onward, her life was going to change forever. As Xanthys she had a very different life to lead—a life of honor, loyalty and truth. A life in which there was no place for lies, or even mild exaggerations, no matter how well-meant they might be. From what Springer had told them, the world of dreams was deceitful enough, without them deceiving each other.

She climbed out of bed and picked up the scrap of paper that Springer had given her. Then she stood in front of the mirror with the paper held up high. She thought that she looked different somehow. There was something in her eyes. A *sharpness* that she had never had before.

You have to recite this invocation three times, Springer had told her. *So—if I change my mind after reciting it twice, I still won't be committed, will I?* She cleared her throat and read out, "Now when the face of the world is hidden in darkness, let us be conveyed to the place of our meeting ..."

That was as far as she managed to get before her cell phone played "Wake Up, Little Susie."

She tried to ignore it and carry on, but the ringtone went on and on. Eventually she picked it up and said, "Listen, I'm busy, okay?"

"Since when have you been too busy for the Great JH?"

"Joe Henry! When did you get back?"

"Flew in about an hour ago. Everything went great! I met a producer from Sony and they want to sign me! The Great JH is going to be rich and famous, babe!"

"That's terrific. I'm so pleased for you."

"You should have seen me, Sash! We did a set at the Crocodile Café and we blew the whole place away! You know that song I wrote for you, 'Sashay Like Sasha'? They was up on their *feet*, babe, and they was waving their arms and I felt like *God*."

"You deserve it, Joe Henry, you really do. Haven't I always told you how talented you are?"

"You was always my muse, babe. You was always my guiding light. If it hadn't been for you—well, I gotta show you how much I love you. All of that adulation, that gave me such a hard-on, babe, and I've been saving that hard-on especially for you."

"Maybe we can meet up tomorrow?"

Joe Henry coughed in disbelief. "You're telling me what? *Tomorrow?* Are you kidding me? I got to see you tonight, babe! I got to see you now, this instant. I'm on such a high. And this hard-on, this hard-on can't wait a minute longer. It's sticking up higher than the Kaden Tower."

"Joe Henry ... I'm so sorry ... but I'm busy tonight."

"You're busy? You're *busy?* Busy doing, like, what?"

"Just busy, hon. I promised somebody I'd do them a favor and I can't back out of it."

"What kind of a favor?"

"I can't really explain it."

"Oh, *that* kind of a favor."

"Joe Henry, there's nobody else here tonight, I swear it. I really want to see you. I really, really do. But I can't put this off, not even for you."

She heard Joe Henry slap his hand against the wall. "Sash, baby, I've been away in Canuckland for eleven days and in all of that eleven days I haven't even blown smoke in another woman's direction because I've been keeping myself for you and you only. You listen to me, babe, I've had women crawling along the carpet to get to me. I've had propositions that the *Pope* wouldn't have turned down. I gotta see you, Sash. I'm in very dire and desperate need."

"I'm so sorry, Joe Henry. But what I'm doing tonight—it's something really important."

"So what is it? This really important thing that's so

much more important than ministrating to your lover's frustration?"

For a split-second, Sasha almost gave in. Joe Henry was such fun. So mad, and spontaneous, and great in bed. He wasn't a stylish lover, but he was tireless. He even managed to keep his erections when asleep, so that Sasha could sit on top of him while he gently snored, and pleasure herself at her own, undulating pace.

But then she thought of those babies screaming at the Ormsby Clinic, and the dead woman at the Colonnade, and the way that she had turned the clock forward using nothing but her finger. The Night Warriors needed her, and she couldn't let them down.

"Joe Henry, believe me, I'm really dying to see you."

"Oh yeah? Freaking sounds like."

"Joe Henry, if there was any other way ... but I've made these people a promise, and it's a promise that I have to keep."

"Sure. I can dig it. Well, don't worry. I'm sure that I can find some other washed-out blonde who won't mind relieving me of this load that I'm carrying."

"Joe Henry—tomorrow, I give you my word."

"Tomorrow and tomorrow and tomorrow, babe. I don't believe in tomorrow. Today's the day and if you can't do it today you can't do it at all, so far as I'm concerned. Have a nice life."

"Joe Henry—"

But he had hung up; and when she tried to call him back, his line was busy. Phoning around for somebody to replace her, she imagined. She tried again, and then again, but after a while she tossed her phone back onto her bed and thought: Forget it. He had probably been lying, anyhow, about saving himself for his return. She couldn't really believe that Joe Henry had turned down any propositions from any girl, let alone propositions that would have tempted the Pope.

She held up the piece of paper again. Her hand was trembling, but she took a deep breath and steadied it. For some reason she felt even more determined. Very slowly and clearly she recited the invocation to Ashapola. Once, and then a second time.

She closed her eyes for a moment. *You don't have to do this, Sasha. Nobody's forcing you. Nobody's going to give you a hard time if you're a no-show. The other Night Warriors can manage without you. Think of all their fantastic weapons. Think of all of their knives and their guns and all of the other amazing things they can do. And what's your special talent? You can turn the clock backward and forward. Big deal. Not much more than a conjuring trick.*

She opened her eyes again. She looked at herself in the mirror. She watched herself, expressionless, as she repeated the invocation for a third time.

That's it, you've done it. She climbed back into bed and switched off the light. The people in the apartment downstairs were watching a comedy show on TV, and every now and then she could hear roars of studio laughter.

CHAPTER NINE

She opened her eyes and she could still hear the television downstairs, although now it sounded like a horror movie. She lifted her head from the pillow. Her bedside clock said 11:37 P.M. She must have been asleep, but only for twenty minutes or so. Her lips felt dry, as if she had been breathing through her mouth.

"*Xanthys*?" said a seductive voice.

She blinked and looked around. Springer was standing at the end of her bed, wearing a loose white robe, so that he looked like one of the Twelve Disciples. He had a calm, beatific smile on his face. His long auburn hair floated around his head as if it were being blown by a summer breeze.

Next to him stood Dom Magator, although he was still dressed in nothing but shorts and his saggy sweatshirt. "Hi, Xanthys," he said, raising his hand. "Bet you never thought that this was really going to happen for real, did you? I sure didn't."

Xanthys turned around and looked down at her pillow. With a tingle of shock, she saw that she was still lying on it, fast asleep, with one hand drawn up on the pillow and her mouth slightly open. Her hair was bedraggled with perspiration.

It was almost as if she were conjoined twins, who shared the same pelvis and the same pair of legs.

"What's happened to me?" she said. "Springer—*what's happened to me?*"

"Nothing at all," Springer reassured her. "All you have to do now is climb out of bed and leave your sleeping self behind."

"What?"

"Try it. Come on … you won't feel anything more than a very faint tingle."

"I did it," said Dom Magator. "It's like taking a shower in ice-cold seltzer, that's all."

Sasha cautiously eased herself out of bed. Dom Magator was right: it gave her a light, prickling sensation, but that was all. She stood up and took three or four paces away from the bed and then looked back. She was still there, sleeping.

"That's *so-o-o* weird," she said. Cautiously, more than a little scared she'd wake herself up, she leaned over and examined her sleeping self more closely. "You know, I never knew that I looked like that. I always thought my face was thinner. And my *nose!* I didn't know it tilted up as much as that. You can see right up my nostrils!"

"I took one look at myself and I swore to go back on one of my diets," said Dom Magator. "I always knew I was kind of bulky, for sure. But when I saw myself tonight … I make John Goodman look like Slimmer of the Year."

Sasha looked down at her striped shirt. "I'm still dressed the same. I thought I was supposed to turn into Xanthys?"

"Be patient," said Springer. "The others will be here soon, and when they arrive, you will all transmogrify together. I decided that we should assemble here, at your apartment, because it is secluded, and most of all because it is closest to the first sleeper whose dream you are going to penetrate."

"How do you pick whose dream we're going to go into?" asked Dom Magator.

"Ambient temperature," said Springer. "The Winterwent freezes everything he touches, so I can detect where he is by the cold spots he leaves dotted around the city. It's rather like the fire department looking for victims buried in collapsed buildings by using infrared heat-imaging ... except I'm looking for extreme cold instead of heat. I am highly sensitive to even the slightest changes in temperature, and that is why I can locate your enemies for you with a high degree of accuracy."

While he was speaking, the air on the opposite side of Sasha's bedroom began to ripple. With the softest slithering sound, like a heavy silk bedspread sliding onto the floor, Perry descended out of the ceiling, feet first, and landed gently on the rug. He was followed immediately afterward by Dunc, who was bent forward with his arms extended as if he were trying to fly, or at least trying to stop himself from falling.

"We *flew,* dude!" he burst out, teetering from side to side to regain his balance. He looked around at Springer and Sasha and John and said, "We *flew!*"

"To be accurate," said Springer, "your dream personality was filtered from your physical body and drawn across the city by psychokinetic attraction."

"Whatever, it was totally awesome! We floated right up out of our beds like we didn't weigh nothing at all! And then we floated right through the roof and we were way up high, right over the rooftops! I saw the river, and the riverboats, and all of the cars, and I saw the planes landing at the airport, *neeeooowwww,* like they was tiny little toys!" He stopped, breathless, and then his face rearranged itself into a frown. "It was real scary, though. I thought I was going to fall and get smashed to bits like that kid who jumped off the Humana Building and his arms and legs came flying off."

Springer said, "Kalexikox—while you are a Night Warrior, nothing in the real world can hurt you."

"What? So even if I *had* fallen, I would have been okay?"

"That's right. This is your *dream* self. Your physical body is still lying in your bed asleep, dreaming that you're here. Of course, if somebody were to kill your physical body while you lay sleeping, you would find yourself in trouble. You would have no body to return to when the sun came up, and you would have to stay forever in the world of dreams, running from one dream to another."

Kalexikox looked worried. "Maybe I should of locked my bedroom door."

Springer smiled. "Think about it, Kalexikox. You don't have any enemies, do you? So the chances of anybody attacking your physical body while you're asleep are very remote. Don't forget, though, that your dream self can be killed or hurt by things that happen to you in dreams. There are many people in hospitals all across America who are believed by their doctors to be in long-term vegetative states. In fact, most of them are Night Warriors whose dream self has been killed in a dream world conflict, and who could never return to revive their physical body."

Kalexikox grimaced at his brother. "I thought you said this was going to be all party-party-party."

The Zaggaline gave him a reassuring slap on the back. "It is, Kalexikox. It will be. Party-party-party till we drop. Just so long as we don't get ourselves mutilated or killed."

At that moment, the air rippled again and Dr. Mazurin appeared, slowly sinking down through the ceiling. She was wearing a loose kaftan with yellow squares and diamonds printed on it.

"Dr. M," said Dom Magator. "Honored you could join us."

Springer raised his hand. "Please, Dom Magator, call her Amla Fabeya! As Night Warriors, you must use only your Night Warrior names and no others. Your names were given to you by Ashapola, the creator of the universe, and so nobody else can use them or steal your identity."

"Sorry," said Dom Magator. "I was just wondering how the babies were getting along. The doc here—I mean, sorry, Amla Fabeya—she was thinking of trying to hypnotize them, weren't you?"

Amla Fabeya pressed her fingers against her forehead, as if she were suffering from a migraine. "Before I went to sleep, I heard that three more babies died this evening at the Ormsby Clinic, and eleven more in other hospitals in Jefferson County."

"Oh, shit," said Xanthys. "That's terrible."

Amla Fabeya nodded. "Yes. It's a tragedy. But I think that I managed to make some progress today. I hypnotized two of the babies at the Ormsby before they died, and I believe I got very much closer to finding out how the Winterwent and the High Horse were trying to steal their dreams."

"How can you hypnotize a baby?" asked The Zaggaline. "Babies can't talk, can they?"

"Of course not. But babies can tell you much more than you would imagine. You can regress babies to the time when they were back in the womb, and you can get them to relive the stresses and strains of their fetal development. By the way they behave, the way they move their arms and legs, the way they kick, you can tell exactly which stage of their growth they're reenacting."

"So what did you find out?" asked Dom Magator.

"It's obvious that the Winterwent and the High Horse haven't had any success in penetrating the dreams of newborn infants, so I think that they've been trying to get into the babies' subconscious through their *mothers'* dreams, before the babies are actually born. After all, there's considerable evidence that expectant mothers and their unborn children share the same brain waves. I'm not entirely sure how they're trying to do it, but I'm hoping that I can find out some more tonight, especially if we encounter the Winterwent face-to-face."

"Hey, I'm really looking forward to that," said The Zaggaline. "A giant insect, right, who can freeze your nuts off as soon as say 'good morning' to you."

"I'm not going to pretend that the Winterwent will be an easy opponent," said Springer. "But you—all of you—you're well-armed, and you have skills and natural intelligences that have been passed down through hundreds of generations of Night Warriors."

"Well," said Dom Magator with a sniff. "I'm ready, if the rest of yous are."

"Yes," Springer agreed. "It's time." He tossed back his hair and raised both arms and said, "Now each of you must dress in your armor and venture into the world of dreams, so that you can carry on the centuries-old struggle between the light of Ashapola and the raging forces of chaos."

He beckoned to Sasha. She came forward, a little hesitantly. "Kneel, please," he asked her, and she knelt on the rug in front of him, making a face at The Zaggaline as she did so. The Zaggaline gave her a reassuring thumbs-up.

Springer drew a circle in the air, directly above her head. As he did so, his fingers left a trail of liquid golden light, so that he formed a halo, which gradually spread wider and wider, like a ripple on a sunlit pond.

He repeated the invocation to Ashapola and then pressed his fingertips to his forehead for a few moments, as if he were thinking hard. Then he said, "Rise, Xanthys, in the arms and armor of a true Night Warrior."

Xanthys slowly stood up, and as she did so, the golden halo sank all around her until it reached the floor. She was now transformed into a Night Warrior, with huge crystal goggles with multi-faceted lenses and a tight cluster of shell-shaped earphones. Her hair was densely knotted with silver beads, so many of them that they almost formed a protective helmet.

She wore upcurving silver epaulets and silver boots with V-shaped vanes on them. The silver was densely carved with hieroglyphs and symbols and interlocking lizards.

Around her waist hung a jointed metal belt that was densely clustered with keys of all kinds—clock keys, watch keys, skeleton keys, master keys and change keys. When Springer had first shown Xanthys what she would look like as a Night Warrior, her armor and her belt had been optical illusions and weighed nothing, so she was surprised to discover how heavy they were, especially the keys, which made a thick *chunking* sound whenever she took a step.

Apart from her goggles and her epaulets, her boots and her belt, she was completely naked, although her skin shone a deep metallic coppery color.

"Xanthys the Time Curver," said Springer, his eyes sparkling with pride. "The keys you carry can unlock any mystery, any treasure chest, any door. Throughout history, keys have been a protection against disease and demonic possession—and they know everything. Have you ever heard of clidomancy? That is when you place a key on the Fiftieth Psalm, and then close the Bible and bind it tightly with a virgin's hair. You suspend the Bible from a string, and when you mention the name of somebody whose honesty you suspect—a thief, perhaps, or a liar—the Bible will twist and turn, because the key is turning to unlock your suspicions.

"Your keys can do the same. They can unlock time itself, and open doors that for most people have closed behind them forever, or which they have yet to encounter."

"Why is my skin this weird color?" asked Xanthys.

"Copper," said Springer. "Copper was the first metal ever fashioned by man, and it has great healing and mythological powers. You need to be quick and light as a Time Curver—faster than time itself—but this copper skin will protect you from injury as well as any armor, and from evil, too."

"Melting point of copper—1,083 degrees Celsius," put in Kalexikox. "Boiling point of copper—2,567 degrees Celsius."

"Dom Magator?" said Springer, and Dom Magator stepped forward and knelt in front of him. Again Springer recited the invocation, and he traced a circle of shimmering light in the air above Dom Magator's head. Dom Magator climbed to his feet, and as the circle slowly descended around him, he appeared in his cubelike helmet, encrusted with knobs and switches and bolt-heads, and his huge black cloak and his black beetle armor. He seemed to be carrying even more guns around his belt than he had before, and the harness on his back was filled with more than a hundred different knives, as well as three rifles, one of them triple-barreled, and a fiendishly complicated crossbow.

"Now *that*," said The Zaggaline, "is truly awesome."

"And heavy," said Dom Magator. "And *hot*. I won't need to go on a diet, walking around like this. I've got my own portable sauna."

"I am sure that you will be glad of that warmth when you meet the Winterwent," said Springer.

Now it was Kalexikox's turn to be dressed in his Night Warrior armor. He was so excited that he kept clenching and unclenching his fists like a small boy. The shining circle sank, and he appeared in his glass globe helmet, in which tiny sparks of light circled around his head, and his brass and stainless steel suit that bristled with every known measuring instrument, from medieval compasses to modern micrometers. He checked his pistol, expertly releasing its safety catch as if he had been using it for years, and loading its five silver spheres. Then he adjusted the sensors on his forearms and said, slowly and soberly, "Time, eleven-oh-six and six seconds precisely. Temperature, seventy-two point three degrees. Air pollutants— ozone, carbon monoxide, lead, nitrogen dioxide and particulate matter—all well within the recommended safety levels."

"Great," said Dom Magator. "At least we won't splutter to death."

"High levels of air pollution can cause respiratory irritation, which disturb people's sleep," said Kalexikox in a matter-of-fact tone. "We wouldn't want to be caught in somebody's dream when they suddenly woke up, would we?"

"You tell me. We might be glad of it."

Springer said, "At best, it's frustrating. At worst, it's very dangerous. If a dreamer wakes up right in the middle of a critical attack, you might find that all of your plans and preparations have gone for nothing, and that your enemy has been alerted without your having had the opportunity to finish him off. Next time you go after him, he will be ready for you."

Amla Fabeya nodded. "That happened when we were trying to trap the Night Cobra in New York. We spent night after night working out a complicated maze, so that we could trap the Night Cobra in a sewer. But right at the crucial moment, when we almost had it snared, the dreamer woke up and the whole scenario vanished. The next time we tried a variation of the same plan, the Night Cobra was wise to us, and it attacked Jyn Baraqys as soon as we had reached the sewer. Jyn was bitten in the side, and his system was flooded with Night Cobra venom. It took him twenty-two nights to die ... twenty-two nights filled with nothing but terrifying nightmares and the absolute knowledge that he was going to die."

Springer laid a hand on The Zaggaline's shoulder, and The Zaggaline knelt in front him. "Are you ready?" Springer asked him.

The Zaggaline nodded. It was too late to say no.

Springer drew a shimmering golden circle above his head. As it sank around him, The Zaggaline felt as if every vein in his body was transfused with light instead of blood. He felt as if he were actually shining inside. He slowly stood up and found that he was wearing his clinging scarlet suit and his chrome-plated helmet with its dazzling complexity of colored lenses, and he felt as if he had the strength and the skill to take on anyone or anything. Not only did he feel physically strong, he felt almost ridiculously fearless, too. He almost wished that he could go back to his house and shake his father and say, "Look at me, Dad. You don't have to be disappointed in me ever again. You may have thought that I was a slacker, but this is who I really am. I'm a Night Warrior. I'm The Zaggaline, the Character Assassin."

"You can do something for us right now, Zaggaline," said Springer. "I want you to create a dog that can lead you through a snowstorm."

"A dog?"

"Well, any species of animal will do, so long as it can find its way through a blizzard."

The Zaggaline was embarrassed. All of the other Night Warriors were looking at him and he couldn't think what to create. But then Xanthys took hold of his arm and leaned close to his helmet, and said, "How about a husky?"

He turned to her. "You're right. One of those sledge-pulling dogs. But maybe bigger, with longer legs, because it won't have to pull a sledge. And with a longer neck, so that it can see further. And incredible eyesight. And a thick shaggy coat to keep it warm. And a high-intensity bark that we can hear from fifteen miles away, so that it can guide us."

"Sounds cool to me," said Dom Magator. "So long as I don't have to take it out in a blizzard to do its business."

The Zaggaline rotated one of the lenses on his helmet until it covered his left eye. The lens was crisscrossed with trigonometric curves and parabolas, and when he rotated a second lens on top of it and turned both lenses counter-clockwise, he found that he could build up the structural outline of the creature he had in mind.

How he had suddenly acquired the expertise to manipulate all of these lenses he couldn't understand, but he found that he could twist them and focus them just as quickly as he could work on his computer keyboard. Once he had completed the creature's basic shape, he rotated a third lens over his eye, this one with three-dimensional images, to give it a skeleton. A fourth lens gave it internal organs and muscles, while a fifth lens covered it with skin. Finally, he used a prismatic lens to give it a shaggy fur effcct, and a clear lens to bleach out any color, so that it couldn't be seen in the snow.

When he was satisfied with his creation, he swung down a cylindrical lamp from the back of his helmet and lined it up with all of the lenses. There was a blinding flash of light, which left them all blinking, but the animal appeared on the rug in front of him, panting and looking utterly bewildered. It was thick-haired, like a husky, but it stood almost three feet tall, with a long neck and a sharply pointed nose. Its eyes were enormous, and a piercing shade of green, as if it were wearing night-vision goggles.

The Zaggaline knelt down beside it and stroked the white fur on top of its head, and tugged at its ears. "Look at you, dude! You're amazing! I just made you! I'm your daddy!"

The dog let out a sharp, piercing bark that was louder than a gunshot and left their ears singing.

"For God's sake," said Xanthys. "I'm not supposed to have pets in my apartment."

"This is no pet," The Zaggaline told her. "This is a fighting dog." He scruffed up the dog's hair again, and the dog rubbed itself against him and arched back its head so that he could stroke it under its chin.

Kalexikox said, "We weren't allowed to have a dog when we were kids."

"Well, that was a pity," said Dom Magator. "Every boy ought to have a dog, as well as a catapult and a secret hoard of *Hustler* magazines."

"I was scared of dogs, that's why," said Kalexikox.

"Oh. You're not scared of this mutt, are you?"

"Of course not. It's nothing but a collection of light-interference patterns, like a moving hologram, with molecular restructuring to make it feel as if it's real. It's just like one of the animated characters that my brother creates on his computer, except that it's visible and palpable in ordinary white light."

Dom Magator hitched up his heavy belt. "I see. I was going to offer it a saltine, but I don't think I'll bother."

"What are you going to call him?" asked Xanthys.

Dom Magator said, "If he's going to be up to his armpits in snow all the time, you ought to call him Numnutz."

"Dogs don't have armpits. Besides, I've already decided. I'm going to call him Nanook."

Springer said, "Please, it's getting late, and we have very little time to waste. Amla Fabeya ... will you come forward, please?"

The Zaggaline pulled Nanook out of the way by the scruff of his neck so that Amla Fabeya would have room to kneel down on the rug. Nanook whined in the back of his throat, but obediently sat close to The Zaggaline's feet, panting. His long black tongue hung out as if he were being throttled.

Amla Fabeya knelt, and Springer stood over her and drew the golden halo above her head as he had before, but his words of incantation were different than those he had used for the rest of them. "Ashapola, I ask you to recognize this your fearless and devoted servant and this your truly faithful warrior. Give her the power to continue her struggle against the tides of darkness and chaos, and protect her against evil and the fear of evil."

The golden halo slowly encircled Amla Fabeya, and as she stood up she was wearing an extraordinary helmet like the head of a striking eagle, with flared-up metal feathers rising from the collar. She wore a skintight suit of shiny black material and a broad black leather sash that was thickly covered with climbing equipment— cable picketts and daisy straps and speed stirrups and ice-ax handcuffs, as well as a selection of "screamers," in case of a fall. On her feet she wore high lace-up ice-climbing boots, in shining silver, with a variety of claws and hooks on them.

"Now we are ready," said Springer. "We are going to rise up and travel through the night, and I am going to guide you to the woman whose dream you are going to enter first. Dom Magator will open a nexus into her dream, and after that you will be on your own, because I cannot follow you."

"I thought you said you were going to train us," said Xanthys.

"In the landscape of dreams, the only useful training is through practical experience. But there is one thing I will show you how to do, and that is to link yourselves together when you find it necessary to move from one dream to another. Each of you will find that you have a grip or a handle on your left shoulder. When you move to another dream, you will all take hold of the next Night Warrior's grip with your right hand, and lock it with the clasp that you will find on your right wrist.

"The night is full of dreams—it is like a huge invisible palace with millions of rooms, one room for every dream. It is not difficult to lose one of your warriors as you move from dream to another. Sometimes, this can be perilous. Occasionally, it can be fatal. It can take a long time to trace your way back to one specific dream, and by that time it may have changed beyond recognition. Dreams change and many dreams are more frightful than you can imagine."

He ushered them into a circle and said, "I have asked you to take up the task of being Night Warriors because each of you has inherited a mystical quality which makes you a skillful hunter of demons and a talented enemy of evil. But even now, you may still decide not to take up your dream identity. If you wish, you may still return to your sleeping body and choose never again to wear this armor or carry these weapons. I will not pretend that you do not face appalling dangers. But if you succeed in this struggle, you will know the ecstasy of great achievement, and you will become exalted. Your names will be inscribed forever in the *Great Book of the Night*, in which every struggle against wickedness and chaos is recorded, and that is an honor as great as having your names included in the Bible."

"That's cool," said The Zaggaline. "Moses, David, Jesus, Perry and Dunc."

Springer said, "Are you all decided?"

"Well, I am, for sure," said Dom Magator. "Anything's better than spending the rest of my life driving a hired tumbrel around this godforsaken city and stuffing my face with Ollieburgers."

Xanthys thought of those babies at the Ormsby Clinic, screaming for breath, and all of the tiny coffins she had seen on the TV news. "I'm ready, too."

"Let's proceed, shall we?" suggested Kalexikox. The Zaggaline couldn't help staring at him. It was totally weird to hear Dunc talking with such authority.

They held hands, more than a little self-consciously. For a split-second, Xanthys saw them all for what they were— five ill-assorted people wearing fancy dress-up costumes. But she had seen enough of Springer's power to know that this was far from being a practical joke or some kind of group hysteria. She had tried very hard to convince herself that the fate of those babies had nothing to do with her, but she knew in her heart that she was personally responsible for every one of their short and tiny lives, just as much as each of her fellow Night Warriors, and for what might happen to the world if the Winterwent and the High Horse were allowed to plunder their dreams.

Springer stayed outside their circle, methodically pacing around them with his hair floating in that unfelt wind. He stared at each one of them in turn, and Xanthys saw that his eyes were frighteningly empty, as black as windows which looked out into infinite space. Beyond his eyes there were galaxies and spinning star systems and light-years of unthinkable distance.

Xanthys began to feel dizzy, and Dom Magator gave a slight lurch. Nanook stayed close to The Zaggaline's thigh, making a high-pitched keening noise.

Springer circled them again and again, faster and faster, so that his image flickered in between them like a figure in a zoëtrope. Jerkily, he began to ascend into the air, and as he did so his image began to fade. Within a few moments he had vanished into the ceiling. Dom Magator thought, What the hell do we do now? He's gone. He's abandoned us, all dressed up like carnival freaks and no place to go! He could tell by the bewildered way in which his fellow Night Warriors were looking at each other that they were thinking the same.

But just before he could tug his hands free from Xanthys and Kalexikox and break the circle, he felt a sudden surge of buoyancy, as if he were bobbing in a swimming pool, instead of standing on the floor. He turned to Amla Fabeya and she was smiling, because she had done this before and she knew just what to expect. He smiled back at her, even though she couldn't see him smiling inside his heavy cube-like helmet.

Still holding hands, the five of them rose silently towards the decorated plaster ceiling, and then *through* the ceiling, and up through the dark, musty attic, and out through the roof. Xanthys felt as insubstantial as a ghost, even though she heard a thick *shushing* sound as her molecules passed through the plaster, like blood rushing in her ears, and then a soft biscuity crunch as she penetrated the roofing felt.

Then they were way up in the air, rising over the tree-lined squares and courtyards of Old Louisville, with the whole glittering city gradually spreading out wider and wider in every direction. They dipped and angled in the humid wind, their arms outstretched as if they were kites. Below them, Xanthys could see late-night traffic crawling along Second and Third Streets, and the sparkling lights of the Ohio River, and Clarksville, Indiana, on the other side, and even as far as New Albany. Her fellow Night Warriors flew on either side of her, with The Zaggaline slightly ahead. She noticed that he left behind a trail of absolute blackness, extinguishing every light that he passed over, and when she turned her head around she realized that she was doing the same.

They were shadows, and when they flew through the night, they left nothing but shadows in their wake.

CHAPTER TEN

After a minute or two, they caught sight of Springer. He was flying about fifty feet below them, his arms held tightly to his sides like an expert ski jumper. He was angling to the right toward Clifton, one of the older neighborhoods on the east side of Louisville. They all swooped after him in a straggling formation, nearly colliding with each other in their efforts to keep up. After only a few minutes, without looking back to see if they were following him, he started a steep descent toward Cedar Street, until he was flying below the treetops. He flew diagonally between the houses, barely higher than the picket fences, and they flew after him, jinking frantically from side to side so that they wouldn't fly into swing-sets or bushes or garden lights. Springer tacked to the right and then to the left, and then he spun around and landed with practiced neatness in the backyard of a small camelback house on Peterson Street. With a flurry of arms and legs, the rest of them landed next to him, panting with effort.

"Is this it?" asked The Zaggaline. "Is this where the dreamer's at?"

The house was in darkness except for a single bare bulb shining on the back porch, surrounded by a cloud of moths. The Zaggaline released his grip on the scruff of Nanook's neck, and Nanook immediately started to snuffle around the apple trees, his eyes flashing unearthly green.

Springer swept back his hair with his hand. "The rear bedroom on the second floor belongs to Judith Meiners, a nurse from the Jefferson County Pediatric Unit. Nurse Meiners is in a profound sleep. She came home three hours ago after working a twenty-six hour shift, trying to ease the suffering of seventeen dying babies. Before she left the hospital, she had already lost five of them, and three more were not expected to survive the night. She was very distressed, and she went home only because she was ordered to."

Dom Magator looked uneasily around. "Hope nobody catches us here. Wouldn't like to be shot at by some over-enthusiastic householder before I get the chance to have a crack at the Winterwent."

"To waking eyes, we are all completely invisible," Springer assured him. "After all, what are you? Nothing but a figment of your own unconscious mind."

"So long as you're sure. My cousin Nathan was shot in the rear end with a squirrel rifle and it took them the best part of two days to pick out all the pellets. You ever hear anybody say 'Ouch!' two hundred eighty-seven times? Gets real monotonous, I can tell you."

"Come," said Springer. "Let's go up to Nurse Meiner's room."

"What if the door's locked?" asked The Zaggaline.

"We don't need doors," said Springer. "We can fly, remember, and we can pass through walls as if they were water."

He made a beckoning gesture with both hands, like a priest encouraging his congregation to stand up and sing. He rose into the air, and hesitantly, one by one, they followed him. Together they floated up the back wall of the small nineteenth-century house, until they were level with the second floor.

Springer hovered for a moment, his fingers pressed against his temples. Then he said, "Yes ... good ... Nurse Meiner took two Ambien tablets to help her sleep and I think she's still having the same dream. Most important, though, I can still feel that coldness."

"So what do we do now?" asked Xanthys.

"You go hunting for the Winterwent and the High Horse."

Without any further hesitation, Springer floated straight toward the wall and vanished into the white-painted clapboard like water soaking into white sand. Kalexikox looked at The Zaggaline and jerked his head toward the wall, as if to say "How about it?"

"I don't know, dude," said The Zaggaline, warily. "That's like a solid wall, right?"

But Kalexikox said, "You heard what Springer said. None of us have any physical substance. We're just dreams that we're dreaming. We can fly, can't we? We can float right through solid ceilings. By the same token, we must be able to pass through walls."

"Okay, then," said The Zaggaline, dubiously. Kalexikox took hold of his arm and pulled him toward the wall. The Zaggaline shouted out, "Watch it, dude—!" but his voice was immediately swallowed up, and so was he; and then both of them had disappeared.

The night was silent except for the distant honking of a firetruck. Dom Magator turned to Amla Fabeya. "After you," she said, smiling.

"No, no, after you," said Dom Magator. "I guess I'm finding it a little difficult to get used to this idea of passing through walls. In real life, I can't even go through *doors* without getting myself wedged."

"This is your dream self, Dom Magator. In dreams—if you have enough faith—you can do anything you want to."

"Okay, then," said Dom Magator. He closed his eyes and said, "I have enough faith. I have enough faith. I have enough faith." Then he opened his eyes and held out his hand. "I have enough faith. Or at least I hope to hell that I have enough faith. Let's go through together."

They materialized in Nurse Meiner's bedroom side by side. Springer and the rest of the Night Warriors were already standing around her bed. The bedroom was cramped and stuffy with a sharply sloping ceiling, and it was crowded with local antiques. On the left-hand wall stood a stained pine chest of drawers with framed photographs and china ornaments on top of it, mostly cats. Beside the bed hung a large nineteenth-century lithograph of a cat dressed up as a magician, with an opera hat and an evening cloak. The cat was entertaining a theater crowded with rats, all of them nattily dressed in checkered tweed vests and cloth caps and smoking cigars—but much to their horror he was sawing a rat in half. Blood was dripping onto the stage, and the caption read "A Pussy-Cat *Saw* A Rat."

Nurse Meiner was sleeping in a brass bed with a red and yellow patchwork quilt. On the nightstand, beside her alarm clock, lay a travel guide to Venice with a brown plastic comb tucked in between the pages to keep her place. She looked thirty-six or thirty-sevenish, with frizzy black hair and a plain, oval face, with a large mole over her right eyebrow. The prune-colored circles under her eyes betrayed how hard she must have been working and how stressed she must have been. She lay completely still, barely breathing, but underneath her eyelids her pupils were dancing from side to side.

"Rapid eye movement," said Springer. "She's dreaming very vividly."

"I thought you said it was going to be cold," Xanthys complained. "It's *sweltering* in here."

"Oh, it'll cold, believe me. You'll find out for yourself,

once you enter Nurse Meiner's dream. The Winterwent's still hiding in there, although he's never easy to track down."

"Nanook can find him, can't you, boy?" said The Zaggaline, and Nanook whined in anticipation.

Springer came up to Dom Magator. "You, Dom Magator—you carry all the basic energy that the Night Warriors need for entering dreams and for relocating from one dream to another. You see these power switches here, and here?"

He clicked two large toggle switches on either side of Dom Magator's belt. Instantly, with a sharp electrical crackle and a wavering hum, two parallel lines of bright blue light shone along each of Dom Magator's forearms, from his elbows to his wrists.

"All you have to do now is draw a portal in the air, as close to the dreamer as you can. That will give you access to her dream. If you wish to leave her dream, and return to the real world—or if you wish to move to another dream—then all you have to do is repeat the process and create another portal."

"So how do I do that?" asked Dom Magator.

"Like this," said Springer. He moved around so that he was standing behind Dom Magator, and he held up both of his arms for him. "Now ... concentrate, and point your index fingers and your middle fingers."

Dom Magator did what he was told, and instantly two narrow streams of sapphire-blue light extended from his fingers and shone above Nurse Meiner's bed. They made a sharp crackling noise, and the bedroom was filled with the pungent smell of burned electricity. Nanook jumped up onto his hind legs in excitement and The Zaggaline had to grip his muzzle to stop him from barking. One of Nanook's barks would have woken up half of Clifton, not to mention Nurse Meiner.

Springer guided Dom Magator's arms upward, outward

and downward, so that he drew an octagon in the air, an eight-sided geometric figure of brilliant blue light that was large enough for them to step through.

"There," he said. "This is the way through to the world of dreams."

The Zaggaline peered into it, deeply impressed. "Eat your hearts out, *Stargate SG-1*. This is the real deal!"

Springer said, "I wish I could come with you, but I am only a guide and a messenger. All I can do to help you is to bless your endeavors and wish you good fortune."

Kalexikox joined his brother beside the octagonal portal. The sapphire-blue light was so bright that he found it almost impossible to see anything on the other side apart from a faint luminosity, but he could distinctly hear a high whistling sound, like the wind blowing through an ill-fitting window frame, and a few flecks of snow came tumbling onto the hand-woven bedroom rug. Springer was right—it was stunningly cold in there. Kalexikox stepped closer, so he could put his hand through the portal to test the ambient temperature. The front of his globelike helmet was immediately covered in fingers of frost.

After a few seconds pause, he took out his hand and consulted the maximum and minimum thermometers on the back of his wrist. "Minus thirty-four-point four Celsius. That's one-tenth of a degree colder than the coldest temperature ever recorded in Helsinki, Finland."

"In that case, there is no question about it," said Springer. "Nurse Meiner's dream has been taken over by the Winterwent, and frozen solid."

Nanook was keening and quivering and raring to go, and The Zaggaline had to cling tightly to the fur around his neck to hold him back.

"Why don't you release him?" Springer suggested. "He can sniff out your enemy for you, and all you have to do is follow."

"Are you sure he's not going to get hurt?"

"He isn't real. You invented him, remember."

"I know. But look at him. Man's best friend. I don't want anything bad to happen to him, even if I *did* invent him."

"He will be in no more danger than you yourself."

"Well ... okay, then," said The Zaggaline. He released his grip on Nanook's fur and smacked him on the rump. "Go on, boy! Go get 'em!"

Nanook jumped through the portal, displacing the rug with his hind legs. They heard him barking—once, twice, three times—and each bark sounded further away, and flatter. Then there was silence.

The Night Warriors stared at each other, unsure what to do next. Dom Magator said, "I guess I'd better go through first. That way, when the rest of you come through, you'll have plenty of weapons to protect yourselves with."

"No, let me," said Amla Fabeya. "Remember that woman at the Colonnade restaurant? The Winterwent has been eavesdropping on us, and it's more than likely that he's set up some kind of a trap. If he has, I think I will be able to detect any warning signs more readily than you."

"Whatever you say, Amla. Beauty before tonnage."

Without any further hesitation, Amla Fabeya stepped through the portal and disappeared.

"She *did* it," said Kalexikox in an awed voice. Despite his huge scientific knowledge, there was still something of Dunc's simplicity about him.

Dom Magator waited for a few seconds. Under his black insect armor, his heart was thumping hard. Then he closed his eyes, said "Forgive me, Jesus," and followed her.

He felt a soft *whoomph* and a buffeting sensation, like the one and only time he had ever played football, and then he was through. He slithered and stumbled and almost lost his balance, but he managed to seize a handrail that was close beside him. When he had steadied himself, he squinted through his visor and saw that he was standing on a verandah, overlooking a landscape that was utterly frozen.

Even in his helmet and his armor he could feel how piercingly cold it was.

"Jesus," he said. "This reminds me of the time I got locked in a deep freeze with a whole lot of hog carcasses. Three-and-a-half hours I was in there and when I came out I stuttered for a whole week."

Behind him, in quick succession, he heard three more *whoomph*ing noises. Tumbling up against him came Xanthys, Kalexikox and The Zaggaline. Xanthys slipped over, too, but The Zaggaline managed to catch her arm.

"You okay?" Dom Magator asked her. "Welcome to the happy Land of Freezyabuttoff."

Jumpily, his weapon held high, The Zaggaline looked around at their immediate surroundings. "So where's the Winterwent and the High Horse?" asked Xanthys, peering through the snow.

"Relax," Amla Fabeya told her. "We don't have to worry. Not just yet. So far as I can see, the Winterwent hasn't set any traps. Maybe he feels that he doesn't need to."

"Because of why?" asked Kalexikox. "Because he doesn't think we're any kind of a threat, or because he can zap us whenever he feels like it?"

"I don't know," said Amla Fabeya. "The Winterwent and the High Horse don't look at life in the same way that we do. To them, death is nothing, even their own. They exist only in dreams, remember, so they don't behave with any kind of human feeling."

"Sounds like my mother," said Dom Magator. "Her idea of human feeling was to open up a can of spaghetti hoops instead of leaving us kids to open it ourselves."

"Where is this place?" asked Xanthys. She felt very anxious here, although she wasn't entirely sure why. From what she could make out through the snow, it could have been any small South End town, like Beechmont or Shively. It was little more than a wide street with an untidy little collection of storefronts on either side. At the far end of town she could see the blue and red T sign of a Thornton gas station and a small Episcopalian chapel with a squarish spire. The spire was thickly clustered with crows, because it was far too cold for them to fly.

Even in the depths of winter, no South End town had ever looked as grim as this. The clouds that hung over the snow-covered rooftops were dank and septic and greenish-black, like ragged bandages stained with gangrene, and they seemed to move in convulsive jerks, contrary to the direction to the wind. The unhealthy looking snow in the street was at least three feet deep, and much deeper where it had drifted up against walls and fences. Icicles hung from every gutter, some of them forming grotesque shapes, like wolves or hunchbacked witches or misshapen children. And the wind kept blowing, pitiless and steel-cold, so that the Night Warriors were fenced in on all sides by ceaselessly whirling snowflakes that blotted their visors and heaped up their shoulders with thick white epaulets.

"Check it out, Kalexikox," said Amla Fabeya. "Is this a real community or is it some kind of metaphor?"

Kalexikox rubbed ice crystals from the array of glass dials along his right forearm. He flicked a series of switches and slid two metal bars along his arm. He waited for a moment, with those tiny sparks of light circling inside his helmet, his face deeply serious. Then he said, "This is a real community. Kenningtown, a trolley stop development nine-point-seven miles southeast of Louisville. Nurse Meiner was raised here, and her mother still lives in the neighborhood. The snow is genuine, too, although it contains something else besides frozen water and the usual motor vehicle pollutants."

"Like what?" asked Dom Magator. "Don't tell me—that stuff that makes it yellow and you're not supposed to eat."

"Well, there's a little of that. But it contains unusually high traces of eicosapentaeonic acid, as well as decosa-hexaenoic acid. I'm not too sure about the streets, either. They're not made of asphalt and crushed rock, like you'd cxpect. They appear to be solid ice, with a high saline content."

"So they're not streets at all?"

"Not in the conventional sense, no. They're more like frozen canals."

"Did you see that travel book on her nightstand?" said Xanthys. "She's dreaming about Venice."

"That would make sense," put in Amla Fabeya. "And maybe she's worried about leaving her mother at home while she goes away."

"What about this iko-hiko-pentatonic acid?" asked Dom Magator.

"It's present in the ice, too," said Kalexikox. "Both acids are. They're both ingredients of fish oil."

"Fish oil?" said Dom Magator.

"That's all I can tell you. Maybe she ate a tuna melt before she went to sleep and it's playing havoc with her digestion."

At that moment, Nanook appeared, running full-pelt down the street toward them, barking his ear-shattering bark.

"Jesus—doesn't that dog have a volume control?" asked Dom Magator. "He's giving me tinnitus already."

"He's found something," said The Zaggaline. "Look—he wants us to follow him."

"What do you think?" Dom Magator asked Amla Fabeya. "This isn't going to be some kind of an ambush, is it?"

Amla Fabeya shook her head. "Doubtful. Nanook is *our* creation, after all. He can't deliberately guide us into any kind of danger."

"Okay, then, let's see where the mutt takes us," said Dom Magator. "Anything to shut him up. Everybody together?"

They stepped down from the verandah and followed Nanook along the street. The snow was so deep that they had to wade through it, rocking from side to side. Amla

Fabeya said, "Keep your eyes wide open. If anything un- usual catches your attention—anything at all—assume that it could be dangerous. It may be something that would be completely harmless in the real world. A scarecrow, maybe, or an animal or a statue. But here, in the dream world, you never know."

The Zaggaline thought: *God, even if I was suffering from serious depression I couldn't invent a place as downright miserable as this.*

The main street was deserted, although there were cars parked all the way along it. They were old cars, early 1960s or thereabouts, with tail fins—Galaxies and Falcons and Impalas. Most of them were buried under thick blankets of snow. The Zaggaline cleared two or three windshields with his hand, just to make sure that there was nobody hiding in them, but they all appeared to be abandoned. There didn't seem to be anybody in any of the stores, either, even though some of their doors were half-open and snow had drifted across the floors inside.

"Ghost town," said Dom Magator.

But Amla Fabeya suddenly stopped and laid her hand on his arm. "There," she said, and pointed to an upstairs window over Hankey's Hardware store. Dom Magator frowned. A dirty net curtain had been pulled to one side and somebody was standing close to the window. It was a woman with very long gray hair. Her face was as white as a church candle, and her eyes were closed.

Dom Magator immediately touched the buttons at the right side of his helmet and brought the woman into focus. He could see right through the wall below the window, and he could see that she was wearing a plain gray dress with yellow flowers on it. He could calculate exactly how far away she was and at what elevation she was standing, and when he touched the Destruction-Option buttons on the left side of his helmet, his instruments told him that he could destroy her most effectively with his Vacuum Carbine, which would instantly evacuate all of the air out of the room, causing all four walls to rush together and crush her to a half-inch thick.

"Palook her?" he suggested.

But Amla Fabeya said, "She's not armed, is she?"

"I don't think so."

"Well … she doesn't appear to be any kind of threat. It's more than likely that she's nothing more than an incidental character in Nurse Meiner's dream. Maybe she's some old blind woman who used to frighten her when she was a child. Or an elderly patient that she knew when she was training as a nurse."

"She's a real person," Kalexikox confirmed. "Her body chemistry is normal—sixty-five percent oxygen, eighteen percent carbon, ten percent hydrogen, three percent nitrogen, four percent calcium, phosphorus, sulfur, sodium, magnesium, copper, zinc, selenium—"

"Okay, Einstein," The Zaggaline interrupted him. "We get the picture."

"Not completely. She has a serious chemical imbalance in her brain and she has no eyes."

Dom Magator frowned at his viewfinder and made an adjustment, and then another. "There's something else. I didn't notice it before. That room she's looking out of—it doesn't have a floor."

"What?"

"It has four walls and a ceiling but it doesn't have a floor. She's suspended about seventeen feet from the ground, with no visible means of support."

Xanthys stared up at the woman's pale, unperturbed face. It could have been a death mask except for the way she occasionally pursed her lips, as if she were sucking on her false teeth; and although Kalexikox had said that she had no eyes, she still gave Xanthys the unnerving impression that she was watching them. "So she's *floating?*" Xanthys asked. "What does that mean?"

"I can't guess," said Amla Fabeya. "I think we'd be wiser

to leave her alone—for now, anyhow. She could be very important to Nurse Meiner, and we don't want to upset her, do we, and wake her up?"

Kalexikox said, "Nurse Meiner has enough zolpidem tartrate in her bloodstream to keep her asleep for another six hours and twenty-three minutes. But I agree with you. We shouldn't risk rousing her unless we really have to. It could be psychologically damaging for her, too."

Dom Magator checked his instruments again. "I go along with that. There's nothing on any of these dials here to indicate that this old biddy can do us any kind of mischief. She doesn't have a weapon and she's not giving off any gamma radiation and her alpha waves are pretty much what you'd expect for a levitating geriatric."

He sniffed, and said, "Besides—look at Nanook. He's still jumping around like he's got a Scotch Bonnet chili pepper up his rear end, and I think our number one priority should be checking out what *he's* trying to show us."

"Let's go, then," agreed Kalexikox.

They left Hankey's Hardware and carried on plowing through the snow. The eyeless woman was still floating behind her upstairs window, but she didn't turn her head to follow their slow progress up the street.

The Zaggaline turned around and stared up at her one last time. When he turned back he found that Xanthys was looking at him.

"What?" he asked her.

"That woman is seriously spooky," said Xanthys. "I think Dom Magator should have palooked her. I mean— supposing she's one of the Winterwent's spies, like that woman in the Colonnade?"

"Why don't you check her out?" asked The Zaggaline.

"What do you mean?"

"You're a Time Curver, aren't you? How about turning the clock back to find out where she came from?"

Xanthys hesitated. The rest of the Night Warriors were already so far ahead of them that she could barely see their outlines through the flying snow. Her instinct was to hurry up and join them, but she also felt that The Zaggaline could be right and that there was no harm in making absolutely sure that the eyeless woman was nothing more than a bystander in Nurse Meiner's dream. Or a hy-levitator, anyhow. Because what if she weren't? What if she were something else altogether, masquerading as a human being? And what if she came after them when they least suspected it?

"Okay," she said. She adjusted the large luminous dial on the side of her insect-like goggles. "Let's take this scene back ... say two hours, forty-five minutes." A series of soft, pastel-colored lights ran across the display at the top of her goggles. Then, with a subtle chime, the shining image of a key appeared. At the same time, the corresponding key on her belt flashed brightly on and off.

Xanthys unhooked the flashing key. It was small but complicated, like a Yale key. She turned to face the hardware store and pointed it up at the window where the woman with no eyes was suspended.

She turned the key counterclockwise, and as she did so, the clouds started to hurry in the opposite direction, and the wind turned around, too, so that it was blowing from the southwest. The faster she turned the key, the faster time was curved back. Snow flew *upward* into the sky, so that roof shingles reappeared. The blind woman in the upstairs window suddenly vanished, but then she came out of the brown door next to Hankey's Hardware and walked quickly backward to the edge of the street.

Something else was happening, too. As Xanthys took the little community of Kenningtown back to the time before the Winterwent had arrived and frozen it to the bone, the ice in the streets started to melt. In a matter of minutes, the streets were turned back into Venetian-style canals, filled with slushy rafts of ice and oily green water, which is what Nurse Meiner had been dreaming about. None of the parked cars sank. When Xanthys looked at them more closely, she realized that they were gondolas more than cars, and although they still sported tail fins, they had varnished wooden hulls, too, and all they did when the street melted away beneath them was to bob up and down and jostle each other, as gondolas do.

At the far end of the street she glimpsed the eyeless woman, still hurrying backward. When she reached the intersection close to where Xanthys and the rest of the Night Warriors had emerged from the portal, the eyeless woman didn't hesitate. She crossed over the street, still walking backward, but she was *walking on water*, as if the canal were still frozen over, or she stubbornly refused to believe that it wasn't asphalt. She reached the other side and disappeared backward through a small alleyway at the side of one of the houses. It was beginning to grow dark again, and Xanthys found it hard to see exactly where she had gone. She had vanished like a cockroach into the crevice between two stones.

Xanthys was about to curve time back further when she heard Amla Fabeya shout out, "*Xanthys!* Take us back! This is the time before the Winterwent appeared! We need to find him *now!*"

Xanthys lifted one hand in acknowledgement and turned the key clockwise. At once, the clouds began to run from left to right and the wind turned around, and snow began to fall so thickly that it was almost ludicrous, as if every down comforter in the county had burst open. Beneath their boots, the ice began to thicken again. One island of semi-frozen slush would collide with another, and then the two of them would crackle into hardness together with a noise like pistol shots, and others would join them, too. In less than a minute, Kenningtown was back to its silent, bitter, snow-buried present.

"What did you do that for?" asked Amla Fabeya, as Xanthys and The Zaggaline caught up with them. "You should be much more careful, tampering with people's dreams like that."

"I'm sorry. I wanted to see where that eyeless woman came from. I know you don't think that she's going to do us any harm, but I have a really bad feeling about her."

"So what did you find out?" asked Kalexikox. "The readings I took ... I can guarantee to you that she was one hundred percent human. And like Dom Magator said, she wasn't carrying any kind of weapon."

Xanthys pointed back along the street. "I couldn't see exactly where she went. She disappeared into that alleyway, can you see it? Right next to where we came through the portal. But I swear that she crossed over the street when it was nothing but water, and she didn't even get her shoes wet."

"Now *that's* interesting," said Kalexikox. "It might have something to do with differential densities."

Dom Magator had come battling back through the snow. "It might have something to do with the fact that this is a dream," he said, impatiently. "Right now, I think that we ought to be doing what we came here to do, which is to look for this raving homicidal ice-individual and his animal-abusing barbarian sidekick."

"Dom Magator is right," said Amla Fabeya. "Nurse Meiner is very deeply asleep, but time is passing very quickly. We have to move on."

Nanook came running back toward them, even more excited than he was before. He barked, and barked again, and his bark was so loud that clumps of snow dropped from the gutter of a nearby building.

Dom Magator said, "For Christ's sake, let's follow him, before he busts our eardrums."

Xanthys glanced quickly back at Hankey's Hardware. They were so far away now that it was impossible for her to see if the eyeless woman was still floating in the window, but Xanthys had the feeling that she probably was. For some reason, the eyeless woman reminded Xanthys of a time when she was seven years old. Two of her friends had badly frightened her when one of them had climbed on to the other's shoulders and they had walked into the room wearing her mother's long black overcoat. The sudden appearance of an adult-sized figure with a child-sized head had left her breathless with terror, and she could feel that same terror now.

CHAPTER ELEVEN

They slipped and struggled across the main Louisville high-way while Nanook bounded on ahead of them. He led them up a wide side street with substantial frame houses on either side. The street was lined with leafless, canker-encrusted oaks. There were no vehicles parked here, and every window in every house was empty and dark. The only sign of life was a red tricycle, lying sideways in the snow like an abandoned childhood. Above the trees the clouds flickered fretfully toward the northeast, a black and white movie of clouds that was running at the wrong speed. Nanook stopped at the very last house in the street. Beyond this house there was a scrubby half-acre of briars and tangled undergrowth, and beyond that lay the Kenningtown ceme-tery, surrounded by a gray picket fence, with black marble headstones and sorrowing angels.

Outside the house, Nanook's fresh tracks in the snow showed that he had been circling around the front yard and running backward and forward to the front door.

The house was plainly constructed and traditional, with a pillared portico. Its boarded walls were painted a strange streaky pink, as if the decorator had cut his fingers and bled profusely into his pot of white paint. All of the flower beds were heaped in snow, through which the gnarled branches of rosebushes protruded. Xanthys thought that they looked like the fingers of half-cremated corpses trying to claw their way out of their shallow graves.

Nanook ran up to the front door and barked twice; his bark echoed for miles.

Dom Magator came up close to Amla Fabeya. "Think the Winterwent's here?"

Amla Fabeya looked around uneasily. "I can't see his sledge, or any of his army. But this is only a dream, so you can never tell for sure."

"Maybe I should just badoom the house completely," Dom Magator suggested. "I have a Seismic Cannon here … it sends out this really low sound frequency so that the house will literally shake itself to pieces. It's a portable earthquake."

"Oh, sure, let's do that," said Kalexikox. "And let's destroy every piece of forensic evidence at the same time."

"Look around you, *mon ami*," said Dom Magator. "Snow, ice, more snow, more ice. The Winterwent must be here, or hereabouts. What more forensic evidence do you need?"

The Zaggaline said, "Maybe I could invent a House Breaker. Somebody to go into the house like a one-man SWAT team and check that it's clear."

"You see?" retorted Kalexikox. "The kid has intelligence."

"You wouldn't recognize intelligence if it snuck up behind you and kicked you in the rear end."

"Leave him alone, okay?" said The Zaggaline. "He's wired different, that's all."

"Sure. I had a TV like that. All it could pick up was *The Mickey Mouse Club*."

Amla Fabeya said, "The Zaggaline's idea is a good one. Can you make such a person as a House Breaker?"

"Sure," said The Zaggaline. "I can do it right now."

The Zaggaline stood back a little way and started to hinge down the lenses on the side of his helmet. First, he used his limning lens to create the House Breaker's outline. Then he used a variety of colored lenses to fill in his body structure, his skeleton, his muscles and his skin. The House Breaker had a low, Neanderthal forehead and deeply buried eyes, like a wrestler squashed under a fifty ton truck. His shoulders were piled up with muscles. His waist was narrow, but each of his legs were like three tree trunks, twisted together. He wore brown leather body armor and huge multi-buckled boots, and he carried a black two-handled battering ram that doubled as a six-barreled rotary machine gun.

As soon as he had aligned all of the necessary lenses, The Zaggaline focused his cylindrical lamp through them, double-checked the settings and then flicked the switch. There was a dazzling flash that made Dom Magator blink, even behind his darkly tinted visor, and the House Breaker was standing in the snow right in front of them, nearly seven feet tall, his breath fuming out of his nostrils. Nanook barked and jumped around him, as if he recognized a fellow creation.

"Well, very impressive," Dom Magator had to admit. "I could have used this guy when I was trying to get back my collection of Johnny Dodds records from that ditsy broad from Mobile with the big gazongas I wished I'd never moved in with."

They all stood in the snow, waiting. Xanthys looked at Kalexikox and Kalexikox looked at The Zaggaline and The Zaggaline looked at his House Breaker.

"Well," said Amla Fabeya, at last. "Aren't you going to give him his orders?"

"Me?" asked The Zaggaline.

"You created him. Only you can tell him what to do."

"Oh. Oh, sure. Okay." The Zaggaline hesitated for a moment, and then he began to narrate his instructions in the most commanding voice that he could manage. "The

House Breaker smashes down the front door and searches the house room by room, searching for the Winterwent or any of his warriors, and spraying them with high-speed machine-gun fire whenever he finds them."

The House Breaker grunted and started to walk with a ponderous lope toward the house, his huge shoulders swaying.

"Wait up a minute!" called The Zaggaline. "The House Breaker stops for a few seconds, while The Zaggaline charges up his battering ram for him. He knows that he can't go into battle without his weapon being loaded!"

The House Breaker halted in midstride and stayed motionless in the same hunched position while The Zaggaline struggled to disentangle the long-barreled Lethal Energy Transmuter that was slung to his back. Once he had wrestled it free, he fitted the Y-shaped butt into the crook of his arm and began to adjust the slides and buttons that would power up the House Breaker's weapon. Energy—one hundred percent. Virtual ammunition—ten thousand rounds of .50 armor-piercing bullets. Speed—thirteen hundred rounds per minute.

Once The Zaggaline had set the LET, he connected it to the end of the House Breaker's battering ram and pressed the trigger. All of the Night Warriors felt a jolt, as if a high-explosive bomb had gone off somewhere deep in the ground beneath their feet.

The Zaggaline uncoupled the LET and announced, with renewed bravado, "The House Breaker, his battering ram fully charged, continues with his mission."

The House Breaker stepped onto the porch, gripped his battering ram in both hands, and struck the front door with a deafening crack. The door splintered, but it held. The House Breaker swung back his battering ram and hit it again. One of the panels was split apart, but still the door didn't yield.

"The House Breaker uses his machine gun to blow the door down," said The Zaggaline, a little desperately.

They heard a sharp whine as the rotary machine gun barrels inside the battering ram began to whirl around. Then there was a continuous blast of noise as virtual bullets ripped through the door, smashing away the lock and the side-panels and half of the architrave. Pungent black smoke drifted across the garden and into the briars. The House Breaker kicked the teetering door with his buckled boot and it toppled sideways onto the floor. He stepped into the hallway, his battering ram raised, looking left and right, and then he moved sideways into the living room.

The Night Warriors waited outside while the House Breaker went from room to room, shining his flashlight and pointing his battering ram. From time to time they could see him through the windows, his deep-set eyes glowering beneath his sloped forehead, but he never looked back at them. The Zaggaline had invented him for one job only, and this was it.

Eventually he emerged from the front door and trudged up the driveway toward them. He stopped, and stared down at The Zaggaline as if he couldn't remember who he was.

"Is the house clear?" asked The Zaggaline. He might have created the House Breaker, but the creature loomed over him in such a menacing way that he couldn't help feeling a little apprehensive.

The House Breaker nodded.

"Nobody hiding in the closets? No booby traps?"

"*Mrrgghh,*" said the House Breaker.

"*Mrrgghh?*" said Dom Magator. "What the hell does *mrrgghh* mean?"

But The Zaggaline said, "Exceptional." With that, he switched off the House Breaker connection, and the House Breaker vanished as if he had never existed, which in reality he hadn't. "*Mrrgghh* is teenage for yes," The Zaggaline explained. "Like, your dad says, 'Get out of bed and sweep the backyard,' and you say, '*Mrrgghh.*' "

"Okay," said Dom Magator, with an exaggeratedly weary sigh. "Let's check this place out for ourselves. I want to know what Nanook finds so darned exciting about it. Kalexikox ... how about running another test, just in case it isn't a real house, but a figment of Nurse Meiner's digestive tract?"

Kalexikox rapidly checked his instruments. "As far as I can tell you, the house appears to be good."

"It only *appears* to be good?"

"Well, it no longer exists in reality. It was pulled down seven years ago to make way for a new housing development. But when it was still standing it was a genuine house, made of wood and brick and cement, and what you see here isn't indigestion, and it isn't any kind of metaphor."

"So it's a real house that isn't really here?"

Kalexikox nodded.

The Zaggaline said, "That's good enough for me. Go on, Nanook. Let's go inside and take a look."

Nanook went panting ahead of them into the hallway, but he immediately stopped and looked back at The Zaggaline in perplexity.

As Kalexikox had assured them, the house was just an ordinary Kentucky house, with 1940s-style furniture and brown flowery wallpaper. An upright piano stood between the living room windows, which were clustered with family photographs, and in the corner sat a television set with a ten-inch screen.

It was an ordinary house, yes. But it was an ordinary house that had been totally deep-frozen. Everything was thickly encrusted with ice—from the lamps to the fringes around the couch cushions.

As they walked around, the Night Warriors' feet crunched on the frozen carpet pile. Icicles hung from the lampshades like wind chimes, and the windows were completely blinded by feather patterns of frost. Even the velvet curtains were frozen solid, rigid. As the Night Warriors went cautiously from room to room, their breath smoked out from the ventilators in their helmets and they left crisscrossing footprints on the rime-covered floor.

In the center of the dining room table, on a frosty lace tablecloth, stood a large bowl of fruit—apples and oranges and persimmons. The fruit was white with cold and sparkling with tiny grains of ice. Dom Magator reached out with his black leather glove and picked up an apple. He squeezed it gently, but it cracked and fell apart, and he was left with nothing but a handful of glittering dust.

"So where's the Winterwent?" asked The Zaggaline. "He's obviously been here. But where's he gone now?"

"The Winterwent is very calculating," said Amla Fabeya. "He never does anything without a good reason. Not like the High Horse, who will attack anything and everything, just because he feels the bloodlust for it."

"So why did the Winterwent come *here*, to this particular dream? And why has he frozen this particular house?"

Xanthys had been picking up silver-framed photographs from the piano and rubbing them with her fingers so the frost was cleared away from the glass.

"Look at these pictures," she said. "This is Nurse Meiner, when she was a young girl, and these people must be her parents, and her brothers. Look how they're all smiling! This must be Nurse Meiner's family home."

"So Nurse Meiner had a happy childhood, and she's dreaming about it, and the Winterwent comes into her dream and freezes it solid. Why the two-toned tonkert does he do that?"

"Why does anybody freeze anything?" said Kalexikox. "To preserve it, maybe, like perishable food. Or maybe, in this case, to make it go numb. You know, like a doctor freezes a wart."

"I don't get it," said The Zaggaline. "Okay—Nurse Meiner is looking after newborn babies, so she can get closer to them than anybody ... but I thought that the Winterwent was trying to get into the babies' dreams through their *mothers'* dreams."

"My guess is that the mothers won't allow him," said Amla Fabeya. "He's a pretty terrifying apparition, after all.

He's a nightmare. And what pregnant woman isn't going to protect her unborn child from a nightmare?"

"But the babies are still dying," said Xanthys.

"Yes, and I can't explain why. But my guess is that the Winterwent is trying to find a different way to infiltrate their mothers' dreams. Maybe he's using the dreams of people that the mothers really trust—people like Nurse Meiner."

Dom Magator picked up a persimmon, and crushed that, too; and then an orange, until the dining room table was heaped with frozen dust. "Kalexikox ... what you said about preserving food ..."

"What about it?"

"Well, what's the similarity between dreams and food?"

"What are you talking about?" said The Zaggaline. "There's no similarity between dreams and food. You can dream that you're eating fifty-eight cheeseburgers, but that isn't going to stop you from being hungry, is it? Won't make you fat, either."

"You're wrong," said Dom Magator. "Dreams and food have this in common: they're both perishable. If you don't put food in the freezer, it goes off, right? And what happens to dreams, when you wake up in the morning? *Poof!* They vanish, like they never happened."

"So what are you suggesting?" said Amla Fabeya.

"I don't have a clue, to tell you the God's honest truth. But supposing the Winterwent has frozen this dream so that it won't vanish when Nurse Meiner wakes up ... Supposing he can *keep* it frozen, and thaw it out later, and use it himself."

"Interesting theory," said Kalexikox. "I can run some calculations on that."

"We don't have time for calculations," protested The Zaggaline. "We have to find this Winterwent dude and wipe him out, whatever he's doing, and however which way he's doing it. Otherwise he's going to get into one of those babies' dreams and all creation is going to be toast."

At that moment, Nanook started barking again, and this

time he didn't stop. It was deafening—as loud as a series of
.45 pistol shots.

"What is it, boy?" The Zaggaline asked him. "Is there
somebody outside?"

Kalexikox checked his instruments. "Weird. I'm getting
that fish oil reading again. Very strongly this time. And it
seems to be getting stronger."

Before The Zaggaline could grab his fur, Nanook bolted
out the front door and into the snow. He kept on barking,
and leapt wildly from side to side and chased his own tail.

Dom Magator reached the front door just in time to see
the most chilling sight that he had ever witnessed in his life.
From the roadway, a huge white fin was sliding through the
snow toward the house. It advanced on Nanook with incredible speed, and before the dog could leap out of the
way, a massive white shark exploded out of the frozen
ground and snatched him in its jaws.

Dom Magator's helmet was equipped with micro-
sensitive listening equipment, and he could hear the crunch
as the monster's teeth crushed every imaginary bone and
muscle in Nanook's body and bit him in half. Blood sprayed
across the front yard and even up the wall of the house.

In a split second, the shark had plunged back into the
snow and vanished.

"*Nanook!*" screamed The Zaggaline. "*Nanook!*"

But all that was left of Nanook was a single twitching leg
lying in the snow with white tendons trailing from it.

The Zaggaline was about to step down into the front
yard, but Amla Fabeya gripped his shoulder and held him
back. "*Don't*—that shark could go for you, too."

Xanthys came up to him, too, and took hold of his arm.
"Nanook was imaginary. I know how much you liked him,
but you *invented* him, that's all. You can always invent another Nanook."

The Zaggaline said, "Sure. I guess you're right. But he
was so—well, we never had a dog at home. He was the first
dog I ever had."

Dom Magator gave him an affectionate punch in the ribs. "You'll get over it, kid. The first time a woman leaves you, losing a dog will seem like nothing at all."

Shading her eyes against the reflected glare from the snow, Amla Fabeya looked around the front yard. "The Winterwent knows we're here," she said, and she sounded worried. "That's where that ice-shark came from. We need to find ourselves someplace safer."

Kalexikox had been checking his meteorological instruments. "Can you feel the temperature dropping?" he said."There's a very cold weather front approaching from the north-northeast. It's a little over nine-point-seven clicks away, and it's closing fast."

"That'll be the Winterwent," said Amla Fabeya. "It looks like we won't have to track him down, after all—he's coming for us."

"So how do we get out of here, with a shark-infested front yard? Or maybe Nanook was enough for it, and it's taken off?"

Kalexikox checked his chemical analyzer. "No ... there's still a very high incidence of fish oil acids in the soil around the house. That means the shark is in very close proximity." He moved the analyzer from side to side. "It looks like it's circling us, too."

Dom Magator flicked on his scanners, but he couldn't detect anything beneath the ground except for a thick blur of black and white speckles, like a TV screen. "You can tell where it is?"

"Sure ... look, it's swimming around and around the house, about six feet under the soil, and every time it comes close to the front door here, the acid indicators go up."

"I can't see a damn thing."

"If it's totally frozen, then you wouldn't. Your scanners wouldn't be able to distinguish it from its immediate surroundings."

"But you can pinpoint it for me?"

"Within two or three feet, yes."

"Right," said Dom Magator. "Let's see if we can do a Louisville special and have a fish fry." He reached around to the rack on his back and unclipped a heavy, single-barreled shotgun. It had an ugly, short muzzle and a huge sliding bolt, which he pulled back to cock it. "This what they call a Sun Gun. For a millionth of a second, it creates a single spot of intense heat exactly where you want it, equivalent to the core temperature of the sun."

"Fifteen million degrees Celsius," said Kalexikox.

"Whatever. When it hits that ice-shark, there's going to be a whole lot of sizzling going on. Just wish we'd brought some Green River batter."

They leaned over the railing around the porch, trying to spot any disturbance in the snow that would betray the presence of the ice-shark, deep beneath. Toward the northeast the sky was already growing blacker, and the wind kept on keening like a knife blade rubbing against a sharpening stone, but apart from that the street was eerily still.

"We can't stay here for the rest of the night," said Xanthys.

Almost immediately, there was a sharp flurry of snow beneath the briars, about thirty feet away, and The Zaggaline shouted, *"There, dude! There!"* Dom Magator hefted up his Sun Gun, but Kalexikox was frantically checking his instruments and said, *"No ... that's nothing but a small bird, or maybe a minor rodent."*

"Where's the ice-shark now?" asked Amla Fabeya in an urgent voice.

"I don't exactly know for sure," said Kalexikox. "It's still within twenty feet of us, but it seems to have dived even deeper. All of its chemical signals are very distorted, and delayed. I'm getting no seismic readings at all."

They waited and waited. Dom Magator impatiently shifted his Sun Gun on his hip. Xanthys said, "Maybe it's swum away, and decided to leave us alone."

"You think?" said The Zaggaline.

"Well, if it hasn't swum away, we could be stuck here until Nurse Meiner wakes up, and then what?"

"Don't you worry, little lady," Dom Magator reassured her. "The Big DM will get you out of this."

At that instant, the ice-shark burst out of the snow right in front of them with a sound as loud as a car crash. It was huge, nearly thirty feet long, and its jaws were a forest of serrated teeth. It smashed into the railings and collided with the left-hand pillar, bringing down the portico in a shower of tiles and snow and wood splinters. The Zaggaline was hurled backward, tripping over a row of shattered plant pots and colliding with the window shutter. He twisted around and looked up, and he could see the shark's eye staring at him—not black and dead, like a real shark, but stony-white and all-knowing.

Xanthys screamed, but she managed to stumble through the front doorway into the hall, with Amla Fabeya close behind her. Dom Magator stood his ground, his back jammed hard against the right-hand pillar, his Sun Gun raised high. Just behind his left shoulder Kalexikox was furiously stabbing at his instruments.

The ice-shark's mouth gaped open again, so that Dom Magator could see nothing else but its forests of teeth and death-white skin. The beast's breath fogged up his visor and filled his helmet with the smell of rancid fish oil, and cold blood and imminent death.

"Fire!" Kalexikox screamed at him.

Dom Magator fired the Sun Gun's double trigger, but as he fired, the pillar that he was leaning against toppled over sideways and backward, and he fell with it.

There was a ripping noise, like winter thunder, and then a *krakkkkk!* as his Sun Gun's charge exploded, right next to the chimney. The charge was smaller than a pea, but it gave off a light so intense that the world was turned inside-out and nobody could see anything. The light was instantly followed by a wave of heat, and then another, so that the snow melted on the trees and on the rooftops, and patches of brown soil appeared in the garden. Water gushed out of the gutters, but instantly froze before it could reach the ground.

Even before the first wave of heat could hit it, the ice-shark plunged itself back into the ground, leaving nothing but mashed-up snow. Dom Magator saw its white tail flap just once, and then it vanished. He dragged himself onto his feet, reloaded his Sun Gun, and stormed along the verandah, screaming "Come on up, you bastard! Show yourself! Think you can hide from Uncle Dom? I'll turn you into sushi before you can blink!"

Xanthys and Amla Fabeya cautiously re-emerged from the house and looked around.

"You didn't fry it?"

"Oh, you wait, I'll get it next time. No doubt about that."

The Zaggaline said, "We're going to have to think of something. We're running out of time."

"Three-thirty-six and eleven seconds A.M., in waking time," said Kalexikox. But then he flicked one of his switches again and peered at the dial on his forearm, and said, "Dom Magator?"

"What?"

"I believe that it might have gone."

"The ice-shark?"

"Look … very low fish oil acid readings. Negligible, in fact. No sonar reading at all. No soil displacement reading. It's gone."

"It couldn't be hiding someplace?" asked Xanthys.

"Where? There's no place around here to hide. My sensors cover everything within a three-kilometer radius, and down to a depth of seven hundred fifty feet. Even an ice-shark can't go down to seven hundred fifty feet."

"You're sure about this?" asked Amla Fabeya. "I've told you how cunning the Winterwent can be."

Kalexikox nodded. "Double-checked. Triple-checked. It's gone, or else the Winterwent has simply un-invented it."

"All right then," said Amla Fabeya. "Let's get out of here. If the Winterwent is headed this way, that's just what we want. But we can't afford to let him trap us here in this

house, or anyplace else. He could freeze us rock-solid before we got our weapons out of their racks."

Reluctantly, Dom Magator returned his Sun Gun to its
holster. "Okay, then," he said, "let's hit the bricks. What we
need to do is to set up an observation post, so that we can
watch for the Winterwent when he arrives and hit him quick
and accurate before he knows what day it is."

"What about the High Horse?" asked Xanthys.

"Like I say, he's extremely unpredictable," said Amla
Fabeya. "I haven't seen any signs of him so far. Maybe he's
in somebody else's dream … some other nurse or midwife.
Maybe he's still trying to make a breakthrough with the
mothers."

"But he could be here, too?"

"Oh, for sure. It's just that I haven't seen any hoofprints
yet, and I haven't smelled horses, and I haven't felt anything
that makes the hairs on the back of my neck stand on end. I
haven't heard any animals screaming, either. That's when I
know that the High Horse is close."

Kalexikox was standing at the top of the porch steps,
looking out over the front yard. "All right … not only have I
triple-checked, I've fourble-checked. I can't detect any sign
of that ice-shark anywhere."

"Let's go, then," said The Zaggaline, and together they
stepped off the porch and into the snow. Dom Magator
hesitated for a moment, but then he followed them, with
Amla Fabeya close behind him.

"Come on," called Kalexikox, who had now reached the
mailbox by the road. "The weather front's going to be
reaching us in eight-point-seven minutes."

The Zaggaline said, "Where's Xanthys?"

Dom Magator turned around. Amla Fabeya was still
there, but there was no sign of Xanthys. She still hadn't
emerged from the house.

"Xanthys?" he called into his intercom. "Xanthys, you
have to get out of the house, honey, *prontissimo,* if not
quicker."

There was no reply, nothing but a soft white-noise crackle. "Xanthys," Dom Magator repeated. "Xanthys—are you okay in there? You really need to shift your ass."

Still no reply. He turned back to Kalexikox. "There's something wrong with my walkie-talkie. I'll have to go get her."

"Well, don't take all night," said Kalexikox. "The weather front is going to be here in seven-point-nine minutes."

Dom Magator began to trudge back down toward the house. He tried his intercom again, but he still couldn't contact Xanthys. He went in through the front door, crossed the hallway and pushed open the living room door. Xanthys was still in there, looking through drawers and gathering up family photo albums.

"What the Sam Hill are you doing?" he asked her. "The Winterwent's coming and we only have about five minutes to get the hell out of here."

"It's such a good story," said Xanthys. "I wanted some family photographs to back it up."

"Xanthys, you're here as a Time Curver—a Night Warrior—not a reporter for the *Daily Asswipe* or wherever you used to work."

"But if I can write this story—"

"You don't have the time, honey, and if we don't succeed in palooking the Winterwent and the High Horse, there won't be anybody left in the world to read your story, let anybody to print it."

Xanthys reluctantly stood up. "It's all so *human*."

"Sure, it's human. Most people are, with some notable exceptions. But what we're fighting here, it isn't human at all, and it's not going to give us any concessions, okay?"

He flicked his intercom switch. "Amla Fabeya? It's okay, she's here. We're coming on out. You all better get your butts in gear."

There was no reply, only that thin hiss of static. Dom Magator tried again, but there was still no response. He switched on his location sensors so he could determine exactly where the rest of the Night Warriors were, but the screens and displays were all blank.

He suddenly realized what was wrong. The Meiner house was a dead zone. The Winterwent had frozen it so solid that it was impervious to radio signals. No messages could get in and no messages could get out, and the whole building was impervious to radar, sonar, thermal-imaging equipment or any other kind of scanners.

"I think we need to exit the premises right now," he told Xanthys.

As they made for the living room door, however, he was sure that he heard something. A low creaking noise from the floorboards beneath his feet.

"You hear that?" he asked, lifting one hand.

"I'm not sure."

"Well, I'm not sure, either."

But then he heard it again. It was coming from the cellar. Or maybe not. Maybe it was coming from someplace *deeper* than the cellar. Maybe it was coming from beneath the foundations. There was another creak, like ice breaking, and then a pause, and then a thick dragging noise, like somebody trying to pull a sackful of dead dogs across recently laid concrete.

"The ice-shark!" he shouted. "That's why Kalexikox couldn't detect it! It was hiding underneath the house!"

He barged across the hallway, with Xanthys close behind him. As they ran through the front door, he could see the rest of the Night Warriors gathered around the mailbox waiting for them.

"It's under the house!" he screamed. *"The ice-shark! It's under the house!"*

They turned toward him, and Kalexikox gave him a mock salute. Dom Magator stumbled down the porch steps and started jogging toward them, frantically waving his arms. But before he was halfway up the path, the ice-shark's fin broke the surface of the snow, only seven or eight feet in front of him, and it sped toward the Night Warriors as fast and straight as one of his knives.

The ice-shark detonated from the snow right in front of them, scattering the Night Warriors. It towered over them for a few seconds, staring with its white eyes, and then it crashed back into the snow, twisting around so that it could attack them from behind. The Zaggaline swung his LET rifle at it, but he was knocked off his feet and into the briars. The creature's tail thrashed furiously from side to side, but Amla Fabeya managed to somersault over it and then handspring backward out of its way.

Dom Magator struggled to free his Sun Gun from his rifle rack. He managed to take it out and pull back the bolt, but before he could take aim, the ice-shark had vanished again. Kalexikox was standing by the mailbox, feverishly trying to locate it, while Amla Fabeya was circling around on the other side of the road, keeping her distance.

The Zaggaline shouted, "Dom Magator—give me a gun for Christ's sake! Anything!"

Dom Magator unclipped an Existence Dart Pistol from his belt, checked that it was loaded with darts, and tossed it across to him.

The Zaggaline caught it. "What the hell does this do?" he asked, turning the three-barreled pistol from side to side.

"Hit the shark anywhere you like ... the darts have a drug in them, moralox. It goes straight to the brain and destroys the shark's belief in its own existence."

"What about something to palook it?"

"I can palook it with the Sun Gun. The dart gun ... that's for stopping it at close quarters, in case it's too near to any of us."

Kalexikox called, "It's under the road ... it's circling back this way!"

"Where, exactly?"

"There ... right there! Off to my right! It's coming in fast!"

Dom Magator lifted the Sun Gun. "Give some coordinates, man! Give me some goddamn coordinates!"

"It's three-point-three meters under, but it's coming in much too—"

Dom Magator didn't even have time to adjust the Sun Gun's sights. The ice-shark reared out of the snow and snatched Kalexikox's left arm between its seven rows of jagged teeth. Kalexikox screamed and tried to pull himself free—he even kicked against the ice-shark's snout with his boot. But with one contemptuous shake of its head, the ice-shark ripped his arm right out of its socket. Dom Magator could hear his armor buckling and his muscles tearing. Then blood jetted across the rose beds and Kalexikox dropped sideways onto the ground, his legs twitching with shock.

The Zaggaline fired his dart pistol at the ice-shark's flank. There was a sharp report, and a long dart flew across the garden, but it hit the mailbox and bounced off. The Zaggaline fired again, but by now the ice-shark was already diving down beneath the snow, and the dart only nicked its tail before spinning off harmlessly into a hedge.

In spite of the danger, the Night Warriors all hurried up to Kalexikox, who was lying on his side, quaking with pain. Even the circling fireflies inside his helmet seemed to twitch and flicker and grow dimmer, as if they could feel his agony, too. His empty arm socket was dark red and glossy with exposed gristle, and his metallic armor and all of his scientific instruments were smothered in blood.

"My *arm*," he protested, in bewilderment, and now he sounded much more like Dunc than Kalexikox. "Freaking fish bit off my freaking arm."

The Zaggaline took hold of his brother's right hand and squeezed it. "Hold on, dude. You're going to be fine. Just stay with us, okay? Just keep breathing."

He turned to Amla Fabeya, and inside his helmet his face was distraught. "He's not going to die, is he? What am I going to tell my dad if he dies?"

"He won't die," said Dom Magator.

"Oh no? And you're some kind of medical expert?"

"So long as we can get some dressing on that shoulder, he's going to be okay."

"Which particular dressing did you have in mind, fatso? Blue cheese or Thousand Island?"

"Hey, you skinny runt. Stand down, will you? We're all on the same side here."

"I'm sorry, dude. But look at him. He's, like, bleeding to death."

Amla Fabeya knelt down beside Kalexikox and opened up her shoulder bag. "I have pressure-bandages, Kalexikox, and coagulants to stop the bleeding. Try to lie still."

"What about the ice-shark?" asked Kalexikox.

Dom Magator stood up. "Oh, we'll skewer that baby for you, don't you worry. Might even get your arm back, too."

But as she applied the pressure-bandage, Amla Fabeya glanced up at him with a question in her eyes, and she didn't even have to say it out loud.

With Kalexikox out of action we have no way of telling where the ice-shark is, and it can move three times as fast as any of us—how are we going to catch it, let alone "skewer" it, before it catches us?

Chapter Twelve

The Zaggaline said, "Maybe I could invent an Ice-Shark Hunter. Kind of a multitasking Inuit. Maybe he could smell the ice-shark coming, and maybe he could sense its movements under the ground, and maybe he could be a crackshot harpoonist, too."

"Not such a bad idea," said Dom Magator. "The only snag is, we don't have a whole lot of time. Look at that goddamned weather."

By now, the sky over their heads was almost totally black, and they could see columns of icy rain falling from the upper atmosphere, as if great gray buildings were collapsing from the clouds. Down at ground level, it started to snow—only a few flakes at first, but then thicker and thicker, and at the same time the wind began to rise.

Kalexikox groaned and whimpered, and tried feebly with his right hand to find out where his left elbow had disappeared to. Amla Fabeya had stopped the bleeding, but Kalexikox was going into shock. His face was newspaper-gray, and his blood pressure was dropping as fast as the barometer.

"Looks like we're faced with a pretty stark choice," said Amla Fabeya, packing up her first-aid kit. "We can make a run for it and hope that the ice-shark doesn't come after us, or else we can stay here and see if The Zaggaline's Inuit can kill it for us. But we've pretty much run out of time, so we'd better make up our minds fast."

"*Time*," said Xanthys. "That could be the answer, couldn't it? I mean, time could solve everything."

"What do you mean?"

"We want to kill the ice-shark, don't we? And we want to save Kalexikox too?"

"The ice-shark bit his arm off, there's nothing we can do about that. He won't have lost his arm in his waking life, not physically, but he probably won't be able to use it again."

"But supposing we kill the ice-shark *before* it bites his arm off?"

"You want to try some of that time-curving stuff?"

"Why not? We could kill two birds with one stone."

Amla Fabeya said, "I'm not sure about this, Xanthys. It could be incredibly dangerous. Moving the timeline forward so that your enemy gets killed or injured by a future event, that's one thing, provided you make all the necessary compensations. But to reverse the timeline so that somebody doesn't get killed or injured when they've *already* been killed or injured …"

"We *need* him, though, don't we?" Xanthys argued. "Without Kalexikox, we can't tell if a hole in a wall is a hole in a wall or if it's somebody's dream about screwing their best friend's wife."

The snow was falling so thickly now that they could hardly see each other, and the wind was blowing in a soft, panicky scream.

The Zaggaline said, "She can do it. She reversed the timeline back along Main Street, didn't she? Why don't we give it a shot, huh? If it doesn't work, okay—I'll try to invent my Inuit. But if she can give Dunc his arm back—"

Dom Magator turned to Amla Fabeya. "What do you think?"

Amla Fabeya thought about it for a moment, and then nodded. "So long as she doesn't take the timeline back too far. No more than five or six minutes, at the most. We don't want this whole dream going out of synch, or we may never get out of here."

Xanthys said, "That doesn't give me too much room to maneuver, does it?" She checked the chronometer in her helmet. "Six minutes will only take us back to the moment before Kalexikox was attacked."

"We'll have to be quick off the mark, that's all. And even quicker on the trigger."

"All right," said Xanthys. "I'll do my best, I promise you."

Dom Magator reloaded The Zaggaline's dart gun and handed it back to him. Then he picked up his Sun Gun, cocked it, and adjusted the sights.

"Okay, Xanthys. Here goes nothing."

Xanthys fine-tuned the large dial on the side of her helmet. She edged it up to six minutes, fifty-seven seconds, as far back as she dared. With a soft chime, a pale green key appeared on her display, and the corresponding key on her belt started to flash. She unhooked the key and turned around to face the east, where time always comes from.

"Ready?" she asked, and twisted the key in the air.

Instantly, right in front of them, the ice-shark reappeared, monstrous and white, its teeth bloodily tearing at Kalexikox's shoulder. Kalexikox was screaming and falling sideways, his eyes wide with terror. But then time reversed itself. The thin bloody strings of scarlet muscle unraveled themselves from the ice-shark's incisors, and its jaws stretched open wider to release their grip, and the blood vanished and Kalexikox's armor magically unbent itself. Kalexikox stopped screaming and swung up into a standing position. He briefly turned his head toward the retreating ice-shark, and then he turned back to jab at his instruments.

There was a fraction of a second when the ice-shark was

almost completely clear of the snow, with only the tip of its tail buried beneath the ground. It looked almost graceful, like a marble statue of a leaping dolphin. Dom Magator leveled his Sun Gun and fired.

Nothing happened, only a complicated *whirr-click* noise, like an old-fashioned camera. Unharmed, the ice shark slid backward into the snow and disappeared.

Dom Magator looked down at the Sun Gun in incredulity. "It *jammed!*" he screamed at it. "It's supposed to be a dream gun, and it *jammed!* Stupid imaginary piece of shit!"

The time curve reached six minutes, fifty-seven seconds, and with an odd, sideways shiver, they were all looped back into the present—back into the teeming snow, with Kalexikox lying on his side, his arm still missing, and the sky as dark as a storm-cellar.

Amla Fabeya came over to Dom Magator and inspected the Sun Gun. "Look," she said, pointing to a small gold lever. "The power-reserve switch has tripped. That's why it didn't fire."

"The which switch?"

"Whenever we enter a dream, we have only a limited amount of power to keep us going, which *you* carry, in your batteries. If we exhaust all of that power, there's no way for us to open a portal and escape the dream before the dreamer wakes up. That means we have to stay in the dream world until another contingent of Night Warriors comes to get us out … that's if they can find us." She paused, and then added, "That's if they come at all."

"So what are you saying? We're running low on juice?"

"The Sun Gun burns up a massive amount of energy every time you fire it. And I mean *massive*. If you had taken that shot, you would have fried the ice-shark, for sure, but your weapons system knew that there was a high risk that we might be marooned here, without enough power to get back to the waking world, probably ever."

"Why didn't you tell me this before?"

"I'm sorry, Dom Magator. I didn't realize how much power we'd already used up. When The Zaggaline created Nanook and the House Breaker, he must have depleted our reserves much more than I thought he would. Creating guide dogs and solid people out of electrons, that's a very energy-intensive operation. And time-curving isn't exactly economical when it comes to power."

"So what the flap-doodle do we do now?"

The temperature had dropped so far that fine ice crystals were forming around their lips as they spoke, so that they looked like bearded Arctic explorers. The Zaggaline came over and said, "We have to get Dunc out of here ... we have to get him home. He's going to die if we don't."

The snow was piling down so fast that Kalexikox looked as if he were covered by a blanket. "Maybe we should just risk it," said Dom Magator.

"We can't," said Amla Fabeya. "We're the only people in the world who are capable of stopping the Winterwent and the High Horse, and if the ice-shark gets all of us—"

"You said something earlier," put in Xanthys. "Something about sushi."

"What?" said Dom Magator. "That was merely an intemperate expletive."

"But I have an idea. Do we have enough energy for another time curve?"

Amla Fabeya checked the small panel of telltale lights on Dom Magator's belt. "Yes, we do. In fact we have quite a reasonable amount of energy left. It's just that we don't have enough for a fifteen-million degree gunshot."

" 'Ware shark!" shouted The Zaggaline, and pointed through the falling snow toward the house. A triangular white fin was slowly circling around the garden, cleaving through the rosebeds, cutting across the snow-covered lawns, and it was gradually widening its circle, coming closer.

"Okay, then," said Dom Magator. "Let's sic this sucker before he sics us."

Xanthys stood back a little way and retuned the dial on the side of her helmet. Four and a half minutes had elapsed since Dom Magator's Sun Gun had misfired, so she had to risk a setting of nine minutes, thirty-seven seconds. A pale purple key appeared on her head-up display, and another key on her belt lit up, small and shiny with a hexagonal pattern on it.

"Are you sure you're ready?" she shouted to Dom Magator.

"You bet your badoopy!"

As she raised the key toward the east, however, they heard a deep rumbling sound in the distance, toward the north. They could feel the ground shaking beneath their feet—not the unbalancing motion of an earth tremor, but a steady, relentless vibration, as if thousands and thousands of trains were coming down thousands of parallel tracks.

The Zaggaline cleared the snow from his visor and switched on his helmet lights. At first he could hardly see anything, but when he looked back toward the house, he glimpsed the ice-shark's fin less than thirty feet away, and starting to speed up.

"Now!" he yelled at Xanthys.

Xanthys turned the key. The ice-shark appeared yet again, savaging Kalexikox's shoulder. It released him, and arched backward through the air. For an instant it looked almost graceful, like a marble statue of a leaping dolphin, and in that instant Xanthys flicked down the Static switch on the right-hand side of her helmet.

The ice-shark froze in midair, utterly still. Time passed for everything around it. The snow continued to fall. The distant rumbling gradually grew louder. But the ice-shark was suspended in a curve in relativity, held by physics in its own temporal limbo.

Kalexikox remained frozen, too, caught at the moment when the ice-shark had first reared out of the snow.

"Hurry, Dom Magator!" Amla Fabeya urged him. "This is draining too much power!"

But Dom Magator had already taken three rows of knives from the rack across his shoulders, seventy-three knives altogether, all in soft black leather scabbards, and laid them in the snow. He picked out the first one, a small *deba* knife, tilted it back behind his head, and hurled it toward the time-frozen ice-shark. It flew unerringly, as if somebody had ruled a line through the air with a metallic silver pen. The tip of the ice-shark's nose flew off.

The rest of the knives came flying after it—*santuku* knives, *oroshi* knives, *usuba* knives, *yanagi sashimi* and *takor sashimi*. They sliced through the ice-shark one after the other, spinning and glittering, each with a high-pitched chopping sound, but the air was so cold that the ice-shark appeared to stay intact, one slice still frozen to the next. In little more than a minute, Dom Magator had emptied his scabbards and was finished.

"Now what?" said The Zaggaline.

"Now I switch out of static mode," said Xanthys triumphantly.

She flicked the switch on the side of her helmet. Time, instantly, unfroze. Kalexikox saw the ice-shark hurtling toward him and instinctively raised his left arm to protect himself. But this time, instead of the ice-shark seizing his arm with its teeth, the entire thirty-foot creature collapsed onto the snow only three feet away from him, immaculately cut into seventy-two five-inch slices.

"*Awesome!*" said The Zaggaline, punching the air. "Totally and utterly ridonkulous!"

He battled his way through the snow to Kalexikox and flung his arms around him. "I love you, dude! I totally love you!"

"What's happening?" asked Kalexikox, trying to push him away. "What the hell happened to that *shark*, man? It looks like a cut loaf."

"You're okay, dude, that's all that counts! Look at your arm, it's stuck back on again! Look, you can flap it up and down!"

"I don't have any idea what you're talking about," said Kalexikox. "Leave my arm alone, will you? What the hell happened to that shark?"

Dom Magator was gathering up his knives. "Let's just say that it was feeling a little cut up."

By now, however, the ground was shaking so violently that they were finding it difficult to stay on their feet. Small fragments of grit and soil began to fall on them amongst the snow and clatter on their helmets.

"The Winterwent ... he's nearly here," said Amla Fabeya.

Kalexikox checked his seismograph and his ground temperature indicators, "You're right ... there's a center of intense cold approaching us, at about thirty kph, and it's less than a kilometer away. Not only that, there's a ripple of seismic shock bearing down on us, about two hundred meters ahead of it."

"What's a ripple of seismic shock when it's at home?" asked Dom Magator.

"*That*," said Kalexikox, pointing toward the woods.

Xanthys had been resetting her keys, and it was only when Kalexikox said, "*That*" that she looked up. At first she couldn't see what it was that Kalexikox was pointing at. The sky was so dark and the snow was falling so thickly that it was difficult to distinguish anything at all apart from the house, the briars and the snow-laden trees. But as the ground shook even more she gradually made out an even darker line, like a high wall, only about a half-mile away and coming closer.

"Holy shit," said The Zaggaline.

Dom Magator said nothing, but watched the approaching darkness with a greater feeling of dread than he had ever experienced in his life. This wasn't just fancy guns and dreamlike battles. This was end-of-the-world stuff. Apocalypse now.

"What *is* that?" shouted Xanthys. "It looks like a tidal wave!"

"It *is* a tidal wave!" Amla Fabeya shouted back. "But it's not water! It's rocks and dirt and trees! The Winterwent is so cold that he turns all the moisture in the ground into ice. That makes it the earth expand—so wherever he drives his sledge, he builds up a huge wall of soil ahead of him!"

"So what the hell do we do?" asked The Zaggaline.

Dom Magator was already backing away. "In my humble opinion, folks, we head for the hills, and fast!"

"No!" said Amla Fabeya. "Don't lose your nerve. We can't outrun it … and we have to face the Winterwent!"

"Oh, yes," said Dom Magator. "I almost forgot."

As the Winterwent came nearer, the rumbling grew louder and louder and the rocks and debris that fell through the snow were even heavier. A heavy tree branch struck Dom Magator on the right shoulder and almost knocked him over. The wall of soil was less than a quarter of a mile away now, and it was over a hundred feet high.

"We're going to be buried!" said Xanthys.

But Amla Fabeya was rapidly unhooking climbing clips and lengths of rope from her belt. "Here," she said, tossing a rope to The Zaggaline. "There's a clip on the side of your belt. Run the line through it, and make it fast, and then pass it on to Kalexikox."

"What the hell are you going to do?" asked The Zaggaline. "We can't *climb* that thing … it's moving!"

"Just do it!" said Amla Fabeya. "Have Kalexikox fasten himself next, then Xanthys, then Dom Magator. And *hurry!*"

While the Night Warriors roped themselves together, the huge wall of soil thundered closer and closer. Dom Magator could see oaks and birch trees being torn out of the ground and hoisted high up into the mass of soil and rocks. He saw wooden fences lifted up like ladders and then broken into firewood. When he looked up, right at the rim of the wall, he could see freezing cold fog pouring over it like dry ice, and he could *smell* it, too, as foul as the stench from an open sewer in wintertime.

"Here," said Amla Fabeya, and hooked him up to her climbing rope.

"I hope you're kidding me," said Dom Magator. "The last thing I climbed was a kitchen chair, to change a light-bulb, and even then I got vertigo."

"You're a Night Warrior," Amla Fabeya insisted, tightening the knot around his belt.

"I know, but suddenly I'm beginning to wish I *had* joined the Mexican Army."

The wave of soil had already reached the far side of the cemetery. The gray fence collapsed in front of it, and grave-stones and crosses and weeping angels were all heaved up into the air, followed by dozens of caskets. The soil rose up underneath them and the caskets broke open, one after the other, and a terrible congregation of decayed bodies in suits and dresses rose to their feet and were carried upward, as if they were riding a moving staircase.

Bones began to drop around the Night Warriors, and three or four skulls rolled across the front yard. Xanthys lifted her hands over her head and screamed, "God, oh my God! Oh my God this is *disgusting!*"

Skulls were followed by detached arms and legs and cof-fin lids, which bounced on the ground like skateboards. By then the wall of soil had passed through the cemetery and was crashing through the briars, only a few feet away from them.

Amla Fabeya shouted, "Are you ready for this? When I say climb, *climb*, and follow me. Remember, this is a dream, not the real world. Have faith in yourself, and keep on climbing and don't lose your confidence!"

Amla Fabeya crouched down, facing the wall. The rest of the Night Warriors strung themselves out behind her, and crouched down, too.

"If this is a dream," said Dom Magator, "give me a night-mare any time."

"You heard what the lady said," Kalexikox told him.

"Have faith. But just to reassure you, this climb is scientifically possible."

But Dom Magator didn't have time to think about faith or what was scientifically possible, because the thundering wall of soil was less than ten feet away from them. He swallowed air and he didn't even have time to curse.

Amla Fabeya literally *ran* toward the wall, and started to climb up it as if she were scaling a near-vertical sand dune. The Zaggaline followed her, and then Kalexikox, and Xanthys and Dom Magator.

Dom Magator didn't believe that he could do it, but the massive upward surge of soil beneath his feet did most of the climbing for him. So long as he kept his legs pumping to stop his feet from sinking into the earth, and as long as he kept his balance, he found that he could scramble higher and higher. He trod on rocks and bushes and broken-open coffins, and halfway up the wall, a woman's partly mummified body rose out of the soil right next to him, grinning at him, still wearing her pearls. He almost lost his footing, but he grabbed hold of a tree root and managed to keep on climbing.

Through his misted-up visor, he saw Amla Fabeya reach the top of the wall and roll herself over it. The Zaggaline followed her, and then Kalexikox. We've made it, he thought, but his thighs were trembling, and he was sweating like a cheese, and he was beginning to doubt his ability to climb any further.

Xanthys made it over the top, and Dom Magator was just about to follow her. As he caught hold of the edge, however, his left foot penetrated something that felt like a bear trap. He tried to kick it off, but when he kicked he lost his balance and his right foot plunged into the soil. He twisted around, his back against the wall of debris, but more debris kept rising up, tons of it, and before he could twist himself back round again, he was buried. He was totally blind, and he felt as if his chest was being crushed.

"Mayday!" he gasped into his intercom. *"Mayday!* I'm—"
More debris poured on top of him, and he thought, This

is terrific, buried alive a hundred feet in the air, in some
homely nurse's nightmare. Just the way I wanted to go. What
happened to a massive heart attack after too many helpings
of crawfish gumbo, and a slow parade along Gayosa Street,
with a jazz-band playing "Didn't He Ramble"?

Yes—but you wanted to be a Night Warrior, didn't you?
You wanted to prove that you were more than a self-pitying
waste of calories. So this is how you die. Uncomfortably,
maybe. But heroically—yes!

He was still arguing with himself when the rest of the
Night Warriors dragged him out of the soil and rolled him
over onto his side. Coughing and wheezing, he struggled
into a sitting position. He was almost up to his neck in
freezing fog, which was rolling past them in a thick, white,
fast-flowing tide. They had managed to climb over the crest
of the wall, and as it rolled across the landscape of Nurse
Meiner's dream, they were gradually sinking back down to
ground level.

"You okay, DM?" Xanthys asked him.

"I got caught by some kind of goddamned animal trap. I
lost my balance."

"Animal trap?"

Dom Magator peered down through the fog and saw that
his left leg was caught inside a human ribcage.

"Jesus! Jesus, this is so disrespectful." He kicked the
ribcage, and kicked it again, and it fell apart.

"You're okay, DM. You're free of it now."

"Yuck. That's the trouble with death. It doesn't matter
what a terrifically nice person you were when you were
alive, death turns you into nothing but a waste disposal
problem."

Amla Fabeya came over and held out her hand. "We have
to move fast," she said. "The Winterwent is only minutes
away from us now."

Dom Magator allowed her to help him up. The wave of
debris was already more than a half-mile behind them, still
rumbling its way south-westward, with trees and fences and

rooftops occasionally rearing out of it. Underneath the freezing fog, they could hear the soil crackling with rapidly forming ice, and up ahead of them, all they could see was a blizzard, a complete whiteout.

"So, what's the plan?" asked The Zaggaline.

"We spread out," said Amla Fabeya. "When the Winterwent comes closer, I'll try to create a diversion, so that the rest of you can pick your moment and open fire. With any luck, he won't be expecting us at all. He'll be thinking that the ice-shark got us." She checked her equipment belt, and then she said, "Dom Magator—how about a weapons issue?"

"Okay," said Dom Magator. "We can't use the Sun Gun, but why don't we try this?" He lifted a long-barreled rifle from his back and handed it to Kalexikox. "You're the science genius, this should suit you. It's a Brainbreaker. It sends out a power surge, which blows out the thinking processes in your target's cerebellum. In other words, the Winterwent may *think* that he wants to attack us, but his synapses will have shorted, so that his central nervous system won't get the message, and his muscles won't respond. That should give us a few seconds' grace to palook him with the heavy stuff."

He unfastened another gun, an elaborate blue-black weapon with a large bell-shaped flash-suppressor on the muzzle. "Skinny, you can use this. It takes a few seconds before it starts working, which is why we need Kalexikox to jam up his brain."

"Hey—I seriously *love* this," said The Zaggaline, jiggling the weapon up and down in his hands to enjoy its weight. "So, er, what does it actually, you know, like, *do?*"

"It's a Helix Rifle. Doesn't matter where you hit the Winterwent with it—arm, leg, chest, ass, any place at all—it will kick off a chain reaction in his DNA. All of the genetic information in his body will start to be progressively dismantled and rearranged, which will eventually turn him into somebody else altogether. Or *something* else. It's kind of an unpredictable process, so he may turn into an Emperor penguin or a double cheeseburger with extra onions or he may turn into nothing but mush."

"How about me?" asked Xanthys, anxiously. "I have to tell you, DM, I'm not very good with guns."

Dom Magator lifted a large platinum-plated revolver from one of the holsters around his belt. "I think you can manage this, sweetheart. It's an Opera Pistol. Fires a shell which sends out a very loud, high-pitched note. It can shatter crystal, but it can also shatter ice."

Already the blizzard was blowing so hard that they could barely stand up straight. Xanthys took the Opera Pistol, and as she did so, she thought she could hear a distant distorted warbling. She turned to Amla Fabeya, who nodded. "You can hear them, too? Those are the wolves which pull the Winterwent's sledge. They can't be very far away now."

"The children of the night, what music they make," said Dom Magator. He lifted out a weapon for himself, a Hot Shotgun. It was a pump-action rifle that fired a full load of incandescent magnesium pellets. The pellets burned so fiercely that they carried on burning even when they were immersed in water or buried in ice. He loaded one metallic-purple cartridge into the chamber and clipped on an extended magazine with twenty more rounds.

Now the howling of the ice-wolves was quite distinct. It sounded as if the inspection cover had been lifted off hell and a thousand tortured souls were crying out for deliverance. Gradually, through the blizzard, the Night Warriors began to see the ice-wolves running toward them, hundreds of them, all in harnesses, their heads lowered, their pelts spiky and glittering and sharp, their eyes burning like red-hot coals.

"Don't let the ice-wolves get around you, or behind you," warned Amla Fabeya. "They can bring you down like a deer and drag your guts out in seconds."

"Hear that?" Dom Magator told Xanthys. "If you see any

of those suckers trying to outflank us, let them have it with that falsetto .45 of yours, okay?"

Xanthys felt close to panicking, but she suddenly thought to herself: My father did this, my father was brave enough to be a Night Warrior. Wherever he is, whatever he's doing, I'm not going to let him down.

But for the first time since she had taken on the role of Xanthys, the Time Curver, she was conscious of her near-nakedness, and how physically vulnerable she was.

Over the howling of the ice-wolves, she heard a *scraping* noise, so harsh and metallic that it made her feel as if her teeth were loose; and beneath her feet the ground began to shake.

Then, out of the furiously tumbling snow, the Winterwent's sledge appeared.

It towered over them, more like a fortress than a sledge. It was over seventy-five feet high and more than two hundred feet long, sliding through the snow on six main runners and dozens of side-runners and steering runners and skate-blades on outriggers. Above this complicated undercarriage rose tier after tier of balconies and turrets and fortifications, all of them thickly encrusted with ice, and all of them bristling with spikes and spears. There were scores of white banners flying from every level, but none of them moved because they were all frozen stiff.

On the uppermost deck stood a tall-backed throne, dark frosty red, and on this throne, managing the reins of his thousand ice-wolves, sat the Winterwent.

When Xanthys had asked Springer to describe the Winterwent, he had told her to imagine what it was like to be lying in the snow all night, with no hope of being warm ever again. Springer was right. She saw the Winterwent, yes; but much more than that, she *felt* him, and he was infinitely cold.

He was gigantic, much bigger than Xanthys had imagined, ten or even eleven feet tall. He was dressed in a cloak of frozen white rags, hundreds of them, and around his bony neck he wore a necklace of human femurs, most of them children's, by their size. He had a tapered, elongated skull, with dead-white skin, more like a reptile than a human; but as he turned his head from side to side, and the perspective was distorted, Xanthys occasionally glimpsed a human face, eerily handsome, with dark, elated eyes. It reminded her of art class, at school. The Winterwent's head had the same anamorphic effect as the stretched-out skull in Holbein's painting *The Ambassadors*.

Six arms protruded out of the Winterwent's cloak, as spiny as a spider's, with vicious-looking claws. But out of his wrists grew six long-fingered hands, so that he could control dozens of tied-together reins all at once and still steer his sledge with a complicated Z-shaped tiller.

"You know what that throne's made out of?" said Amla Fabeya. "Frozen blood, more than a hundred gallons of it."

"Think I'll stick to my La-Z-Boy," said Dom Magator.

The Winterwent's throne was surrounded by railings, and dangling from every railing were dozens of human scalps, furry with frost, as well as necklaces, bangles, stiffly frozen fragments of human skin, like eyeless faces, tattooed shoulders, withered penises and empty gloves that had once been human hands.

The Winterwent's own penis stuck out of the front of his cloak like a yard-long icicle, permanently frozen into an up-curving erection. Xanthys felt both fascination and dread. How could a creature so cold and terrifying feel any kind of carnal lust?

As the sledge overshadowed them, Amla Fabeya shouted out, "Cover me! And for Ashapola's sake—watch out for those ice-wolves!"

Dom Magator let out a piercing whistle. "Kalexikox, ready with that Brainbreaker! Aim straight for his bean, okay? Skinny—got that Helix Rifle armed? Doesn't matter where you hit him, so long as you hit him!"

"Locked and loaded, dude, whatever that means."

Amla Fabeya unclipped a flare from her belt and tugged

at the fuse. There was a second's pause, and then it burst into flame—a dazzling crimson, trailing a long streamer of smoke. Immediately, she began to run diagonally across the front of the Winterwent's sledge, waving the flare above her head.

The Winterwent caught sight of her immediately, as she had hoped. He swung his Z-shaped tiller to one side and heaved on the reins that controlled his wolfpack. A hundred ice picks immediately folded down from the underside of the sledge and bit into the ice, bringing the immense vehicle to a slithering, grinding halt. It stopped in such a short distance that the ice-wolves skidded into each other, howling and yelping, and tangled up their reins, and for a few seconds there was utter confusion.

The Winterwent reared up in his throne like a praying mantis, shielding his eyes from the blizzard so that he could follow Amla Fabeya as she ran around to the other side of his sledge. And she was running as fast as an Olympic gold medallist. Dom Magator was amazed how graceful she was, in her eagle's head helmet and gleaming black suit—lean and powerful and utterly determined. Hard to believe that this was the same doctor he had picked up from the airport in her beads and bangles and her white silk dress.

"Okay, Kalexikox, go for the noodle!" he shouted, slapping Kalexikox on the back.

Kalexikox raised the Brainbreaker and squinted through the sights. As he did so, however, the Winterwent lowered the claw that had been covering his eyes and slowly turned his elongated skull around, so that he was staring intently in Kalexikox's direction. Again Xanthys saw that extraordinary optical illusion, in which the Winterwent's face looked almost human, and almost handsome, and his eyes seemed to be wide with delight.

"*Fire!*" yelled Dom Magator.

But there was silence. Kalexikox stayed where he was, still squinting through the telescopic sights, unmoving.

"Fire, Kalexikox! For Christ's sake! Any time this month will do!"

But still Kalexikox remained motionless. Eventually The Zaggaline circled around his brother and screamed into his face. "Dunc! What's the matter, dude? You have to shoot him, or we're screwed!"

Dom Magator pushed Kalexikox's shoulder. Kalexikox fell sideways into the fog, making no attempt to break his fall. His arms and legs were completely rigid, like a store window mannequin.

"He's frozen!" said Xanthys.

Dom Magator immediately hunkered down on the ice and tried to wrench the Brainbreaker out of Kalexikox's hands. "Let go, will you?" He waggled the rifle furiously from side to side, and then tried to pry Kalexikox's fingers away from the trigger one by one, but no matter how hard he tried, he couldn't force Kalexikox to release his grip.

"Skinny—fire the Helix Rifle!" he ordered. "Quick—before he freezes you, too!"

The Zaggaline lifted his weapon but it was already too late. The Winterwent was climbing down from his throne, and before The Zaggaline could take aim, his pointed skull had disappeared from view on the other side of his sledge.

"Where's he gone?" said Xanthys, beginning to feel hysterical.

"Can't you time-curve?" The Zaggaline asked her. "If you can take us back just a couple of minutes, that should be enough!"

"Jesus, he's gone after Amla Fabeya!" said Dom Magator. He slung his Hot Shotgun over his shoulder and started to run through the snow, heading for the other side of the Winterwent's sledge.

Xanthys tried to adjust the dial on the side of her helmet, but it wouldn't budge.

"It's frozen!" she said. "I can't move it!"

"Then we'll have to shoot the bastard! Come on!"

Together, they started to run after Dom Magator. But

they hadn't covered more than twenty yards before sixty or seventy ice-wolves that had been resting under the shelter of the Winterwent's sledge suddenly scrambled to their feet. They broke away from the main pack and came hurtling toward them, baying and barking. They were trailing their reins behind them, and The Zaggaline realized that the Winterwent must have set them loose on purpose.

"Back to back!" The Zaggaline shouted to Xanthys.

"What?"

"You heard what Amla Fabeya said! We mustn't let them get behind us!"

They stumbled together, and stood back to back. Without any hesitation, the ice-wolves came streaming around them, and surrounded them on all sides.

Close up, the ice-wolves looked even more terrifying than they had from a distance. Their noses were much more pointed than real wolves, and their lips were constantly curled back, revealing their chipped and broken teeth, and their lolling, white, fish-fillet tongues. Their bodies were covered all over in sharp splinters of ice, with taller splinters sticking up along their spines. They stood in a circle, panting, and started to edge their way inward.

The Zaggaline leaned back so that their helmets touched. "You okay?" he asked Xanthys.

"Great. What did Amla Fabeya say about them dragging your guts out?"

"You still have that Opera Gun?"

"Sure."

"Okay, I'm going to say 'fire,' and we're both going to fire. Hit as many wolves as you possibly can. That should hold them off for a couple of seconds, while the helix effect begins to work."

"Okay."

The Zaggaline checked his Helix Rifle to make sure that it was properly armed. Then he aimed at the largest ice-wolf that he could see. The ice-wolf stared back at him, its red eyes giving nothing away. Right, you bastard, thought The Zaggaline. Let's see how you like your polymers unraveled.

"Fire," he breathed, and then he realized that he had said it so softly that Xanthys hadn't heard him.

"Fire!" he repeated, and this time he said it so loudly that he frightened himself.

CHAPTER THIRTEEN

The Helix Rifle let out a bright blue flash and a bang like a cellar door slamming. The Zaggaline's first shot hit the ice-wolf in the neck, and fragments of sparkling shrapnel exploded into the air. The ice-wolf yelped, shook its head and took two or three cautious steps back, but it was clear that the shot had only stung it.

The Zaggaline swung his rifle around and hit five or six more ice-wolves. *Slam! Slam! Slam! Slam! Slam!* Again, the ice-wolves did little more than yelp and retreat a little way before they started closing in again.

It was then that Xanthys fired her Opera Pistol. The bullets were fluted, so that they set up a simultaneous chorus of five high-pitched screeches. One of the five screeches was tuned to oscillate at exactly the same frequency as ice. Instantly, the ice-wolf right in front of her burst apart, leaving nothing in the snow but broken white lumps.

Most of the ice-wolves jumped back a few paces, alarmed. But a big battered male wolf with only one eye started to snarl at Xanthys and to creep in closer, his jaws stretched wide to reveal five higgledy-piggledy rows of jagged teeth. He gave a long menacing growl from the depths of his throat and then started to bunch up his hindquarters, as if he were preparing to leap on top of her. Xanthys fired again. One of the ice-wolf's front legs disintegrated and he rolled sideways onto the ground, underneath the fog, howling in pain and bewilderment. She fired again and again and he was shattered into slush.

"Way to go, babe!" whooped The Zaggaline. "Remember the Alamo!"

Xanthys fired again and again, until her ears were singing and ice-wolves were exploding all around her. Some of them tried to retreat out of range, but she adjusted the sights of her Opera Pistol and blew up six or seven of them who had obviously thought that they had run too far away for her to hit them.

Now The Zaggaline shouted, "Xanthys—look, babe, I think it's working! Its whole DNA is coming undone!"

The first ice-wolf that he had shot with his Helix rifle was beginning to lurch unsteadily on its feet. What had looked like an inconsequential wound on its shoulder had already boiled up into a huge beige tumor with dark brown cancerous scabs on it. Right in front of their eyes, like a speeded-up nature movie, the tumor spread itself all across the ice-wolf's back and down the upper part of its legs. The creature's genetic makeup was rapidly being taken apart and rearranged at random, and what it was eventually going to turn into, God alone knew. Already it was hunched up and grossly misshapen—more like a warthog than a wolf.

Within a few seconds, similar lumps started to appear on all of the other ice-wolves that The Zaggaline had hit with his Helix Rifle—nine or ten of them at least. The warthog-wolves were not only grotesque, they were highly aggressive. When any of the other ice-wolves tried to approach them, they turned on them, barking and slavering and snapping.

The first warthog-wolf threw back its head and tried to howl. All that it could manage was a strangled scream, like a slaughtered pig, but it must have unnerved the rest of the ice-wolves, because they started to back away. The warthog-wolf screamed again, and this time it sounded almost human. The rest of the ice-wolves hesitated for a few more seconds, but then one of them turned around and started to lope back toward the shelter of the Winterwent's sledge, and one by one the others followed.

Soon, only the warthog-wolves were left behind. The Zaggaline and Xanthys circled around them, keeping their weapons lifted, but the warthog-wolves didn't seem to be interested in them any longer. After their first display of ferocity, they were all beginning to weaken. Their chests were rising and falling as if they were finding it almost impossible to breathe. One by one their legs gave way and they dropped down beneath the freezing fog, their red eyes dimming, their bodies so swollen with scab-encrusted tumors that they looked like corpses in the very last stages of decay.

"We killed them," said The Zaggaline, soberly. "Did you see that? We turned them into animals that don't exist, even in nightmares."

Xanthys said, "God, I hope so. They're hideous."

When the last of the warthog-wolves had collapsed, Xanthys and The Zaggaline turned and looked warily back toward the Winterwent's sledge. Nearly a thousand ice-wolves were crouched down beside it, and they were all staring at them, so many hundreds of red eyes shining that they looked like a city at night. But not one of the ice-wolves howled, and not one of them stood up and tried to come after them.

"Is that cool or is that cool?" said The Zaggaline. "We beat them off, babe, and they *respect* us. Remember that movie *Zulu*, when twenty British dudes stood up to about a million Zulu warriors? In the end, the Zulus quit trying to kill them, and gave them this big Zulu salute."

He lifted his Helix Rifle over his head and called out, *"Respect!"*

Instantly, one of the ice-wolves leaped to its feet and

started tearing toward them. The Zaggaline said, "Oh, shit! Less respect than I thought!"

The ice-wolf was less than twenty feet away from them before Xanthys could cock her Opera Pistol, aim it and fire. The shell left the barrel with an ear-splitting screech, and the ice-wolf detonated in a cloud of ice. None of the other ice-wolves looked as they were inclined to follow, but all the same, The Zaggaline took hold of Xanthys' arm and pulled her away, as fast as the slippery ground would allow them.

The snow was falling so thickly now that they could barely see six feet in front of them. But as they came around to the far side of the Winterwent's sledge, they heard a deep, booming shot, and then another.

"That's Dom Magator's shotgun," said The Zaggaline.

They struggled forward, gripping hands so that they wouldn't lose each other. Visibility was so poor that they almost tripped over Dom Magator, who was lying on his side, holding up his Hot Shotgun.

"What's happened?" said Xanthys. "Where's Amla Fabeya?"

"Where's that freaking Winterwent?" said The Zaggaline.

"There," said Dom Magator, coughing.

They had to wipe their visors before they could see clearly through the teeming snow. The Winterwent was standing less than thirty feet away, and he was holding up Amla Fabeya with the self-satisfied callousness of a hunter holding up an injured rabbit. His spider-like talons were hooked up in her climbing belt and snagging the fabric of her shiny black skintight suit. Even though she was twisting and struggling and kicking him with her spiky climbing boots, the Winterwent seemed to be quite unconcerned, and when he turned his human face toward them, The Zaggaline saw him smile.

"Okay, asshole!" shouted The Zaggaline, stalking toward the Winterwent with his Helix Rifle held high. "You let her go or I'll turn you into something so disgusting that you'll make *yourself* gag!"

"Night Warriors," said the Winterwent contemptuously. His voice was like every note on a church organ playing at once. Bass, tenor, treble—with a reedy, breathy, metallic echo. "I could hardly believe it when the High Horse told me that he had picked up the smell of *Night Warriors*. I was sure that you had all disbanded, decades ago, and returned to the lowly callings for which you were much more suited."

"Well, you and your horsey friend were very much mistaken," Dom Magator retorted, climbing to his feet. "Night Warriors never disband. So long as the universe has mugwumps like you in it, we'll always be here."

"Hah! Still so self-righteous! Still so moralistic! You don't change, do you? But this time you don't have to concern yourselves with keeping the universe safe for the human race. After three more nights have passed, the High Horse and I will have the secret of creation, and when we have *that,* my friend, there will be no more universe for you to worry about. There will be nothing but chaos and old night."

"Let her go," The Zaggaline repeated, aiming his Helix Rifle at the Winterwent's head.

The Winterwent hoisted Amla Fabeya even higher, so that his head was obscured behind hers. "You'll have to kill *her* first. Go on, why don't you? She's going to die anyhow, as you all are. What difference does it make if you blow her brains out, so long as you blow *mine* out, too?"

He shook Amla Fabeya so violently that she screamed. Dom Magator shouted, "You bastard! Let her go!"

The Winterwent shook her again, and then gripped her between the legs and clutched her so tight that his spider-claw penetrated her climbing suit and went right up inside her. Amla Fabeya screamed again and struggled like a beetle transfixed on a pin. "You're hurting me! Ashapola! You're hurting me!"

"Ashapola?" the Winterwent mocked her. "Ashapola can't save you!" And with that, he thrust his claw into her even more fiercely, and then added another claw.

The Zaggaline yelled, *"Leave her alone!"* and fired at him, but the Winterwent disappeared and reappeared eighteen inches off to the left, and the charge from the Zaggaline's Helix Rifle missed him by more than a foot. However, just as the Winterwent jerked back to his original position, Dom Magator fired, too.

His Hot Shotgun let out a deafening report, and a load of white-hot pellets hit the Winterwent in the elbow of his second arm. The magnesium pellets were so hot that they crackled, and they burned so fiercely and so quickly that before the Winterwent could smother them with rags from his cloak, they had eaten right into his muscles and started to burn at his bones.

The Winterwent threw Amla Fabeya onto the ground. Smoke was pouring from his clothing, but he didn't hesitate. He took hold of his burning arm with two of his other arms, gripped it tight, and twisted it backward. He bellowed in pain, so loudly that Xanthys lifted her hands to the sides of her helmet in a vain attempt to protect her ears. Then he wrenched his arm from its socket, and twisted it around three more times to tear away the skin and the tendons. It took only one more twist to rip it off altogether.

"Oh my God," said Xanthys, as the Winterwent tossed his disconnected arm across the snow. It landed thirty feet away, still smoldering.

"Amla Fabeya!" shouted The Zaggaline. *"Kalexikox, go help her!"* He lifted up his Helix Rifle and tried to aim it, but the Winterwent flickered to one side, like a character in a shadow play. He tried to aim it again, but again the Winterwent was gone.

The Zaggaline waved his weapon from side to side, wildly trying to get a fix on his target. Amla Fabeya was crawling toward them, and Kalexikox was charging through the snow to rescue her. But the Winterwent lunged forward with three double-jointed steps and snatched her ankle before Kalexikox could reach her.

"I warned you!" shouted Dom Magator. He pumped his

Hot Shotgun to reload it, but the Winterwent heaved Amla Fabeya right up in the air and swung her from side to side, so that it was impossible for Dom Magator to get a clear shot.

"You warned me? You *warned* me? Well, Night Warriors, this is how I warn *you*."

He held Amla Fabeya even higher. She was still fighting, but it looked as if her ankle were broken, because her right foot was twisted almost at a right angle. The Winterwent reached up with two of his claws and unscrewed her eagle's head helmet, flinging it into the blizzard, where he had thrown away his burning arm. Amla Fabeya's eyes were squeezed tight with terror and she was gritting her teeth. She was hurting now, but she knew from experience as a Night Warrior that there was even worse pain to follow.

Three claws and five long-fingered hands appeared like spiders between Amla Fabeya's thighs, and parted them. Then yet another hand appeared, holding up the Winterwent's icicle-like erection.

"No!" shouted Dom Magator, and started to run forward. But the Winterwent ignored him, and maneuvered his erection between Amla Fabeya's legs, pointing directly upward. Dom Magator had covered less than a quarter of the distance between them when the Winterwent's cloak shook with a sickening spasm, and his huge glasslike glans disappeared inside Amla Fabeya's body. Dom Magator stumbled and stopped where he was, unable to run any further, his chest heaving. There was nothing he could do but watch as the Winterwent impaled Amla Fabeya with his erection, a few inches at a time, all three feet of it. He must have penetrated her vagina, her uterus, her stomach and her lungs—all the way to her chest cavity.

Amla Fabeya screamed in pain, but if there was one mercy about the Winterwent's rape, it was his utter coldness. She screamed for only a few seconds before she began to freeze, from the inside of her womb outward. Her stomach, her liver, her lungs—one after another they were all solidified. Her blood slowed to a chilly creep and then froze in her arteries and her heart was suspended in mid-beat. Her beaded hair turned white as an old woman's, and her black leather climbing costume was gradually coated in a thickening layer of frost. Her body stiffened and her head fell forward. After little more than a minute, she was turned to ice, with both of her arms held out as if she were still pleading for somebody to save her.

The Zaggaline shouted, "*Now*, dude! Fire!" But even though he knew that Amla Fabeya was dead, Dom Magator hesitated to blow her apart.

In that split second of hesitation, the Winterwent reached behind his back and produced a double-headed ax made out of brightly shining metal. It looked like a weapon out of a Norse legend, with concave blades and a demon's head on the pommel.

"*The Kattalak*," whispered Xanthys.

Dom Magator hefted up his Hot Shotgun, but he was too late. The Winterwent cracked Amla Fabeya in the back of her head and her whole body disintegrated, suddenly exposing his erection.

Dom Magator fired, but the Winterwent was too quick for him, and the blazing buckshot disappeared into the darkness. The Winterwent whirled his five remaining arms around his head and the snow began to blow harder and thicker, until the Night Warriors were blinded.

Kalexikox tilted his helmet toward Dom Magator and yelled out, "Wind speed one hundred thirty kph and rising! I think we need to get out of here!"

Dom Magator knew that he was right. He could use his scanners to locate the Winterwent, but none of his readings would be accurate, because the Winterwent's body temperature was exactly the same as the air that surrounded him, and there was so much interference from the blizzard that Dom Magator couldn't be sure how close he was or in which direction he was heading. The danger was that the Winterwent might circle around them and pick them off one by one with his Kattalak—or even worse, he could penetrate them with his ice cold erection and freeze them to death where they stood. Dom Magator was pretty sure that the Winterwent wouldn't discriminate between men and women.

"Follow me!" Dom Magator called out, waving the Night Warriors away from the Winterwent's sledge. "Tactical retreat, guys!"

"Give me one more shot!" shouted The Zaggaline.

"We don't have the time!"

"Just one more! Tell me where he is!"

"Over there!"

"What do you mean 'over there'? I need coordinates!"

"I can't give you any! I'm only picking up static!"

"How can I hit the bastard if I don't have coordinates?"

"Try this!" said Dom Magator. He unlocked another rifle from the rack on his back and tossed it over. The Zaggaline caught it in his left hand and tossed back his Helix Rifle with his right.

"What is this?" he wanted to know. It was covered in leaf-springs and flat-headed levers and it looked more like a crossbow than a rifle.

"It's a Daisy Cutter!"

"A what?"

"It fires five-inch titanium disks!" He made a quick circling motion with his forefinger. "They fly straight for about a hundred feet, then they start to spiral, six inches above the ground! If the Winterwent is standing within a fifty-foot radius, they'll chop off his feet!"

"Only his feet? I'd like to chop more than his goddamned feet off!"

"Tell me about it! But at least this will give you a half-decent chance of hitting him!"

The Zaggaline pulled back the Daisy Cutter's cocking bar. "So where did you say he was?" he frowned, peering into the blizzard.

Dom Magator squinted at the display screen inside his

helmet. Through the interference, he could vaguely make out something moving between him and the Winterwent's sledge. It walked with a stilted, insect-like gait, so it was a pretty reasonable bet that it was the Winterwent.

"There!" he told The Zaggaline, pointing into the snow.

The Zaggaline fired twice without any hesitation. The Daisy Cutter was almost silent, except for two hollow noises like a slide-whistle.

"Did I hit him?" asked The Zaggaline.

Dom Magator tried to fine-tune his scanner so he could see if the Winterwent had stopped moving. But the interference was so furious now that even his sledge was invisible.

"Did I *hit* him?" The Zaggaline repeated.

"I can't tell you. No, I can't get any kind of picture. Listen—we have to get out of here."

"I just want to know if I hit him, for Christ's sake!"

"Let's put it this way—if he was standing up anyplace between us and his sledge, the chances are that he's walking around on his ankles. You'll have to be satisfied with that."

They caught up with Xanthys and Kalexikox. Kalexikox said, "It's four-oh-seven now, in the waking world. It's probably time we called it a night. It's going to be sunrise in fifteen minutes and Nurse Meiner's alarm clock was set for four-twenty-nine."

Dom Magator looked back in the direction of the Winterwent's sledge. "Okay ... I guess that discretion is the better part of getting your butt frozen off by some sub-zero sodomite with five arms and a dong the size of a submarine sandwich."

"I just want to take one more shot at him," said The Zaggaline.

"You'll have your chance," said Dom Magator. "I think we learned a lot tonight, all of us. We made some crappy mistakes, but we won't make them a second time."

"We're going to come back?"

"You bet. And we're going to take our revenge for Amla Fabeya."

"Amen to that," said The Zaggaline.

Xanthys lifted her hand to show that she, too, was determined to return. Kalexikox shouted, "We're Night Warriors, yes? We don't give up until the bad guys are chopped shallots!"

"Chopped shallots?" said Xanthys.

Dom Magator clicked the power switches at the side of his belt. The lights on his forearms made the snowflakes sparkle, so the Night Warriors looked if they were surrounded by a thick swarm of bright blue fireflies. Then Dom Magator drew a hexagon in the air—a portal back to Nurse Meiner's bedroom, and the waking world. *"Go,"* said Dom Magator, and Xanthys stepped through first, and then Kalexikox.

Just as The Zaggaline was about to follow, he turned to Dom Magator and said, "We're definitely coming back, yes? You weren't just talking gung-ho?"

Dom Magator shook his head. "Let me tell you something, son. I used to wonder what was the point. That's why I always ate so much. I mean, if there's no point, why worry about anything? But what we've been through tonight ... that proves it, as far as I'm concerned. There *is* a point, and this is it."

The Zaggaline nodded and stepped through the portal. Dom Magator was just about to follow him when he heard an appalling scream, only about fifty yards away. He turned and switched on his scanners.

It was still impossible to see anything clearly, but he was sure that he could distinguish something lurching in his direction. Something tall, awkward and off-balance. He heard another scream—but this was a scream of rage, rather than pain.

"Night Warriors! I will murder you all! I will freeze you and smash you and crush you in my claws! I will suck your frozen blood! I will come after you, wherever you are, waking or dreaming!"

Dom Magator switched off his screen and stared into the

blizzard through his visor. It might have been nothing more than a windblown whirl of snow, but he thought that he could see a pale, blurry shape approaching him. He pumped the action of his Hot Shotgun, and lifted it up to his shoulder. But then he thought: Suppose I miss, and the Winterwent hits me with that Kattalak? Suppose he freezes me and smashes me and crushes me in his claws?

If that happened—apart from him being seriously hurt, and then killed—the rest of the Night Warriors would have to go looking for another armorer. By the time they had done that, the Winterwent and the High Horse might well have found a way to penetrate a baby's first dream, and discovered the key to unraveling the whole of creation.

The ghostly shape appeared to be much nearer now. He held his breath and fired once, and felt the shotgun kick against his shoulder blade, but he didn't wait to see if he had hit anything. He took a lumbering jump through the portal and immediately shut down the power.

CHAPTER FOURTEEN

Dom Magator arrived back in Nurse Meiner's bedroom in a furious gust of snow, and it was only by grabbing her bed rail that he managed to stop himself from toppling over. Behind him, the portal collapsed with a deafening *pssshhhtt!* like a tractor trailer's air brakes.

Springer had been waiting for them. Dom Magator immediately saw from the look on his face that Xanthys and Kalexikox had already told him about Amla Fabeya. This morning Springer appeared to be at least twenty years older than the previous night, with cropped white hair and eyes as pale as agates, and he was wearing a tan-colored collarless suit that looked as if it had been designed for a 1960s science-fiction movie.

It was still dark outside, but Nurse Meiner was beginning to grow restless. She was lying on her back and whistling through one nostril. Springer said, "We have to hurry. You really need to be back in your physical bodies before sunrise."

Dom Magator said, "Listen ... I don't know what to say about Amla Fabeya. I feel like I really let her down."

Springer pursed his lips as if he had tasted something bitter; but that was the only emotion he betrayed. "She knew the risks, Dom Magator, as you all do."

"What's going to happen to her body?" asked Xanthys.

"The same thing that happens to all Night Warriors killed in action. Her doctors will think that she's inexplicably lapsed into some kind of catatonic trance, and they'll keep her alive until they decide that she's never going to recover and it's no longer worth the expense."

"Jesus," said Dom Magator. "Doesn't bear thinking about, does it?"

"No. But from what The Zaggaline has been telling me, Kaiexikox was very lucky. He could have permanently lost the use of his arm."

"So what do we do now?" asked Xanthys.

"What you do now is, you go back to your sleeping bodies and get as much rest as you can. We'll meet again tomorrow, in the afternoon, and discuss what happened tonight. Then we can decide on a new plan of action."

"Can't we talk it over now?" said The Zaggaline. "I need to wind down, dude. I'm pumped up with so much adrenaline." He couldn't stop jiggling up and down and punching the air.

"That's the trouble," said Springer, laying a hand on his shoulder. "You're so overexcited, you won't be able to think straight."

"But don't *you* want to know everything that happened?"

"Of course I do. But only when you've all had the chance to work it all out in your own minds."

Nurse Meiner suddenly turned over and snorted. "Come on," said Springer. "It's time for us to leave this poor woman in peace. We've disturbed her dreams enough for one night."

Xanthys looked down at her and said, "When we were inside her dream ... did she see us there? I mean, was she dreaming about *us*, as well as that town?"

"Of course."

"God, I feel so sorry for her. I hope I never have a dream like that, ever."

Springer led them away from Nurse Meiner's bedside and out through the wall of her bedroom. After the sub-zero blizzard in Nurse Meiner's dream, the early morning air felt blissfully warm. They floated away from the neat suburban streets of Clifton just as the sun was edging its way up over the distant trees of Tom Sawyer State Park. They flew higher now, and slower, and with much more confidence, and they didn't need Springer to show them the way home. The Zaggaline and Kalexikox peeled off to the left as they passed over the Highland District, and then, when they reached downtown Louisville, with its streetlights still glittering, Xanthys and Dom Magator parted company.

"Later," said Xanthys, softly, in Dom Magator's earphone.

"You bet," said Dom Magator, and angled himself north-westward along the riverfront, his arms outstretched, as if he weighed nothing at all.

"Perry!"

"I'm still asleep, Dad! I can't hear you!"

"Perry, do you know what time it is?"

"No, and I'm seriously begging you not to tell me."

Perry's father managed to force his bedroom door open, even though Perry's sneakers were wedged against it. He stepped over his jeans and his cushions and a scattering of DVDs until he reached the side of Perry's bed.

"Come on, son. It's way past nine o'clock."

Perry buried himself even deeper in his comforter. He found it difficult enough to wake up after a normal night, let alone a night of trudging around in a blizzard and battling with the Winterwent.

"Dad, I didn't sleep too good, honest. Just leave me alone for a couple more hours."

"What the heck is the matter with you boys? I can't even get *Dunc* out of the sack, and he's usually up and eating his

Cap'n Crunch while it's still dark. Don't tell me you were listening to that pod gizmo of yours all night?"

"I'm okay, Dad, honest. I've been suffering from amnesia, that's all."

"Amnesia? That's okay, then. I'm truly relieved. So long as you haven't been suffering from insomnia." He went to the window and opened the drapes, so that the whole room was flooded with sunlight.

"I *meant* insomnia," said Perry. "I forgot what it was called, because I've been suffering from amnesia."

Perry's father sat down on the side of his bed and dragged down the bedclothes. Perry said, "I'm blinded!" and covered his face with both hands. "I'll never see again! I'll have to do all of my homework in braille!"

"Perry, it's past nine o'clock already, which is almost lunchtime, and something totally wonderful has happened."

Perry parted his fingers and stared at his father through the chinks. He hadn't seen him smiling for a long, long time. Not a *happy* smile, not like this. George Beame, beaming? Totally out of character. Perry covered his face again.

His father said, "I hope you're not suffering from amnesia, because if you are, you won't recall who *this* is."

Perry heard somebody walk into the room and felt them sit down on the end of his bed. He thought he could smell perfume, too, something light and flowery. He stayed where he was for a count of ten, trying to think who it was. His cousin Millie, more than likely. His father had always wanted him to spend time with Millie, because she ran her own Bible class and was a shining example of young American womanhood, in spite of her corrective dentistry and her frizzy ginger hair.

"Perry?" said a girl's voice. Perry lifted his head and opened his eyes. He could hardly believe what he saw. Sitting next to his father in a loose pink linen dress was his sister Janie. He knew at once that it was really her, and not

Springer pretending to be her, because she looked so different from the last time that he had seen her. She had cut her long dark hair very short, like a pixie's, and the tips had been dyed a vivid pink. Not only that, she had a gold hoop pierced through the middle of her lower lip.

"Janie? Janie! You *did* come back!" His father caught the intonation in his voice and looked to him with one eyebrow raised. But Perry could hardly tell him that Springer had predicted Janie's return. At best, his father would have thought that he was talking gibberish, and at worst, he would have thought that he was being blasphemous.

Right now, though, George Beame seemed to be full of nothing but delight that Janie was there—which, considering the screaming matches that had led to her walking out—was almost miraculous. He stood up and laid his hands on her shoulders with fatherly pride.

Janie said, "Look at you, Perry. You haven't changed one little bit."

"I know," said Perry, soberly. "It's the diet."

"The *diet?*"

"It's not Dad's fault, but the only thing he can cook is Brunswick stew."

"Now that isn't so!" George protested. "I make you a whole mess of different dishes these days. What about that Mexican turkey we had last week?"

"Exactly, your honor. I rest my case. Will the jury stop gagging, please?"

"Your sense of humor hasn't changed, either," said Janie.

George leaned forward and kissed Janie on the top of the head. Then he said, "Janie asked me if she could move back home for a while. I admit that I took the time to think twice about it, but then I said yes." He paused for a moment, and Perry could see that his eyes were glistening. "I know we had some pretty horrible arguments, and a lot of bad words were spoken between us, but that was then and this is now. No matter what we say to each other, we're still family, and families have to forgive."

Perry said, "You don't have to persuade me, Dad. So far as I'm concerned, this is totally radical. Now I won't have to help out in the store anymore. Janie—you realize that your coming back home has probably saved my life. I think I've developed a potentially fatal allergy to the smell of Swiss cheese."

"Er, Janie won't be helping out in the store, Perry. Janie came back for a very special reason. She told me all about it over the phone, and we've talked it all through."

There was a lengthy silence, but Janie didn't take her eyes off Perry, and she didn't stop smiling. Her eyes were very dark brown, brown as Hershey's chocolate sauce, and when she smiled they crinkled just like their mother's eyes, as if she were thinking about something mischievous, as well as affectionate.

George reached around and laid his hand gently on Janie's stomach. "Janie's going to have a baby."

"Wow," said Perry.

"You and Dunc, you're going to be uncles," said Janie.

"That is *so* cool. Hey! Now I can call him Unca Dunc!"

Janie said, "I thought I could manage on my own, but I was down to my last fifty dollars. Then I talked to this really understanding nurse at the prenatal center. She said—well, she said that I should swallow my pride and think about my baby."

"Hey, what about the baby's father? Where's he in all of this?"

Janie shook her head. "He didn't want to know about it. In fact, he never wanted me to have the baby at all. I guess I can't blame him. He has kind of, like, other commitments."

"Other commitments more important than his own baby? Don't tell me he has a season ticket for the Cards?"

"He has a wife, and three other children."

"Jesus! How *old* was this guy?"

"Thirty-four."

Perry smacked his forehead with the flat of his hand. "My God! My sister got herself knocked up by a senior citizen!"

"Perry," George cautioned him. "Third commandment."

"Sorry, Dad. This is all such a total surprise."

"Well, it's been a surprise to me, too, son. But it's obliged me to think about myself, and how selfish I've been. I was grieving for your mom and I forgot that you kids were grieving just as much as me."

Perry climbed out of bed. He rummaged around the floor until he found a reasonably clean pair of red and green-striped Bermuda shorts. He put them on, almost toppling over as he did so. "So where have you been living?" he asked Janie.

"New Albany. I had a job in a hairdresser's until the baby started to show."

"New Albany? So the baby's father, he's not only a geriatric, he's a Hoosier? Jesus, Janie! Bring shame on your family or what?"

Janie laughed and whacked him with his pillow.

Just then Dunc appeared in the doorway with his hair sticking up, wearing his saggy gray pajamas. He looked like Lenny in *Of Mice and Men*.

"Got my family back together again," said George, holding out his arm so that he could embrace Dunc, too. "Why don't we go downstairs and have ourselves a family breakfast? Haven't done that in far too long."

He started off downstairs. Janie stood up to follow him.

"Janie," said Perry. "I got to tell you … it's really great to have you back."

Janie came up to him. She tweaked his hair between her finger and thumb, just like she used to fuss over him when he was little. "You know … I thought you didn't look any different, but you do."

"What do you mean?"

"I don't know. It's something. Maybe you just grew older."

"Well, it happens to everybody, doesn't it? Just think. One day, *I'm* going to be thirty-four, too."

Janie said, "He didn't take advantage of me, Perry. I knew what I was getting myself into."

Perry nodded. "Trouble is, babies never know what they're getting themselves into, do they?"

"Believe me—this one is going to be cherished, no matter what."

Perry hugged her close. Underneath her loosely fitting dress, her stomach was huge and rock-hard. "Hey ... this sucker is way bigger than he looks. I didn't ask you when it was due."

"Any time. Could be tomorrow, could be next week. Could be *now,* if you keep on squeezing me like this."

"So soon? Are you kidding me? And you came back here to Louisville to have it? You must have seen the news—all those babies dying around here because they can never get to sleep?"

"Of course I've seen it. But Dad's going to take me down to Aunt Bethany's in Bowling Green. One of Aunt Bethany's friends is a midwife at the Greenview Regional."

"Okay, then. That's okay. Did Dad tell you that Dora's granddaughter died at the Kosair Children's Hospital? I was there when it happened, and it seriously sucked."

"They haven't had any outbreaks down at Bowling Green, so I guess it's going to be safe."

"Well, let's hope so," said Perry.

Janie stared at him for a moment. "There is definitely something different about you, Perry. You're so—I don't know—like, *mature.*"

"Mature? *Moi?* You make me sound like one of Dad's cheeses."

"Well, serious, then."

"Maybe I grew up. Listen, give me a moment to get dressed, and I'll see you downstairs."

Janie gave him a kiss on the cheek, and kissed Dunc, too, and followed George down to the kitchen.

If anybody was looking serious, it was Dunc. "I just thought of something," he said.

"I know, Dunc. You and me both."

"The Winterwent and the High Horse are going to come looking for us. You heard what Dom Magator said— *waking or dreaming*. That means they could come sniffing around here, trying to get into Dad's dreams, or Janie's dreams, and then they wouldn't only find us, but Janie's baby, too."

Perry said, "Maybe I can talk Dad into taking Janie down to Bowling Green today. Whatever, we need to tell Springer about this, and we need to tell him like *urgent*. If the Winterwent and the High Horse get into Janie's baby's dreams, that's it, dude. The end of the universe as we know it."

"You want pancakes?" called Janie.

John dreamed that masses of spiders were crawling into his mouth, and when he woke up, they were. He sat up, flailing his arms and furiously spitting, but then he saw that a seam in his pillow had split apart and that his face was smothered with duck feathers.

"*Tfff, ptttfff,* shit."

His room was filled with blinding sunlight. When he squinted at his wristwatch he saw that it was almost 10:00 A.M. God, he felt bushed. He hadn't realized that fighting as a Night Warrior meant that he wouldn't get any sleep. It reminded him, unexpectedly, of a Dr. Seuss book that his mother used to read to him when he was little. "We fight all night, we play all day."

He eased himself out of bed and loudly farted. Being a Night Warrior was playing havoc with his digestion, too. He was badly in need of bacon and fried eggs and waffles and sausage links and waffles, with a large mug of coffee, but it was almost lunchtime already and he had been craving the chopped mutton barbecue at Paul Clark's Owensboro Bar-B-Q for over a week, with half a loaf of onion rings and buttermilk pie to follow.

He used a dinner knife to chisel a can of Dr. Pepper out of his icebox and then shuffled to the window to drink it.

Before he opened it, though, he pressed the can against his forehead and held it there until his brain began to hurt. He wondered what kind of pain Amla Fabeya had suffered in the seconds before her flesh had been solidified.

"Charlie Mazurin," he said out loud, as a kind of requiem. He hadn't known anything about her: how old she was, where she was born, what kind of life she had led. He didn't know if she was ever married or if she had any relatives that he ought to talk to. But he felt as if there had been some kind of connection between them, from the time that he had first picked her up at the airport and thrown his roast beef melt in the trash can, to the shattering moment when the Winterwent had frozen her to death and then cracked her into smithereens with his Kattalak.

He took a hefty swallow of ice-cold Dr. Pepper and burped twice. "Sorry, Amla. Didn't mean no disrespect."

He showered and dressed in a black T-shirt, gray Bermuda shorts and black Jesus sandals, which was the nearest thing he had to a mourning outfit. Then he took the bus to Barret Avenue and called into Lynn's Paradise Café for a breakfast burrito to-go. He shambled into the Sunshine Cabs garage at five after eleven, sucking his fingers and wiping his mouth on a crumpled napkin.

Leland was lighting another Kent Light. "Your shift started three hours ago."

"I'm sorry, Leland. I had a personal setback."

"Don't tell me. You started to eat breakfast and you found that you couldn't stop."

"As a matter of fact—" John began, and then he suddenly found that he couldn't swallow the last lump of burrito and his eyes begin to fill up with tears. Leland blew out smoke and filled in three columns of figures before he realized that something was wrong. He looked up and saw that John's shoulders were shaking with grief.

"John? What's wrong, John? What happened?"

John managed to swallow and sniff and wipe his eyes

with the back of his hand. He was tired, more than anything else. Charlie Mazurin? For Christ's sake, he had scarcely known the woman. He said, "Family bereavement. She wasn't especially close. Came as a shock, that's all."

"You want to take the rest of the day off? I could ask Larry to fill in for you."

"No, no. I'll be fine. Really."

"So long as you're sure. I don't want you to get blinded by tears on I-65 and wreck your vehicle. Think of my insurance premiums."

"You're all heart, Leland."

He climbed into the bright yellow Voyager and started the engine. In the rearview mirror he could see that his eyes were still bloodshot, but after all, he told himself, he had been up all night battling against ice-sharks and crystallized wolves, so it was hardly surprising. He was *fat*, right? And he had learned from an early age to keep his feelings to himself, especially his feelings about women, and he didn't want to start getting all emotional, not now. He was Dom Magator, the Armorer. The Night Warriors needed him to stay solid.

As John was turning west onto River Road, Leland called him on the radio and told him to pick up a party of Girl Scouts from Schnitzelburg. "And don't yell at them if they sing, okay, like you did with those Legionnaires."

"Okay, Leland, whatever."

"Yell?" he told himself. "Who needs to yell? A quiet garroting, that's all it takes."

He stopped at the next red light, indicating that he intended to turn right. But while he was waiting for the signal to change, his attention was caught by a bright yellow van parked on the opposite side of the street, with BLIZZARD WINDOWS printed on the side. A man in greasy blue overalls was opening up the back doors and reaching inside. After a moment he lugged out a large brown carpetbag, which he dropped onto the sidewalk, *clank*, as if it were cramful of tools.

It looked so much like the carpetbag that Amla Fabeya had asked him to carry to her room at the Ormsby Clinic that it gave John a crawling sensation in the palms of his hands. It was like the time he thought he had seen his dead father staring at him through the window of a 7-11.

And what had Amla Fabeya said to him? *The equipment in this bag—well, I hope you never have to find out what I designed it for. But you know where it is, if you should ever need it.*

Back then, her words had meant nothing. Me? Why should *I* need it? But of course she had known from the moment that he had introduced himself that he was a Night Warrior. And she had brought that carpetbag with her to Louisville for a very specific purpose, whatever it was. Something to do with fighting the Winterwent and the High Horse. Something to do with saving babies, and the cosmos.

"You want to give me your ETA?" said Leland.

But John had already forgotten about going to Schnitzelburg and picking up Girl Scouts, whether they were singing or silent. Instead, he switched off his intercom, swerved over three lanes of wildly honking traffic, and made his way south. Within fifteen minutes he had reached the Ormsby Clinic, turned into the parking lot and stopped his Voyager under the shade of a wide-spreading cedar tree.

He sat in his vehicle for a moment, his hand pressed over his mouth, wondering if he was going to be able to face the sight of Amla Fabeya, still breathing, but essentially dead.

"You have to stay *solid*, John," he told himself.

"Oh, sure," he replied. "Solid—solid as a rock. And where has it ever got you, may I ask, this solidity? Everybody depends on you but where is *your* share of the good life? Where for you is all the mazumah and the panting cuties?"

"Just quit feeling so sorry for yourself, will you? Life is

just as tough for everybody, and the price of lobster keeps on going up."

He heaved himself out of the Voyager, waddled up the marble steps to the clinic's revolving doors and squeezed his way through.

The girl in the glasses looked up from the reception desk. "Help you, sir?" she asked, coldly.

He held up his Sunshine Cabs badge. "Dr. Mazurin, please? She called me to collect some bag."

"Room Five, in the residential block. Go all the way along to the end of the corridor, then turn right, and it's second on your right."

"Right," he said, although he already knew where it was.

He passed through the obstetrics suite. More than a dozen parents were still waiting for news of their babies, although John could hear only one infant crying, and that was very weak.

The residential block was chilly and hushed except for the distant nagging of a vacuum cleaner. John went up to Room 5. He raised his fist to knock on the door, but then he remembered that there was no point. Amla Fabeya would never hear anybody knocking, ever again. He tried the handle and the door opened. Amla Fabeya must have left it unlocked on purpose. Maybe she had guessed that she wouldn't make it back to her sleeping body, and that her fellow Night Warriors would come looking for her personal possessions.

John stepped cautiously inside. The drapes were drawn and the room was gloomy. Amla Fabeya was lying on her back, covered with nothing but a single sheet. He approached the bed and looked down at her. She looked completely serene, as if she were dreaming of nothing at all, and of course she wasn't. In one hand she was holding a necklace made of green and gold beads, and in the other she was holding a small ivory crucifix.

John bent forward and kissed her forehead. Not only was she still breathing, she was still warm. Only the Night Warriors would ever know that her consciousness had been extinguished in the screaming blizzard of Nurse Meiner's nightmare, and that there was no hope that she would ever wake up.

"*Adios,* Amla Fabeya," said John.

He found her carpetbag in the bottom of her closet. He lifted it out as quietly as he could, but it still clanked and jingled. He went to the door, opened it, and looked along the corridor to make sure that there was nobody around. He turned back to Amla Fabeya and tried to think of one last blessing, but he couldn't, so he closed the door behind him and made his way back to the reception area. The girl in the glasses was chatting to one of the cleaners about her vacation in Mexico and didn't even see him leave.

CHAPTER FIFTEEN

Sasha was woken up by her doorknob furiously rattling and somebody calling, "Sasha! Come on, baby, I know you're in there!"

She stretched herself so extravagantly that she almost dislocated her neck. Then she opened her eyes and tried to focus. It was nearly 11:20 in the morning, according to her bedside clock, and the ceiling was dappled with sunlight. She sat up and looked around her apartment, and everything was tragically normal. Her clothes strewn over her couch. Her unwashed pots on the stove. She could hardly believe what had happened the previous night, that she had been stalking through the snow, dressed as Xanthys, the Time Curver, in helmet and boots and a belt that was jangling with keys.

"Sasha, come on, baby! It's me! I know you're in there, your landlady told me!"

Sasha climbed out of bed, went to the mirror and scrabbled her hair with both hands, so that she looked like a madwoman.

"What are you doing around here, Joe Henry? I thought you went to find yourself a replacement! Some other washed-out blonde, that's what you told me!"

"I never even went looking, babe! It's you that I've been pining for! I swear it!"

"Oh, grow up, Joe Henry! You're talking to HRH the Princess of Liars here!"

"I promise you, babe, I was all on my own last night! I was watching Frankenstein movies and smoking skunk and eating Cheetos and missing you so much it was like having my heart ripped out!"

"Sure you were." She peered at herself closely in the mirror and thought that she looked terrible. She had dark circles under her eyes, and she was wearing nothing but a grubby pink T-shirt with a faded image of Donna Duck on it, as well as some dried splatters of minestrone soup.

"Come on, babe. What if I said I was truly sorry?"

Sasha went to the door. "Why would you say you were truly sorry? Truly sorry for what?"

"Truly sorry that we didn't get it on last night. Come on, doll. You know how much I love you."

Sasha thought: I have a choice here. Either I can tell Joe Henry to go away and never come back, or else—or else I can tell Joe Henry to go away and never come back. But maybe not just yet.

She opened the door. Joe Henry was standing on the landing with a bedraggled bunch of roses that looked as if he had rescued them from a dumpster. He was tall and scrawny, with blond streaked hair that stuck up like a cockatiel's, and a thin, angular face, like a young Clint Eastwood. He was wearing his usual uniform of tan leather pants and a baggy white satin shirt, fastened with cords, and a ton of chains around his neck.

"Sasha … hey, baby, you look really great!"

"Don't tell lies. I look like shit."

"All right, I admit it, you look like shit. But you look like really fantastic shit!"

He came loping into her apartment without waiting to be invited.

"Where do you want to me to put these?" he said, holding up the roses.

"The window's open."

"Oh, come on, baby. Don't be hostile. I'm sorry about last night, but my brain was totally sautéed and I wasn't thinking in a straight line. I've come round to make it up to you. How about lunch, anyplace you like? Kunz's? Cunningham's?"

"I haven't even had breakfast yet."

"Okay, then, forget lunch. How about a hump?"

Sasha closed the door. "You know something, Joe Henry? That's the most seductive thing that any man ever said to me."

She came up so close to him that her bare feet were standing on his pointed cowboy boots. She wrapped her arms around his waist and kissed him on his pointed nose. In spite of his South End accent and his chronic unfaithfulness, he had three things going for him that really turned her on: he was as skinny as a half-starved goat, which she adored, and he could wring such emotion out of his guitar that she had to squeeze her eyes tight shut whenever she listened to him play. And he was always ready to make love to her. *Always*.

She tugged loose the string of his shirt and lifted it over his head. His shoulders were covered in tattoos of angels and devils and there were deep hollows over his collarbone. He kissed her and grinned and said, "Hey, I knew you'd forgive me. You're the forgiving kind."

"Who says I've forgiven you?" she retorted, unfastening his belt and pulling open his fly-buttons. He was hard already, and since he never wore underwear, his purple-headed penis sprang out of his pants like a greyhound springing out of its starting trap.

Sasha pushed him back onto her scrumpled-up sheets.

"The trouble with you, Joe Henry, is that you think that you can treat me like one of your rock hoes."

"Rock hoes? I don't have no rock hoes. I'm as chaste as the driven snow."

The driven snow. For a split second, Sasha's mind was filled up with the snow that had teemed across the frozen landscape of Nurse Meiner's nightmare. She could feel the wind, cutting against her like knives and salt. She could hear the wolves howling.

Joe Henry sensed her hesitation and said, "What?"

"I thought of something, that's all. Something I did last night."

"Oh, yeah? Me—all I was doing was watching Frankenstein movies and smoking skunk and eating Cheetos."

"Of course you were, Joe Henry."

Sasha climbed astride him. She curled her fingers around his penis and steered it up between her legs. Although Joe Henry was so skinny, his penis was enormous, so she had to sit down easy and slow. For all the care she took, he still touched the neck of her womb and made her jump.

She gently rode him up and down, her eyes half-closed, as if she were nearly asleep. As he always did, Joe Henry kept up a nonsensical running commentary. "Oh, baby, that is totally ludicrous. Oh, baby, you don't know how electrified this feels. You make my skin frizz, darling. You're turning my bones into rubber."

Sasha really needed this. As she rode on Joe Henry's erection, she emptied her mind of all of the stress that she was still suffering from last night's encounter with the Winterwent. She thought of Amla Fabeya and the way that she had burst apart, but she allowed that image to dissolve. She thought of the ice-shark, too, and how it had torn off Kalexikox's arm, and how she had turned back time to save him.

As her stress gradually dissipated, she felt a warm, expanding feeling between her thighs. She began to push herself down more forcefully on Joe Henry's penis, and she could hear herself panting, almost as if somebody else were panting, close behind her. Without warning, her toes curled and her fists clenched and a climax overwhelmed her, temporarily blinding her like an atom bomb in a 1950s newsreel. She quaked and quaked, and she thought that she would never stop quaking.

She lay on top of Joe Henry for a long time, not moving. Eventually, though, she heard the traffic outside her window, felt the breeze blowing across the back of her sweat-soaked T-shirt, and she opened her eyes.

"That was some coming," said Joe Henry with a grin. "Reckon it's my turn now. The second coming!"

Sasha sat up, but as she did so, she heard a screech of brakes in the street outside and somebody shouting.

"What was that?" she asked.

"Who cares? Come on, baby, I didn't come yet. I'm busting my cojones here."

But Sasha climbed off him and went over to the window.

"Hey!" said Joe Henry, holding his erection in his fist. "Don't you know that a man can suffer from all kinds of serious and potentially fatal complications if you get him all excited but he doesn't get to come?"

Sasha pushed up the window a little further and leaned out. Three or four vehicles had stopped in the street, including a metallic green SUV, and a small crowd had gathered. A golden Labrador was lying on its side in the gutter with blood trickling out of its mouth. A teenage girl was standing close by, white-faced with shock.

"Dog got run over."

"Hey, too bad. But how about coming back to bed?"

Sasha turned away from the window. "That poor dog. I can't bear to see animals hurt."

"What about poor *me*, baby? I'm hurting, too."

Sasha started to walk back toward the bed, but halfway across the carpet she stopped and looked back toward the window.

"Take your time, why don't you?" said Joe Henry.

"Take my time? Yes."

"What do you mean, 'yes'?"

"I mean taking my time—that's a really great idea."

"I don't know what the hell you're talking about, and I don't think I'm interested."

Sasha hesitated, but then she lifted her right arm and pointed her index finger at him, and frowned at him in concentration.

"What the hell are you *doing*, baby? Look at this thing! I got the water tower here, girl, and it's in urgent need of flushing out!"

But Sasha continued to frown at him, and now, very slowly, she started to rotate her index finger in a counter-clockwise direction. At first, she didn't think that anything was going to happen, and that she was simply making a fool of herself. She concentrated harder. *I want time to go backward. I am Xanthys, the Time Curver, and I want time to go backward.*

Joe Henry said something blurry and unintelligible, and she realized that he was talking in reverse.

He swung up from the bed at an impossible angle, until he was standing on his feet again. His pants were rapidly re-buttoned and his shirt jumped up from the floor and dropped itself over his head. He snatched up his bunch of roses and disappeared backward out of the door.

She heard a blurt of backward-speak and then her door-knob rattled. Then silence.

Sasha stood in the middle of the room, hardly able to believe what she had done. It fascinated her that when she turned time backward, she didn't see herself going back through her previous actions. She hadn't seen herself making love to Joe Henry backward, and she hadn't seen herself opening the door for him. Maybe Night Warriors weren't as solid as other people. Maybe they were ghosts, of a kind, living halfway between the waking world and the world of dreams, and never quite occupying either.

It was 11:20, and suddenly the doorknob rattled.

"Sasha! Come on, baby! I know you're in there!"

Sasha opened the door. It was Joe Henry, holding up the same bunch of bedraggled roses that looked as if he had rescued them from a Dumpster.

"Sasha! Hey, baby! You're looking really great!"

"Just get out of my way."

"What? What kind of a welcome home is that?"

"This isn't your home and you're certainly not welcome. Now, get out of my way!"

Joe Henry stood right in the center of the doorway so that Sasha couldn't get past him. "I'm not getting out of your way until you tell me how pleased you are to see me."

"I had a zit on my nose last Friday. About as pleased as that."

"Sasha—"

"Get out of my way, Joe Henry, this is a matter of life or death!"

"What? What the hell are you talking about?"

Sasha pushed her shoulder against him, but he still wouldn't budge.

"Get out of my way, you asshole!"

She reached down between his leather-covered thighs, grabbed hold of his testicles and squeezed them as hard as she could. Joe Henry screamed out "*Je*-sus!" and fell backward against the wall. Sasha skirted around him and hurried down the stairs.

Outside her apartment building, on Third Street, the morning was sunny and warm. She ran along the sidewalk barefoot, still wearing nothing but her Donna Duck T-shirt. One or two passersby turned and stared at her, and three teenage boys whistled and called out, "Hey, darling! How's about it?" But she didn't take any notice. She was looking for a teenage girl with a golden Labrador dog, and so far she couldn't see her.

How long had she been making love to Joe Henry before she climaxed and heard the accident outside? Five minutes? Ten minutes? How far could a girl and her dog walk in ten minutes? Had they been walking north, or south, or had they been crossing the street east to west?

Sasha was about to give up when she saw them. They were ambling toward her, on the same side of the street. The girl was talking to another girl, a little shorter and plumper than she was, wearing a red headscarf. The dog looked as if it were on a leash, but as they came nearer, Sasha could see that it was only a length of knotted string.

The girls crossed West Magnolia. Sasha wasn't sure what she was going to say to them. How do you warn somebody about something that hasn't yet happened? But then she saw the Labrador lift his head, cock up his ears and stare intently across the street, where the white oak stood. Two squirrels had jumped down from the tree and were scurrying madly along the top of the fence.

Sasha looked up Third Street. A metallic green SUV was approaching, the same vehicle that she had seen from her upstairs window. The golden Labrador was straining at his length of string, desperate to chase after the squirrels.

Sasha started to run. The two girls saw her coming toward them and stared at her in bewilderment. Sasha shouted, "His collar! *Hold his collar!*"

It was too late. The Labrador yanked at his makeshift leash and the string broke. He raced across the sidewalk toward the road. Sasha dodged between two elderly shoppers and caught him just as he reached the curb. She seized his left front leg, and then his collar, and brought him around in a circle, his claws scrabbling on the concrete. At that instant, the metallic green SUV came speeding past and disappeared down the street.

The girls came up to Sasha, shocked. "Thank you *so* much. He could have been run over! You're so quick-thinking!"

"That's okay," said Sasha, handing him back. "Sometimes—you know—you can just *tell* when something bad is going to happen."

The girl in the red headscarf stared at her curiously. "Did anybody ever tell you that you look so much like that girl in the newspaper? What was her name?"

"Oh, you mean Sasha Smith, the Tender Heart of Kentucky."

"That's her. She's not your daughter, is she?"

"No," said Sasha. "No relation. It's just a trick of the light."

Joe Henry was still waiting for her when she climbed back up to her apartment. He was sitting on the end of her bed, both hands cupped between his legs, and he was looking very pale.

"I came back to say I was sorry," he told her. "You didn't have to crush my goddam nuts like that."

"I'm sorry."

"I was hoping that maybe I could take you out to lunch or something. Anyplace you like. Kunz's, or Cunningham's."

Sasha felt deeply at ease now that Joe Henry had made love to her, and brought her to such a satisfying climax. Her back muscles were relaxed, her neck muscles had lost all of their tension and her post-traumatic stress seemed to have melted away. She came up to him and kissed him on the forehead.

"I don't think so, Joe Henry. Not lunch. Not even 'or something.' "

"Sasha, baby, listen. All I did last night was—"

"I know what you did last night, Joe Henry, but I really don't care."

"Listen, baby, my brain was sautéed. I wasn't thinking in a straight line."

"Good-bye, Joe Henry."

He stared at her. "You're not serious. Looky here—I brung you roses."

"Look at them, Joe Henry. They're all droopy."

"Well, maybe. But *I'm* sure not."

"Too bad. I'm not the one you need, babe. Go find yourself some other washed-out blonde."

Joe Henry stared at her, one eye half-closed. "You've *changed*," he accused her. "There's something different about you, but I'm damned if I can put my finger on it."

"You're right," said Sasha. "I think I found myself a purpose in life."

"And that means you don't want one last hump just to say *hasta la vista?*"

"Got it in one."

By 3:00 P.M. Perry was beginning to worry that they hadn't yet heard from Springer. Dunc seemed to have forgotten all about being Kalexikox, and was happily tearing down gypsum board in the store next door, singing "Sixteen Tons" and sending up billows of chalky dust; but Perry couldn't stop checking the old mahogany-cased clock that hung over the display cabinets at the far end of Beame's Provisions, and wondering if Springer had decided not to give them another assignment in the world of dreams.

Maybe last night's tragedy had convinced him that this particular band of Night Warriors were too inexperienced and too incompetent to be trusted with saving the cosmos.

Perry kept turning over everything that they had done wrong. They had spent far too long exploring Nurse Meiner's childhood home, and they had failed to post a guard outside. They had allowed the Winterwent to catch them by surprise. Not only that, they had failed to kill the Winterwent outright, and they still had no idea where the High Horse was or what he was planning to do.

Worst of all, Amla Fabeya had been killed, their only experienced Night Warrior, and Perry could never forgive himself for that. He kept thinking that he could have created any kind of character to rescue her—a Snow Archer, an Ice Runner, a Blizzard Beast—but he had been far too panicky.

"I'll take some of that knockwurst, too," said the henna-haired woman at the counter in front of him.

"I'm sorry?"

"I said I'll take some of the knockwurst. About a quarter of a pound, sliced medium. But watch your fingers, son. It seems to me like you're half asleep."

"I'm sorry. I stayed up kind of late last night. I was studying."

"Oh, yes? So what are you studying?"

"Graphic art. I'd like to work in the movies one day."

"The movies? You'd be better off running this business. This is a good business. I've been coming here for my sausage ever since your father took over."

"I know. But I have this fatal allergy to Swiss cheese."

He was slicing the knockwurst when John walked into the store. He was followed almost immediately by Sasha, wearing a tight sleeveless top, a very short denim skirt and wedge-heeled sandals.

John stood in the middle of the store for a moment, looking around him with a bewildered expression on his face, until Morris said, "Yes, sir? What can I get you?"

"I'm supposed to meet some people here. Perry Beame? And Duncan Beame?"

"Oh, sure," said Morris. "That's Perry, right over there, working the slicer. Dunc's out back, doing a little demolition work."

As if to emphasize his words, they heard a muffled crash from the other side of the PVC curtains, and Dunc shouting out, *"Yesss!"*

John came over and waited patiently until Perry had finished serving. Then he said, "This is your dad's store, right? Springer told us to meet you here at three-twenty."

"Don't you just adore the smell of this place?" said Sasha, closing her eyes and breathing in.

"It's amazing," John agreed. "Look at this stuff. Smoked turkey, chorizo. Why didn't you tell us you lived in heaven?"

"It kind of loses its appeal after a while," said Perry. "In fact, I only have to smell this stuff and I get nauseous."

John peered into the glass case in front of him. "Green chili lasagna," he said in a reverent whisper. "Lemon basil tortellini."

It was then that Springer came in. He looked much younger than he had yesterday, when he had been waiting for them in Nurse Meiner's bedroom, and much more androgynous. In fact it was difficult for Perry to decide if he were a man or a woman. He was wearing a natural-colored linen suit, with a loose coat and flappy white pants, and two-tone tan and white Oxfords. His hair was coppery and very shiny, combed back straight from his forehead.

"Good, you're all here," he said, strutting toward them across the boarded floor. "I was concerned that one or two of you might have lost your nerve."

"I'll go call Dunc," said Perry.

Springer nodded. "The sooner the better. We have a great deal to talk about. Tonight, you have to find out where the High Horse has been hiding himself, and hunt him down, if you possibly can."

Perry pushed his way through the plastic curtains and found Dunc jumping up and down on a piece of gypsum board.

"Demolition derby!" said Dunc, gleefully.

"Dunc—Springer's here. He wants to talk about tonight."

"Tonight?"

"We have to be Night Warriors again. You have to be Kalexikox."

Dunc stopped jumping and looked at Perry with a strange expression that Perry couldn't interpret. It was wistful, almost, as if he knew that he could never be Kalexikox in the waking world.

Perry put his arm around him. "Come on, dude. How about you take off those dusty old overalls and come and talk strategy."

"And what if I don't want to?"

"You know you want to. You're not going to let me down, are you? You're not going to leave me stuck in somebody's nightmare, with Winterwents and High Horses coming after me?"

Dunc unbuttoned his overalls and stepped out of them. Underneath he was wearing a brown striped shirt and baggy brown shorts. These were his favorite clothes, and George Beame had been obliged to wash them so often that they had faded to a light milk chocolate color.

Perry led the way back into the store. Springer was talking to John about Dom Magator's weaponry, while Sasha was talking to Morris about strawberry fondants.

"Do you want to go someplace private?" asked Perry. "My father's not here right now ... we could use his office."

"I don't think we need to be any more private than this," said Springer, looking at Morris.

"What do you mean?"

"The reason I convened today's meeting here in your father's store is because Morris and May both know who you are, and what you are fighting for, and after last night's debacle I think you could use their help."

"Morris?" said Perry. "May?"

Morris, who was usually so sour, gave Perry a crinkly, avuncular smile. "Sorry if it comes as a surprise, son. I've known that you came from Night Warrior stock ever since I first started working here, and you were no more than a boy of three and a half years old. The Zaggaline, that's what you were born to be, and that's what you are today."

"But even my dad doesn't know."

Springer explained, "Morris comes from a very long and respected line of Night Warriors, going right back to the War of Independence, and probably before. He's Jek Rekanter, the Night Map Maker. He used to draw campaign maps of people's dreams, so that Night Warriors would be able to work out plans of attack."

"Retired, though, these nights," Morris told them. "Haven't gone through a portal in thirty-five years. Can't say I miss it, neither."

"And May?" said Perry.

May couldn't help grinning at him. "Raquasthena, that's me. Morris saw me one night at Union Station, jobless and pretty much penniless, but he recognized me as a Night Warrior right away, before even *I* knew it. I'm the Dream Wrangler. I can tame just about any animal that anybody ever dreamed about, ever. Dogs, cats, crocodiles, coyotes. You only have to put a name to them, and I can have them jumping through hoops."

"Why didn't you say anything to me before?" asked Perry.

"There was no necessity, was there?" said May. "So long as the world of dreams was peaceful and quiet, you didn't need to know who I was, and you didn't need to know who *you* was, either. If the Winterwent and the High Horse hadn't come looking for babies' dreams, you could have lived your whole life without even realizing that you was a Night Warrior. Many people do. They go their whole lives and Springer never calls on them, and they go to their graves without ever understanding what they might have been."

Springer said, "Raquasthena will accompany you when you pass through the portal tonight. Not only to make up your numbers, now that we have lost Amla Fabeya, but because you will need her. You will be hunting down the High Horse, and you will require a Night Warrior who can handle livestock. And when I say livestock, I mean any kind of beast that you can imagine, and a few that you wouldn't dare to."

"Is our mapmaker coming with us?" asked John.

"Jek Rekanter? He's staying here. But he will prepare you a map, based on the algorithms of the dreamer we choose, and that should give us a good idea of where you can start looking for the High Horse."

Sasha said, "What about the Winterwent? He's going to be looking for us, isn't he?"

"Too damn right," John agreed. "I don't know if I managed to bazook him last night, but he's going to be pretty damn mad at us, don't you think, even if I missed?"

Springer raised one hand, as if he were pledging an oath. "I very much doubt if the Winterwent is too concerned with seeking his revenge on you. He wants to destroy the fabric of the universe, after all, and compared with an ambition like that, I don't believe that getting equal with a few stray Night Warriors will be occupying his thoughts too much."

"Oh, *excusez-moi*. Sorry if I overestimated our importance."

"No, no," said Springer. "Don't think for a moment that I am belittling you. You are capable of doing great things. But it will do you no harm if the Winterwent believes that you are no serious threat."

"So what's the plan?" John asked him.

Springer waited until May had finished serving a young woman potato salad. Then he said, "Today I have been thinking very deeply about last night's mission. When Amla Fabeya hypnotized those babies at the Ormsby Clinic, I am sure that what she discovered was right: the Winterwent and the High Horse are trying to penetrate the babies' subconscious minds through their mothers' dreams. For some reason they found that if they tried to enter the infants' subconscious minds *after* they were born they were unable to gain access to the knowledge that they so desperately seek.

All they did was damage or destroy the babies' ability to dream, which is why so many of them are dying. So now they are trying to do it while the babies are still in the womb.

"Of course their mothers will do everything they can to protect their babies, and to keep the Winterwent at bay. But the Winterwent is very calculating, and he has no illusions about how terrifying he looks. I believe that *you* were on the right track, too, Dom Magator, about the way in which he is trying to deceive those mothers into sharing their dreams with him.

"The reason he froze Nurse Meiner's home was to prevent it from melting away when she woke up, as any building in any dream will always do, whether you are dreaming about single houses or whole cities. He froze her home, and he has kept it frozen, as Dom Magator suggested, to preserve it."

"But why would he want to do that?" said Sasha. "The house was covered in ice, yes, but you could tell that Nurse Meiner was very happy when she lived there, and her family was, too."

"*Exactly*," said Springer. "The Winterwent understands that he is far too cold, and far too frightening, and that expectant mothers will do everything they can to protect their babies whenever they feel him approach. So my guess is that he has been trawling the night for pleasant memories. I believe that he has been preserving each of those memories by freezing them. He has probably frozen other houses, too, from other people's dreams; and gardens, and beaches. Any place where people have been cheerful and felt that they were welcome. All he has to do now is allow them to thaw and make sure that the sun appears to be shining, and he has the happiest place that anybody ever dreamed of—"

"And because the mothers have been feeling so anxious, and so stressed …" said Sasha.

"That's right. They'll be tempted to stroll right into it. We all like to share happy memories, don't we?"

"And then?" asked Perry.

"I'm not exactly sure. But I suspect that the High Horse and his beasts will be able to circle around them, so that they're trapped."

Dunc nodded and kept on nodding. "I get it. Once they're in *his* dream, he'll be able to enter their sleeping minds, and then the minds of their unborn babies, and then he'll have what he and the High Horse have been looking for. The secret of all creation."

"And *that*," said John, "that will be good night, Vienna."

When Perry and Dunc arrived home that evening, they were disconcerted to find that Janie was still there, sitting cross-legged on the couch eating popcorn and watching *The Simpsons*.

"Hey, I thought dad was driving you down to Bowling Green."

"They just said on the news that seventeen more babies have died," she told him.

"Yeah, we heard it on the radio. Pretty scary, huh? But you're going tonight, aren't you?"

"Dad couldn't do it. I was all packed and everything but he had to go downtown to talk to his bank."

"But you *are* going tonight?"

"I don't know. I don't think so. Dad said we'll probably have to leave it until tomorrow morning."

"Shit," said Perry. "Dunc and me, we *told* him you had to go today."

"We *told* him," Dunc echoed. "We *told* him you had to go today."

"What's the big rush? You guys aren't tired of having me around already, are you? The baby isn't due for at least a couple more days."

"Listen, the baby could be in danger right now, before it's actually born."

"How do you know that?"

"I was talking to these people from the hospital who have inside information."

"Oh, come on, Perry, you're scaring me."

"You should be. You should be scared. We should *all* be scared."

CHAPTER SIXTEEN

George Beame said, "I don't see how one more day is going to make any difference."

"Dad, believe us. I was talking to these people from the hospital and they have this theory that the babies start to get sick while they're still in the womb."

"Come on, Perry, let's be realistic here. How is Janie's baby going to get sick? She hasn't left the house all day, and she hasn't had a single visitor."

"Dad—these people from the hospital think this isn't your normal kind of disease. It's, like, airborne."

"I haven't heard anything about that on the news."

"That's because they're keeping it secret, so that people won't panic."

George took out a crumpled Kleenex and blew his nose. "Exactly who are they, these people from the hospital?"

"They're doctors. Gynecologists."

"Gynecologists came into the store and told you all of this stuff, even though they're trying to keep it secret to stop people from panicking?"

"That's correct."

"So what did they buy, these gynecologists?"

"Nine-grain rolls," said Perry.

"Fruity muffins," said Dunc, simultaneously.

"Both," said Perry. "Nine-grain rolls *and* fruity muffins."

George asked, "How are you feeling, Janie?"

"Good," said Janie. "And baby's kicking like Lenny Lyles."

George turned back to Perry and Dunc. "I don't understand what your agenda is, you boys, but I've had a long and tiring day and I'm not really inclined to drive a hundred miles to Bowling Green because of what some imaginary gynecologists might have told you."

For a split second, Perry was tempted to tell his father that he was The Zaggaline, one of the Night Warriors, and that Dunc was Kalexikox, another Night Warrior, and that Janie's unborn baby was in critical danger from the Winterwent and the High Horse, and that if he didn't take Janie to Bowling Green before nightfall, Janie's baby's dreams could be stolen and the whole of God's creation could be ripped apart from seam to seam.

Dunc blurted out, "Dad, we really know what we're talking about here, believe me. Perry and me, we're not the people that you think we are. Well, we *are* who you think we are, but we're somebody else, too."

"What?" said George. He turned to Perry, bewildered, as if Dunc had been talking in Klingon.

"Forget it, Dad," Perry told him. "Dunc's kind of stressed out, that's all. It's my fault. I've been making him do too much work in the store."

George approached them and laid a hand on each of their shoulders. "Janie's here because I invited her here, because I wanted to make amends and bring our family back together again. The least you two can do is to make her feel welcome, and not cook up excuses to get rid of her at the first possible moment."

"Dad," said Perry, "we love having Janie here. It's cool. But we're not making this up, I promise you."

"Leave it, Perry," George ordered him. "We can talk about this tomorrow, when I come back from Bowling Green."

If Bowling Green still exists in the morning, thought Perry. If *anything* still exists.

On his way home, John stopped off at Jay's Cafeteria on Muhammad Ali Boulevard and bought himself a double portion of fried chicken and barbecued rib tips. Back in his room, sitting on the bed, he managed to finish the whole bucketful, leaving only well-gnawed bones, but he had to confess to himself that he hadn't felt at all hungry. He was too worried about what he would have to do tonight as Dom Magator, and whether any more Night Warriors would have to die, including himself.

He took a very long shower, even though the water was running cold. These days, when his hair was wet, he could see an ever-widening bald patch on top of his head, which he found deeply depressing. *You might be able to stop the Winterwent, my friend, but you can't stop your follicles from betraying your age.* He stepped out of the shower to discover that he had forgotten his towel, so he had to wobble back across the landing with his T-shirt wrapped around his middle like a loincloth.

He had just reached the door of his room when Nadine came out, dressed in tight white Spandex matador pants and high stiletto heels. "Hey John!" she said. "You feeling better now?"

"Better than what, Nadine?"

"Yesterday evening you told me you was feeling kind of logie. That's why you had to hit the sack so early."

"Oh, that's right! Twenty-four hour virus, that was all! I'm feeling much better now, thanks for inquiring. Hundred and fifty-eight percent."

Nadine maneuvered her way around him and started to strut down the stairs.

"By the way," she said. "Nice ass."

John opened the door of his room, slammed it behind him and flung his wet T-shirt onto the floor. Shit, shit, *shit!* He could almost believe that Nadine had rigged up a red warning light in her room so that she always knew when he was coming out of the bathroom. He lay back on his bed and banged his head against the pillow, so that even more duck feathers came flying out and stuck to his scalp like a sad attempt at a home-made toupee.

"You're a dumb-ass *fool*, John, you know that? What makes you think that Nadine would consider you as a potential partner for one nanosecond, even if you were dressed up like Andre Benjamin?"

"Who are you calling a dumb-ass fool? Don't be such a defeatist. Any woman worth having can see through a man's outward appearance. Underneath your modest apparel, she can tell that you're a love machine."

"Maybe she can, but your apparel wasn't exactly modest, was it, with your bare posterior protuberating halfway across the landing? Surprised the highway authority didn't put up a detour sign."

Less than fifty minutes later, however, John was asleep, and softly blowing feathers off his pillow and onto the floor. It wasn't surprising that he had managed to drop off so quickly; he had slept for only four hours in the past twenty-four, and even though he was overweight and badly out of condition, he had battled his way through blizzards and waist-deep snowdrifts as furiously as the rest of the Night Warriors.

It was just past 11:00 P.M. when his dream self opened his eyes. He yawned and snorted and rolled onto his back and then he heaved himself up into a sitting position. His physical self continued to snore softly and blow feathers with every snore, and he promised himself that if he returned from tonight's mission in one piece, he would buy himself a new pillow.

That's if he still had the nerve to go on tonight's mission. He felt as if he had been pummeled all over by boxing kangaroos, and he didn't seem to have any reserves of energy left at all. Not only that, he was beginning to wonder if there were really any point in them trying to stop the Winterwent and the High Horse. So the universe was going to be ripped apart? Maybe it was high time that somebody ripped it apart, with all its wars and its diseases and its federal and local taxes. It wouldn't matter to any of them, would it, if they were dead?

He went to the window, scratching himself. He could see red and yellow lights glittering on the river, and he suddenly felt nostalgic for Baton Rouge. Maybe the universe *was* worth saving, if it meant that he could see his old friends again, and sit in the Jones Creek Café over a large slice of Mississipi mud pie and a cappuccino with three spoonfuls of demerara sugar.

Man, those had been the days. Days of good companionship and high calories when none of them gave a rat's ass for anything.

He stood there a few minutes longer, then he closed his eyes and gradually rose from the floor. He was Dom Magator. He had a duty to perform, even if it was nothing more than saving his own happy memories. He was a Night Warrior, armed and armored.

Before his head had touched the ceiling, however, he stopped rising upward and opened his eyes, staying where he was, hovering. *What about Amla Fabeya's carpetbag?* It must have some critical importance in their fight against the Winterwent and the High Horse, or else Amla Fabeya wouldn't have bothered to drag it all the way to Louisville.

He allowed himself to sink slowly back down to the floor. He opened his closet and lifted the bag onto the bed. It was very clanky and very heavy, and he wasn't sure if he would be able to fly with it, but he had a strong feeling that he was supposed to take it with him if he could.

He took off a second time. The weight of the bag unbalanced him, and he had to make an extra effort to rise as high as the ceiling. Eventually, however, he managed it, and tugged the bag through the plasterboard with a soft, dry *choosh*. Although the bag felt so heavy, it had no more physical substance than he did, and he was able to lift it through the attic space, where the water tanks dripped and rumbled, and out through the roof.

Gradually, like an overladen jet plane, he climbed into the wind, and soon he was flying five hundred feet over the sparkling lights of downtown Louisville. But he didn't feel elated the way he had the previous night. Instead, he felt resigned to whatever fate the night was going to bring him; almost mournful.

After a few minutes, he caught sight of a white fluttering shape approaching him from the direction of Old Louisville, like a kite. It was Sasha, flying much higher than him. He swung heavily to starboard and gained some more altitude, and after two or three minutes he managed to catch up with her. Together they veered southeastward toward the Highland District.

"I almost chickened out!" Sasha shouted.

"You and me both!" John yelled back. "Suddenly this isn't fun anymore!"

"You mean you're scared, too?"

"Scared? I'm shitless!"

Sasha waved toward the carpetbag. "What's that? Don't tell me you've brought a change of clothes?"

John flew closer, so close that they were almost nudging. "Amla Fabeya had it with her when she first arrived. I don't have any idea what it's in it. For some reason she seemed to think that we might need it."

"Looks heavy."

"Heavy? Damn thing weighs nearly as much as I do."

Sasha pointed down through the trees. "Hey, look! That's Ray Avenue, isn't it? We're almost there already."

Below them and slightly off to their right they could

see the pale orange shingles of the Beame's house, where they had all agreed to rendezvous. Perry had left a flashlight shining on his windowsill so that the Night Warriors wouldn't mistakenly descend through the wrong bedroom ceiling—his father's, or Janie's.

They sank through the roof into Perry's room, and the other Night Warriors were all there to greet them. Perry and Dunc were sitting on the edge of Perry's bed, where Perry's physical self lay sleeping, pale-faced, with his hair tousled. Morris was seated at Perry's desk, wearing an old brown cardigan with a shawl collar, like Starsky used to wear in *Starsky and Hutch*. May was leaning over him, in a shocking pink tracksuit, watching him work. On his left hand, Morris had a giant-sized metal gauntlet with complicated knuckle-joints and lights that shone from the fingertips. He was systematically passing it from side to side over the surface of the desk, like a scanner, and as he did so, he was creating a three-dimensional map.

Springer was standing in the corner, next to the door. Tonight, he looked fretful and even more feminine than he had this afternoon. His hair was combed back, and his lips and his fingernails were painted gold.

"Dom Magator! Xanthys! I was beginning to worry!" Even his voice was higher than usual.

"You didn't think we were going to come?" asked Dom Magator.

"Let's just say that I'm very sensitive to people's reluctance."

"Well, I *was* a little reluctant, I admit it," said Dom Magator. "But I came anyhow."

Springer said, "I didn't think for one moment that you wouldn't. This could be the most critical night in the history of all creation." He hesitated, and then he said, "What's that you're carrying?"

Dom Magator lifted up the carpetbag and gave it a vigorous shake. "I'm not too sure, to tell you the truth. Some junk that Amla Fabeya brought with her."

He dropped the bag down on the floor. Springer immediately stalked across the bedroom and opened it. Inside lay a tangle of strange metal shapes, about twenty of them. Most of them were fitted with hooks, and several had protruding bars and springs.

"Did Amla Fabeya tell you what these were?"

"She said they were specially designed. But she also said that it would be better if I never had to find out what they were designed for."

Springer lifted up one of the pieces of metal and turned it this way and that. It was some kind of mechanical pincer, fashioned out of titanium and chrome. "Amla Fabeya was the Ascender, so I think it would be logical for us to assume that this is climbing equipment."

Kalexikox stood up and examined it, too. Then he picked up a second piece and clicked the two of them together, so that they formed two claws, one above the other. "I think you're right. It's climbing equipment, but it's highly specialized. It looks to me as if it's been designed to climb up one surface and one surface only—and a very difficult surface at that. Look—all of these various segments are designed to lock together, and then quickly come apart again. See these springs and these catches? You don't usually get moving parts like this with any normal climbing gear."

"So, any idea what Amla Fabeya was thinking of climbing?"

Kalexikox picked up another piece of metal, and then another, and tried to fit them together, too. In the end, however, he gave up and dropped them back in the bag. "I can't even begin to guess. But whatever it was, I'll bet money that it wouldn't stay still while she climbed it, which is why most of this equipment is so highly articulated."

"What kind of a mountain doesn't stay still while you climb it?" asked Dom Magator.

"We are talking about the world of dreams," Springer reminded him. "In a dream, a mountain could instantly turn into water, or sand, or a huge heap of rats."

Dom Magator looked at the equipment dubiously. "Do you think we should take it along with us?" asked Dom Magator.

"I don't know," said Springer. "Maybe you should take it through the portal, but conceal it close by, so that you don't have to carry it everywhere. You don't want to be encumbered, do you? You're hunting down the High Horse tonight, and you'll have to be very fast on your feet."

Over at Perry's desk, Jek Rekanter shook his head and said, "Shoot! This is a darn complicated dream! I'm not sure that I can make heads or tails of this."

Springer went across to see what he was doing, and the rest of the Night Warriors gathered around, too. It looked to The Zaggaline as if Jek Rekanter had almost finished his map. It was molded out of shiny shadows and tiny sparkling lights, and it showed hills and mountains and trees and cities. It even had moving trains and miniature cars, hundreds of them, pouring their way along the highways like red and white fireflies.

Springer explained, "This is the dream in which I think that the Winterwent and the High Horse have set up their trap. Just after nine o'clock, I sensed the Winterwent's coldness moving across the city and I followed him to this particular dream. He has left the dream now, and I can no longer feel him, but he won't be very far away. I have not yet felt the High Horse, but I will smell him when he comes closer. I can always smell the High Horse. He reeks of spoiling meat and rotten blood."

"Me, I always *hear* him first," said Raquasthena, wrinkling up her nose. "He wears living animals, and they're always screaming in pain. He does it partly to scare off his enemies, but he also does it because he enjoys it so much."

"Sounds like something of a sadist, then," said Xanthys.

"Sadist? You have no conception. To the High Horse, the agony of other living creatures … it's like *oxygen*. It's his food and drink."

"So whose dream is this?" asked The Zaggaline, nodding toward the miniature landscape on his desk.

"Dr. Steven Beltzer. He's one of the most respected obstetricians at the fetal diagnostic center at Norton Audubon Hospital. Currently, he is supervising the progress of seventeen pregnant women and investigating the deaths of eleven newborn babies. They have a sleep disorder center at Norton Audubon and he is liaising with them, too. So he is an obvious choice for the Winterwent and the High Horse to get close to expectant mothers."

"And this is a map of what Dr. Beltzer's dreaming?" asked Kalexikox.

"Correct," said Jek Rekanter. "The problem is, this map is really misbehaving itself. Some of the places you see here, like this small farming community down here on the left, they're pretty much holding steady. But most of the other places, they make no sense, or else they keep altering themselves from one darn thing into another."

The Zaggaline studied the map more closely. Jek Rekanter was right: tiny as it might have been, the entire landscape was ceaselessly changing. Small towns disappeared and reappeared. Hills rose and immediately sank. Waterfalls gushed down narrow creek beds and then dried up. Roads changed direction, bridges were constructed and then instantly dismantled. Every place on the map was clearly named, as were schools and hospitals and cemeteries, but their names faded and changed just as quickly as they did.

"How the hell are we going to find our way with a map like this?" asked Dom Magator. "One second we'll be walking through a wheat field, and the next second we'll be up to our necks in a lake."

"Wait a minute," Kalexikox interrupted. "This Dr. Beltzer ... he can't be a stupid man, can he? I mean, he wouldn't be suffering from any kind of mental disorder?"

"Of course not," said Springer. "He's one of the most respected young obstetricians in Kentucky."

"So what we're seeing on this map, all of this apparent chaos, all of this jigging and shifting and moving about, that's not because he's psychologically unstable?"

"Not all. He's a very brilliant man."

"Then I think this dream is some kind of intellectual exercise," said Kalexikox.

The Zaggaline raised one eyebrow. He still found it difficult to come to terms with Dunc talking to him so coherently. His daytime self would probably be saying, "Look at all those teentsy-weentsy women on that map, Perry. Bet they got teentsy-weentsy bongaroobies!"

Sasha said, "I don't understand what you're saying. What kind of intellectual exercise?"

"A puzzle, maybe. Jek—can you enlarge this area here?"

Using his illuminated gauntlet, Jek lifted a small cube-shaped section out of the map and enlarged it twenty times bigger. It showed an undulating field full of pale blue flowers.

Kalexikox said, "About a minute ago, I saw a building standing here, like the Kentucky state capitol, with about thirty flags flying in front of it."

"Sure, I saw it, too," Jek agreed. "But now it's gone. There's nothing here but this field."

"Exactly," said Kalexikox. "A field full of blue irises, to be more specific. *Iris virginica,* the Southern iris. But another name for 'iris' is 'flag.' So what we have on this map is a location with a double meaning. A place where flags are flown and a place where flags are grown."

"I hate to say this," The Zaggaline told him, "but I think you've seriously lost it."

"No, look," Kalexikox persisted. "Here at the top end of the map, there was Back Bay Beach, in Virginia. Now that's gone, and what's standing here in its place? The Brigham Isolation Hospital for infectious diseases. A beach is a seaside and 'disease' is an anagram of 'seaside.' "

"I can't even pretend to know what you're talking about, dude."

"I'm sure I'm right. I'm convinced of it. Every place you see on this map is the answer to a cryptic crossword clue. It's like *Wheel of Fortune*, where they give you the answer and you have to work out the question. *That's* how we're going to find our way through this dream and find out where the Winterwent and the High Horse have set up their ambush."

Rasquathena said, "Are you absolutely positive about this, Kalexikox? Because if you're wrong, and the High Horse gets us ... believe me, you'll pray that he rips off your head before he rips off any other part of you."

Kalexikox was examining the night map even more intently. "Here—here's another one. Can you bring this section up? Look—here's a boat, tied up at a pier, but the boat is totally black and the pier is totally black and even the water in the lake is totally black. The answer is 'jetty'—which means 'the same color as jet' as well as 'pier.' "

"Even supposing you're right," said Dom Magator, "how the hell is the word 'jetty' going to help us locate the High Horse?"

"Because it's part of a cryptic crossword, and the cryptic crossword will help us to find our way around Dr. Beltzer's dream. He's obviously a cryptic crossword enthusiast, and that's what his brain does when he's asleep. It works through his day's problems by creating clues, puns, anagrams and *double entendres*. To him, it's easy. It's the way he makes sense of everything."

"That's all very well," said Raquasthena. "But how are *we* going to know what's real and what isn't?"

"Strictly speaking, none of it's real," said Kalexikox. "But that's why you have a Knowledge Gunner with you, i.e., me. I can solve the clues for you and tell you which is a clue and which is an answer, how the answers fit together and what they mean once they have."

The Zaggaline shrugged and said, "He's the man. No question about it."

Springer was becoming increasingly edgy. "Does this mean that you're ready to go now? Time is pressing, believe me. It's eleven fifty-two, and the High Horse could easily have trapped those expectant mothers by now."

"I guess we're about as ready as we're ever going to be," said Dom Magator. "Kalexikox ... how about you go through the portal first? That'll give you the chance to check out where the hell we are and what the hell we're going to do next. The Zaggaline—you go through right after him, and sharpish, in case he needs some firepower, or some of your imaginary friends to help him out. I'll go through next, and Raquasthena and Xanthys can follow me."

"Oh, I see," said Xanthys. "We're the two little women, tripping along three steps behind you. Chauvinistic, or what?"

Dom Magator turned to her. "Honeybee, you want to go first? You're more than welcome. It's just that I was brought up in Baton Rouge, where women are always protected like fine porcelain."

"Oh, I do declare, Mr. Magator, you are a caution!"

Springer was so anxious that he was biting his thumbnail. "Let's hurry, people, shall we, before we're too late?" He lifted his arms and drew his dazzling halo in the air.

"Come on," said Dom Magator. "Springer's right ... we should be hustling here."

The Zaggaline knelt in front of Springer so that he could be invested with his Night Warriors armor. This time, Springer used the same incantation that he had used for Amla Fabeya. "Ashapola, I ask you to recognize this your fearless and devoted servant and this your truly faithful warrior. Give him the power to continue his struggle against the tides of darkness and chaos, and protect him against evil and the fear of evil."

The halo sank to the floor and The Zaggaline stood up in his huge helmet and his glossy scarlet suit with its golden scroll work.

Kalexikox was next, followed by Dom Magator and Xanthys. Once they were fully armored, they waited with curiosity to see how Raquasthena would appear. The golden halo sank around her, and when she stood up, she was wearing an expressionless mask of polished black metal, like a character in a classical Greek play, and a flexible black suit that was completely covered with tiny metal hooks, like a vicious version of Velcro. Her breasts were protected by two black metal disks with spikes on them, and she also wore a triangular black metal plate between her legs, with an even longer spike jutting out of it, like an artificial phallus. Around her waist was coiled a jointed black metal whip with a forked tongue on the end, like a cobra's, and diagonally across her back she carried a short trident with barbed prongs.

Dom Magator nodded his head toward the spike between her legs. "Doesn't matter how good we do tonight," he said. "Stop me if I rush up to you and try to give you a hug."

Jek Rekanter held his gauntlet over the map of Dr. Beltzer's dream, his fingers spread wide. He pressed a switch on his wrist and the map shrank into a chrome-plated button in the palm of his hand. He detached the button and passed it to Kalexikox, who snapped it into the neck-ring around his helmet. Now, whenever he wanted to, Kalexikox would be able to bring up a three-dimensional holographic display of the map, right in front of his face.

"And *now* we're ready?" said Springer, tetchily. Without waiting for an answer he rose from the floor and vanished through the ceiling.

"I get the feeling he's kind of anxious for us to get going," said The Zaggaline. He rose up, too, immediately followed by Kalexikox and Xanthys. Dom Magator picked up Amla Fabeya's bag and held out his free hand to Raquasthena. "Shall we, my dear?" he said, with exaggerated courtesy.

They rose through the ceiling and into the air.

Silently, the Night Warriors followed the blackness of Springer's wake southwestward across the city sky, in the direction of the airport. The night was still very humid, and they could hear distant thunder, like an omen of serious trouble. After less than five minutes they were flying over the redbrick hospital complex at One Audubon Plaza. They circled around the parking lot, and then Springer beckoned them to follow him downward to the lower level. Like the spirits in *Fantasia*, they streamed through the outside wall, across a brightly lit corridor and then through another wall, into the rooms where the duty doctors slept.

Dr. Beltzer was lying in a plain lavender-painted room with a large print of Churchill Downs racecourse hanging on the wall. His clothes were crumpled up on a chair, and a half-eaten slice of pizza was congealing in a grease-spotted box. As they gathered around his bed, the Night Warriors could see that Dr. Beltzer was dreaming, because his pupils were darting wildly from side to side underneath his eyelids, and his half-open hand kept twitching on the pillow. He was youngish for a senior consultant—no more than thirty-seven or thirty-eight—snub-nosed, with scruffy blond hair and three days of stubble. He looked to Xanthys like Brad Pitt's younger brother.

Kalexikox had guessed right about Dr. Beltzer's addiction to cryptic crosswords: a folded newspaper with a half-finished puzzle lay on the floor beside the bed, next to his duty roster.

Springer said, "The Winterwent visited Dr. Beltzer's dream about an hour ago, and I am reasonably sure that he has set up a trap in it. He has gone now, but one location in Dr. Beltzer's dream is still detectably colder than anyplace else."

"In that case," said Dom Magator, "let's go there and blow the bastards to smithereens. Just tell us where it's at."

"In the far northeast corner of Jek Rekanter's map, about five kilometers due north from the seaside—or the isolation hospital, whichever definition applies when you eventually arrive there. But I would caution you not to rush there directly. The High Horse will undoubtedly be watching and waiting, and he will set his creatures on you as soon as you step out of the portal."

"Okay," said Kalexikox "Let's try some alternative locations." He flicked the switch at the side of his helmet, and instantly an image of a storm-swept lake appeared in the air in front of his face. The water was black and the boats were dancing a sinister fandango at their moorings. "Mmh, maybe not." He flicked the switch again and a range of sunlit mountains appeared. "How about this?" he suggested. "It's only about three clicks to the west of the seaside, and the mountains should keep us well shielded from view."

"Looks good to me," said Dom Magator. "Let's get it on."

"Before you go ..." Springer interrupted. He picked up Dr. Beltzer's duty roster and pointed to shifts that had been underlined with magic marker. "Dr. Beltzer will have an alarm call at three-twenty tomorrow morning, sharp. Whatever you do, you have to do it before then."

"We'll be in and out like gurr-eased lightning," Dom Magator promised him. He raised his arms, adjusted his levers, and drew a bright blue hexagon of light next to Dr. Beltzer's bed. The portal spat and sizzled with electrical energy, and Dr. Beltzer stirred and said something indistinct, but he didn't open his eyes.

"Anyone for dreamland?" asked Dom Magator.

Kalexikox stepped through the portal first, with The Zaggaline close behind him. Dom Magator followed, heaving the carpetbag with him.

He hadn't even had time to drop the carpetbag on the ground, however, before he realized that something was badly wrong. There was no sunshine and the mountains had disappeared. Kalexikox and The Zaggaline were both lying flat on their stomachs on a scrubby plain, under a sky that was overcast with dull purplish clouds.

"Down!" shouted Kalexikox; and, as he did so, a bullet sang past Dom Magator's helmet, and then another. He threw down the carpetbag and dropped to the ground.

"What in hell's name is happening here?" he demanded. "Who the hell's shooting at us?"

CHAPTER SEVENTEEN

The Zaggaline didn't answer. Panting with effort, he rolled over and over until he reached the portal. He had only just reached it when Xanthys stepped through, and he reached up and grabbed her, hurling her down to the ground.

"What are you *doing,* asshole?" she protested, but when she tried to raise her head, three or four bullets came flying past her shoulder, and then another three.

"Somebody's using us for target practice," said The Zaggaline. "Keep your head down, unless you want to lose whatever brains you got left."

At that moment, Raquasthena came through the portal. The Zaggaline seized her ankles, too, toppling her over, but immediately he flapped his hands in agony. The tiny metal hooks on her armor had ripped his fingers, and he was flinging droplets of blood in every direction.

"Jesus, you're more dangerous to *us* than anybody else!" he protested.

"Kalexikox!" shouted Dom Magator. "What's all this shooting about?"

Kalexikox called back, "It's a range, I think!"

"I thought you said it was going to be mountains!"

"I did, but the definition must have changed while we were going through the portal. From *mountain* range to *shooting* range!"

"Oh, brilliant! What the platinum-plated hell are we going to do now?"

"I don't know. I don't have any way of telling how long this definition of 'range' is going to last!"

Dom Magator looked up to see if he could make out who was firing at them. Instantly, another fusillade of bullets flew overhead, and this time one of them struck a glancing blow to the top of his helmet—slamming his head backward with a hefty neck-wrenching jolt.

He shook himself like a wet dog. "Christ almighty!" he protested. "What the hell are they using? Elephant guns?"

"No," Kalexikox corrected him. "From the sound of them, they're using weapons much more lethal than that— Barrett XM one-oh-nine sniper rifles with twenty millimeter HEDP ammunition. These bullets can penetrate forty millimeters of armor plating from five hundred meters away. You're very fortunate that you were hit at such an oblique angle."

"Oh, I'm very fortunate, am I? I'd sure hate for my luck to run out."

The Zaggaline raised his head, too, although he did it much more cautiously than Dom Magator, bobbing down whenever he saw anything move. About two hundred yards away he could make out seven or eight figures lying flat on their bellies among the scrub. Each of them was armed with a long-barreled rifle supported on a bipod. Their heads were wound around with long black scarves, with only their eyes showing, and they had long scarlet ribbons tied around their foreheads. They were all dressed in black and khaki combat fatigues, except for one of them, who was wearing dusty red. A tattered black banner with scarlet lettering was flying on a pole behind them, but The Zaggaline didn't have time to read it before the men suddenly started shooting again.

He ducked his head down. "I'd say they were terrorists," he told Dom Magator. "I mean, they *look* like terrorists."

Kalexikox nodded, as much as he could nod with his helmet pressed against the ground. "It seems likely that Dr. Beltzer has conceptualized the 'rifle range' clue in his cryptic crossword as an al Qaeda training camp, or some place like that."

Dom Magator checked his orange-lit chronometer. "Whoever they are, we can't afford to be pinned down here for very much longer. Zagga—how about you conceptualize some kind of crack antiterrorist dude to go kick their highly irritating rear ends? You know … like Jean-Claude Van What's-his-face or Steven Seagal?"

"Sure … good idea … I'll give it a try." The Zaggaline turned over onto his side and swung down two lenses from the side of his helmet. He tried three or four experimental outlines—a High-Speed Samurai, a Bulletproof Commando, and even a Mechanical Camel—but none of them gave him the tactical flexibility he was looking for. He needed a *team*—an antiterrorist squad that could attack the snipers from several different directions at once. The technical problem was that his lens equipment could produce only one character at a time.

"How about conjoined twins?" suggested Kalexikox.

"No … too easy a target. Hit one and you hit them both." But the idea of twins suddenly gave him an inspiration. Twins were a single egg, weren't they, which had divided in the womb? Split in half, like an amoeba. "Hey—how about the Amoebic Avenger … one guy who can instantly split into two more guys, and then four more guys, and then eight more guys? Amoebas are made of nothing but protoplasm, so bullets should whiz straight through him without hurting him."

"One guy who can turn into eight guys?" said Raquas-thena. "That sounds *sweet*. When this is all over, you can make one specially for me."

The Zaggaline flicked on the dozens of multicolored lights that illuminated his lenses. Almost immediately there was a vicious crackling of gunfire, and scores of bullets shrieked over their heads. One came so close that Xanthys was showered in grit.

Frowning with concentration, The Zaggaline used his limning lens to create the outline of a huge, jellyish man-creature—jellyish, because he had no skeleton. In the real world, a man with no skeleton would find it physically impossible to move, even if he wasn't suffocated by his own wallowing body mass. But this was the world of dreams, where anything was possible. The power of the human imagination ruled here, not the laws of physics.

The Zaggaline folded down three more lenses—aquamarine, amber and crimson—one after the other. He traced in the intricate details of the Avenger's veins and arteries and nervous system. Blood vessels ran down the Avenger's arms and legs like tree roots spreading in a speeded-up movie.

The Amoebic Avenger's skin was as white as a fogged-up window and semitransparent, so that The Zaggaline could dimly see his internal organs floating around inside his body. He had eight hearts, which looked like ripe crimson capsicums, all clustered together on the same vine and throbbing in sequence. He also had a crowd of bulging stomachs and eight mahogany-dark livers, and miles and miles of slippery intestines.

The Zaggaline used a crystal clear optical lens to cover the man-creature's entire forehead with sixteen eyes—all different colors—staring, blinking, rolling and turning.

"How's it going?" asked Dom Magator. "Any chance of us getting out of here by the Thanksgiving after next?"

"No, I'm done," said The Zaggaline. "The Amoebic Avenger is all ready to go on the rampage. What kind of weapons do you think we should give him? A dozen or so handguns maybe?"

"I don't know. I'm not so sure about guns. If he's going to be splitting himself up like an amoeba, we'd better give him a weapon that he can share out between himself. Or him*selves*. Or whatever."

Dom Magator awkwardly reached around behind him. From a rack beneath his bristling collection of knives, he produced a four-foot steel bar made of shining surgical steel. He tugged one end and a throwing knife appeared with a wickedly barbed tip. He tugged again and yet another appeared.

"Ten knives fitting together in a single stick," he explained. "When your guy splits himself apart, all he has to do is pull out another one and then another one, and share 'em out, so that his various selves have a knife each. And believe me, one of these knives is as deadly as a handgun. They're made of hypnotized steel, so they always hit their target smack between the eyes."

"Hypnotized steel?"

"I don't know, it's some kind of samurai thing."

"Not exactly," said Kalexikox.

"Well, of course. I should have known *you'd* know."

Kalexikox said, "In the year 794, the Buddhist monks in Kyoto found a way to hypnotize just about everything, animate or inanimate. Jugs, hats, buckets—you name it, they could hypnotize it, and make it behave exactly how they wanted it to. Hat—jump onto my head! And the hat would do it."

"You're kidding me."

"Think about it. Buddhist monks and Night Warriors have a whole lot in common. The Buddhists believe that the material world is an illusion, and that the only reality is inside of your head. Which—as we know—it is."

"Okay, then," said The Zaggaline. "Let's go for the hypnotized knives."

He lined up his various lenses and then adjusted his animation light. "Cover your eyes, guys," he warned his fellow Night Warriors. "Recommend that you keep your heads down, too." It was good advice: when he pressed the switch there was a blinding flash of light that turned the whole landscape inside out, like a photographic negative, and which immediately provoked another furious storm of bullets.

Only a few feet away, the Amoebic Avenger began to materialize. He was lying on his side, because The Zaggaline had been lying on his side when he had visualized him—a huge mass of glistening white tissue that roughly resembled a man.

"Jesus," said Dom Magator. "And I thought *I* needed to lose weight."

The Amoebic Avenger uttered a thick, asthmatic groan, and his myriad eyes looked everywhere at once, as if he were desperate to find a way out of his predicament.

"Can you hear me?" asked The Zaggaline.

"Of course he can hear you," said Kalexikox. "You gave him eight pairs of ears, didn't you?"

The Zaggaline crawled awkwardly over to the Amoebic Avenger and waved his hand in front of his sixteen eyes to make sure that he had his attention. "Listen to me, dude, this is what the story is. You're a war hero, okay, and I'm your commanding officer. I'm sending you over in that direction, got it? There are some seriously bad guys spread out on the ground over there, okay, and I need you to take them out for me, all of them. You'll recognize them when you see them because they're all wearing black scarves with red ribbons around their heads. You can take this weapon with you. This is your favorite weapon—a samurai knifestick, made up of throwing knives, and I am reliably informed by a well-known panel of experts that when you throw one of these babies, you can't miss whatever it is you're aiming for. So how about it?"

The Amoebic Avenger groaned again.

"I mean, if you don't feel *well* enough ..." said The Zaggaline. He was beginning to regret that he had created anybody so hideous. Fantasy was one thing, but suffering was another, even if this suffering wasn't *real* suffering, but only dream suffering. While he was hesitating, the terrorists fired three more shots. One high-explosive bullet blasted up a fountain of soil only inches away from Raquasthena's boot, but she didn't even flinch. The Zaggaline had to admit to himself that he was totally impressed. This was only May from the sandwich counter, but under fire she was totally fearless.

The Amoebic Avenger climbed to his knees, his white skin rolling and floundering, and held out one shapeless hand.

"What?" said The Zaggaline.

"*The weapon*," demanded the Amoebic Avenger in a thick, watery voice.

The Zaggaline hesitated for a moment, but then he handed him the samurai knife-stick. The Amoebic Avenger looked down at The Zaggaline with all of his differently colored eyes, and The Zaggaline thought for a moment that he was going to curse him for having brought him to life, like Frankenstein's monster—or worse, that he was going to take out one of those hypnotized knives and stick it in his head.

Instead, he said, with unexpected gentleness, "I will not disappoint you. I will do what you have asked me to do, and I will do it willingly."

"You're sure about that?"

"As you have told me, I am a war hero and this is my story. Each of us has a story, and this is mine."

At that moment, a bullet hit him in the chest. Shockwaves shivered across his translucent white skin, and for a split second The Zaggaline saw a bullet hole, although it instantly closed up. The Amoebic Avenger was hit again, and then again, and then again. The Zaggaline pressed himself flat against the dirt, not daring to raise his head. Each time the Amoebic Avenger took a hit, his skin rippled violently, but the bullets passed right through him and his wounds were swallowed up as if they had never existed.

The Amoebic Avenger reached down and laid his right hand gently on The Zaggaline's shoulder. His hand was heavy and soft and shapeless, like a latex glove filled with warm jelly, but The Zaggaline could feel that it was teeming with energy. Amoebas were life in its most elemental form: single cells that divided and divided and never stopped dividing, ceaselessly driven by the imperative of continuing existence.

It was then that The Zaggaline realized why he had been inspired to create the Amoebic Avenger: he was using creation to *save* creation. The war between life and death had at last come full circle, back to the moment when it had started.

The Amoebic Avenger stood up straight. He took one dragging step and then another. So many bullets were hitting him that he shuddered as he walked, but he didn't stop making his way forward.

"I do believe he's going to make it, goddammit," said Dom Magator, winking at The Zaggaline through his visor. "I do believe he's going to nail those suckers good and proper."

But the Amoebic Avenger had covered fewer than fifty feet when the terrorists found his range. There was a tremendous, ear-splitting barrage of gunfire, and high-explosive bullets began to detonate *inside* him. He walked slower and slower, and at last he was brought to a standstill. Through his semitransparent skin, inside his body, The Zaggaline could see orange flashes and smoke and splatters of blood.

The Amoebic Avenger swayed and undulated. He looked like a great building about to collapse. The terrorists fired and fired until he dropped to his knees and lowered his head. Smoke began to pour from his ears and his rudimentary noses.

"Oh, my God," said Raquasthena. "This is an execution Dom Magator—can't we do something?"

"Raquasthena, lighten up," Xanthys told her. "He's not a real person. The Zaggaline just invented him."

"What do you mean he's not real? Right now, he's as real as you are."

Dom Magator said, "Whether he's real or not, he's giving us one hell of a great diversion. Methinks this is a cue for the Successive Detonation Carbine."

He detached from the rack on his back a short, thick, gold-plated carbine. He cocked it by pulling back a slide on the right-hand side and flicked over the safety catch. The carbine immediately started to make a high singing sound, more like a saintly choir than a weapon of mass destruction.

Dom Magator unlatched a squat, ugly handgun from his belt and handed it to The Zaggaline. "What's this?" asked The Zaggaline.

"Perforation Pistol. It fires tungsten needles—three thousand rounds a second. In the right hands, it can tear you into seventy-two equally sized pieces, like a sheet of commemorative stamps. It's got a hell of a kick, though, so careful how you use it. And don't start blasting off in all directions. All I need you to do is to cover me."

He gripped his Successive Detonation Carbine and began to elbow his way across to a low hillock, which would give him a few inches of cover.

Meanwhile, the Amoebic Avenger had sunk to the dust. He barely resembled a human being anymore. The terrorists let off one more burst and then stopped shooting at him, and one or two of them raised their heads and inspected him through red-lensed binoculars.

"Well ..." said Xanthys. "Some invincible antiterrorist squad *he* turned out to be."

"Will you give the poor guy a break?" said The Zaggaline. "This is the Amoebic Avenger. He hasn't even *started* yet."

Kalexikox lifted his hand, asking for silence. "The Zaggaline's right, ladies." He adjusted a microsensor in his helmet, and the tiny fireflies of light that circled around his head began to revolve even faster. "I'm definitely picking up some tremors."

"Tremors? You mean like an earthquake?"

"Unh-hunh. These sound like the first vibrations of a major binary fission event."

"A *what*?"

"Binary fission is how single amoebas split themselves into two separate entities."

Dom Magator had reached the hillock and was nestling himself into a firing position. As he did so, the Amoebic Avenger started to tremble. His right arm stretched out sideways, transparent and gluey, until he had planted his hand flat on the ground about three feet away from him.

"That's his pseudopod," said Kalexikox. "That means 'artificial foot.' Amoebas use them to move around."

As soon as the Amoebic Avenger's hand was firmly planted on the ground, protoplasm began visibly to flow out of his torso and into his arm. His hand and his forearm quickly swelled up, and in only a few seconds his arm had taken on the shape of a second Amoebic Avenger. Each figure was only half the size of the original, but their human form was much more clearly defined. They looked like hairless, heavily built young men—still white-skinned and semitransparent, but far less lumpy and monstrous than their parent cell. All the same, The Zaggaline found it strangely difficult to keep them in focus, as if they had both moved while having their photograph taken.

Both were still kneeling, their heads bent forward, joined

together from the shoulder to the hip. The Zaggaline was worried that the terrorists would start shooting at them again, but the terrorists seemed to be too mesmerized by what was happening to open fire.

The original Amoebic Avenger suddenly convulsed, and the Night Warriors saw half of his internal organs passed in a slimy clump to his new companion—hearts, lungs, livers and a great snakelike mass of intestines.

When that was done, the skin that connected them immediately began to shrink, and then to separate, until there were two individual Avengers kneeling side by side.

"Binary fission. Wow," said Raquasthena. "If you ask me, that beats sex any day of the week."

The Amoebic Avengers slowly stood up. They may have been far less bulky, but they were still very tall. The only way in which The Zaggaline could tell which one was the original was that he was holding the samurai knife stick. But without hesitation, the original pulled the stick in half, and handed five of the knives to his double. The two of them stepped forward again.

The terrorists must suddenly have realized that they were renewing their attack, because they abruptly opened fire. This time, however, the two Amoebic Avengers were much quicker on their feet than the original, and as they made their way toward the terrorists' position they swerved and jinked and dodged sideways, and none of the first volley of bullets found their mark. As they got closer to the terrorists, though, one of Amoebic Avengers was hit in the shoulder. The bullet passed right through him, but it caused him to hesitate.

From his vantage point on the hillock, with the tip of his tongue clenched between his teeth, Dom Magator had been carefully focusing his crosshairs on the terrorist on the far right of the group. This terrorist seemed to believe that he was better shielded than the rest, because the ground to his left rose higher, so he was kneeling up to shoot at the Amoebic Avengers. From where Dom Magator was lying, however, he was almost fully exposed.

As soon as Dom Magator saw that one of the Amoebic Avengers had been hit, he steadied his aim and squeezed the wide spoonlike trigger of the Successive Detonation Carbine.

CHAPTER EIGHTEEN

Dom Magator wished to God that he had worn ear protectors. The Successive Detonation Carbine screamed louder than a tour bus full of evangelists toppling off a cliff. He rolled over onto his back, his eyes squeezed shut, his hands clamped to the sides of his helmet. He didn't even see the detonation round hit the terrorist and throw him ten yards backward into the bushes. The terrorist lay there twitching and jumping and screaming in pain.

"Haaawesome shot, Dom Magator!" said The Zaggaline, over his intercom.

"What did you say? I can't hear you too good!"

"Haaawesome shot, dude! My friend Lennie couldn't hit squirrels any better than that!"

"I hit him?"

"Right in the badonka, man."

Two of the terrorists had abandoned their guns and were hurrying across to their screaming companion. But the remaining four continued to fire at the Amoebic Avengers, and now they were beginning to get their eye in. They were triangulating their sights so that the Amoebic Avengers were caught in a hammering crossfire. One of the Amoebic Avengers was hit seven times in the chest in rapid succession, his white skin erupting like a panful of boiling grits. The second Amoebic Avenger was hit in the groin, the thighs and the side of the head.

The first Amoebic Avenger pulled out one of his throwing knives, tilted it back, and hurled it toward the terrorists. The Night Warriors could see it flashing as it turned over and over in the air. It struck the left-hand terrorist directly in the forehead, and he dropped sideways onto the ground, one arm flung up as if he were waving good-bye.

The remaining three terrorists redoubled their shooting. The crackling noise of gunfire was deafening, and Dom Magator winced because his ears were already hurting from the Successive Detonation Carbine. The second Amoebic Avenger was hit again and again, so many times that his skin wouldn't stop rippling. He pitched face forward onto the ground, less than seventy meters away from the terrorists' position, and lay there motionless.

"Looks like your Amoebic Avengers *can* be killed," said Xanthys.

Kalexikox was frowning at his microsensors. "He's not dead. But I'm not picking up any pre-indicators of binary fission."

"He'll make it, man," said The Zaggaline. "In the story, he definitely makes it."

"Trouble is, have these terrorists heard the same story?"

The two terrorists who had left their guns to help their fallen companion had reached him now. They both knelt down beside him and tried to lift him up. Dom Magator couldn't see them very clearly because they were partially obscured by the ridge. They were obviously trying to find out where he had been hit, but Dom Magator knew that the Successive Detonation Carbine left no visible injuries. Instead, it charged up its victim with a massive amount of destructive energy, enough to demolish a six-story hotel.

One of the terrorists took hold of his companion under

his arms. As he did so, Dom Magator saw a fine tracery of white lightning crawl up over his shoulders. The energy was passing from one victim to the next.

"Come on, fellow," he urged the third terrorist, under his breath. The third terrorist looked back down the slope to see how his companions were coping with the Amoebic Avengers. Dom Magator thought for a moment that he was going to go back and join them, but when the terrorist saw that one of the Amoebic Avengers was lying prone on the ground and that the second Amoebic Avenger was taking very heavy fire, he turned back again. He took hold of the wounded terrorist's ankles and attempted to drag him behind the ridge. As he did so, the white lightning crawled over him, too, and Dom Magator knew that he had got them—all three of them. He aimed at the back of the third terrorist's head, set the carbine's catch to successive detonation, and fired.

Without any warning, the first terrorist exploded, his bloody intestines thrown up into the air like the Indian rope trick, and his head blown ten yards clear of his body. In a terrible chain reaction, the second terrorist was ripped apart, too, his right arm and half of his ribcage flung across the desert floor. He was still alive, but he was screaming with shock, and Dom Magator could tell that he wouldn't last for long.

The third terrorist seemed to think that he could escape by running away. He disappeared behind the ridge and started to jog toward the distant horizon. But Dom Magator knew how much energy had been stored up inside his body and that he didn't stand a chance. There was only one way in which the energy inside him could be released, and that was by violent detonation.

Dom Magator waited and waited, and then he heard a devastating bang from the middle distance. After a few seconds, blood came sifting from the sky like warm rain, and body parts started to fall all around them. The last fragment to fall was a foot in a torn black combat boot.

"Got 'em," he said, twisting around toward the rest of the Night Warriors and giving them a thumbs up.

"Can you hit the others?" asked The Zaggaline. "I'm not so sure these Amoebic guys are going to make it."

Dom Magator lifted his head, but as he did so, a terrorist bullet hit the dust right in front of his face.

"They've spotted me, kid. I don't think I can get a bead on them without them blowing my nut off."

The remaining Amoebic Avenger was only a few yards away from the terrorists now. Two of the terrorists stood up so that they could fire at him even more relentlessly, from almost point-blank range, but still the Amoebic Avenger didn't fall. He drew out a second knife, aimed it, and flung it at them. It hit one of the terrorists in the forehead—so accurately that it cut his red ribbon in half. He tipped backward as if somebody had given him a hard shove in the chest, and lay on the ground with both of his hands raised, looking surprised.

"Yes! One more down, only two more to go!" said The Zaggaline. The remaining Amoebic Avenger was so close to the terrorists that he could have reached them within four or five steps, but they were both pouring high-explosive bullets into him, and he began to stagger under the sheer volume of firepower. He stopped, swayed and then fell. The two terrorists stood over him and raked him from head to foot, blowing his protoplasm into the bushes in pale, gelatinous lumps.

"Dom Magator!" shouted The Zaggaline. "Can't you hit them now?"

Dom Magator raised his head again, but again one of the terrorists swung around and fired at him, to keep him down.

"I caught them once. I don't think they're going to let me do it again."

Xanthys said, "Look—they're starting to head toward us!"

The Zaggaline raised his Perforation Pistol and cocked it. He had been frightened last night, when they were fighting the Winterwent, but there was something much more grim about this battle. Whatever Springer had said about the Winterwent taking no notice of a few marauding Night Warriors, he was sure that the Winterwent had specifically dreamed up these terrorists to eliminate them—all of them, before they could interfere with his ambitions.

The two terrorists broke into a purposeful trot. Dom Magator lifted himself up, but before he could level his carbine at them, three or four bullets banged into his armor-plated chest and knocked him back down again.

"Dom Magator! Dom Magator—are you okay?" Raquasthena demanded urgently.

Dom Magator was lying on his back in a low pebble-filled gully, like a shallow grave. He was whining for breath. He hadn't been winded so badly since a four-hundred-pound bouncer at the Baton Rouge Diner had punched him in the gut with a fistful of dimes. "Can't breathe—otherwise—perfect!"

"Weapons, Dom Magator!" shouted The Zaggaline. *"We need weapons!"*

"Sorry—I'm sorry—winded—can't get up—you'll have to come get them!"

"What can you give us?"

"A Density Rifle—that should do it."

"What?"

"Density Rifle—to compress them—and a couple of High-Intensity Incinerators. You can use the Density Rifle to squash the bastards—then you can cremate them. That way—they can never come back to life again—not even in dreams."

"On my way!" said The Zaggaline, climbing to his feet. Immediately, a shot snapped past his helmet and he dropped back down to the ground. "On my way in just a minute, okay? These guys have got us seriously nailed down."

Raquasthena quickly glanced up. "They're only a hundred yards away! We have to think of something *now!*"

Xanthys suggested, "Maybe I could turn back time. Then we can hit them before they can get here."

"You can try it. How about it, Dom Magator?"

Dom Magator was coughing so much that he could hardly speak. "Okay by me. Whatever."

Xanthys fumbled with her dials, turning the numeral display back by three minutes, ten seconds. A crimson key appeared on her face-up display, and a corresponding key started glowing on her belt. She detached it and held it up toward the east, slowly turning it counterclockwise.

Time reversed itself. Bullets glided slowly backward in the direction from which they had been fired, and disappeared back into rifle barrels. The Zaggaline rose from the ground and then fell back down again. Dom Magator rolled sideways, holding his ears, and then he propped himself up with his carbine pressed against his shoulder.

Body parts flew up in the air, accompanied by fountains of blood. The next thing that Dom Magator knew, the three terrorists that he had blown apart had reassembled themselves. Arms and legs tumbled backward and found their original sockets. Flesh grew rapidly back over exposed ribcages and was instantly wrapped up in skin. It took only a few seconds before the terrorists were whole again and rising to their feet. With a curious backward lope they returned down the slope to their original positions and settled themselves down behind their rifles. Before Xanthys could do anything about it, they were furiously shooting at the Amoebic Avengers, as if they had never been dead.

"*What's happened?*" screamed Xanthys. "*Everything's gone back way too far!*"

Dom Magator sat up and three bullets narrowly missed his head. "What the hell are you trying to do, get me executed?"

"I'm so sorry," Xanthys told him. "Somehow I must have worked out the time lapse wrong. But I can't see how I did."

Kalexikox checked his chronometer. "No—no, you didn't ... it's the dream. Dr. Beltzer is under so much pressure at the hospital that he perceives time moving at variable rates. For instance, he thinks that his afternoon shift goes past three times more slowly than his time off. So time in this dream time isn't constant ... it keeps speeding up and slowing down."

"But I've brought those three terrorists back to life," said Xanthys. "I've taken us right back to square one."

"Sure, but *look*," said The Zaggaline. "That Amoebic Avenger they shot to pieces ... *he's* back together again, too."

He was right. The glutinous lumps of protoplasm that had been plastered all over the dust and the bushes had slithered back together into a human-like shape, and the Amoebic Avenger was already starting to rise from the ground.

"He's not waiting around this time, ladies and gentlemen!" said Kalexikox, shouting like a wrestling promoter. "I can feel the preliminary tremors already! A major binary fission event, coming right up!"

The fallen Amoebic Avenger stretched out his left arm and placed it firmly on the ground. Immediately, his arm filled up with protoplasm, swelling bigger and bigger until it had grown to the size and shape of yet another Amoebic Avenger.

Inside the murky interiors of their semitransparent bodies, hearts, lungs and livers slid from one Amoebic Avenger to the other. Then the two Amoebic Avengers separated. They stood up, still well-built, but only half the size of the body from which they had split. Their faces were much more sharply defined, with noses and lips. They still had four eyes each, but it was obvious that they were humans, rather than shapeless blobs of protoplasm.

They even had the rudiments of genitalia——ambiguous bulges to represent penises and testicles.

One of them picked up his half of the samurai knife-stick

and passed two throwing knives to his companion. Then, without any hesitation at all, he flung one of his own knives toward the terrorists, hitting one of them in the top of the head as he bent down to reload his sniper rifle.

"Hey!" said Kalexikox. "*More* binary fission!"

Not far away, the second Amoebic Avenger was starting to split in half, too, and in less than half a minute there were four Amoebic Avengers. The terrorists kept firing at them, but now they were even more difficult to hit, because they advanced on the terrorist position in a complicated crisscross pattern that even the Night Warriors found difficult to follow. As they passed in front of each other, they seemed to fade from sight and then reappear twenty or thirty yards away.

But one of them fell, and then another, and for a moment Dom Magator thought that the terrorists must have found their distance.

"Sun Gun," he said. "We have to incinerate these bastards for good, or else we're never going to get anyplace at all."

"Don't—not the Sun Gun—" Raquasthena protested. "We're going to need all of that power when we find the High Horse."

"What else do you suggest I do? At this rate we're going to be trapped here all night."

"They're splitting again!" said Kalexikox. "My binary fission sensor's gone right off the dial!"

The two Amoebic Avengers who had fallen to the ground were now dividing into two more Amoebic Avengers. As soon as they had seperated, the other two Amoebic Avengers dropped to the ground, and *they* began to divide, too. Within less than half a minute, there were eight Amoebic Avengers advancing on the terrorist position. They approached the terrorists so quickly, and their advance was so complicated, that the terrorists abruptly stopped firing, abandoned their weapons and started to run away.

They didn't get far. Each Amoebic Avenger knew the

story The Zaggaline had devised for them. In The Zag-galine's story, they had to pursue the terrorists and kill them—all of them—and nothing in the dreaming world was going to stop them.

Dom Magator, winded as he was, rose to his feet. It was one of those moments when the Night Warriors defeated their enemies, and he wanted to witness it. Xanthys stood up, too, and then Kalexikox and Raquasthena. The sky rolled over them, purple and unforgiving, but they had beaten the terrorists, and they had every hope now that they were going to beat the Winterwent and the High Horse.

The terrorists were running now, their ribbons flying in the wind, but the Amoebic Avengers were faster. When the terrorists leaped from the second ridge below their original position, the Amoebic Avengers were there already, waiting for them. Even The Zaggaline couldn't understand how they had got there so quickly. Confused, frightened, the ter-rorists turned left and right. But now the Amoebic Avengers were surrounding them. Eight Amoebic Avengers, tall and semitranslucent and ghostly, their hearts visibly pumping, their arteries visibly throbbing with blood.

The terrorists dropped to their knees. Their leader called out, "Save us! High Horse! Save us! In the name of all that we have sacrificed for you! Save us!"

"What are you going to do now?" Dom Magator asked The Zaggaline.

"Exterminate 'em—what do you think?"

Dom Magator said nothing, but looked away. He had used the Successive Detonation Carbine, and he would probably find himself using many different weapons before this war was over, but somehow he was beginning to feel that killing was no longer the answer.

Maybe goodness, in itself, was enough to defeat evil. Maybe reality, in itself, was enough to defeat dreams.

By now the eight Amoebic Avengers had encircled the terrorists and joined hands. One of the terrorists jumped to his feet and tried to break away, but the Amoebic Avengers wouldn't allow him to break the circle, and pushed him back.

"I'm a mercenary!" he screamed at them. "I was doing what they paid me to do, that's all!"

The Amoebic Avengers didn't answer him. Their faces were as bland as melted altar candles. They drew their circle in closer and tighter. One by one, the rest of the terrorists climbed to their feet, and now they were were jostling against each other in panic.

Slowly but unstoppably the Amoebic Avengers joined together. First they intertwined their arms. Then their torsos seemed to flow into each other. Their hearts and lungs intermingled and swam together through their collective body. At last they had formed themselves into a single vast lump of protoplasm, one huge Amoebic Avenger, as The Zaggaline had first created, instead of eight. Inside him, the Night Warriors could dimly see the hysterical terrorists struggling to escape. Their arms and legs jerked spasmodically, like insects trapped in glue.

"Oh my God," said Xanthys. "They're being *digested*."

Although it was difficult to see the terrorists clearly, Dom Magator could make out their combat outfits being reduced to rags, and then their skin turning into liquid. As his digestive juices began to dissolve the terrorists' flesh, the inside of the Amoebic Avenger filled up with clouds of scarlet blood. All that Dom Magator could see now were thighbones, a ribcage, a fleshless pelvis, gradually sinking downward.

He turned to The Zaggaline and said, "I think you can switch him off now."

Raquasthena nodded her approval. "I think he's more than served his purpose, don't you?"

"Okay," said The Zaggaline. He switched off the Amoebic Avenger program and instantly the huge heap of protoplasm disappeared. The terrorists' skeletons fell to the ground with a muted clatter—that was all that was left of them.

The Night Warriors gathered around them. Raquasthena hunkered down and picked up one of their skulls. It didn't resemble a human skull at all. It was narrow and pointed, with long incisor teeth and eye sockets that were far too close together. All the other skulls were similar.

"What the hell are they?" asked Dom Magator.

Kalexikox made some quick measurements with his biological instruments. "That is the skull of a very large example of *canis lupus,* the North American gray wolf."

"These were *wolves?*" asked Xanthys incredulously.

Raquasthena turned the skull over. "Wolves with men's bodies, or men with wolves' heads, whichever way you want to look at it. A typical creation of the High Horse. He's trying to hunt us down, right? I guess he figured that the best animal for doing that would be something between a gray wolf and a human being."

"Makes sense, in a weird kind of way," said Kalexikox. "The wolf is only second to man in the variety of habitats it can thrive in. It's highly sociable and hunts as a team, like men do, but at the same time it's much more aggressive and has no qualms about killing its prey as quickly as it possibly can."

"Well, we've licked them, all the same," said Dom Magator. "It's time we headed out of here, before the High Horse catches those women. That's if he hasn't done it already."

"You're going to leave Amla Fabeya's stuff here?"

"I think I have enough to carry, don't you?"

They left the littered bones of the terrorists and started to walk northeastward. As they did so, the sky, which was already overcast, began to darken, until it was charcoal gray. A chilly wind rose up and long snakelike streaks of dust blew across the desert.

After they had covered nearly a mile, they saw a cluster of posts standing in the distance and they heard a repetitive clacking sound, like somebody knocking two pieces of wood together.

The posts varied between twenty and thirty feet high, some of them upright and some of them leaning at an angle. As the Night Warriors came closer, they saw that they were wooden effigies— strange and ferocious faces with staring eyes and vicious teeth. They were all hung with beads and necklaces fashioned out of dead vegetation, and some of them had shriveled decorations that looked as if they could have been human ears or strips of human intestine. There was something infinitely horrible about these effigies, as if they represented the depths of human hopelessness. They looked like the gods who reigned in a world in which cruelty and pain were inescapable.

The clacking sound was coming from the largest of the figures. It had eyes made of grimy mirrors and a headdress made of thorns, like a parody of Christ. Its body was represented by a small wooden box, and there were two doors in the front of it that flapped open and shut in the wind. Inside the box, they could see a dried-up maroon object no bigger than a man's fist, which could have been a human heart.

"You, dude," said The Zaggaline, squinting up at it, "are seriously homely."

Raquasthena looked around at the effigies with obvious unease. "Any idea what they are?" she asked.

"Whatever they are," said Xanthys, "they give me the heebie-jeebies."

Kalexikox circled around them, checking them against his mythological registry. "It looks like they're all well-known Mexican deities. This figure here with the mirrors for eyes and the doors in his chest, this is Tezcatlipoca, sometimes called the 'smoking mirror' or 'night wind.' He can bring sickness and death to any community, so people often give him offerings of fruit and roosters, and build seats for him so that he can rest himself while he's prowling around looking for victims. If you can reach inside the doors of his chest and snatch out his heart without having your hand chopped off, Tezcatlipoca will grant you whatever you wish, so that he can have it back.

"Here—this one with the long hair and the face like a skull—this is Xipe Totec, the 'night drinker.' Xipe Totec shows up whenever blood is being spilled—in war, fatal accidents, childbirth—so that he can drink his share. The Aztecs used to make sacrifices to him by cutting off their enemies' tongues so that they would bleed all over the floor, and he could lick it up."

"What about this one?" asked The Zaggaline. He pointed up at an effigy with crooked teeth and gray painted lips. "It's more like a dog than a god."

"Zotz," said Kalexikox. "He was supposed to guard the treasures of hell. But anybody who tried to creep into his chambers to steal any of his riches would have their head bitten off. I guess he was kind of a cautionary tale against venture capitalism."

"So what are they doing here, all of these highly unpleasant individuals?" asked Dom Magator. "Do they mean anything? Are they another crossword clue or what?"

"I think they must be. But maybe only part of a clue. What we have so far is *range* and *flags* and *seaside* and these could be *deities*. They have a lot of letters in common and all we have to do is figure out how they fit together."

"Sounds simple enough to me."

"Well, no, it isn't. But it's the only way we're going to find our way through Dr. Beltzer's dream."

"Okay ... but whatever we do, we'd better do it quick."

They carried on walking across the desert, leaving the effigies far behind them. All the same, Xanthys found herself turning around every few yards to make sure that none of the effigies were following them. In dreams, anything can pursue you, even a Mexican deity carved out of wood, and she could still hear the clacking of Tezcatlipoca's doors even when he was out of sight.

The rubbly ground beneath their feet began slowly to rise, and eventually they found themselves standing on top of a low hill. Ahead of them, less than a half-mile away, they could see the isolation hospital that had appeared on Jek

Rekanter's map. It looked as if it were abandoned, with flaking white paint on its outside walls and its metal window frames rusted, yet there were six or seven cars parked outside and a red flag flying.

"That flag is showing us where to go next," said Kalexikox. " 'Flag' meaning 'signal' rather than 'banner' or 'iris.' "

"If you say so. I guess we're headed in the right direction, anyhow."

CHAPTER NINETEEN

When they reached the hospital parking lot, they realized that the automobiles parked outside were all old and corroded, 1950s and 1960s models, their windows milky and their tires flat. The Zaggaline recognized two of the cars that he had seen last night as they walked along the snowy streets of Kenningtown. This disturbed him, because he couldn't think how Nurse Meiner and Dr. Beltzer could dream about the same cars.

They walked up to the front entrance of the hospital and peered through the smeared windows of the art deco doors. They could see a receptionist sitting at the desk inside, wearing a folded white wimple, like a nun.

"Looks like the place is still open for business," said Raquasthena.

"Terrific," said Dom Magator. There was something about nuns that had always disturbed him.

"Meaning, we need to go inside and find out what's happening."

"Oh? Oh, for sure. Let's do that."

He pushed open the doors and entered the lobby. It was

gloomy and stale inside, with only a dim yellowish light filtering down the staircase, and a million specks of dust sparkling in the air. The marble flooring obviously hadn't been swept in years, because it was covered with fine grit, so that he made a loud crunching noise as he walked across it.

On the wall behind the reception desk hung a faded picture of Pope Pius XI, in his wire-rimmed glasses, and the exhortation: *By what things a man sinneth, by the same also he is tormented*. Close behind Dom Magator, Kalexikox murmured, "That's a quote from Pope Pius's encyclical of May, 1932, about the depression."

Dom Magator turned and stared at him through his visor, but said nothing. He didn't want to be offensive about it, but sometimes Kalexikox told him just a little bit more than he wanted to know.

He approached the reception desk, but the nunlike woman didn't seem to notice that he was there. He cleared his throat noisily, but when she still didn't raise her eyes he looked at a small bell at the far end of the counter, and a sign that said RING FOR ATTENTION.

"Can you ping that?" he asked Kalexikox.

"You ping it."

"You're supposed to be a Night Warrior and you're too chickenshit to ping a bell?"

At that moment, however, the nunlike woman looked up. She was very pale, with skin that was beige and withered like dried-out chamois leather, and she wore intensely dark glasses, so that Dom Magator couldn't see her eyes at all. Around her neck she wore a crucifix made of seashells. Seaside, disease, he felt that he was beginning to understand this cryptic crossword stuff.

"You're looking for Dr. Beltzer's patients," she whispered.

"I am? I mean, yes, I guess I am."

"First of all, you have to fill out this form."

"I do?"

The nunlike woman took a faded sheet of typewritten paper out of a metal in-tray and laid it on the counter in front of him, along with a pencil. Dom Magator peered at the form and couldn't understand any of it. Not only was it difficult for him to read through the visor of his helmet, it didn't seem to make any sense.

It was headed *Brigham Isolation Hospital For Infectious Diseases,* Louisville, Kentucky. The first question was: *How long have you been sleeping?* The second question was: *Where has your happiest memory gone?* The third question was: *Do the gods take this document to become misshapen?*

"I, uh —I'm not too sure that I can fill this out."

"You don't need to, sir. So long as you're aware of what it says."

"I don't need to?"

The nunlike woman groped along the counter as if she couldn't see, and took the form back. "Third floor, fifth door on the left."

"Thank you," said Dom Magator. The Zaggaline had joined him now and was looking around.

"What's happening, man?" asked The Zaggaline.

"Third floor, fifth door on the left," said the nunlike woman.

Dom Magator stared at her more closely. "Didn't I see you last night?" he asked her.

"Third floor," she repeated. "Fifth door on the left."

"That was you, wasn't it, in that building in Kenningtown? That building that didn't have any floors, and you were just floating in it?"

The Zaggaline stared at her, too. "Hey, yes! It *was* you! I recognize you! You were up in that window, watching us!"

The nunlike woman turned her head away, but The Zaggaline was sure that she allowed herself a small smile. Very quietly, she said, "You think you recognize me, but you don't, I'm afraid. Perhaps you never will. Let us sincerely hope not."

"I don't get it," The Zaggaline persisted.

But without saying anything else, the nunlike woman rose from her seat behind the reception desk and disappeared through a varnished oak door. Dom Magator frowned. He was sure that the door hadn't been there when he had first walked into the lobby.

"Do you know something?" he said. "I could have sworn—"

"Don't you think we need to get moving?" Raquasthena interrupted him.

Dom Magator checked his chronometer again. "Yeah, you're right. We don't have more than an hour of reality time before Dr. Beltzer's next shift starts."

They couldn't see an elevator anywhere, so they had to climb the stairs. Their boots clattered and echoed on the marble steps. Inside, the building was just as dilapidated as it was outside. Doors stood half-open, revealing empty hospital beds and sagging venetian blinds. Gurneys had been abandoned in the corridors and pictures were tilted at odd angles. There didn't seem to be anybody around, and yet Xanthys was sure that she could hear a soft, blustery fluffing, like a draft blowing under a doorway, and far away, from out on the desert, a clacking noise.

"What did she say?" wheezed Dom Magator. "Fifth floor, third door on the left?"

"Third floor."

"Thank God for that. Thank you, God."

They reached the third floor. Here, heavy green blinds had been drawn down over the windows, so that it was dark and stuffy and claustrophobic. Both Dom Magator and The Zaggaline switched on their blue halogen helmet lights. The corridor was an obstacle course of upturned chairs and oxygen cylinders and soiled, discarded mattresses. As they negotiated their way forward, their lights threw nightmarish shadows on the walls, which hopped and jumped every time they turned their heads.

The fifth door on the left was closed. It was painted a dull hospital gray, but it was covered in crisscross scratches, some of them very deep, as if lions had been trying to get in. A sign on the door said, MOBIUS SYNDROME WARD.

Dom Magator tried the handle. "Locked," he announced. "Maybe we've made a mistake here."

"I don't think so," said Kalexikox. "Dr. Beltzer happens to be an expert on treating Mobius syndrome."

"Yes, but what is it?" asked Xanthys.

"Mobius syndrome? It's a very rare congenital birth defect—a kind of facial paralysis caused by the absence or underdevelopment of the sixth and seventh cranial nerves. It makes it very difficult for the baby to suck, or even to smile."

"That's terrible."

"Well, that usually isn't the half of it. Mobius babies often have other symptoms, such as strabismus—severely crossed eyes—or club foot, or webbed fingers. It's also associated with Pierre Robin syndrome, which can result in a child having an unusually small jaw, and Poland's anomaly, where babies have irregular development of one side of their chest."

"And?"

"We're talking about deformities here, aren't we, and that was the answer to the crossword clue. Question three on that form that the receptionist gave you was 'Do the gods take this document to be misshapen?' Gods are 'deities' … insert the word 'form' into the middle of 'deities' and you get 'deformities.' Which is what we're going to find behind this door."

"Say *what?* I really believed that I was getting the hang of this crossword malarkey."

"So," said Raquasthena, "are we going to kick this door down or what?"

The Zaggaline unholstered his Perforation Pistol. "I could open it with this."

"Sure, why not," said Dom Magator. "Go ahead. Just remember that it kicks like a mule with a jalapeno pepper up its rear end."

"I can handle it." Gripping the Perforation Pistol tightly in both hands, The Zaggaline pointed the muzzle at the door, half-closed his eyes, and squeezed the trigger. There was a roar like a ripsaw, and the middle of the door was torn into hundreds of fragments. The Zaggaline staggered back against the opposite side of the corridor, shaken but triumphant.

"Wow," he said. "That is some bodacious pistol, man."

"Way to go, Zagga," said Dom Magator, slapping him on the shoulder.

They stepped into the dimly lit ward. Lined up against the opposite wall were six cream-painted iron cribs, of which four were occupied. The Night Warriors approached them very cautiously. They looked into the first three and saw sleeping children, two girls and a boy, their cheeks hot, as if they were baking.

"They don't look deformed to me," breathed Xanthys. "Look at them, they're absolutely *perfect*."

They went over to the fourth crib. A boy about six years old was lying in it, wearing a simple blue nightshirt with an appliqué picture of Popeye's Swee' Pea on it. His hair was blond and curly, and he had intensely green eyes; he was smiling up at them with a dreamy expression on his face, as if he had just woken up.

"Hallo, sweetheart," said Xanthys, leaning over his crib. "Don't be frightened … we've only come here to talk to you."

"I'm not frightened," said the boy. "I've been waiting for you."

"You know who we are?"

"You're my friends. You're my mommy's friends."

"Who's your mommy?"

"My mommy's in the hospital. I'm going to have a baby sister."

"Your mommy's in the hospital? Do you know which hospital?"

"Or-bad-on."

"Norton Audubon," said Raquasthena. "So that's it. His mother must be one of the expectant women that the High

Horse is going after. In real life this boy is asleep now ... but he's joined us here in Dr. Beltzer's dream to help us."

"What's your monicker, kid?" asked Dom Magator.

The boy blinked at him, bewildered. "Your name," Xanthys prompted him.

"Michael," the boy told her. "Michael John Russell. But my mom calls me Michael-Row-The-Boat-Ashore-Hallelujah."

"Well, Michael, are you going to show us where your mommy is?"

Michael sat up in his crib. The Zaggaline reached inside and lifted him out. "Hey, dude, you weigh as much as half an elephant. The back half."

"I always eat all my Cheerios," said Michael, "and all my eggs and all my toast and I always drink all of my milk."

Raquasthena said, "I'm sure you do, honey," but at the same time she gave The Zaggaline a sad and meaningful look. It was then that The Zaggaline understood what was happening here, in Dr. Beltzer's dream. In the real world, Michael was probably suffering from severe facial deformities, which made it impossible for him to eat or drink properly. But here, in the world of dreams, he could imagine that he was perfect, and that he could eat and smile and talk as clearly as any other child.

Xanthys took hold of his hand. "Okay, Michael-Row-The-Boat-Ashore-Hallelujah, let's go find your mommy, shall we, and make sure that she's okay? Then maybe we can go get pizza."

"Yes, pizza!" said Michael. "And doughballs! And ice cream sundaes!"

"To be honest with you," said Dom Magator, "that doesn't sound like a bad idea at all."

They clattered back downstairs to the hospital lobby. The nunlike woman had returned to the reception desk, and was typing on an old-fashioned Underwood typewriter, even though the only sound it made was a very faint clacking.

Xanthys went up to the desk and said, "We're taking Michael."

The nunlike woman carried on typing. "You mean Michael is taking *you*."

"Well, whatever. But we'll take very good care of him, I promise."

"You're not a mother yet," said the nunlike woman. "But one day you'll understand what's happening here."

"Who *are* you?" Xanthys asked her.

The nunlike woman stopped typing and raised her head. As she did so, a ray of amber sunlight came through the smeared glass in the art deco doors and illuminated her face. Her wrinkles seemed to dissolve, and for a split second she looked no more than twenty-five or thirty years old. Behind her dark glasses, though, it was obvious that she had no eyes, only smooth sockets covered in a web of skin.

"Who am I?" she smiled. "Let me just say this ... the day you no longer need to ask, then you will know who I am."

Raquasthena said, "Xanthys ... we really have to get moving."

Xanthys hesitated. For some reason she couldn't take her eyes off the nunlike woman—couldn't bring herself to leave her without understanding who she was. She felt for a fleeting moment that if only she could talk to her, if only she could ask her what her life meant, and what mistakes she was making, all of her problems would rattle away like dried leaves.

"Xanthys," said Dom Magator. His tone was sympathetic but insistent.

"Sure," said Xanthys. "Come on, Michael-Row-The-Boat-Ashore-Hallelujah, let's hit the trail."

They left the hospital and headed northward. The dusty desert gradually gave way to thick rustling grass. High above their heads the clouds were clearing and a milky sun was beginning to shine through. Michael walked a little way ahead of them, swinging his arms like a toy soldier, and shouting out, "Left! Right! Left! Right!"

Although she was aware how strange and dangerous this expedition was, Xanthys began to feel much happier, and she caught up with The Zaggaline and took hold of his hand. "Hey," he said, and smiled at her. Even Raquasthena relaxed, and talked to Kalexikox about various species of wolf and how she had once wrestled a Fire Fox, a blazing creature in a convicted arsonist's nightmare.

Only Dom Magator was silent. He was feeling tired after all of the walking, but he was also feeling very unsettled. The weather was too perfect. When he turned around and looked back, the Brigham hospital had vanished, and instead he could see the sunshine sparkling on the ocean, and red-sailed yachts bending in front of the wind.

Up ahead of them, the gradient rose even more steeply. Along the top of the ridge, a line of tall silver birches stood glittering in the wind. If he hadn't known that this was all a dream, he would have stopped, sat down on the grass, and relaxed for an hour or two, just to smell the salty air blowing off the ocean.

"Left! Right! Left! Right!" Michael chanted.

Kalexikox came across, closing the U-shaped bio-medical scanner on his right forearm. He nodded toward Michael and said, "I just gave him a physiological once-over. In the real world, the poor kid has very serious maxillary and skeletal deformities. Can't walk, can't talk, drools all the time."

Dom Magator looked at Michael sadly. "I guess that's what dreams are for." He sniffed, and then he said, "Any idea where he's leading us?"

Kalexikox flicked the switch at the side of his helmet-ring and brought up a three-dimensional section of Jek Rekanter's map. As the holographic map wavered in the air in front of him, Dom Magator was able to identify the shoreline off to their right, and the grassy hill that they were climbing. The line of silver birch trees ran diagonally from the southwest to the northeast; and beyond that the ground gradually sloped down again, until it reached a small town.

The town was surrounded by farms, with a wide slow-moving river branching around it. The lettering on the map said it was called New Mile Branch.

"You think this could be the place?" asked Dom Magator.

"Ninety-nine-point-nine percent sure of it," said Kalexikox. "It's sunny there, it looks like paradise, but the air temperature is still two degrees lower than the surrounding countryside, which is an indication that the Winterwent was there, less than two hours ago. But it's the cryptic crossword that's convinced me."

"Huh?"

"The Winterwent and the High Horse have chosen Dr. Beltzer's dream to set up their ambush, right, because Dr. Beltzer is closer to these expectant mothers than anybody. He thinks about them even when he's asleep, which means they're almost certain to be here.

"But I'm pretty sure that, even in his dreams, Dr. Beltzer has definitely gotten wind that something is wrong. In the real world, he's a clever enough doctor to have realized that some malignant entity is trying to invade his patients' subconscious thoughts, so it makes sense that his dreaming mind has been thinking along the same lines. In the real world he probably thinks that this malignant entity is some kind of virus. After all, there's no way that he could found out anything about the Winterwent and the High Horse, and if somebody *did* try to tell him—well, he would probably think that they were off their chump.

"He may not be sure exactly what it is that wants to trap his patients, but he's aware that *something* is, something seriously hostile, and his dreaming mind has sensed that it's going to happen here, in this pretty little town, because this pretty little town is made up of these women's memories, not his. That's why he's named it New Mile Branch."

"You've lost me again," said Dom Magator.

"If you put the letters of the word 'mile' in a new order,

you get the word 'lime.' Another word for 'branch' is 'twig.'
A 'lime-twig' is a trap for birds."

"Why didn't he just call the place 'Ambushville'?"

"Because that's not the way his mind works. He solves
his problems by turning them into clues and riddles and
anagrams and puns. Besides, I think he may have realized
that his patients are being threatened by sentient beings,
who would be inclined to realize that he was on to them if he
named their ambush 'Ambushville.' "

Dom Magator said, "I'll tell you something, Kalexikox,
when this is all over, I hope I get to keep my Successive
Detonation Carbine and you get to keep some of those
smarts."

Measured by Dom Magator's chronometer, it took them
another half hour to reach the outskirts of New Mile
Branch, but their subjective perception was that it took
them only five or six minutes. This was Dr. Beltzer's dreaming mind, playing tricks on them again.

As soon as they reached the first houses Michael broke
into a run.

Raquasthena said, "I guess he's eager to find his mom
and show her how good he looks."

There was no question that the Winterwent had made
New Mile Branch a tempting place for anyone who was suffering from stress. The sun was shining warmly now, and
the sky was intensely blue. Katydids were chirruping, bees
were droning, and orange butterflies were blowing everywhere. Off to their right, through some shady lime trees, the
Night Warriors could see a sloping picnic meadow and a
small lake where children were swimming.

Dom Magator was gripped by an unexpected pang of
nostalgia, and stopped. He used to splash around in a lake
just like that when he was a boy. He could almost smell the
water drying on his sunburned skin and hear his friends
shouting at him from their makeshift raft. "Come on,
Porky, you can make it!"

"Dom Magator?" said Xanthys, peering into his visor. "Is something wrong?"

It was only then that he realized that he had tears in his eyes.

"Everything's fine. Hay fever, I guess."

"Hay fever, in a dream?"

"He's a doctor, isn't he? I'll bet this dream is absolutely crawling with symptoms."

The first property they came to was a large two-story frame house of the kind found in Louisville's Crescent Hill neighborhood. It was painted a fresh cream color, with olive green shutters, and the porch was overgrown with climbing roses. A red and white-striped swing seat on the verandah was still swinging, although there was nobody sitting in it. A coppery spaniel was lying asleep in a woven dog basket, and the Night Warriors couldn't even guess what he was dreaming of; perhaps a dream dog dreaming of dream rabbits.

As they passed the picket fence, the front door opened and a young woman appeared, wearing a flowery hospital gown. She was pale, with auburn hair and freckles, and she was very heavily pregnant. One hand shaded her eyes and the other hand rested on her stomach.

The Night Warriors stopped, and Xanthys walked up to the front gate. "Excuse me for asking, ma'am ... did you come from the Norton Audubon Hospital?"

The young woman hesitated, and then she nodded.

Xanthys opened the gate and walked up the warm brick path. "Do you know where this is?" she asked.

"What? Of course I know where this is. This is my grandparents' house."

"Are your grandparents here?"

The young woman looked behind her, into the house. "Not right now ... they must have gone to the market."

"They've left you alone?"

"They'll be back soon. There's always ice cream, and I can help myself."

Xanthys said, "Can I ask you what your name is?"

"Ellen—Ellen Rohrig. Who are you? And who are those other people?"

"Ellen, my name is Xanthys. Me and my friends here, we've come to protect you. You and your baby are in very great danger."

Ellen Rohrig frowned at Xanthys in disbelief. "No ... I'm safe here. This is my grandparents' house. I was always safe here, even when my mom and dad were divorced."

"Ellen, think about it. Are your grandparents still alive?"

"They—they must have gone to the market."

Doin Magator came up behind Xanthys. "Ma'am, I have to tell you that this is nothing but a dream. Your grandparents' house, it never stood right next to a bungalow like that, now did it?"

Ellen Rohrig glanced at the neighboring house, a single-story property that looked as if it had come from the Deer Park district. Its paint was peeling and its yard was cluttered with children's toys: colored bricks and tricycles and a leaky paddling pool.

"I don't understand," she said. "The Wattersons used to live next door ... and they had a big green house. What happened to that?"

"Nothing happened to it. None of this is real. This isn't even your dream ... you've been enticed here because you've been feeling stressed and because you're so anxious about your baby. To you, this is like a sanctuary, but I have to warn you that it isn't, and we're here to get you out of here as quick as we can."

Ellen Rohrig bit her lower lip. "Is this true? You wouldn't lie to me, would you?"

Kalexikox said, "We know this is difficult to believe, but your grandparents' house was stolen from a dream you had several days ago, specifically so that it could be re-created here tonight."

"It was *stolen?* How could anybody steal a house?"

"It's not a real house, it's like a memory of a house, an

image of a house. Can you remember when you last dreamed about it? What was the weather like?"

"I dreamed about it ... I'm not sure when, but only a few nights ago. It was Christmas, I think, because it was snowing outside, and there were icicles hanging from the porch. It was very, very cold."

"Your grandparents' house was frozen solid, that's why, so that when you woke up, it didn't dissolve, like it should have done. It stayed right here, in this dream existence, ready to be used as a trap."

"A trap?" Ellen looked back at the house again, and then stepped nervously off the porch and onto the path. Two quail were flirting with each other on the chimney, but somehow the house had already taken on a slightly sinister appearance. The upstairs windows were blind and black, and the front door was creaking backward and forward as if it were trying to coax Ellen back inside.

"There isn't time to explain it all now," said Raquasthena. "But there are two entities who are trying to enter your baby's dreams, and the only way that they can do it is through *you*, and *your* dreams."

"And if they manage to do that," Kalexikox put in, "the result will be universal molecular disassembly."

"*What?* What does that mean?"

"It means that none of us will ever be stressed or anxious about anything, ever again, because there won't be any anything and there won't be any *us*."

"How many of you ladies came here tonight?" asked Dom Magator.

"Seven of us altogether. We're all in the same maternity unit."

Michael had been marching up ahead, but now he had come marching back again and was waiting impatiently by the gate. "I know where my mommy is! I can see my Aunt Susan's house!"

"That's great, Michael, well done. Let's go get her, shall we, and all of her friends," said Xanthys.

Ellen Rohrig was close to tears. "I've been so worried about my baby ... he's a little boy, and my husband has always wanted a boy. But when all those other babies started to die ... I've been so *frightened*. And then I found myself here, and it was just like always ... quiet and safe and peaceful."

"That's exactly how the Winterwent wanted you to feel."

"The Winterwent?"

Xanthys put her arm around Ellen Rohrig's shoulders. "Ellen ... you can trust us, I promise. I know this all sounds crazy and confusing, but it's like a war, a night war, and crazy and confusing is how wars always are."

"You should be a news reporter," said The Zaggaline.

Behind Ellen's back, Xanthys gave him the finger.

They walked next to the far end of the street, to Aunt Susan's house. It was a modest brick house, of the kind constructed in Louisville's southern suburbs after World War Two, but its owners were clearly proud of it, because the window frames and the garage doors were newly painted, and there were terracotta pots filled with geraniums on either side of the front door, and a concrete Bambi with glass eyes.

A brand-new 1955 Chevrolet Bel-Air was parked in the driveway, two-tone turquoise and cream, its chrome sparkling in the sunshine.

"Look at those wheels," said Dom Magator. "What I'd give to have an automobile like that."

"It used to belong to my grandpa," Michael told him. "I've seen it in photographs."

Xanthys went to the front door and rang the bell. They waited for a while and then a petite dark-haired woman appeared, wearing a similar nightdress to Ellen Rohrig, but with a red candlewick robe on top of it. She was pretty in a brown-eyed Spanish way, although her skin was sallow, as if she had been cooped up indoors for a very long time.

"Mommy!" shouted Michael, and ran right up to her.

"Michael?" said the woman. "Michael, is this you?"

"I was asleep in the hospital and when I woke up my face was all better!"

The woman looked at Xanthys with bewilderment and gratitude. "I don't know who you are, or how you managed to do this, but thank you. Thank you from the bottom of my heart."

The voice of an elderly man came from inside the house. "Maggie? Who is that?"

"Some people, Dad. I don't know who they are. But they brought Michael with them, and somehow they've cured him!"

"Ma'am," said Dom Magator, "before you get too excited, you have to be aware that this is only a dream."

"I don't understand."

"You're dreaming this, Mrs. Russell. This house, your father being here. In real life, you're asleep, back at the Norton Audubon maternity unit."

"I still don't know what you mean. This must be real. This is my sister's house."

"This is only your memory of your sister's house. You've been led here by some very bad characters who are trying to get into your unborn baby's dreams."

"I don't believe you! This *must* be real!" She slapped the fin of her father's car. "See? It's solid! I can feel it!"

"We're real sorry," put in Raquasthena. "We really are. But think about it: do you ever see people walking around dressed like we are in normal life? Is your father still alive? You're dreaming, Maggie. It's a very happy dream. But for all of that, it's nothing more than a dream."

Maggie Russell held Michael tightly against her side. "Does that mean that ...?"

"I'm sorry," said Raquasthena. "Michael still has Mobius syndrome in real life. Here, he's dreaming that he doesn't, and you can't blame him for that."

Ellen Rohrig said, "I believe these people, Maggie. Look

around you. Was your home street ever like this, really? It's all too perfect."

The woman shook her head. "I feel *safe* here. My baby can be safe here, too."

"I'm afraid not, ma'am," Dom Magator told her. "You may feel safe for now, but it won't be long before these bad characters show up looking for you, and believe me, you don't want to be here when they do."

CHAPTER TWENTY

Time was passing quicker and quicker, and now the Night Warriors had to hurry urgently from one house to the next, gathering together all of the expectant mothers that Dr. Beltzer had been dreaming about. All of them were reluctant to leave, and one or two of them became argumentative and even tearful. These houses, after all, were the places where they had felt happiest and most secure.

They found Nurse Meiner's house, exactly as it had looked the previous night, except that it was filled with sunshine. In the sitting room they discovered a young black girl, nineteen years old, watching TV.

"This isn't your house, is it, sweetheart?" said Dom Magator.

"I know ... but I always wanted to live in a house just like this."

Dom Magator looked at Raquasthena and pulled a face. The Winterwent and the High Horse certainly knew what they were doing. Even if one of the mothers hadn't had a happy childhood home, they had provided one.

As they reached the outskirts of New Mile Branch, however, the weather began to turn. A chilly wind began to blow from the east, and huge gray clouds started to pile up behind the trees. Leaves scuttled along the street as if they were panicking, and yard gates slammed and hesitated and slammed again, like a slow handclap.

They coaxed a young mother called Kelly Pittman to leave her parents' two-story brick house from Chenoweth Lane, and then they had seven mothers altogether, as well as Michael, who was possessively holding his mother's hand. "Is that everybody?" asked Dom Magator.

"Yes, this is everybody," said Ellen Rohrig. "What do we now? How do we get out of here?"

"We have to return to the portal where we first entered this dream," Kalexikox told her. "It's a little more than a mile-and-a-half, but Dr. Beltzer's perception of time is accelerating as he gets closer to waking up, so it shouldn't take us more than a few minutes to get there."

Raquasthena ushered the expectant mothers close together, so the Night Warriors could protect them as they walked along. They were worried and silent, most of them, although one older woman kept pleading, "Don't let anything happen to my baby, will you? Please don't let anybody hurt her."

Ellen Rohrig leaned close to Xanthys and said, "That's Sylvia Bellman. She's thirty-seven and she had her baby by IVF."

Xanthys said, "We're not going to let anything happen to you, any of you—you or your babies."

The Zaggaline gave her a quick look that meant "We sure hope so, anyhow."

The sky was much darker now, and the women's nightdresses were rippling in the wind. Michael was holding his mother's hand very tightly and looking worried.

"We really need to get out of here *schnell*," said Dom Magator.

As they walked back along the main street, however, The Zaggaline saw something that he hadn't noticed before. In the backyard of one of the three-story properties stood a huge spreading oak, and perched in its branches was a ramshackle treehouse. He didn't recognize the main building, but when he caught sight of the treehouse, he felt a tightness around his chest and a terrible sense of dread.

"Wait up a second, man," he said to Dom Magator. "That treehouse ... see it? That's the treehouse that our dad built for us when we were little."

Kalexikox said, "You're right. There was a really bad storm one night and the whole thing collapsed. We were really pissed, because we kept our comic collection in it. But that's it, all right. Same blue checkered drapes made out of an old kitchen tablecloth. That's the actual treehouse."

"But I haven't dreamed about it for years," said The Zaggaline.

"Me neither."

"So how did the Winterwent get hold of it and bring it here?"

They stared at each other, and then they both said, *"Janie."*

They opened the gate and hurried together across the overgrown yard. When they had first passed this house, the grass had been neatly trimmed and the rose trellis had been crowded with fragrant pink flowers. Now the grass was nearly waist high and tangled with thistles, and the roses had turned tobacco brown and their heads were drooping.

"Janie!" yelled The Zaggaline, as he reached the foot of the oak tree. *"Janie, are you up there?"*

"Janie!" bellowed Kalexikox.

At first there was no answer. But then they both screamed *"Janie!"* at the tops of their voices and Janie drew back the old blanket that covered the "door."

"What do you want?"

"Janie, you have to get out of there, now!"

"But I'm having such a good time up here! I'm having a tea party for all of my dolls."

"Janie, something really bad is going to happen to you if you don't get out of there."

The wind was rising, and The Zaggaline felt the first few pellets of hail rattling against his helmet. "Janie, there's going to be a real bad storm and the treehouse is going to come crashing down to the ground. So, please come down."

Janie hesitated, so The Zaggaline started to climb up the makeshift wooden ladder. When he reached the top he held out his hand and said, "Come on, Janie. You don't want your baby to get hurt, do you?"

"My baby? These are *all* my babies!"

Inside the treehouse, Janie had arranged dozens of dolls—Barbies and Cinderellas and teddies and clowns. Here was her childhood, before their mother had died and she had grown up to be sulky and rebellious. Here was innocence and safety.

"Janie, you have to get down here right now."

The oak tree's branches were swaying in the wind and the treehouse was making deep creaking noises. George Beame had never pretended that he was a great carpenter, and the structure was held together with not much more than rusty old nails and enthusiasm.

Janie balanced her way across the floor and put her bare foot on the upper rung of the ladder. "You won't let me fall, will you?"

"I'm The Zaggaline now. I'll take care of you."

They climbed down the ladder together. The wind was screaming at them now, and bursts of white hail were scattering across the street. The Night Warriors were doing their best to shield the mothers from the storm, but it was growing increasingly violent and they were already soaked, their hair bedraggled and their cheeks red from cold.

"Who's this?" shouted Dom Magator, as The Zaggaline and Kalexikox brought Janie out of the front gate.

"This is our sister, Janie. She's expecting a baby any day

now. Our dad was supposed to take her down to Bowling Green, but he didn't have the time."

"There's no time left for anything, now," said Raquasthena. "Look!"

On the crest of the slope up ahead of them, hundreds of figures were pouring through the silver birch trees. They were hunched and gray, and they were running very fast. At first they looked like soldiers dressed in armor, but as they came nearer The Zaggaline could see that they were animals of some species, with bristly gray fur and warty gray shells protecting their bodies. They had narrow, sleek skulls, with eyes as yellow as fermented pus, and snaggles of barbarous teeth. Some of them appeared to be carrying machetes and three-pronged baling hooks, although they all had claws that looked capable of tearing off somebody's face with a single rip. Even from a distance of a half-mile, the Night Warriors could hear them chittering and screeching, and their body-plates knocking together.

"Holy moly," said The Zaggaline. "There has to be a thousand of them!"

"What the hell are they?" asked Dom Magator.

"I've seen them before," said Raquasthena, her voice sounding grim behind her expressionless mask. "They're Armadillo Rats, one of the High Horse's favorite war species. They're totally vicious, they have no pity whatsoever and their shells are so dense that normal weapons don't make any impression on them."

"In that case, it looks like we're going to need some non-normal weapons." Dom Magator lifted two handguns out of his belt. "Here, Zagga—try this one. It's a Deathwatch Torpedo Pistol. Works in the same way as a wood-boring beetle, only at very high velocity. It can drill a fifty-caliber hole through ten inches of solid teak timber, so it should be able to go through armadillo shell."

"How about me?" asked Xanthys.

"Did you ever fire a gun before?"

"No. But then I never turned back time before, and I didn't have any trouble picking *that* up."

"Okay, try this one." Dom Magator gave her a gold-plated pistol with a flared muzzle. "Optical Automatic ... it shoots out a burst of bio-halogenic light that changes the chemical composition in your targets' eyes, so that they instantly go blind. Hey, be careful—for God's sake don't point it at any of us, or we'll be walking around with white sticks for the rest of our lives."

Ellen Rohrig suddenly said, "Look—there's more of them!"

She was right. Hundreds more Armadillo Rats were running over and surging down the slope toward them. Not only could they hear them, but they could *smell* them, too. They gave off a sour, damp, rancid odor like decaying fur coats, and their odor was carried ahead of them on the wind.

Behind the Armadillo Rats they saw even bulkier creatures swaying through the trees with huge heads and bulky backs and enormous black claws. "Bull Crabs," said Raquasthena. "Half fighting bull, half giant crustacean. They have as much strength as a mechanical digger. I've seen a Night Warrior in a titanium helmet have his head torn off by one of those claws."

"You're making me feel more and more cheerful by the minute," said Dom Magator. He unlocked a heavy-duty rifle from the rack on his back, a multi-barreled Gatling that detonated the oxygen and hydrogen molecules in the air and set up a shattering chain reaction. He called it his Einstein Gun.

Raquasthena unwound the jointed metal bullwhip that she wore around her waist. "You want a gun, too?" Dom Magator asked her, but she shook her head. "How about you, Kalexikox?"

Kalexikox nodded, and Dom Magator passed over the crossbowlike Daisy Cutter that had been used to shoot at the Winterwent's ankles. "You be careful, too," he cautioned him. "You blow my feet off, that's going to be the end of my career as a tap dancer."

"Dom Magator," said The Zaggaline soberly, and pointed into the distance. Far off to their right, even more Armadillo Rats were appearing through the trees and pouring toward them like a gray *tsunami*.

"Jesus," said Dom Magator. "I think we're outnumbered."

Raquasthena aggressively snapped her whip, and it made a series of deafening bangs like gunfire. Kalexikox looked up from his calculator and said, "There's no way that we can fight off this many rats. I've worked out the mathematical odds according to the weaponry that we have available to us and even if every single shot finds its target and every single knife we throw causes a fatality, they will overwhelm us in three minutes, eight seconds."

"So what the hell are we going to do?" asked The Zaggaline.

"How about another Amoebic Avenger?"

"If The Zaggaline creates another Amoebic Avenger ... let's take a look ... that will enable us to survive for another seventeen seconds."

"Great. Won't even have time to eat a last cheeseburger."

"What if I turn back time?" Xanthys suggested.

"That won't help us," said Kalexikox. "We're Night Warriors, and if we turn back time *we* may be able to escape, but all of these mothers will find themselves back in New Mile Branch, and we'll be right back to square one."

"Then supposing I turn it *forward*?"

"What good will that do? The rats will be on top of us even quicker."

"No—forward to the point where they've actually *passed* us, so that we can attack them from behind."

Dom Magator said, "Hey ... that's a really neat idea. And these mothers will be that much nearer the portal."

"Whatever we decide to do," Raquasthena put in, "we'd better do it pretty damn quick."

The first of the Armadillo Rats were less than a hundred

yards away now. Their smell was so strong that it filled the Night Warriors' helmets, and Xanthys couldn't stop herself from retching. She could taste Armadillo Rat in her mouth, as if she had been eating one.

As they came closer, the Night Warriors could see that the Armadillo Rats were infested with tiny brown vermin, and that their arms and their legs were covered in suppurating sores. They were like creatures from some dark medieval triptych, a vision of hell and damnation made flesh.

Raquasthena said, "Be warned. Even if it doesn't kill you right off, one scratch from an Armadillo Rat's claws will give you a really serious disease, like leprosy or plague or ebola."

One of the mothers started to wail—a high-pitched, quavering song of utter terror. Two or three others started to sob. Even Michael was biting his lip. But Xanthys held up her hand and said, "Don't be frightened. Please don't be frightened. We're going to save you, I promise."

With that, she turned around and faced the oncoming hordes of Armadillo Rats and Bull Crabs. She selected a key from her helmet display—a bright scarlet key that immediately lit up on her belt. *Two minutes and fifteen seconds ahead, that should do it.* She pointed the key toward the Armadillo Rats and turned it.

For a long, airless moment, she thought that her time-curving hadn't worked. But then she felt an immense wave of insubstantial flesh surging past her as the Armadillo Rats passed *by* them and *through* them and into the immediate future. The wave seemed to rush on and on forever, but in real time it took less than three seconds.

Abruptly, they found that the High Horse's army was behind them. Some of the Armadillo Rats had even managed to run as far as the outskirts of New Mile Branch. The seven expectant mothers, with Janie hurrying close behind them, were halfway up the slope toward the silver birch trees. The sky was even darker and more menacing than ever.

"Fire!" shouted Dom Magator, and the Night Warriors

opened fire with everything they had. Kalexikox fired the Daisy Cutter, and its titanium disks sliced into the crowds at ankle level, dropping scores of Armadillo Rats and four or five Bull Crabs, too. The Armadillo Rats screeched in pain and frustration, while the Bull Crabs let out a reverberating roar that distorted the entire landscape, because it disturbed Dr. Beltzer's dream.

Xanthys held her Optical Automatic in both hands, aiming it at the Armadillo Rats as they turned around in disarray. Every time she squeezed the trigger, a blinding blast of blue-white light illuminated the whole battle scene, giving it a jerky, stroboscopic effect. Armadillo Rats appeared to be frozen as their heads were blown apart. Bull Crabs were caught in mid-collapse, their heavy claws flung upward.

The Zaggaline got down on one knee and rested the long barrel of his Deathwatch Torpedo Pistol against his upraised forearm to steady it. He fixed an Armadillo Rat in his sights and fired. The pistol made a sharp Doppler noise, as if a huge truck had sped past him. A torpedo hit the rat on the side of his gray abdominal shell. The impact flung it backward two or three feet so that it collided with the Armadillo Rats behind it. Then it blew up, and a stringy mess of fur and intestines were flung up into the air.

The Zaggaline fired again and again, until the barrel of his pistol was so hot that it was scorching his arm. Armadillo Rats were exploding on every side, their disintegrated remains jumping up and down in a grisly parody of an ornamental fountain.

Dom Magator used his throwing knives first. With great steadiness and balletic poise, he took one knife after another out of the sheaths on his back—lifted it, aimed it and then flung it into the struggling, screaming mass of Armadillo Rats. His victims fell without a sound, their brains pierced seven inches deep by surgical steel.

But it was Raquasthena whose skill impressed Xanthys the most. She advanced toward the Armadillo Rats swinging her whip and beckoning them to come closer. Two of them rushed toward her, hissing and screeching and lashing at her with their baling hooks. But as they came nearer, she snapped her whip and their heads flew off, both of them. A third ran toward her, its claws upraised, but she snapped her whip again and it wrapped itself tightly around the creature's waist. Raquasthena yanked the Armadillo Rat toward her with such force that it thumped into her. Its spinal column was penetrated by the penis-like spike between Raquasthena's legs and its fur was immediately snared by the thousands of hooks that covered her armor. The Armadillo Rat thrashed and kicked and tried to pull itself free, but Raquasthena reached behind her, lifted the trident from her back, and forced it into the crevice at the top of its chest plate. She worked it from side to side until it had penetrated deep, and all the time the helpless creature was jerking in agony and rage. At last she pushed the trident forward, and with a sickening crackle the Armadillo Rat's chest plate was torn away like the shell being torn off a turtle, revealing its bloody, glutinous insides. Raquasthena flicked her wrist so that her whip unwound itself from the Armadillo Rat's body. It fell onto the ground in front of her, still shuddering and quaking and arching its back in agony.

She stepped back, looking for more Armadillo Rats to decapitate, but as she did so a wounded Bull Crab reared up from the heaps of bodies all around her.

Xanthys shouted, "Raquasthena! *Raquasthena—look out!*"

The Bull Crab had a massive black head like a minotaur, and curving black horns and eyes that burned as red as incandescent coals. Kalexikox had cut through its lower legs with one of his Daisy Cutter disks. One its feet was severed completely, while the other was hanging from a shred of black skin. But its enormous knobby claws were still intact, and as Raquasthena took one more step backward, it seized her left leg just below the knee.

Xanthys heard the crunch even above the screeching of the Armadillo Rats and the ceaseless detonations from The

Zaggaline's pistol. Raquasthena didn't scream, but she fell sideways, almost on top of the Armadillo Rat whose shell she had ripped off. The Bull Crab shifted itself forward to give itself more leverage.

Xanthys aimed and fired her Optical Automatic. Again, the battlefield was lit by a dazzling blue flash and the Bull Crab's burning red eyes instantly went black and blind. But the Bull Crab already had Raquasthena firmly in its grip, and it was trying to sever her leg by sheer force of compression.

"Zagga!" Xanthys yelled, and pointed to Raquasthena.

The Zaggaline fired, too. A Deathwatch Torpedo hit the Bull Crab in the breastbone and black blood sprayed all over Raquasthena's impassive faceplate. Seconds later, the Bull Crab exploded, a messy lump of meat and guts and connective tissues.

"Cover me!" shouted Xanthys. The Zaggaline and Dom Magator fired wildly into the crowds of Armadillo Rats while Xanthys ducked forward and knelt down beside Raquasthena. Her bare knee squidged into one of the Bull Crab's slippery lungs, and it let out a wet, rubbery exhalation, as if that were the Bull Crab's last breath.

Raquasthena's leg had been crushed so badly that it was obvious that she was going to lose it. Gently, Xanthys unfastened her faceplate. Raquasthena looked sweaty and gray with shock, and she was breathing in shallow, panicky gasps.

"You're going to be okay," Xanthys reassured her. "I can curve time back, before this happened. I did it with Kalexikox, when he lost his arm."

"You can't," Raquasthena panted. "There's too many of them ... we have to kill them all now or we never will."

"But we can't let you lose your leg!"

"Xanthys, I'm a Night Warrior. I know the risks. So what if I walk with a limp from now on ... I'll be proud of it, if we win this battle tonight."

Xanthys looked up. She could see that Raquasthena was right. There were still hundreds of Armadillo Rats left alive, and the Night Warriors were almost out of ammunition. Dom Magator had only three or four throwing knives left and Kalexikox had run out of titanium disks for the Daisy Cutter. If she curved time back, all of the Armadillo Rats that they had killed in that time span would be revived, but the Night Warriors' weapons would still be empty. They would be overrun within minutes, and horribly slaughtered, and the High Horse and the Winterwent would be free to do whatever they wanted.

"Kalexikox!" Xanthys called out. "Come help me!"

She couldn't move Raquasthena herself because she had no gloves and she was almost naked, and in spite of her protective copper skin-covering, Raquasthena's hooks would have torn her to pieces.

Kalexikox dodged forward and joined her. "She's hurting bad," said Xanthys. "We have to move her away from here."

Kalexikox maneuvered his hands under Raquasthena's armpits. He tugged her, and lifted her, and she cried out *naaaaah!* with pain. Kalexikox hesitated, but then he tugged her again, and again, and at last he managed to pull her clear of the blood and the bones and the sickening heaps of blown-apart Armadillo Rats. Raquasthena's leg was twisted sideways at an impossible angle and she shouted in agony every time he shifted her, but in a few minutes he had managed to drag her back to the other Night Warriors.

Now that his last throwing knife was gone, Dom Magator had been rapid-firing at the Armadillo Rats with his Density Rifle. It used a dangerous amount of energy, but it compressed whatever it hit to a thousandth of its normal size. With a sharp rattling noise like a hundred pairs of castanets, the Density Rifle was reducing scores of Armadillo Rats into tiny knots of hair, bone and shell, and scattering them all across the battlefield like gravel.

Soon there was only a rabble of thirty Armadillo Rats left standing, and all of the Bull Crabs were dead. Dom Magator said, "Right ... I've had enough of this shit," and picked up his Einstein Gun. The remaining Armadillo Rats ran toward them, screeching in fury. They weren't afraid of dying, because they didn't know what dying was. They were nothing more than cruelty turned into living creatures.

They came nearer and nearer in a horrible round-shouldered lope, until they were no more than twenty yards away. The Zaggaline coughed and said, "Dom Magator? Are you going to fire that thing? Any time now would be good."

"Don't shoot until you see the turmeric yellow of their eyes, that's what I always say."

"Dom Magator!"

The Armadillo Rats were so close now that The Zaggaline took hold of Xanthys's hand and took two involuntary steps back.

Dom Magator said, "Practical physics in action!" and fired his Einstein Gun. There was an explosion so loud that it was unhearable and the whole universe went white. The Zaggaline felt as if he had seen God.

CHAPTER TWENTY-ONE

He opened his eyes, and all of the Armadillo Rats had been turned to ashes, like the victims of Hiroshima. Their flesh had been charred from their skeletons, and smoke was rising from their eye sockets.

The Zaggaline took off his helmet and screwed a finger into his ear. "I'm deaf," he said, and his voice sounded funny and flat.

"Yes," said Kalexikox. "Next time you decide to set off a nuclear chain reaction, Dom Magator, I think it would be more prudent not to do it quite so nearby. The recommended safety distance for an explosion of that magnitude is something over a mile."

"Palooked the bastards, though, didn't I?" said Dom Magator. "Palooked them good and proper."

"Yes, you palooked them all right."

Lightning flickered on the northern horizon, and the Night Warriors could hear the black collision of distant thunder. Xanthys looked up the slope and she could see that the expectant mothers had almost reached the line of silver birch trees. "I guess we'd better catch up. We still haven't seen the High Horse, have we?"

"Oh, I think we will," said Dom Magator. "I think he'll probably want to have a word with us about flattening his entire army."

"What about Raquasthena?" asked Xanthys. "We can't leave her here."

"You can," said Raquasthena. "I'll be okay. You can come back for me tomorrow night."

"If there *is* a tomorrow night," said Kalexikox.

"What if Dr. Beltzer doesn't have this dream again?"

"He's bound to, sooner or later."

Dom Magator said, "Raquasthena, this is all very heroic, but in the Army we never left a buddy behind, and as far as I'm concerned the same applies to the Night Warriors."

He unclipped the toboggan-like weapons rack that was fastened to his back. There were three carbines left, but all of the knives had gone. He took out the carbines, including his Sun Gun, and dropped them onto the ground. "Here … if you lie on this rack, we can take it in turns to carry you."

"You're not going to leave these weapons behind?"

"I'll take the Sun Gun, in case we need some ultimate force. Otherwise we'll just have to take our chances."

Dom Magator's weapons rack was complicated, but it was made of very light alloy, and what was more, it was extendable. It was a little short for a stretcher, but Raquasthena was able to lie on her side with her right leg bent. Her left leg they tied with a strap to one of the carbine clips so it didn't swing loose from the side of the stretcher and give her too much pain. The Bull Crab's claw had pinched her flesh so completely that it had sealed off her arteries and she had lost almost no blood at all. All the same, she was already going into deep shock, and the Night Warriors knew that they had to get her out of this dream as soon as they could.

The Zaggaline and Kalexikox carried her first. She weighed very little and they made good progress climbing the slope. The expectant mothers saw that they were coming and waited for them. Behind them, they heard more thunder, and there was an ominous smell of ozone on the wind.

Janie joined The Zaggaline and looked down at Raquasthena. "Oh my God, her *leg!* Is she going to be okay?"

"We hope so. She won't actually lose her leg in the real world, but she'll always have to dot and carry when she walks. We just have to get her out of here like real quick, that's all. And all of *you, too.*"

Janie looked confused. "I don't understand what happened. How did we climb up this hill? One minute all those horrible rat things were coming toward us, and then we were up here, and you were back down there, fighting them."

"This is a dream, Janie. Some weird stuff happens in dreams."

They topped the rise and then they walked down the long incline that took them back between the Mexican effigies.

This time, the effigies looked even more sinister, as if they were grave markers rather than gods, and they knew that the Night Warriors were going to die in this dream. The wooden doors in the figure of Tezcatlipoca were still clacking, and his carved face looked as if it were mocking them.

Clack—clack—clack— Xanthys thought that she would never forget that sound for the rest of her life, however long that was going to be.

They passed the hospital—or rather, in a strange way, the hospital appeared to pass *them,* rotating like a building seen from a train window. The hospital looked empty now. Its windows were boarded up and its paint was peeling in long tattered pennants.

But it was here that Michael-Row-The-Boat-Ashore-

Hallelujah came up to Dom Magator and held his hand. "I'm going to leave you now."

"What? What are you talking about?"

"I'm going back to the hospital."

"Michael, none of this is real. This is a dream being dreamed by Dr. Beltzer, and you were sent into this dream to help us. In a little while, though, Dr. Beltzer is going to wake up, and this dream will be gone. Vanished."

Michael looked up at him with one eye half-closed. "I'm still going to go back. If it all vanishes, then I'll vanish, too, and I don't mind that."

Michael's mother came over. She looked very pale and tired, and her hair was blowing across her face.

"What's wrong?" she asked Dom Magator. "Why have we stopped?"

"Michael says he wants to go back to the hospital."

Michael's mother bent down and put her arm around him. "Michael, sweetheart, you can't do that."

Michael's mouth puckered and his eyes filled with tears. "I don't want to go back. I don't want that face anymore."

Maggie Russell stood up straight and looked at Dom Magator. "If he stays here, what will happen to him?"

"Dr. Beltzer will open his eyes. The hospital will disappear, along with everything else in this dream, and in the real world Michael won't ever wake up."

Tears were running freely down Maggie Russell's cheeks. "Do you know how badly deformed he is?"

Kalexikox had come up to join them. "I checked him over, ma'am, and he's suffering very badly, isn't he?"

Maggie Russell wiped her tears with the back of her hand. "Michael," she said, "if you want to go back to the hospital ... if that's what you really want to do ... then, yes, you can go back."

Michael wrapped his arms tightly around his mother's waist. "Thank you," he sobbed. "Thank you, Mommy. Thank you."

They stood and watched him walk back through the hospital parking lot. One second he was only a few steps away from them—then, in the blink of an eye, he had reached the far side of the parking lot—and then, in another blink, he was climbing the steps to the front doors.

As he reached the doors, they opened, and the nunlike woman appeared. She laid both hands on Michael's shoulders and the two of them stood there for a while, looking back at the Night Warriors and Michael's mother. Michael waved. His mother waved back and whispered, "Go on, Michael. Row the boat ashore."

"Hallelujah," said Dom Magator.

Xanthys came up to them. "Who *is* that woman?"

"I think I'm beginning to work it out," Dom Magator told her.

"And?" asked Xanthys.

"I'll tell you later. You don't need me to start bawling, too."

Kalexikox said, "Come on, guys, we really need to hurry now. We only have about twenty minutes before Dr. Beltzer gets his wake-up call."

Within a few minutes, they could see the mountain range. It looked gray and craggy and forbidding, and the clouds were so low that some of the peaks were completely hidden. Thank God, though, it was a mountain range and not a rifle range. The last thing that Dom Magator felt he could face right now was a hostile barrage of sniper fire.

All eight expectant mothers were beginning to show signs of exhaustion, especially Maggie Russell, who was being comforted and supported by Ellen Rohrig and another woman. Raquasthena's eyes were closed, and Dom Magator hoped for her sake that she was unconscious.

He used his helmet sights to check up ahead. He was slightly worried because he couldn't yet see the bright blue lights of the portal. Yet, according to Kalexikox's latest calculations, they should reach it in a little less than eleven minutes.

He fine-tuned his focus. It was then that he realized that something was obscuring the portal. Something that was sixty or seventy feet high, and brindled, and shaggy, like a massive heap of dead buffalo.

"Kalexikox," he said. "Check that out, right up ahead of us."

Kalexikox stopped, and he and The Zaggaline carefully laid the improvised stretcher down amongst the brush. Kalexikox adjusted his instruments, and Dom Magator saw the swarm of sparks circling inside his helmet even faster, as if they were excited, or frightened.

"He's been waiting for us," Kalexikox said, at last. "What do we do now?"

"There's nothing we can do. He's blocking our only way out of here."

"What is it?" asked The Zaggaline. "Is there something wrong?"

"You could say that, yes. Standing between us and getting the hell out of this dream is your unfriendly neighborhood High Horse, in person."

"Listen," said Xanthys.

They listened. Intermittently blown on the breeze they could hear screaming, howling and the baying of wolves. But this wasn't the sound of wild animals hunting for prey. This was the sound of creatures in agony.

"Holy shit," said The Zaggaline. They all looked at each other in trepidation. Ellen Rohrig said, "What? What is it? What's that dreadful crying noise?"

"I could create a character to fight it," said The Zaggaline.

"Well, yes. I think you'd better do that. What do you have in mind?"

"Er—how about a High Horse Hunter?"

"That sounds appropriate. You want to get to work?"

The Zaggaline opened up his limning lens. He quickly

sketched out a tall, attenuated figure, like an early frontiers-
man in a buckskin jacket and a coonskin hat—thin-faced,
sharp-eyed and mean-looking. The Zaggaline gave him a
long-barreled sharpshooter's musket, so that he could pick
off the High Horse from a distance.

He swung down another lens and constructed the
hunter's skeleton, and then another lens to fill in his circula-
tory system. But the hunter's arteries had only wriggled as
far as his abdomen when the lens suddenly went blank.

The Zaggaline furiously jiggled his power switch. He saw
a momentary flicker of pinky-orangey light, but then the
lens went dead again.

"You can take your own sweet time if you like," said Dom
Magator.

"I can't do it, man. I'm totally out of power. That Amoebic Avenger must have drained my system."

"Great. I'd give you a feed, but I'm running on empty,
too. How about you, Xanthys?"

"Just about enough to time-curve us backward or forward about twenty-eight seconds. No more than that."

"Kalexikox?"

"Enough to keep my weapon powered up and my instruments running, but that's it. I certainly don't have enough
to create a High Horse Hunter."

"Well, I still have my trusty Sun Gun. I guess we'll
have to hope and pray that the High Horse is highly
inflammable."

Kalexikox and The Zaggaline picked up Raquasthena's
stretcher again, and together they all began to walk toward
the forbidding outline of the High Horse. Soon the screaming of tortured animals became constant, and several expectant mothers started to whimper in fear.

As they approached, the High Horse started to move
toward them, too, and it was then that they realized the true
horror of the enemy they were fighting.

He sat astride three horses, one on top of the other, a
three-story building of living animals. The lowest of the

horses was a giant warhorse, over 30 hands high, with a jet-black coat and massive hooves. It was hung with brasses and belts and corroded bronze plates, all connected with leather straps, and each plate bristled with barbs and knives. Its head was encased in a bronze helmet that was fashioned into the shape of a grinning skull.

The second horse was a Percheron, a huge draft horse. Its legs had been connected to the elbows and thighs of the warhorse below it with a complicated system of screws and levers, so that both horses were forced to walk in unison. This horse, too, was protected by jointed bronze plates, but it was also wrapped around with razor wire.

Finally, on top, a third horse had been attached, an American Cream, joined to the Percheron with more levers and pistons, so that all three horses had to move their legs together in a terrible swaying march. The topmost horse was decorated with torn and bloodstained flags, as well as bunches of human skulls of all different sizes hanging from chains. A long black studded scabbard was suspended from the side of the saddle, containing a sword with a monkey's skull for a pommel.

Sitting astride the saddle was the High Horse himself, at least fifteen feet tall, wearing a helmet made of three stags' heads, with a forest of antlers. The stags' heads were still alive, with rolling eyes and bloodied tongues, and they kept up an endless screeching of pain and despair. They were joined by a hair-raising descant that came from the scores of living creatures that the High Horse wore as his war cloak—rabbits and otters and beavers and foxes, as well as ravens and owls and other large birds—all of them roughly stitched together to form a crying, struggling, screaming mass.

Many of the creatures had been badly injured, which added to their agony. Some had been burned, some had broken legs or wings and some of them were partially disemboweled. In the real world, they would have been dead, but this was the world of nightmares, where the dead could be kept alive forever.

It was the High Horse himself who made the Night Warriors hesitate. Underneath his stags' head helmet, his face was wide and smooth and leathery-brown, as if the skin of a smaller man had been stretched across a broad, Mongolian skull. His eyes glittered green and black like blowflies, and his mouth was a straight lipless split crammed with tiny yellow teeth. Underneath his cloak of writhing creatures, they could see his bare chest, crisscrossed with scars and pierced with hooks and studs and rings. From each nipple hung several small skulls—birds and rabbits and iguanas.

The tower of horses slowly approached them with a teetering motion, as if the whole living structure was on the point of losing its balance and falling over. The Night Warriors could see the levers and pistons working like the driving rods of twelve steam locomotives, all of them greased with thick yellow fat.

The High Horse stopped right in front of them. The warhorse's hooves restlessly shifted on the stony ground.

"You're—*ahem!*" said The Zaggaline, clearing his throat. "You're standing in our way, dude."

The High Horse spoke to them. His voice was terrifying. It was a thick, suggestive whisper, but it seemed to fill their heads as if he were inside them.

"I have come to take the women."

"Oh, you think?"

"The women are all mine. Their unborn infants are all mine."

Dom Magator stepped forward, holding up the Sun Gun. Xanthys and Kalexikox kept the expectant mothers behind them, shielding them as much as they could.

"I believe that it would be in your own best interests if you stepped to one side," said Dom Magator. His heart was beating so hard that it hurt his ribcage.

"My interests are no concern of yours, Night Warrior,"

the High Horse told him. "I have come to take the women and take the women I will."

He yanked at his reins so that his horses turned sideways. Then he reached down to the side of his saddle with a hand like a spider crab and drew out his sword. It made a slithering sound that set Dom Magator's teeth on edge.

"Is this guy serious?" said The Zaggaline, dismissively. "How's he going to reach us with *that*?"

But Kalexikox had been frantically punching at his databank buttons and he shouted, *"Down! Get down!"*

The High Horse swung his sword and the blade seemed to leap out at them, so that it was twenty feet longer. It struck Dom Magator on the left shoulder and sent him hurtling sideways onto the ground. Gasping, coughing, he looked at his shoulder and saw that the sword had cut clean through his armor and into his flesh. Blood pumped out of his wound, but almost immediately the blood was followed by a boiling mass of whitish-brown maggots.

Kalexikox rolled over to him, keeping his head low.

"Maggots!" screamed Dom Magator. *"You don't know how much I hate maggots!"*

With taut-faced efficiency, Kalexikox unfastened Dom Magator's armor-plated sleeve and wrestled it off. The wound was about four inches across, and maggots were pouring out of it thick and fast and dropping onto the ground, almost as if it were a fountain of maggots.

Out of a clip on his belt, Kalexikox slid a two-pronged metal instrument like a tuning-fork. Within a few seconds the prongs began to glow red, and Dom Magator could feel the heat it was giving out.

"This is really going to hurt," Kalexikox warned him.

"Anything! Just get these damn maggots off of me!"

Kalexikox held Dom Magator's upper arm steady and pressed the red-hot fork against the wound. There was a sharp sizzling sound and a smell like burning lamb fat, and the maggots writhed and wriggled and curled up in agony.

As Kalexikox cauterized the inside of his wound, Dom Magator almost passed out. He had experienced pain before, but nothing like this. He squeezed his eyes tight shut and thought of his mother and the time when he had tried to climb over a fence and caught his knee on some rusty barbed wire. "What are you making such a fuss for, John Dauphin, a little pain ain't nothing, especially when it's not your own. You see *me* crying?"

"That's it," said Kalexikox. "Had to do it quick or you would have been nothing but maggots in three minutes flat."

Dom Magator looked at the wound in fascinated horror. It was blistered and puckered and raging red, and it still hurt like seven degrees of hell, but at least there were no maggots crawling around in it.

"Give me a hand here." With Kalexikox's help, he managed to prop himself up on one elbow so that he could see what was happening.

Thirty yards away, The Zaggaline and Xanthys were trying to keep the High Horse at bay. The Zaggaline had picked up Dom Magator's Sun Gun and was circling around him, while the High Horse wheeled his snorting horses so that The Zaggaline couldn't get a clear shot. He was still swinging his sword around his head and it grew longer and longer every time he swung it. It made a low droning sound like a bagpipe chanter.

"What kind of freaking sword is that?" gasped Dom Magator. "How did he manage to cut me when I was standing so far off?"

Kalexikox helped him to climb to his feet. "According to my data bank, it's a Septic Saber."

"Septic Saber? How the hell does that work? Zagga! Don't get too close, and don't go pulling that trigger until you got a clear line of fire!"

Kalexikox said, "The way I understand it, the Septic Saber uses some kind of liquid nanotechnology to make itself as long or as short as its user wants it to be. Then it uses advanced entomology to infest every wound that it inflicts with face-fly maggots—*musca autumnalis,* the same flies that cluster around horses' nostrils."

"That's disgusting," said Dom Magator, checking his wound again.

"Yes … and this particular strain of face-fly maggots is incredibly voracious. They triple in number every five seconds and they can turn your entire body into one big wriggly maggot pudding before you can dial nine-one-one. I mean, not that there would be any point dialing nine-one-one in a dream."

"No," said Dom Magator. The sky had turned dark green now, and lightning began to strike all around them. The expectant mothers were all cowering together in a low depression in the ground, with Raquasthena lying on her stretcher beside them—conscious now, but still very shocked.

"We have to get these women out of here," said Dom Magator. "How the hell are we going to deal with our wonderful twelve-legged friend here?"

"I don't think that the High Horse is going to be our only problem," Kalexikox told him. "Haven't you noticed? The temperature's dropping. It's gone down three degrees Celsius in the past six minutes."

"The Winterwent," said Dom Magator. "That's all we need."

The Zaggaline kept circling around the High Horse, raising the Sun Gun now and then, trying to get a shot in. But it was obvious that the High Horse was experienced in battle and knew how to keep himself out of the line of fire. There was only enough power in the Sun Gun for one apocalyptic shot, and if he missed, the Night Warriors would be virtually defenseless.

And still it was growing darker. And still it was growing colder.

Dom Magator supposed that the Night Warriors could

take their chances and make a run for the portal, leaving the women behind. After all, as soon as Dr. Beltzer opened his eyes, all of this dream would disappear, and so would the women. But even if Dr. Beltzer woke up within seconds of their return, that would still leave the High Horse and the Winterwent enough time to capture at least two or three women and enter *their* dreams, and Dom Magator wasn't prepared to take the risk. This was it. This was the time. This was where positive good and negative evil were finally going to come head-to-head, and neither side was going to leave anybody standing.

The Zaggaline tried feinting to the left and then to the right, but he could almost believe that the High Horse was capable of reading his thoughts, because the High Horse responded by shifting his horses slightly to the right, and then to the left, so that he was always obscured behind his top horse's head and neck.

Dom Magator and Kalexikox came up to The Zaggaline and Xanthys joined them, too. A few crumbs of snow were tumbling through the air, and some of them were settling on the High Horse's cloak.

"He's *playing* with me, man," The Zaggaline protested.

"You could shoot his horses out from under him," said Dom Magator.

"You can't do that!" said Xanthys. "Those poor horses, what have *they* ever done, except suffer?"

"That apart," said Kalexikox, "there is no guarantee that by hitting his horses you would take out the High Horse himself. And he would be just as dangerous on foot, if not more so, especially if your weapon was empty."

The snow was falling much more densely now. Dom Magator held out his hand to The Zaggaline and said, "Give me the gun."

"What are you going to do?"

"Just give me the freaking gun, okay?"

"Dom Magator—wait," said Kalexikox. He was checking one of his sensors, tilting his head to one side so that he could catch the last reflected light.

"Give me ... the gun," Dom Magator repeated.

Reluctantly, The Zaggaline handed it over. Dom Magator slung it over his back and said, "I'm going to save this for the Winterwent. Payback for Amla Fabeya."

"That could be a wise move," Kalexikox told him. He checked his sensor again, and then said, "I suspected this, from the moment I first saw him. The High Horse isn't a real being at all, and never has been. Not like the Winterwent."

"He's coming for us," said Xanthys. They looked up, and the awkward, lurching arrangement of horses was slowly approaching them through the blizzard. The High Horse was standing up in his stirrups, his gruesome cloak of living birds and animals flying out behind him, his sword slowly rotating around his head—a sword that had grown to thirty feet long. It made a low whistling sound—*whooooww, whoooww, whoooww*—and cut a dark circle in the falling snow.

"Are we going to run or what?" said The Zaggaline, desperately.

"He's not real," Kalexikox insisted.

"What are you talking about? He was real enough to cut a slice out of my arm and fill it with creepy-crawlies!"

"He's *tangible*, yes. But he's nothing more than human cruelty, brought to life."

"What? I don't understand what the hell you're talking about!"

"In a dream—yes?—you can visualize frustration as a cinder block wall. Or some delay in your life—it can seem in your dreams like you're wading through a swamp. The High Horse is just the same. He's not a real entity. He's the very worst of human nature ... and cruelty to animals, above all."

"So what are we supposed to do about it? Call for the ASPCA?"

"No," said Kalexikox. "You call for the Knowledge Gunner."

He unlatched his heavy handgun from his belt, with its gold and silver balls lined up along its barrel. "See these balls? They're anti-illusory shells. When they explode, they disassemble any deceptions, straighten out any refracted light and show things up for what they really are."

"You're kidding me," said Dom Magator. "We could have used some of those at the last elections."

The High Horse was almost on top of them now and they began to back away, fast. But just as they thought he was going to take a swing at them with his thirty-foot broadsword, he steered his horses away. They lurched to the left and headed toward the depression where Raquasthena and the expectant mothers were trying to hide.

"Jesus!" said Dom Magator. "He's ignoring us—he knows we've run out of ammo—he's going straight for the women!"

"Janie!" shouted The Zaggaline. He began to run toward the depression, totally disregarding the fact that the High Horse was less than twenty feet away and could have cut his head off with a single swing of his broadsword.

"Zagga! For Christ's sake watch out!" said Dom Magator, jogging heavily after him. Kalexikox was running, too—beside him at first, but then faster and faster, until he was thirty or forty feet ahead.

"Janie!" screamed The Zaggaline. "Janie, get out of there! Run!"

The expectant mothers had heard the shouting, and one or two of them were already standing up. Even Raquasthena had managed to sit up on her stretcher.

The High Horse gathered speed. From a lurching walk his horses broke into a hideous canter, all three of them working together to keep their balance. The levers on their legs were groaning and squealing, and one or two screws burst out of their thighbones in a spray of blood. The High

Horse obviously didn't care. He was urging them into a gallop and uttering a low, reverberating howl of utter pleasure.

The Zaggaline was sprinting now. He managed to reach the depression and grab hold of Janie as she was climbing to her feet. He threw her sideways a fraction of a second before the High Horse swung his sword, and the blade clanged against the edge of his sharklike helmet. Next to them, Sylvia Bellman was still standing up, and the sword cut her completely in half at elbow-level, cutting her baby in half, too. The top of her body dropped backward, but her legs remained standing for a count of five—long enough for a furious mass of face-fly maggots to come pouring out of her open abdomen and drop down her thighs. The other women screamed in horror.

The Zaggaline helped Janie onto her feet and the two of them made their way back toward Xanthys and Dom Magator as fast as Janie could hobble.

The snow was blinding. The High Horse circled around the depression, trying to keep the rest of the women trapped. But Kalexikox had caught up with him and dodged around behind him, and was trying to grab hold of one of the armor plates that covered the flanks of his monstrous warhorse.

"Raquasthena!" he shouted. *"Raquasthena!"*

As badly injured as she was, Raquasthena was a hardened Night Warrior and she knew what Kalexikox wanted her to do. She managed to drag herself onto her hands and knees and crawl across the ground toward the High Horse. It seemed to take her forever, but the High Horse was so high up in his aerie and the snow was so furiously thick that he didn't see her.

She finally reached the forelegs of the warhorse and dragged herself upright. She hesitated for a moment, gathering her strength, and then she seized the warhorse's foreleg as tightly as she could, driving the spikes in her armor deep into its flesh and snaring its skin with her hooks.

The warhorse screamed and reared, and for three or four

seconds it looked as if the entire three-story construction of horses was going to come crashing over. But the High Horse lashed at them and shouted at them and they managed to steady themselves.

By that time, though, Kalexikox had managed to jump up and seize some of the armor plates, and heave himself halfway up the warhorse's side.

CHAPTER TWENTY-TWO

The High Horse kept on circling and circling, slowly rotating his sword above his head, keeping the expectant mothers trapped. At the same time, though, he kept leaning over the side of his topmost horse in an effort to see why his warhorse was whinnying and tossing its helmeted head and walking with such an uneven gait.

Seventy feet below him, Raquasthena clung on to the warhorse's foreleg, her injured leg hanging loose, too exhausted to pry herself free and try to make her escape.

But each time the High Horse circled around, Kalexikox managed to climb higher and higher. Soon he was standing on top of the warhorse, with one foot on its back and the other on its croup, and he began to force his way up through the razor wire that protected the Percheron. It was far from easy. Although his armor saved him from being cut to pieces, the complex instruments that covered his arms and chest were continually snagged on the wire, and it took valuable seconds to disentangle himself. He felt like the prince in *The Sleeping Beauty,* which his mother used to read to them when they were little, climbing up through the overgrown briars that surrounded the Princess' castle.

Meanwhile, on the ground, there was nothing that Xanthys and Dom Magator and The Zaggaline could do except watch. The Zaggaline held Janie tight and said, "You're going to be okay, babe, okay? We have to go back through the portal, me and the rest of the Night Warriors, but you don't. As soon as Dr. Beltzer wakes up, that's it—you'll be back in your own bed, and you probably won't even remember that any of this happened."

"What about these other women?" asked Janie. "That poor Mrs. Bellman!"

"You'll all be safe, so long as we can make sure that the High Horse and the Winterwent don't get you."

Kalexikox had negotiated the last tangle of razor wire, and now he was pulling himself up the American Cream. He used the chains and bloodied flags as handholds, and he found plenty of toeholds on the levers and pistons that connected the horse's legs to the Percheron below. The High Horse's living cloak would have afforded him a better grip, but Kalexikox thought that the creatures that were screaming and writhing on his back had suffered too much already. He could hardly bear to look at them, let alone pull at their tortured bodies to help himself up.

The High Horse must have felt the flags dragging beneath his saddle, because he suddenly twisted himself around. His eyes narrowed into black crevices and he grinned with delight.

"So, Night Warrior," he said, in that deep, coarse whisper. "You have succeeded in scaling the tower!"

Kalexikox grabbed a chain with his left hand to steady himself and unlatched his handgun with his right. In response, the High Horse tightened his reins and lifted his broadsword high above his head.

"It is many years since I took the head from a Night Warrior! I shall hang it around my horse's neck!"

"I wouldn't be too sure of that, sport," Kalexikox retorted. "Because I know something that you don't know, and that knowledge is going to be the end of you."

The High Horse opened his eyes wider. "What knowledge is this?" he whispered.

Kalexikox pointed his handgun directly at the High Horse's heart. "You are not a man. You are not an animal. You are not even a reptile. All you are is an evil intent, made manifest."

"You speak like all Night Warriors speak, like an innocent fool."

Kalexikox cocked his handgun. "Very well, then. Let's see who's the innocent fool, and let's see who's nothing but the very worst of human nature."

The High Horse didn't swing his sword. Instead, from under his cloak, he stabbed upward with a long-bladed dagger, straight through a tangle of squirming squirrels. The dagger went straight into the front bracket of Kalexikox's handgun just as Kalexikox pulled the trigger, jamming it.

"There!" whispered the High Horse, with undisguised glee. "Now let's be having your head!"

At that moment the first of the anti-illusory shells exploded.

From the top of the tower of horses, there was a detonation like the slamming of a huge door and a bright green flash. The darkness was lit up for miles in every direction, as far as the mountain ranges. Then—even before the first echo could come back to them—there was a second detonation, and a third, a fourth and a fifth.

The first detonation blew the High Horse himself into thousands of glittering fragments—not skin and bone, but lies and perversity and malice, like a shattered mirror. Kalexikox was cartwheeled into the air, his armor on fire. He had fallen only halfway to the ground before the second detonation blew the topmost horse into bloody bits.

The next three detonations blew the other horses apart— bones and levers and pistons and gory hunks of horseflesh.

Raquasthena was still clinging to the warhorse's forearm when the final detonation went off, and she was still clinging to it when she was flung more than a quarter of a mile away, setting the bushes alight.

The High Horse's living cloak was carried high up into the air by the heat of the explosion. As it floated, it burned, and the birds and animals that the High Horse had tortured for so long at last met the death that they had been longing for.

Xanthys and Dom Magator and The Zaggaline stood in silence as they watched the remains of the High Horse blazing in the snow. Janie had turned her back and covered her eyes.

"Dunc always wanted to be smart," said The Zaggaline. "He wanted to be smart more than anything else in the world. Even when he was five years old he used to kneel down beside his bed at night and say 'Please God, make me smart.' "

Dom Magator put an arm around his shoulders. "If you're smart, Zagga, then it's up to you to make a difference. Stupid can sit on its butt and watch *The Simpsons* all day. Smart has to go out and change the course of history."

Xanthys said, "We'd better make sure that these mothers are okay. They're probably going to be so traumatized after this."

Dom Magator checked his chronometer. "You're right. And we'd better get our skates on. Dr. Beltzer's wake-up call is in two minutes fifty-nine seconds flat."

The Night Warriors hurried through the snow to the depression where the expectant mothers had been hiding. They were shivering and sobbing and spattered with Sylvia Bellman's blood. There was nothing left of Sylvia Bellman except for her skeleton. The face-fly maggots had all crawled away, taking her with them.

Ellen Rohrig stood up and said shakily, "Is it over now? Is it really all over?"

"In less than two minutes, Dr. Beltzer will wake up and

then you'll be fine. We're going to stay with you, right up to the last second, just in case the Winterwent turns up. But I get the feeling that he's seen what we've done to his friend, and he's gone away with his Popsicle between his legs."

"And our babies?"

"I don't think that he'll try to take your babies again. This is all over now, thank God, and the good guys came out on top."

"Oh, but you lost your friends. You—Zaggaline, is it?—you lost your brother."

"I know," said The Zaggaline. "But he knew how dangerous it was going to be, and he still wanted to do it."

"Come on," said Dom Magator. "If you can come close to the portal, then we can keep an eye on you—right up until the last millisecond."

The expectant mothers stood up, and together they started to walk back to the portal. Although it was snowing very hard now, the portal still shone dazzling blue, and Xanthys thought that it looked almost like a shining memorial to the Night Warriors they had lost—Amla Fabeya and Kalexikox and Raquasthena. Janie was waiting beside it, chafing her arms to keep herself warm.

Maggie Russell stopped for a moment and looked back into the darkness. Dom Magator knew what she was probably thinking, but said nothing.

"He was such a beautiful little boy, wasn't he?" she said.

Dom Magator nodded.

Xanthys said, "It may be three o'clock in the morning, but I could really use a drink."

None of them heard it coming. The snow was so thick and well-compacted that its runners made hardly any sound at all, and the ice-wolves were silent, too. Out of the darkness, with stunning suddenness, the Winterwent's sledge appeared, sliding at full speed. Its banners were frozen and its towers were thick with stalactites. The ice-wolves were straining at their harnesses, and the Winterwent himself was standing on one of the front runners, with his elongated head sunk low in his shoulders and his cloak frozen stiffly behind him.

"*Janie!*" shouted The Zaggaline. "*Run, Janie! Run!*"

But Janie didn't understand what was happening. She turned and stared at the Winterwent's fast approaching sledge in bewilderment, and she didn't move. The ice-wolves ran past her without slackening their pace, and then the Winterwent reached out with two of his spider-like arms and seized her. She didn't even scream.

"Janie!" yelled The Zaggaline in despair.

The Night Warriors started to run, but all three of them knew that it was too late. The Winterwent's sledge sped fifty or sixty more yards and then it vanished. They stopped running, and Dom Magator had to sit gasping on the ground.

"Fifty-three seconds left," he said.

"So where did they go?" asked Xanthys. "One second they were there, and now they're not."

"Another dream," said Dom Magator, flapping his hand in frustration.

"What?"

"The Winterwent has taken Janie into somebody else's dream. Probably somebody who won't wake up for hours."

"Can he do that?"

"Of course he can do that. He *exists* in dreams. Dreams are the Winterwent's natural habitat."

"Can we go after him?"

"Oh, sure. But if we do that, it'll be too late for us to go back through the portal into Dr. Beltzer's bedroom. In fact, we won't be able to go back at all."

"Explain it to me."

"It's very simple. If we want to follow the Winterwent, I'll have to make another portal through to whatever dream it is that he's taken Janie into. I can do that, but it's going to take every last joule of energy I have left."

Suddenly, the ground shifted underneath their feet, as if they were standing on a rug and somebody had tugged it.

"We have to make up our minds quick," said Dom Magator. "It feels like Dr. Beltzer's waking up."

The Zaggaline said, "Even if you guys don't want to come with me, *I* have to go."

"I think we *all* have to go," said Xanthys. "If we don't, the Winterwent will get into Janie's baby's dream, and everything we did here is going to be wasted."

"Well, you're absolutely right, of course," Dom Magator agreed. "But let me just say this. Goddamn it to hell."

The six remaining mothers had approached them. It had stopped snowing now that the Winterwent had gone, and a weak yellowish sun had risen behind the mountain range.

Ellen Rohrig said, "We all wanted you to know how much we appreciate your sacrifice. We're so sorry for your losses, and we hope that you find your sister."

The Zaggaline mouthed the words "Thank you," but already the landscape was wavering, and the Night Warriors knew that it was time to leave. Dom Magator heaved himself onto his feet and walked as close as he could to the place where the Winterwent's sledge had disappeared. He switched on the lights on his forearms and shone a bright blue portal into the air.

"Ready? God only knows what kind of dream this is going to be."

"Ready for anything," said The Zaggaline. He stepped through the portal without any hesitation, and Xanthys followed. Dom Magator was about to step through it, too, but then he caught sight of Amla Fabeya's carpetbag, thickly covered in melting snow, in the same place that he had left it when they first arrived in Dr. Beltzer's dream.

"Dom Magator!" called Xanthys. The portal to the next dream was beginning to blink like a broken fluorescent light. "Dom Magator, it's closing!"

Dom Magator grabbed the carpetbag and hurried back.

The portal was right on the verge of collapse. Holding the carpetbag close to his chest, he threw himself into it sideways.

"Shoot, man," said The Zaggaline. "We thought you'd changed your mind!"

Dom Magator held up the bag and rattled it. "Still don't know what these are, but I thought I'd better bring them along."

He looked around. They had stepped through the portal into a desert, but Dom Magator could immediately tell that the Winterwent had passed through because the desert was two feet deep in snow. Less than a mile away, there was an oasis with frozen date palms and frozen water, where three frozen camels were standing. It was nighttime, and a cream-colored moon was hanging in the sky, but no stars.

"I don't think he's gone too far," said Dom Magator. "The temperature's down to twenty-five below."

"There—you can see his tracks," said The Zaggaline.

Even though it existed only in dreams, the Winterwent's sledge must have weighed several hundred tons. Several inches of snow had fallen since it had sped across this quarter of the desert, but its runners had left such deep troughs that they were still clearly visible.

"Any idea where this is?" asked The Zaggaline as they trudged through the snow.

Dom Magator checked his navigational instruments. "The Nefud Desert," he decided. "But not the real Nefud Desert. The Movie Nefud Desert."

"The Movie Nefud Desert?"

"Whoever's having this dream, they've never been to the real Nefud. So this isn't a dream about a real desert, it's a desert they saw in *Lawrence of Arabia* or *The Jewel of the Nile* or some movie like that."

Xanthys said, "I think you're right. Look over there."

In the middle distance, they could see a city with crenellated walls all around it. Its towers and domes were covered in snow and all of its windows were dark. Xanthys had seen the same kind of city in every Arabian Nights–type movie she had ever watched—the kind of city where Sinbad jumps from the rooftops and slides down a merchant's awning into the street.

They continued to follow the sledge tracks for a further three miles until the city had disappeared behind whirling curtains of snow, but there was still no sign of the Winterwent's sledge. Eventually, they were so exhausted that they had to stop.

The Zaggaline said, "The speed that bastard was traveling, he could have covered twenty miles by now."

"No, I don't think so. It's too damn cold. Kalexikox could have told us what the mean temperature is supposed to be in the Nefud Desert, but you can bet your left ass cheek they never have a whole lot of snow."

It was then that Xanthys said, "There it is—look."

She pointed off to their right. The snow was so thick that they had almost walked past it. Less than a quarter of a mile away, the Winterwent's sledge had been brought to a standstill. The ice-wolves were lying down resting, while the sledge itself towered above them like a ghostly white galleon in a frozen sea.

"Okay," said Dom Magator, "this is the plan: (a) we get in there, (b) we find your sister, and (c) we get the hell out of there."

"That's like an aspiration, man, not a plan."

"Exactly. What I'm saying is, we're going to have to improvise."

They approached the Winterwent's sledge from the stern, so that they wouldn't alert any of the ice-wolves. The closer they came to it, the more they appreciated how difficult it was going to be for them to get into it. Its sides were sheer and thickly coated with ice, and there seemed to be no handholds or footholds anywhere. Even if they climbed up the runners or the outriggers, they would still be faced with a perpendicular wall that was over sixty feet high and overhung at the top by hundreds of stalactites and knobby lumps of ice.

"I wish to God that Amla Fabeya was here," said Dom Magator, dropping the carpetbag. "She could scuttle up here like a spider up a drainpipe."

"Maybe she is here," said Xanthys. She hunkered down, opened up the bag and took out one of the complicated pieces of equipment. Then she climbed the strut that supported the nearest runner until she reached the vertical side of the sledge.

She didn't know how she understood what she was supposed to do: she had never been techanically minded. But there was perfect feminine logic in this device, a combination of intuition and inspired mechanics. It was like a rectangular bracket with two sharp claws at the top and two more claws at the bottom, and a complex arrangement of levers and springs in the middle. She placed it up against the wall of the sledge and pressed it flat, and immediately the springs opened and the levers clicked into place and the four claws buried themselves firmly into the ice.

"Well, that looks promising," Dom Magator admitted.

"Hand me another piece," said Xanthys. "That piece there, with the clips on."

The Zaggaline climbed halfway up the strut and passed it to her. Without any hesitation she fitted it into the first piece and again pressed it flat. Two more claws bit into the ice and she had her first foothold.

Dom Magator said, "Wait up, I'm coming up, too."

He stepped onto the runner and handed the carpetbag up to The Zaggaline. Xanthys rummaged around until she found a third piece, and she fitted that in, too.

"That's cool," said The Zaggaline. "Trouble is—there aren't nearly enough of them to take us up to the top."

"That's the beauty of this climbing system," Xanthys told him. "You only need thirteen brackets and you can climb anything."

She was fitting in a fourth piece when the sledge suddenly lurched. Dom Magator leaned out from his perch on the runner and said, "Damn it! The ice-wolves, they're up on their feet, and they're moving again!"

"You'd better hold on real tight, then, dude," The Zaggaline suggested.

The sledge lurched again and again as the ice-wolves took the strain on their harnesses. Gradually it began to gain momentum, until they were running over the snow at more than twenty miles an hour. The ride was far from smooth. They jolted over snow-filled wadis and bounced over snow-covered sand dunes. Dom Magator had to hold on to the runner strut so tightly that his fingers began to go numb.

The whole sledge was like some hideous traveling circus, with the ice-wolves howling and baying, the sterncastles creaking and the runner struts and outriggers clanking and banging, and there was that continuous hissing of metal over snow.

Xanthys had fitted in all thirteen brackets now. She climbed back down and beckoned to The Zaggaline that he should go up first. He climbed up the first eight, and then looked back for support. The brackets were cleverly engineered, but they were narrow and cold and difficult to hold on to, and the freezing wind was buffeting him badly.

"Dom Magator—you're next!" said Xanthys.

"I'm not sure I can do it, honey."

"You have to! It's the only way!"

Dom Magator said a small prayer to St. Olaf, the patron saint of the overweight, and then he started to climb up the strut. Xanthys helped him to reach the first bracket and find his balance. The Winterwent's sledge was traveling even faster now and the snow was seething all around them, so that it filled their mouths whenever they tried to talk.

"Come on, dude, you can make it!" shouted The Zaggaline. "Pretend you're Father Christmas, climbing up on the roof!"

"I shall freaking kill you for that when this is all over!"

But Dom Magator managed to get his foot into the first bracket, and then the second, then the third. Inside his armor he was sweating and his legs were shaking with effort, but he was determined that he was going to make it to the top.

Xanthys mounted the brackets now, just below him. When she had climbed to the second bracket, she hooked her boot down and released the springs of the first bracket. Then she reached down, took hold of it and passed it up to Dom Magator.

"Give this to The Zaggaline! It fits into the top bracket! Then all he has to do is press it flat against the ice!"

Next, she climbed to the third bracket and used her foot to release the second.

Once they had got into the rhythm of climbing, it took them no longer than five minutes to reach the top of the sledge. As they went up, Xanthys simply unfastened the bottom bracket and passed it up to The Zaggaline to be fitted into the top—an endless ladder that could have taken them as high as they wanted to go.

One of the brackets even had a special arrangement of hooks and springs so that it fitted over the bulky excrescences of ice that had formed around the sledge's railings. The Zaggaline climbed over it and dropped down onto the deck, and then he helped Dom Magator to swing his leg over, too.

The deck was sharply sloping and icy and extremely narrow, considering the size of the sledge. At the front stood the Winterwent's tall, forbidding throne of frozen blood, but it was empty now, and all the reins that controlled his ice-wolves were elaborately tied to the Z-shaped tiller so that the sledge ran directly forward, in a dead straight line. The Winterwent must have been confident that the dream desert went on and on for hundreds of miles.

Close up, the Winterwent's trophies of war were even more disgusting than they had appeared from the ground. Not only had he hung bones and penises and hanks of human hair to the railings around the tiller, but also the skin from women's faces, stretched over oval frames.

"He must be below someplace," said The Zaggaline, pointing to a circular hole in the center of the deck. They peered down it and could see a winding wooden staircase, which must have been barely wide enough for a monstrous creature like the Winterwent to climb up and down.

"Time for (b), then," said Dom Magator. "I guess I'd better go first :... seeing as how I'm toting the one and only gun."

He had never considered himself to be brave, but as he started to make his way downward he thought: Either you're a hero, my friend, or else you're a prime candidate for the funny farm.

The staircase wound down like a corkscrew, with six or seven turns, and when he switched on his helmet light, Dom Magator could see that its sides were badly scarred where the Winterwent's spider-like arms had continually scratched against it. It seemed strange that the Winterwent should have constructed a sledge with such a tight, claustrophobic interior. Maybe he had grown larger over the centuries, or maybe he had stolen this sledge from some other creature.

At the bottom of the stairs Dom Magator found himself in a long narrow corridor. He shone his light down it and saw a dark, dented, copper-covered door. A circular panel in the center of the door was embossed with the face of a screaming woman with snakelike hair, and a series of runic characters running all around. Kalexikox could have translated them, but Dom Magator could only guess what they meant. Maybe it was *Abandon all hope, you who enter here!*

The Zaggaline came down the staircase to join him, immediately followed by Xanthys.

"I guess he must be in there," said Dom Magator, nodding toward the door. "All we can do is bust in and hope for the best."

"He's got my sister in there, man."

Dom Magator squeezed his elbow. "I know that, son. But I don't see any other way, do you? And if we *don't* do this—well, I think we all know what the consequences are going to be."

Xanthys said, "Whatever happens, Zagga, we'll do everything we can to protect her."

"Yeah," said The Zaggaline.

"Are we ready, then?"

They all glanced at each other. A few days ago—a few *nights* ago—they hadn't even known of each other's existence. Now—with nothing more than a meaningful look——they were telling each other that they were prepared to die together.

Dom Magator lifted the Sun Gun off his back, held it up high and took a deep breath. Then he shouted *"Yaauahhhhh!"* and stormed along the corridor and kicked open the copper-covered door.

Inside, the room was painted completely black, although the walls were rimed with white frost. It was illuminated by nothing more than tiny, fatty candles, which filled it with acrid smoke. The Winterwent was standing with his back to them when they burst in, but he jerkily turned around.

"Night Warriors," he cackled, as if the words made him feel physically sick. His cloak made a sharp splintering sound like somebody treading on very thin glass.

CHAPTER TWENTY-THREE

His face was mesmerizing. Xanthys thought it was the most handsome face she had ever seen, with dark, penetrating eyes, a straight nose and slightly bow-shaped lips. Yet this face was attached to a long, distorted skull and a body like that of a monstrous insect—an insect that now had only five legs. His erect penis stuck up in front of his abdomen as if he were taunting them with it.

Janie was lying naked on a wide black bed. She appeared to be unconscious, and her lips were pale blue with cold. Her swollen stomach was bulging and shifting as her baby kicked inside her.

"What have you done to her, you sicko?" demanded The Zaggaline.

The Winterwent looked amused. "I have done nothing to harm her, Night Warrior. I simply laid my hand on her forehead to reduce her brain temperature and now she has fallen peacefully asleep."

"You're *sick*, man! You're totally sick!"

"Why are you so worried? Now that she is asleep, she will start to dream, and when she dreams, I will enter that dream and the dream of her unborn infant, and that is where the secret of all creation is waiting for me."

"That's right," said Dom Magator. "And you're going to use that secret to take the whole damn universe to pieces."

The Winterwent smiled, and in spite of his grotesque body and his distorted head, his smile was almost convincing.

"Who decided that Ashapola alone should know the secret of creation? Every baby ever born has known what Ashapola knows, but that knowledge is stolen from them within seconds and they spend the rest of their lives trying to remember what they once knew. That is the way in which Ashapola controls you all, you poor pathetic humans! You are always trying to understand your birthright, but you never can!"

"So if *you* acquire all of this knowledge, what are you going to do with it?"

The Winterwent continued to smile. "I will free you all, believe me. Every single one of you will know how and why you were created, and why the cosmos was created. You don't understand, do you? Ashapola has been controlling your lives forever, and I am about to release you from your ignorance."

"By invading the dreams of an innocent child? Is that it?"

The Winterwent clattered his claws in irritation. "What is one child, in the scheme of things, Dom Magator? What is one child, compared with the universe?"

"One child *is* the universe, you malevolent freak."

Just as he said that, Janie murmured something, moved her hand and turned over.

"She's dreaming," said the Winterwent, triumphantly. "She's dreaming, and now you pathetic creatures of Ashapola—now you can't stop me!"

The fatty little candles guttered and swayed, and gradually Janie's dream began to appear. The Night Warriors saw bedroom walls, a bed and a window with pale yellow drapes. Xanthys lifted her hand and touched one of the walls, and she could feel it solidifying underneath her fingertips, which gave her a strange shrinking sensation.

Dom Magator hefted up the Sun Gun and aimed it at the Winterwent.

"You wouldn't dare," the Winterwent mocked him. "If you fired that now, in this room, none of us would survive."

"Maybe we don't care," The Zaggaline challenged him.

"You would incinerate your own sister and her unborn child? I don't think so."

The dream was becoming clearer and clearer. Soon they found themselves standing in Janie's bedroom in the Beame's house in Louisville. The walls were freshly papered with pale blue flowers and there were soft toys stacked on a chair in one corner. In the opposite corner stood a pale blue basketwork crib.

"Yes," said the Winterwent. "Your sister is dreaming that her baby has already arrived."

Dom Magator kept the Sun Gun leveled at the Winterwent while he walked across the room to the window and looked out. The street below was deep in snow, and the trees were frozen, yet it must have been midsummer. Although it appeared as nothing more than a haunted orange disk, the sun was high in the sky and the jacaranda was blooming, like splashes of rabbit blood on the snow.

The Winterwent took a lurching step toward the crib.

"Don't even think of touching that baby!" said Dom Magator.

"Or what? What will you do, Night Warrior? Atomize me, and this innocent infant, which hasn't even drawn its first breath yet, and yourselves, too?"

"Like you said, what is one child in the general scheme of things? If one child has to die to save the whole of creation, well, that's kind of a miserable thing, ain't it, but on balance it's the only solution, wouldn't you say?"

The Winterwent's eyes dropped slyly sideways. "It seems as if I'm bringing you around to my way of thinking, Night Warrior. There's nothing like total ruthlessness, is there?

Or are you still dithering? Here, let me make your mind up for you—spare you the agony of indecision!"

With that, he reached under his crackling cloak and hauled out the Kattalak. It looked even longer and more menacing than it had when Dom Magator had seen it from a distance. Its blade was hooked over like an executioner's ax and it had a sharp curved point. It was so cold that it fumed.

The Winterwent threw it from one claw over to the next, and then swung it so fast that Dom Magator didn't even see it coming. It hit the barrel of the Sun Gun with a loud clank, chopping off the flash-suppressor at the end and bending the muzzle, rendering it useless.

The Winterwent returned the Kattalak to its sheath and smiled. "No need for further discussion, is there?"

He took two more steps and leaned over the crib. The Zaggaline shouted, "No!" and jumped onto his back, but the Winterwent lashed at him with one of his claws and sent The Zaggaline sprawling across the room. Dom Magator approached the Winterwent, too, but the Winterwent turned his anamorphic head around and whispered, "Don't, or I will freeze you solid from the inside out." To emphasize what he meant, he took hold of his glassy penis in one claw and slowly rubbed it up and down. Its glans was the size of a small pear, and the shaft was nearly two feet high, with protuberant veins.

"You are going to get your punishment in hell for this," said Dom Magator, hoarsely.

"By the time I have finished, Night Warrior, there will be no hell, nor heaven, either. Only chaos."

The Winterwent lifted the naked baby out of the crib. It was a little boy with dark curly hair. He was fast asleep, and his rapid eye movements showed that he was dreaming.

"At last," said the Winterwent, and two long strings of saliva slid from the side of his mouth and froze.

The walls of the bedroom began to fade. The crib became transparent and vanished. Dom Magator realized with awe that they were about to enter this baby's dream, and that this baby knew everything about everything: how the stars were created, how the world had been born, why man had developed and where he was going.

He looked at The Zaggaline, and then at Xanthys. "We're not going to survive this," he told them. "But this is some kind of privilege, believe me. Before we die, we're going to find out the secret of the whole goddamned universe."

The Zaggaline said, "I think I'm scared, dude."

Xanthys said nothing at first. She was frowning as if she were thinking. But when Dom Magator was about to put down his damaged Sun Gun, she said, "No ... hold onto it."

"What? It's just a piece of junk now."

"Please—just hold onto it."

Now the bedroom walls had evaporated altogether. They found themselves standing on the sidewalk at the intersection of Fourth and Main, and it was a warm summer's evening. In almost every respect the street looked normal, with lighted store windows and pedestrians crowding the sidewalk. But everything was moving in deep slow-motion. The cars crept along the roadway at such a snail's pace that it would have taken them over an hour just to travel one block. People were talking to each other, but their voices were nothing but a deep, slurry blur.

"This is it?" said The Zaggaline, turning around and around. "Fourth and Main is the secret of the universe?"

But it suddenly began to dawn on Dom Magator what was happening here, in Janie's baby's dream. The secret of the universe *was* here. He felt that extraordinary warm surge of excitement that he had experienced when he was taken to watch the Baton Rouge Bruins by a friend of his father's, who was a professional baseball coach. For the first time he had actually understood what was happening on the field in front of him, and the consequences of every pitch. A similar comprehension was dawning on him now, except on a brain-dazzling scale that included the meaning of everything that had ever been created—not just human life, but *everything,* down to the smallest particle of matter.

"It's a game," he said, in disbelief. "The whole god-damned thing is a game. It's got rules, look at it—*look!* The way that bird's flying—the way that cloud's moving—the way those people are crossing the street!"

He could see and understand the rules of existence as clearly as if they were written in a handbook. He could understand what the universe was—and most stupefying of all—he could actually understand *where* it was. He could understand time and why it kept passing. He could understand why humans had evolved, and how, and he knew what their future was likely to be. History, geography, astronomy, physics—he not only knew everything about them, he knew what they meant and how they interacted.

Everything intersected. Everything fit together. If a British scholar jotted down the word *Newton* in an Oxford University library, a schoolgirl in Newton, New Jersey, would drop the apple out of her lunchbox. If a star exploded in Aquarius, a woman carrying water in Uttar Pradesh would suddenly lose her sight.

Xanthys and The Zaggaline were standing next to Dom Magator in awe. Even the Winterwent was silent, his elongated skull tilted upward.

"You're right, man," said The Zaggaline. "It's like the most amazing X-Box game that ever was. If only I'd known a *millionth* of this stuff when I was in school."

All Xanthys could do was shake her head. She felt elated, almost ecstatic, and yet terrified, too. To see the universe working in front of her eyes was like a religious revelation, and she found that tears were sliding down her cheeks.

The Winterwent turned to the Night Warriors with a beatific expression on his face. "Here it is, then. This is how it was done. And this is how it is going to be undone. All I have to do is freeze one atom in this baby's dream, and it will start a chain reaction that will freeze the whole of creation.

Everything will shatter. *Everything*, except the world of chaos, which is my dominion and always will be."

Xanthys said to Dom Magator, "Give me the gun."

"It's useless," said Dom Magator. "It won't even misfire and blow us all up. I thought of that. I didn't exactly relish the thought, but I thought of it."

"Give me the gun. Please."

"Okay." Dom Magator gave her the Sun Gun.

With no hesitation, Xanthys slid open the power connection in the left-hand side of the Sun Gun's stock and fastened it to her belt. She had scarcely any power of her own, but the Sun Gun contained enough energy to give her one last time-curve. The Zaggaline realized what she was trying to do and stepped between her and the Winterwent to hide her.

Dom Magator, meanwhile, was playing for a few more seconds of time. "Looks like you've beaten us, then," he told the Winterwent. "I guess congratulations are in order."

"I need no congratulations, Night Warrior. Seeing you consigned to oblivion, that will be satisfaction enough, believe me."

"Let me ask you one thing. Won't you be kind of … lonely … when all of this has disintegrated?"

"Chaos is freedom," replied the Winterwent. It was obvious that he didn't really understand the question. "The universe has been ordered for far too long. Now is the time for the liberation of everything."

He looked down at the sleeping baby he held in his claws. If he hadn't been so hideous and distorted, the expression on his face could almost have been taken for affection.

Xanthys had drained the Sun Gun of its very last joule of energy. She disconnected it from her belt and laid it quietly down on the sidewalk. Then she dialed as far ahead as she could—three hours and seventeen minutes. A yellow key appeared on her display, and a yellow key on her belt lit up.

She knew that she was taking a hideous risk. She might simply be delaying their destruction by three hours, or else she might land them instantly into oblivion, after the Winterwent had taken the universe apart—not that they would know anything about it.

But she stepped forward and pointed the shining yellow key toward the east.

"What's this?" demanded the Winterwent, in his thickest, slimiest voice.

"Another game," said Xanthys, although her throat was so tight that she could hardly speak. "In this game, though, the winners are *us* and the loser is *you*."

She turned the key. Nothing seemed to happen at first. The cars continued to creep along Main Street and the clouds continued to roll overhead so slowly that they didn't appear to be moving at all.

Then, abruptly, there was a sound like a thousand pairs of feet running, and a rush of traffic, and jets screaming across the sky. They had jumped three hours and seventeen minutes ahead.

Xanthys thought she had gambled and lost. The Winterwent was still there, and his handsome face was dark with fury. But then Xanthys realized that he was no longer holding Janie's baby, and that Main Street had faded and there was nothing around them but a blurry whiteness.

They were still in Janie's baby's dream, but this was the dream of an infant who knew nothing about the universe or the secrets of creation. This was the dream of an infant whose only conscious experience was warmth, softness and reassuring noises.

"What have you done?" the Winterwent shouted at her. *"What have you done?"*

"I've taken us forward," said Xanthys, and she couldn't stop herself from sounding triumphant. "I've taken us forward three hours and seventeen minutes, and Janie's baby has been born now, and the poor little guy has forgotten all that stuff he knew about the meaning of life. He's a blank page now."

Something was happening to the Winterwent. His shoulders hunched up and then he started to grow taller and taller. His claws went into a jerky, arrhythmic spasm and his whole body trembled. His skull appeared to stretch out longer and longer, and then his face began to blur, as if somebody had been furiously rubbing at it with an eraser.

Dom Magator said, "Xanthys? What the hell's happening to him?"

"The worst fate of all," said Xanthys. "Janie's baby is forgetting that he ever knew him."

The Winterwent stretched open his mouth and screamed. Dom Magator had once seen a vat of boiling vegetable soup tip over and scald a young soldier, but even that young soldier hadn't screamed like the Winterwent. The Winterwent, the lord of oblivion, was facing his own oblivion, and his terror went far beyond pain.

The air grew colder and colder, until a crystalline structure of ice began to grow around the Winterwent, formed of oxygen and hydrogen molecules from the air itself. The Night Warriors could feel the hairs in their nostrils freezing, and their faceplates began to ice over. When Dom Magator tried to step further back, he found that the joints of his armor had seized up and he was immobilized.

But then the Winterwent began to disintegrate. His claws broke off, and then his legs collapsed. There was a sharp creak and his erection snapped like an icicle. Finally, his long skull tilted back and his head dropped from his shoulders. As Janie's baby forgot about his existence, the blurry whiteness all around them seemed to absorb him completely, as if he were disappearing into a dense fog.

Nothing was left of him but the Kattalak, his battle-ax. Then that, too, began to liquefy. It formed a shimmering pool of mercury, which rolled into shining round beads.

There was an ear-splitting crack, like a glacier breaking apart, and then there was utter silence. The Night Warriors felt as if they had all gone stone deaf.

* * *

The Zaggaline said, "You palooked him, Xanthys."

Dom Magator nodded. "You palooked him good and proper."

"What happens now?" asked The Zaggaline. "Is there any way we can get back to real land?"

"Without any power, no. All we can do is make the most of what time we have left before Janie's baby wakes up."

Xanthys sat down cross-legged on the soft, warm, woolly ground. "Do you realize something? We saved the world. We saved the *universe*, even, and nobody will ever know?"

"It's a bitch, ain't it?" said Dom Magator. "I mean, it's bad enough being a martyr, without being an unsung martyr. If I'm going to be a martyr I want to be *sung*, you know?"

"At least we'll die comfortable, man," said The Zaggaline.

They were still talking when they became aware that the nunlike woman from the hospital was standing quite close by. She was wearing a long white dress and eyeglasses with solid white lenses.

"*You*," said Dom Magator.

"Yes," she said. "Weren't you expecting me?"

"I don't know. My own mother ... well, she didn't take care of me too good."

"Who are you?" asked Xanthys. "The last time I saw you ... I felt that I knew you, but I didn't know why."

But The Zaggaline had taken off his helmet and was openly crying. "It's Mom," he said. "It's everybody's mom. It's my mom and your mom and Dom Magator's mom if she'd ever been good to him."

Dom Magator took off his helmet, too. The Night War was over, and they knew that they were safe now. "You're right, Zagga. She's been watching out for us all along, haven't you? And just like all good mothers, she's blind to all of her children's sins and all of their misdemeanors."

The woman smiled and took hold of Dom Magator's hands. "You Night Warriors have been risking your lives to save the mothers of this world, and that's why Springer made sure that I was always there to keep an eye on you."

She turned to The Zaggaline and Xanthys and said, "Come on, now. It's time for us all to go home."

She let go of Dom Magator's hands, turned around, and lifted both her hands. Shimmering blue static flowed from her fingertips and slowly she created a portal of dazzling light. Xanthys stepped through first, then The Zaggaline, and Dom Magator approached it last.

"You're not coming?" he asked the woman.

She shook her head. "I belong in *this* world, John. But the best of luck, and always remember that I love you."

Dom Magator stepped through the portal and found himself back in Dr. Beltzer's room at the Norton Audubon. Dr. Beltzer had gone, leaving his sheets twisted like an escape rope, but The Zaggaline and Xanthys were still waiting for him.

The three of them hesitated for a moment, and then they held each other close. None of them spoke, but they were all thinking of Amla Fabeya, Raquasthena and Kalexikox, who would never see reality again.

George Beame knocked at Perry's bedroom door. He was still unshaven and his hair was sticking up at the back.

"Tried to wake you earlier, son. Shook you and shook you, but I'm darned if I could get you to stir!"

Perry sat up and blinked at him. "What is it, Dad? What's happened?"

"Janie went into labor, about three A.M. I called the Kosair and they took her straight in. They were on the phone just now. You're an uncle. Little boy, seven pounds two ounces. Mom and baby doing real good. She's going to call him Joe, after your little brother."

"That's great," said Perry. Then—with a feeling of terrible dread—"Did you try to wake Dunc up yet?"

"Just doing that now. Can't wait to see his face!"

George left the room and Perry could hear him knocking

at Dunc's door. He knocked and he knocked and then he went in. Perry climbed out of bed and found his jeans.

He was still buckling up his belt when George came back and he was looking pale and worried. "Perry—something's happened to Dunc. He's still breathing, but I can't wake him up."

Perry said, "Call nine-one-one, Dad. I'll see what I can do."

While his father went to the telephone, Perry went across the landing to Dunc's bedroom. His brother was lying on his back, his eyes closed, breathing steadily. Perry sat down next to him and took hold of his hand.

"Good night, Kalexikox," he whispered. "Sleep well."

John came out of the shower and padded toward his door with his towel wrapped around him. He had almost reached it when Nadine came out of her room, wearing a tight red T-shirt and a short red satin skirt.

"John! How's it going, John?"

"Going good, Nadine, thanks for asking."

"That's some scar on your shoulder, excuse me for saying so. How did you get that?"

"Active service. I was in the Army, when I was younger. And thinner."

"Really? And what, you got shot? Where was that? Eye-rack?"

John gave her a noncommittal shrug. "It was nothing. Only a flesh wound, you know?"

"I never knew that you were so *brave*."

"Brave? Nah. Just doing my duty."

Nadine touched the puckered mark on his upper arm with fascination. "You could take me to lunch and tell me about it. I love tales of derring-do."

"You want me to take you to lunch?"

"Sure. Don't you *want* to take me to lunch?"

"Of course. You like fried fish? Give me five minutes to put some duds on."

"I think you look pretty damn good as you are. You've got something, John. Like, *aura.*"

John let himself into his room and closed the door behind him. He let the towel drop to the floor and studied himself in the mirror on the back of his closet door.

"Yesss," he said, punching the air.

Sasha was just leaving her apartment building when her cell phone rang.

"Is that Sasha Smith?"

"This is she. Who wants to know?"

"This is David Charbonneau, from *Checkout News.* I'm a friend of Kevin Porter, from the *Courier-Journal.* Kevin was telling me all about your work, and I was wondering if you were interested in a weekly feature spot."

"Checkout News? You mean 'Man Gives Birth To Own Stepfather'? 'Harley-Davidson Discovered On Moon'?"

"That's the one. Kevin was telling me you got a real talent for human-interest stories."

Sasha looked across the street. A woman in a blue spotted dress was walking along, holding the hand of a small boy who looked exactly like Michael-Row-The-Boat-Ashore-Hallelujah. The boy turned and stared at her, and then gave her a funny little scrunchy-fingered wave.

"No thanks," she said. "I don't do made-up news stories anymore. From now on, I'm only going to tell things the way they really are."

MANITOU
BLOOD
GRAHAM MASTERTON

A bizarre epidemic is sweeping New York City. Doctors can only watch as victims fall prey to a very unusual blood disorder. They become unable to eat solid food, are extremely sensitive to daylight—and they have an irresistible need to drink human blood....

As panic, bloodlust and death grip the city, a few begin to consider the unimaginable: Could the old folktales and legends be true? Could the epidemic be the work of...vampires? Their search for the truth will lead them to shadowy realms where very few dare to go. They will seek help from both the living and the dead. And they will realize that their worst fear was only the beginning.

SARAH PINBOROUGH
BREEDING GROUND

Life was good for Matt and Chloe. They were in love and looking forward to their new baby. But what Chloe gives birth to isn't a baby. It isn't even human. It's an entirely new species that uses humans only for food—and as hosts for their young.

As Matt soon learns, though, he is not alone in his terror. Women all over town have begun to give birth to these hideous creatures, spidery nightmares that live to kill—and feed. As the infestation spreads and the countryside is reduced to a series of web-shrouded ghost towns, will the survivors find a way to fight back? Or is it only a matter of time before all of mankind is reduced to a...BREEDING GROUND

Dorchester Publishing Co., Inc.
P.O. Box 6640   _5741-7
Wayne, PA 19087-8640 $6.99 US/$8.99 CAN

Please add $2.50 for shipping and handling for the first book and $.75 for each additional book. NY and PA residents, add appropriate sales tax. No cash, stamps, or CODs. Canadian orders require an extra $2.00 for shipping and handling and must be paid in U.S. dollars. Prices and availability subject to change. **Payment must accompany all orders.**

Name: _____

Address: _____

City: _____ State: _____ Zip: _____

E-mail: _____

I have enclosed $_____ in payment for the checked book(s).

CHECK OUT OUR WEBSITE! www.dorchesterpub.com
_____ Please send me a free catalog.

JACK KETCHUM

OFF SEASON

September. A beautiful New York editor retreats to a lonely cabin on a hill in the quiet Maine beach town of Dead River—off season—awaiting her sister and friends. Nearby, a savage human family with a taste for flesh lurks in the darkening woods, watching, waiting for the moon to rise and night to fall....

And before too many hours pass, five civilized, sophisticated people and one tired old country sheriff will learn just how primitive we all are beneath the surface...and that there are no limits at all to the will to survive.

Dorchester Publishing Co., Inc.
P.O. Box 6640   5696-8
Wayne, PA 19087-8640 $6.99 US/$8.99 CAN
Please add $2.50 for shipping and handling for the first book and $.75 for each additional book. NY and PA residents, add appropriate sales tax. No cash, stamps, or CODs. Canadian orders require $2.00 for shipping and handling and must be paid in U.S. dollars. Prices and availability subject to change. **Payment must accompany all orders.**

Name: _____

Address: _____

City: _____ State: _____ Zip: _____

E-mail: _____

I have enclosed $_____ in payment for the checked book(s).

***CHECK OUT OUR WEBSITE!* www.dorchesterpub.com**
_____ *Please send me a free catalog.*

RAPTURE

THOMAS TESSIER

Jeff has always loved Georgianne, ever since they were kids—with a love so strong, so obsessive, it sometimes drives him to do crazy things. Scary things. Like stalking Georgianne and everyone she loves, including her caring husband and her innocent teenage daughter. Jeff doesn't think there's room in Georgianne's life for anyone but him, and if he has to, he's ready to kill all the others... until he's the only one left.

"Ingenious. A nerve-paralyzing story."
—*Publishers Weekly*